CASSANDRA CIELO

FROM SAPPHIRE OCEANS

THE BODY, THE SOUL
BOOK 3

Content Warning : There are depictions of violence and death. Heavy topics such as grief and loss. Though it is a closed door romance with no explicit scenes, there are some makeout scenes but characters do not go further than kissing on page.

MT. ARYTHMA
WYCLIFF
CITADEL
ORO
BEZER PLAINS
MT. ERAN
ERASMUS
MT. KIDRISOL
BLUE VOLCANO
N
E
W
S

COINANIA
TYNDALE
PALACE MOREH
KINGDOM OF SHAMAR
CASTLE JUDAHALL
ROMATH
CHARTED
KINGDOM OF GOLAN

CHAPTER 1

Awakening

The Rip

The snowy landscape chilled me to the bones, the white puffs of my breath disappearing in the growing night.

They would come, soon.

The Wraiths.

They would never stop, no matter how many we killed. I would never be safe. Even if what I hoped to accomplish came to fruition. The monsters would live on until Skithian was destroyed. The clothes Lev had given me were tattered and torn from the fight to save Coinania. Even as the Wraiths drew closer, their shadowy forms slipping towards me in the snow-laden night, I did not fear them. No, that wasn't right. Deep down I was still scared, but it wasn't my knowledge of how to kill them that had me standing on the hill unbothered. No, it was something else, something I was forgetting. Something important. Something that changed everything. What was it?

Though my mind told me I shouldn't, not with the

Wraiths approaching, I folded my legs under me, sitting breezily in the snow.

"Shroding?" I whispered into the night, wanting to see him. Fear shot through my chest, not directed at the encroaching Wraiths but at the man before me.

He trudged through the snow, his loose linen tunic billowing open as he lifted his booted feet again and again. Dark gaze locked on me, rich brown locks shadowing his face from my scrutiny.

Something was not right. But what? What was so off about this encounter? Why was the wash of safety I always got in his presence evading me now?

He stalked ever closer, as if I, not the Wraiths at his back, were the enemy. Wait. The Wraiths. Why were they still here?

The night had not lifted into day; the silvery moon above was gradually turning bloodred. And though my senses were sharp, Shroding's presence showing I was in the pocket dimension, everything was all wrong.

The slide of metal, a sword being drawn, did not make any sense, until I fixed my eyes on the prince. For a fleeting second I wondered where he had gotten a sword from, but the thought was completely overridden when he poised the tip inches from my throat.

"Shroding?" I gasped, confused and afraid. He wouldn't hurt me, would he? The Wraiths were behind him—he should be fighting them. He should be protecting me. What was going on?

The side of my neck flared with pain.

"Don't you dare hide behind her," Shroding growled, his face imperious as he glared down at me.

I wanted to turn to see if there was someone else here,

behind me perhaps, but instead my body began to shake with laughter. It was a twisted sound, nothing like my own voice.

It almost sounded like... the man from the dank alley when I was a child. The man from Mama Meod's tent. A flurry of images flashed across my mind as it all came back to me.

Logan.

The Nephesh Maveth.

Right...

I was dying.

"So this is where you have been hiding, my prince." Logan spoke through me. The sensation caused bile to rise in my throat. Was this what it was like to be possessed? No, I would not be seeing this, remembering this, if it was a normal possession, and we wouldn't be in the other dimension.

"Let. Her. Go." Shroding's grip tightened on the hilt, but even with the slight shake of his hand, the blade stayed level, balanced dangerously to the curve of my neck. I was only vaguely aware it was the side Logan had bit.

"Drop the hero act, you're finished," Logan taunted. "I have you completely surrounded." My body moved, rising and standing before Shroding. Smoking Wraiths cavorted at his back, solidifying Logan's point. I wanted to warn him, to tell him to run, but my voice was not my own. "You can raise your blade all you want." He snickered as my hand flicked the tip of the sword in a mocking, unaffected gesture. "You will never hurt this body," Logan scoffed.

Shroding's hard gaze flinched, Logan's words cutting deep, before it steadied into acceptance.

"You can't come back here," Shroding warned.

What did he mean? Was he talking to me or to Logan?

He took a step forward, blade dropping as he wrapped an

arm around my shoulders, his forehead resting against mine as he sighed. "I know you are still in there."

"What are you doing?" Logan wrestled against Shroding's hold, but in my body, it was futile. I did not have the physical strength to go up against someone so much stronger, without using the gift.

"It will all be okay now, trust me."

My body jerked, but he held me firmly. I was glad I couldn't see his face. It hurt so much more than getting burned by the Wraiths. There was pressure, a searing sensation, but worst of all was the hollow cold that seeped through my core, expanding out from where the sword in Shroding's hand pierced clean through my stomach. I closed my shaking hands over his on the hilt of the blade. At my touch he let out a rattled breath that told me he was crying.

It's okay, It's okay, I thought, hoping he could hear me.

I couldn't scream, there wasn't time for it as the dimension shattered around me, and I knew then he meant I was never coming back.

CHAPTER 2

Reckoning

The sun warmed my face. A gentle rocking had me moaning and rolling over, wanting to go back to sleep. I could almost hear Micah's voice calling the kids, the jostling motion so similar to riding in the back of a wagon. For a blissful moment I was there, having fallen asleep in the wagon on the farm, my father steering his dappled horse into town to deliver our harvest.

The air was cold on my exposed face and hands, but the chirp of birds in the distance and thump of hooves on a rocky path only solidified the dream behind my closed eyes.

Theo's teasing voice calling, "Haybale it's time to wake up!"

"Whoa," a voice nothing like my father's, Theo's or Micah's called, and the swaying jerked to a stop.

"Are you awake?" Shroding's voice filled my mind, making my eyes flash open. I took in the worn wooden slats next to where I lay in a narrow cart. The sudden shift in reality left me bereft, the pain of losing my family, my home, crawled over my skin hardening like ice. I shivered.

Soft fur rubbed against my neck from behind, and a cascade of words I couldn't make out scrambled through my thoughts.

"Haya..." was the only sound clear enough to hold on to. The relief at hearing his voice ebbed the sorrow, bringing a soothing peace to my mind instead.

Rolling towards the soft purring, I noticed a few things at once. The sky was a brilliant, clear blue; over the edge of the wagon I could see the white-capped mountains of the Amaranth range; but it was the flat plains covered with cattle that told me everything I'd been wondering. We were no longer in Coinania, and judging by the rolling plains, this land could only be the outskirts of Tyndale. Though the environment was captivating, it paled in comparison to the silver-furred cat curled around my body. His long form stretched the length of me, and though the weight of at least three blankets covered me, his body gave me the most warmth.

"Shroding," I sighed, my mouth sticky from disuse. I cleared my throat, embarrassed.

"Haya," his voice called again, the gentle tone like a balm to my soul.

He was safe. He was here.

His dark gaze held mine, and the moment stretched on forever before a tuft of blond hair caught my attention outside the wagon.

"Glad you are finally awake," Callum grunted, annoyed.

Asher's bright blue eyes appeared next, his comforting smile so much like Micah's that I ached, for just a moment, to have stayed in the dream, between sleep and consciousness.

"What happened?" I muttered, but then held up my hand; the mass of unpleasant memories assaulted my mind, confirming our unfortunate situation. "Never mind. I remember." I touched the side of my neck. A thick bandage covered the spot Logan had attacked. Nephesh Maveth Mama Meod had called it, soul death. So why was I not dead yet?

Asher strode to the back of the wagon and held out his hand for me to take. I slid my hand along Shroding's fur before scooting to the back of the wagon.

"Take it easy, go slowly," Asher warned as my fingers pressed into his palm. He reached around my back, helping me down to my feet. I was still wearing the clothes Lev had let me borrow, and though I was glad for the thick, durable fabric, as it kept me protected from the elements, it was stiff with dirt and blood. I caught a whiff of my hair and winced at the unpleasant sourness. How long had it been since I last bathed? How long had I been asleep for? Judging by how far we were from the mountains it must have been a while.

"I smell awful." I grimaced, tossing my tangled braid behind me and away from my nose. How had Shroding been able to stand lying next to me with such a stench?

"You have been unconscious for nearly four days." Callum crossed his arms, ambling to stand next to Asher. I gripped Asher's arm to steady myself as my whole body protested my upright position. I blinked a few times till the three blond heads merged back into one.

Asher glared at Callum before giving me a placating smile. "Mama Meod used a lot of different herbs and medicine on you. They don't smell the greatest, but we will be at Palace Moreh soon, and you can get cleaned up."

"Not the best idea to tell her where we are," Callum snapped, tapping the side of his head.

"Why?" I asked, confused.

"Logan is listening," Asher explained, gesturing to the bandage on my neck. "Because of the mark."

My hand lifted, hovering over the bandage. Was that a side effect of the Nephesh Maveth? Where Logan was now, I could only guess, but he knew where we were headed, and no doubt exactly what we were intending to do when we got there.

I glanced at Shroding staying low in the wagon to keep his fur hidden, as between the silver strands the sun created little prisms of light.

"It would be good for you to walk a little and stretch your legs, but don't push yourself too much, you are still recovering." Asher pat my hand still wrapped around his forearm. I was grateful he was in no hurry to extricate himself, as I was pretty sure my legs would give out the moment he did.

Callum climbed up to take the reins, and we set off again.

"Why did we leave Coinania?" I asked once my legs stopped shaking from the effort of walking. It was still painful to move—why, I wasn't even sure, as Logan had only bit my neck as far as I recalled. Perhaps it was another effect of the Nephesh Maveth?

Asher kept his eyes ahead on the road, and though his demeanor was relaxed, his free hand rested on the hilt of the sword at his hip, ready for an attack.

"There was nothing else left for us to do there. You were as healed as you could be, and we have a mission to complete."

"Of course, but we don't know when the next attack will come. Will it really be okay, just the four of us going to the summer palace? Shouldn't we have enlisted the protection of Lev or Fealth or some of the other fighters?"

"You are with two of the strongest fighters in all of Shamar; we are plenty of protection," Callum huffed from the wagon seat, where he steered his beautiful white horse.

"And you have the king's power," Asher added, glancing down at me with a cheeky smile. "Plus, we have a plan," he declared with a confidence that almost lifted the shadow from my thoughts.

"One we can't tell you for obvious reasons," Callum interjected again.

I refrained from rolling my eyes. I had to trust these two not only with Shroding's life but mine as well. They would stop at nothing to get Shroding back to himself, and I would do everything in my power, the power I hoped I could still access, to not be a hindrance to their plan.

"You're awfully quiet," I mused, resting my hand on the edge of the wagon. It was odd that Shroding had not made a single comment on the conversation.

Shroding lifted his head, and placed his paw on top of my hand. At the touch his thoughts exploded in my mind. At first they were jumbled and confused, but they quickly coalesced.

"Our connection is weak, so not only can't you move dimensions, but we need to be touching in order for you to hear me."

"Does that mean *you* can't hear *me?*" I asked through our connection, but when he did not respond I got my answer. "I see," I mumbled out loud.

"What is it?" Shroding asked, but at that moment pain so acute, so sharp, burned across my neck, and I jerked my hand back, falling into Asher. I doubled over, crumpled to the cold ground as heat warmed my skin and sweat peppered my brow.

Like the sun breaking through the trees at golden hour, a

wall of soldiers pushed out onto the battlefield before my mind's eyes. They were Shamarian men and women clad in black, silver and gold. I watched from above as they pressed into the sea of Golan fighters and Grieving in suits, tattered, disfigured and terrifying. The freezing wind of winter bit greedily into the soldiers, ice hanging from their gaunt faces like a kiss of death. The death I knew would befall them. All of them.

I wanted to scream at them to turn back. I opened my mouth, but in place of my voice came another.

"Burn." It rumbled in my chest as if I had spoken, as if the voice was part of me.

Out of my mouth shot a burst of flames so great that for an irrational moment I wondered how so much could be expelled out of my small body.

How did it not sear me from the inside out? How was I not charred by the force of the flames?

To my horror, the fire burned all those fighting from Shamar and Golan—no respecter of persons, no loyalty—to oblivion.

When I looked down at myself I saw black talons and enormous white feathered wings thrusting in place against an orange sky.

"This is a warning." A voice I had only heard a few times snaked through my thoughts. His voice was like hot iron on skin.

I coughed and wheezed against the burning that radiated through my whole body. Pressure like thumbs pushing unrelentingly against my eyes permeated the sockets and down my neck, culminating where the bandage was wrapped.

Through clenched teeth I grit back a scream, the sound coming out as a haggard hiss. "Get out of my head!" I closed my eyes, willing his voice to disappear.

"Don't come into my thoughts, love, you won't like what you see." Then silence descended, and I knew he was gone.

When I opened my eyes, Shroding's mouth was clamped over my arm, the spokes of the wooden wheels knobby against my back.

Asher approached me cautiously, his hands raised in front of him, palms out in a gesture that indicated he didn't want to hurt me. I looked at him, confused, then I sensed it, my vibration gift. The weak vibration at my fingertips, though it was not much, had caught his and Shroding's attention because my hand was plastered to my temple, my vibration power ready to be pushed into my own skull, like I was one of those monsters. Someone with the sickness. A Grieving.

What had I been about to do?

Shroding tugged gently, careful not to cut me with his teeth as he drew my arm away and back down to the cold dirt.

Once the power dimmed and faded, Shroding wrapped his body around mine, his chest a pillow for my cheek. The steady beat of his heart and the plushness of his fur against my face calmed me instantly.

"Talk to me, please," he begged, his voice as miserable as the small whimpers still leaving my lips.

"Logan, his voice..." I turned my head, burying it deeper in his warm coat. Tears heated behind my eyes as I tried to rationalize the image I had seen. Was that a vision of what was to come, what Logan was planning?

Carefully and without hesitation he brushed my tangled

hair back, revealing my neck. His paw barely touched the wound, but I hissed in pain as if he had cut me open with his claws. He leaned back, and the pain ebbed.

My hand lifted toward it. What was happening to me?

"Mama Meod healed the wound, but a mark remains because the damage is ongoing." I lifted my head to look up at him, and his dark eyes narrowed. "The Nephesh Maveth is similar to poison."

"What are you saying?" I whispered, terrified.

"Only people with the gift can see this mark. Logan didn't just bite you but something else." His ears flattened. "Something illegal for thousands of years. Something we believed had fallen out of knowledge." His tail flicked. "We were wrong."

I searched his dark eyes; the flecks of gold were there but somehow dimmed, as if a light in him had gone out. "The Nephesh Maveth." I whispered.

He nodded once. "He tainted you with it. Now I can't hear you, *feel* you anymore," he confessed, and the turmoil in his voice nearly brought me to tears. "Even still I won't let you succumb to the poison. I will stand on the edge of danger, holding you back, even from yourself, to keep you safe."

I still did not fully understand what the Nephesh Maveth was, how the poison worked, but if the ultimate end was my death then we needed to act quickly to save Shroding before my time ran out.

"Shroding, you need to return to the wagon," Asher interrupted, his uneasy expression reminding me we were not alone, not just that Asher and Callum were there, but that we were out in the open where anyone might spot Shroding. Might catch sight of the tiny prisms in his fur, might notice the king's powers inside me.

But Shroding ignored his friend and buried his face in the uninjured side of my neck, his silver fur filling my sight as he wrapped himself around me as if he could be a shield.

"I won't let you become a Grieving," he promised.

But how could he shield me from something happening *inside* me?

CHAPTER 3
Unbidden

My eyes adjusted as I tried to focus on my new surroundings. I had fallen asleep a while back when the rolling plains became crowded with the trees of a massive forest. Shroding's soft purring beside me and the rocking of the wagon had swayed me into a dreamless rest. But now the tree line was a few yards behind us, and we approached a huge white stone wall. The wagon rumbled along the gravel path that cut the open garden of the front grounds in half. Garden was unfortunately not the best word, as whatever it was supposed to look like was a distant memory. Overgrown wilting grass leaned over heavily. Sodden with the heavy mist.

The strong smell of salt filled my nose. The bright, sunny day had become shadowed by a heavy drizzle brought about by the ocean waves perpetually rushing and crashing somewhere to the left of the wagon. The haze curled around the towering summer palace, giving it an eerie abandoned appearance instead of a welcoming one. Ivy climbed the white walls. Glass windows of all shapes and sizes plastered the sides at unusual and peculiar placements that made the structure look more like a greenhouse than a palace. As we descended the path, the thick white wall rose from the mist and wilting greenery, the rampart surrounding the perimeter; its once defensive opulence was diminished by pervasive moss and tufts of weeds poking through its defense. Even still the wall and palace before me were bigger than any structure I had ever seen before. I marveled at them. It was like a white and glass giant capped with a blue dome roof, which protruded high up in the middle.

We passed under the courtyard arch and stopped before a massive metal door at least four times taller than Callum.

"Welcome home." Callum sighed, content, as he released the reins and stretched his arms high over his head. The metal pauldrons on his arms clinked with the motion. The emblem of the king etched on Callum's breastplate was also carved into the stately metal doors of the palace. Dropping his arms, Callum vaulted down from the wagon, then did a few quick squats to stretch his legs.

Shroding shifted next to me and stretched, paws out in front of him, rear in the air and claws extending and retracting against my thigh. I shivered as a cool ocean breeze cut through the gravel courtyard.

"Let's get inside and get you warm." Shroding spoke, his voice sleepy as his cat eyes blinked slowly.

I climbed down, finding my feet much more steady than before, and strode up beside Callum, who was standing in front of a much smaller door to the bottom right of the massive metal one. I vaguely recalled a similar entrance set up for the citadel back in Wycliff.

Callum glanced at me with an air of distrust. Shroding growled, stepping up beside me and baring his teeth slightly to Callum. The interaction befuddled me. Before I could question it Callum beckoned me to follow him inside.

The shifting crunch of gravel behind me drew my attention.

I paused in the doorway, looking back at Asher. "Where are you going?" He had climbed up, taking the driver's seat.

"We need some supplies in town, and it would be best to go now while you all clean up and rest. We can't have Shroding traipsing through town." He chuckled, scooping up the reins Callum had discarded, and bid the horse to trot. I watched him leave. Being alone in this massive palace with just Shroding and Callum didn't seem like the best idea if their most recent interaction was any indication of things.

Asher had explained the palace had been empty since King Roark's death, the steward preferring life in the capital to the countryside. No one stayed to keep up any part of the place, and it showed. I tried to imagine what the place would have been like when Shroding was young. Him sitting at this window, watching guests arrive for the parties the king would throw to celebrate the summer harvest or some other glamorous event. I read in one of the books that people from every city would come here to attend the galas the king would throw. Now the palace looked haunted by the splendor it once held. The remnants of roses, hydrangeas, delphinium and foxglove were scattered in clusters that might have been a beautiful scape had the grass and weeds not overtaken them. The ivy that traversed the wall beside us twisted up in tangles of dark purple and green ascending all the way to the highest point of the blue dome. I peeked down at Shroding. Was he happy to be back? Or saddened to see this place in such a state? It was surely a spectacular sight in its heyday. But those days were long gone.

Callum cleared his throat with annoyance, pulling me from my musings; I noticed then that Shroding was missing. With eyes wide I frantically scanned the garden around us.

"He went to look around," Callum answered flatly, but his gaze was sharp and assessing. Relief filled me, followed quickly by confusion.

"How do you know—?"

He pulled out a flat board used in school for teaching kids to read and write, from the satchel he had strapped to his hip.

"He has been communicating with this since you were unconscious."

"Clever." I smirked, imagining how Shroding would push the letters around with his nose. I was actually glad I had not seen him use it. It would have been too cute.

Callum shoved the tablet back in the bag, when a familiar comb caught my eye.

"That brush." I pointed. "That's the one I stole from you at camp."

He stepped forward so close that I could see the drops of water condensing on his breastplate. I lifted my gaze from the bag, meeting his storm gray eyes.

"Shroding explained to us why you did not tell me the truth then—he told us your whole sordid tale." A crease formed between his brows, a water drop sliding down and across his nose. I followed its path till it dripped off the side of his chin.

Surely Shroding hadn't told Asher and Callum everything, right? Not about us. Then again, was there anything to actually tell about us? Sure, we'd kissed, but Shroding had been quick to shut that down. As much as it pained me, it was clear his feelings only went as far as a general concern for the person who had the king's power. But did they know I was in love with him? It wasn't like it was a secret, especially after I made him swear an oath to kiss me once he was human again. Had he told them that? Could they see how completely smitten with him I was? That I would risk everything for him? That it didn't matter to me that Logan had done what he had? That I would die to save Shroding no matter what I lost in the process? I had already decimated everything else good in my life. If Shroding needed what little was left, I had no qualms about giving it.

The taint of Logan's power moved just under my skin, clouding and seeping into my gift. What had been warm and inviting, the pinpricks of the king's power on the tips of my fingers were hard to conjure, far out of reach. Like digging through dry sand; tedious and fruitless. Yet, the king's power was the strongest in the world. It couldn't be so easily snuffed out by Logan, could it? There had to be a way to reverse the Nephesh Maveth. And if there wasn't, then all the more reason to hurry up with Shroding's transformation before the king's power was gone forever, because I highly doubted Logan would show up again without a foolproof plan to finish what he'd started and kill me, or Shroding.

I was a walking death trap, but I would not let the trap close on anyone but myself. I would not give the power to Logan, and I would not leave Shroding trapped as a cat, alone in the pocket dimension.

"I'm sorry I took the brush from you. It seems as though it is important."

He flipped the flap of the satchel closed and took another step forward. At our uncomfortable proximity, I instinctively stepped back but was surprised when I bumped against the metal edge of the doorframe. Callum didn't halt his approach; instead he crowded me, his arm bracing above my head as he leaned down, our noses inches apart. This close I could see a faint green swirl in his gray eyes.

"I was pretty sore when you ran off with it."

"Of course." I shuddered, dropping my eyes to his chest. The metal plate glinted in the misty light. "It is clearly an expensive gift." It was definitely a gift for a woman, and from his displeased tone it must be someone he loved very much. But if he loved the girl with the initials N.M., then why were his lips moving at the shell of my ear, whispering intimately?

"Don't worry," he breathed, and I swallowed so hard I was sure he heard it. "There is no need to be jealous. It's a gift for my sister."

Affronted, I snapped my eyes up to his. What was he talking about? Jealous? Me? Was he mentally unwell? The hesitation in his gaze did not match the sultry, cocky words he had just spoken, but then his lips formed a thin line, resignation I couldn't comprehend hardened in his gray eyes. I had all but concluded Callum hated me. For a while I'd thought he might be warming up to me, but he had iced me out the whole wagon ride, and anytime our gazes had met, his answering glare was riddled with disdain.

He stepped back and started down the corridor.I blinked quickly a few times, trying to flush away the last twenty seconds.

My steps were stilted, hand trailing along the wall as I gained speed, having to jog to catch up to him.

I took in my surroundings. If the exterior of the palace was an unkempt garden of white and glass, the interior was the opposite. Tall twelve-foot stone walls spanned the vista before us, lined with unlit ornate iron wall lamps. The hall was dimly lit by skylights high above. The misty air was like a cloud of gray hovering above us, much like the strange tension between me and the commander.

The squelch of our wet shoes on the hard stone echoed in the narrow corridor. A few twists and turns and we walked out into a massive hallway; the walls' stone facade was replaced with sky blue fabric, scalloped with gold detailing. On either side of the hall were rooms hidden behind thick oak doors. The skylights overhead cast the space in a hazy glow, muting the deep blue of the plush carpet. The passage we stepped out from appeared to be a hidden path within the wall. Callum clicked the wall panel closed behind me, and I marveled at how it completely disappeared, no visible seam in the fabric.

"This way," Callum grunted, back to his surly self. I was not sure how much of Callum's company I could manage. Surely Asher would be back before nightfall?

I bumped into Callum's back as he stopped before one of the doors. He glanced back at me, then, with a faint creak of the old wood, I followed him inside.

"This will be your room."

I walked deeper into the chamber, taking in the two windows that started at the floor and curved up the wall onto the ceiling above us. How on earth could it have been made? A small leather chaise was angled in front of an unusually large hearth—big enough that I could stand upright in it. There were two doors on either side, one of which we had come through from the hall. The doors were a mix of metal and wood with a gold pattern etched into the panels.

"You should get warmed up; the palace is pretty drafty." He pointed at the other door off to the side of the fireplace. A washroom?

I nodded, not wanting to test Callum's patience right

now. He was being kind, but how long would that last? Plus the mist had saturated my body down to my bones, and I was ready to shed Lev's tattered clothes. Though I was not sure I had any other clothes available.

When I closed the door to the bathroom I was surprised by the size. The ceiling curved in a dome, ornate tiles in warm tones decorating the curveThe floor was smooth white stone. A vanity and a porcelain clawfoot tub were off center in the space, and a narrow door off to the side hid a toilet.

I undressed and wrapped a thick fur robe, left draped over the tub, around myself. It was far too big on me and kept sliding off my shoulders. I bunched the extra fabric in my hands so I could walk without tripping.

I peered around the tub for a spigot. Finding none, I got to my knees and crawled around the basin. I spent far too long searching. Perplexed by the odd tub with no way to turn the water on, I got up and left the bathroom, hoping someone was around who I could ask for help. Hoping for Shroding but okay if it was anyone but Callum.

I shuffled the robe awkwardly, the hem tangling around my feet. Frustrated, I hiked the hem up, exposing my legs to make walking easier.

"Ahem," Callum cleared his throat.

I jumped, startled to find him kneeling at the fireplace, stoking a small flame. His face was in line with my now exposed legs. Slowly his gaze traveled up my bare skin, took in the rumpled robe in my arms, my exposed shoulder and mess of tangled hair, before settling on my wide eyes. With a squeak I dropped the fabric to the floor and clasped the robe closed with my hand, covering my shoulder. Under his gaze, I might as well not be wearing anything at all.

I swallowed. My voice eked out as a whisper. "What are you still doing here?"

He said nothing, just stared.

"Callum?" I said with more force.

He blinked slowly. "Hmm?" As if coming back to himself, he looked away and began to work the fire again, which had almost gone out. "Shroding wanted you to have a fire," he said simply, back to his normally gruff self.

"Could that wait?" He looked at me again, keeping his eyes firmly on my face. "I—" Had been about to ask him for help with the bath but quickly thought better of it.

"Ah, right, of course." He stood and turned to leave, but after two steps he stopped and shook his head as if remembering something. "Haya, this probably isn't the best time, but about the betrayal ten years ago..." He rubbed the back of his neck. "I wanted to say thank you."

I stared at his back, unsure why he was thanking me. "What do you mean?"

He pivoted on his heel, strode up to me, and his knees hit the hard stone floor, head bowed as he knelt.

"What are you doing?" I grabbed his arm to pull him. "Stand up."

His biceps flexed, but he didn't budge.

"Thank you for protecting Shroding when I could not."

"I didn't know what I was doing then," I fumbled out honestly. I'd been so scared in that alley as a child, the first time I had encountered Logan. Long before I had the vibration gift to help me.

"It doesn't matter. As the prince's protector, thank you. Thank you for keeping him safe in my stead." His words were rushed, like he did not utter "thank you" often enough to feel comfortable saying it.

"Please, Callum, stand up." I yanked his arm again, my hand almost like a child's against his muscular form.

His gray eyes were unwavering as they looked up at me. Slowly he put his hand over mine.

"Thank you, Haya, for keeping him safe all this time."

I wanted to laugh and tell him it was the other way around, that Shroding didn't need protecting. That I *really* had done nothing for Shroding all this time, but the sincerity in Callum's stormy eyes stopped my words.

"Okay, okay," I accepted gently, placing my other hand over his, forgetting the situation with my robe. For just a second it hit me just how intimate of a moment we were having, and heat flushed my cheeks.

He must have noticed it too because he cleared his throat, breaking the mood and rising to his feet.

"I'll leave you to it, then." He nodded curtly, but before turning to leave he reached out and lifted the robe up over my shoulder, as it had fallen loose again. Then he was gone, and I was left thinking I must have imagined his thumb grazing the curve of my collarbone and the heat in his eyes, like an unexpected summer storm had caught us both unprepared in its downpour.

CHAPTER 4

Visitation

I peeled back the bandage around my neck, revealing the mark. It was clean, the indent of human teeth leaving a half moon over my pale flesh. I ran my hand over the skin. It was smooth, like the mark was not there, but I could see the pattern, and even though it was healed there was a persistent burning growing harder to ignore. Did that mean the power was spreading? The memory of Logan's teeth and tongue sliding over my skin had me leaning over the edge of the tub, dry heaving.

Catching my breath, I slammed the door on those thoughts. Something in me warned that if I thought about him too long, Logan would know and might speak to me again.

"How do I turn this thing on?" I grumbled to myself as I went around the tub again. "Ah, there you are!" I clapped, spying a small button. I pushed it, and water began filling the tub from underneath. I watched in amazement as the water rose.

Reaching down, I tested the water.

"Strings!" I pulled my hand away. It was ice cold.

The door flew open behind me and hit the wall with such force I toppled over onto my rear in alarm.

Shroding bounded to my side and touched me so I could hear him. "What's wrong?"

Hand to my heart I exhaled; he had startled me more than the water had. "I'm okay... It's just freezing." The robe slipped again, the curve of my shoulder and collarbone exposed to the chill of the air. I snatched it, my cheeks warming.

His dark gaze followed my hand, and as usual his expression was unreadable in his cat form, though the flick of his tail might be indicating he was annoyed. Silently he rose to look in the tub then back to me.

"Sorry to barge in like that," he murmured in chagrin, and attempted to dip his paw into the water.

I glanced at the door.

"How did you...?" I asked. I had definitely closed the door behind me, especially after the unnerving moment with Callum. I had not wanted any unwelcome visitors. Not that I expected Asher to disturb me, but Callum had been acting especially bizarre since I woke in the wagon.

"Lever handles are easy to open." He shrugged as if it were the most obvious thing in the world. Then again I suppose if he really thought I was in danger, he would have just broken it down. Did that mean he'd come in just to check on me? Where had he gone after we arrived?

"Glad I didn't get undressed," I teased under my breath.

His ears flicked. "That would have been interesting to say the least."

I frowned, sure he was laughing at me.

"You didn't need to come, for such a trivial thing," I

hedged. "Though I'm not sure I can handle an ice bath—my whole body already feels stiff as stone."

"Things are a little old fashioned here."

"Um, this tub is not old fashioned. I've never seen a basin fill like that." I pointed accusingly at the porcelain. "It took me forever to figure out how to get water in it."

"Well, some things make more sense than others. If you want hot water, you have to turn it on." He moved over to the vanity and opened the cabinet with his teeth. Inside was a cluster of pipes and knobs. He pulled with his mouth and nudged with his nose a few things I could not see. "There, you should have hot water now."

I reached in and touched the new water pooling in. It was hot. Sweet heavenly heat. "It's a lot warmer, thank you."

"I'll be outside if you need me." His tail dropped to the floor, and he turned to leave.

"Shroding." His ears twitched, and he glanced up at me. For a moment it seemed like he wanted me to ask him to stay. I snorted to myself, sure I was imagining things again. "Umm, how do I turn it off?"

"It will stop automatically. Push the same button when you want it to drain."

"Right..." I looked back at the tub skeptically.

"Haya."

"Hmm?"

"You are important to me. So very important, please don't forget that. No matter what happens..." I met his dark eyes. His tail dragged on the floor as his ears flattened. "No matter how things change, please don't forget."

What had him so on edge? What did he think was going to change? I still planned to save him, regardless of the Nephesh Maveth.

I wanted to assure him, but I was uncertain what "important" actually meant to him. Could I be important to him on more than just a "I'm going to make you human again" level? More than a friend? Could I be important enough to love? I didn't know. Just as I didn't know how we would survive what Logan had done to us.

"Why would things change?" I said simply. Because my plan to change him back had not altered in the slightest, even with Logan's power inside me. Even with my impending death.

"I don't know how things will unfold, but I want you to remember." He hesitated, his big dark eyes looking down at the floor. "I want you to remember that the weeks we spent together, for me, were incomparable to anything else in my long life."

The air hung heavy between us. His words were almost like a goodbye. Like he was telling me things *would* be different. More than a warning, it was a promise.

"You're about to become king. The whole world is about to be yours; you can do anything you want," I reasoned, not understanding what he had to fear. I turned to watch the water level rise, as if it were mirroring the rising tension between us.

"My life is still dictated by the laws and rules of this world. Having power doesn't always mean having the power to use it." At that he pulled out of my reach and left.

The door clicked closed behind him, and somehow, though his words were not harsh, tears burned the backs of my eyes.

———

Deliciously pruny, I exited the bath. Hair plaited into a long braid, I wrapped myself up in the robe once more and entered my room.

Asher paced outside the open door of my room. I clasped the robe and tripped my way over to him.

"What is it? What happened?" I panicked, made more worried by his contemplative expression.

"Get dressed, we have a visitor." He held out a bundle of clothes, and without a word I grabbed them, before closing the door to change.

There was a simple Krav suit of black and brown, a light blue dress and a sleeping gown. The dress made the most sense, as Asher wasn't acting like the guest was one we would have to fight. I donned the clean undergarments and gown. It was definitely not like the work dresses I'd had back at the farm, which stopped at my ankles—no, this one trailed on the floor. It fit amazingly well and was buttery soft to my weathered skin. It was tight at the waist, and to my mortification it hung off my shoulders, exposing my skin. The sleeves were long, leaving only the tips of my fingers visible.

I glanced at the mirror. The mark on my neck was so visible. Quickly I unbound my hair and braided only the top half, allowing the underneath to hang loose, covering the mark.

Joining Asher in the hall, I pad barefoot next to him, the plush carpet squishing delightfully between my toes. He pushed open two white-painted double doors embossed in gold filigree, a few paces down the hall from my room.

"This is the solar." The blue domed room I had seen from the outside expanded out before me. Centered in the space was a large rug and an elegant seating area where Callum and the mysterious guest sat. There was a low table in the center, full of fruits, bread, meats and cheeses. My stomach growled viciously at the splendor, but I refrained from stuffing my face. I was not sure what this situation called for.

Shroding was curled on the edge of the rug closest to the massive hearth big enough for all of us to stand under. Which would be ill advised, as a roaring fire currently blazed in the enormous space, casting the room in a strange blur of orange light that clashed with the blue glow from the dome above. The walls were the same blue fabric as in the hall, and though the circular room was lined with wall sconces, only the fireplace was lit.

The men wore simple Krav suits, their metal adornments removed in the presence of the stranger, which only led me to wonder again who had come here? How had they known where to find us? Why had they come?

The guest rose at my arrival. An elderly man draped in an emerald green robe embellished with all sorts of embroidery. He was wiry, with a long beard that twisted into a braid at the end. His tanned skin was pressed with deep wrinkles, and the round bare plane of his head shone in the waning blue light that filtered in from the dome above.

"This girl, here." The elderly man gestured to me. "She carries the king's power?"

I startled, surprised he could still sense the power amid Logan's taint.

"Yes, she does," Asher chimed in, moving around me to sit on the couch opposite Callum and the guest.

"You took on a very dangerous task, dear child. Wielding the king's power is not something just anyone could do." The man smiled warmly at me, and I returned the gesture, still unsure who he was. "You have a very particular task ahead of you. For so young a person I hope you can wield the power well. For if you don't, your life may be forfeit." He shook his head gravely. Shroding visibly tensed at the guest's observation. The older man did not miss it. "Majesty, I'm sorry if I offended you."

Shroding's tail flicked in annoyance . Asher shifted next to me drawing my attention.

"Drink your tea. It's quite medicinal." Asher nudged my shoulder, glancing at the untouched drink in front of me.

I blinked at the change in topic. "Did you study medicine or something?" I asked conversationally.

"Oh yes, Asher is very accomplished." The older man beamed, his thick gray brows lifted. His scratchy voice bounced with excitement as he gushed like a proud father. "As the future leaders, each one of them needed to be well versed in a wide range of areas."

I supposed with four hundred plus years of time, becoming proficient in a field—or in many—shouldn't be so surprising.

"Asher studied medicine." The elderly man rubbed his hand thoughtfully over his braided beard. "Shroding studied languages, and Callum... well, I'm sure you can guess that one."

How to be a complete jerk, I wanted to say but bit my tongue. Callum was a bit all over the place: he was rude, gruff, but also gentle and charming, though it was very off putting.

Callum observed the exchange with boredom.

The old man's beard wiggled from side to side as he shook his head gamely. "He studied people, social physics, and of course they all studied how to fight."

"I would have never guessed that," I deadpanned. "So

you're really a doctor, Asher?" I leaned forward, lifting the tea and taking a sip.

The liquid was lukewarm and a little bitter. I swallowed and grimaced.

"I have studied a lot of things, but medicine has always been a personal favorite." Asher smiled, his face too young for someone so skilled. "I take it dandelion tea isn't a personal favorite?"

"Dandelions and I have mixed feelings about each other right now." I attempted to be good humored, but it came out a bit stilted. The raw edges of all I had lost chafed on me, lacing the words with the truth of my grief.

Asher only smiled and took the tea, then set it down. "Eat, you must be starving," he encouraged me, handing me an ornate porcelain plate with little blue flowers painted along the edges.

Needing no other encouragement, I sat across from Callum and the older man and filled my plate to the brim. My mouth salivated at the sight of the incredible spread. Taking a bite, I had to stop myself from moaning. Had food ever tasted this good?

I had nearly died a few times, and though decorum required me to be a bit more ladylike in this situation, I was over the idea of holding back. Something about knowing I was going to die at any moment relieved some of the inhibitions I had always allowed to govern me back on the farm. I had only so much life left to live, and eating good food when I was desperately hungry and making Shroding human again were at the moment my only goals.

There is a surety that comes with death, a sense of knowing in oneself what actually matters and what will make you happy. I didn't care who this man was; if he wasn't a threat, then it didn't necessarily concern me.

My hair cascaded over my shoulder, and I brushed it back, not wanting it to get in my food. It was slightly damp but closer to dry thanks to the heat of the fire.

"Child." I froze, a berry inches from my lips. "Come here." I lifted my gaze. "Kneel down." And just like that the sense of decorum and etiquette was back, dictating I must listen to my elders. So I put my plate aside, dabbed at my lips, and I did as I was told.

The carpet was soft under my knees as I bowed my head before the older man. He lifted his wrinkled hand to my chin and held it between his finger and thumb. His dark eyes scrutinized me. "You. I know you."

I blinked in surprise.

Shroding began to move the letters around on the board beside the table. Everyone waited, a deference to the soon-to-be king taking precedence over anyone else's words. Once he was finished Asher read the words aloud.

"'She is the descendant of Sir Armond Golden, general to the late king.'"

Callum glared at Asher, who shrugged. The exchange was fueled with unspoken words, and when Callum rolled his eyes, I knew something else was going on.

"Sir Liam did not tell me this. Why hide such wonderful news?" The man beamed, letting go of my face to pat my shoulder. "I knew Sir Armond very well. You have his eyes and golden hair. You even have the same braid. It is a court tradition, to show our solidarity to the king." He reached around and touched my hair. I flinched back, uncomfortable.

"I have not properly introduced myself." He extended his hand to me, and I took it in the traditional greeting, clasping him at the elbow. Despite his frail appearance he lifted me with ease to my feet. "My name is Sir Markel Martus, and I am the head of the king's court."

I bowed my head, embarrassed.

"Oh please, none of that now, child," Sir Martus said, guiding me back to my seat.

"I intend to use the power to bring Shroding back, sir, but..." Hesitation crept in as I considered a major problem to the plan. "I can't move between dimensions anymore." I stared helplessly down at my palms in my lap. How was I supposed to complete the transformation without accessing the other dimension?

"Do not concern yourself with the details." Sir Martus waved me off gently. I sighed, agreeing, since the more I knew, the more at risk we would be with Logan listening. Still it was nerve-racking to think I had to accomplish something without knowing *how* to do it.

Callum sighed loudly. "Enough about all that." He crossed his arms, looking down his nose at me. "We need you to attempt to block Logan out."

My brow knit. "How do I do that?" I asked incredulously. Was it even possible to block him?

"Callum, my dear boy, don't rush things." Sir Martus held up a wrinkled hand.

But I was caught up by the "boy" comment. If Callum was a boy, then I must be a fetus to these men.

"Rush things?" Callum blanched. "All we can do is rush things," he snapped, glaring.

As much as I was not loving Callum's attitude, he was right. A persistent foreboding had settled over me when we arrived. As if something really bad was going to happen if we didn't take action quickly.

"I think we all know time is of the essence," I agreed conciliatingly. "So how do I block him?" I inquired again, inching forward in my seat, my readiness to take action causing me to hit my knee on the edge of the table, jostling the tea Asher had placed there. The contents sloshed over the rim.

"Have you ever shared the king's power with Shroding?" Sir Martus questioned, placing a cloth over the spill and wiping it up.

I nodded, thinking of the times we'd made a fire and shared memories.

"That is good. If you can focus the power in the same fashion, and instead of sending it out, you target it over the mark, it can contain the taint, just long enough for—" He stopped himself by clearing his throat before he expelled any more information that might not be safe for my ears.

"I'm not a fan of that plan, love." Logan's dark snakelike voice twisted through my mind, and I slapped my hands on the table, making it shake and the teacups rattle. "I thought we were getting along so well." He *tsked*, a dry unamused laugh.

I panted, wishing I could try blocking him at this very moment, but his taint was raging inside me now, sending shock waves through me that were so violent, when the episode passed I was on the floor, my hand cut open with a shard of glass sticking out.

"Give her some air," Asher advised, his brilliant blue eyes coming into view above me.

"How did I..." I winced, clutching my hand as Asher helped me sit up.

"Like last time, you were about to use your gift on yourself," Callum answered somewhere behind me.

"But it seems some part of your mind knew what was happening and broke a glass to stop yourself," Asher finished, taking my hand gently and inspecting the wound.

I glanced uneasily at Sir Martus, who looked on with pity. Shroding however was an unreadable mask of tension. From his ears to his tail, he was eerily still, the sound rolling out of him a far cry from the purrs I was so accustomed to. If I didn't know him so well I would be afraid of him.

While Asher tended to my injury—which ended up looking worse than it was—I decided to avoid questions about what had just happened and focus on what mattered most. The transformation.

"As you can see, time is critical, so we need to decide when it's happening. I can't shake the feeling that something worse is going to happen." I didn't need to say more. Everyone understood.

"You have been tormented by nightmares for months now, nearly died a few times; damage to your psyche isn't all that surprising. I would be more surprised if you were not expecting terrible things to happen at every turn," Asher placated me, rinsing my hand with a pitcher of water on the table and dabbing it clean with a napkin.

"What kind of medical doctor did you say you were again?" I teased half heartedly, needing to lighten the mood, if not for Shroding, then to distract myself from how badly my hand hurt.

He raised an eyebrow, huffing slightly but playing along. "How many kinds are there?"

"How would I know—you're the one who is intimidatingly smart, grandpa."

Sir Martus coughed to stifle his laughter.

"In that case just assume I'm every kind of doctor you can

think of." Asher smiled warmly. The expression made him look so young and bright that I almost regretted my grandpa comment. His blue eyes shimmered like the bioluminescent waters I had seen in my school's science books. It gave him an otherworldly look, like how the Wraiths turned the possessed's eyes purple, except this wasn't scary, just beautiful. I was reminded again how Shroding warned that those in the court were all exceptionally attractive. I hadn't really believed him until I met Asher and Callum. They were gorgeous, but not only them, Sir Martus, even for his age, was striking. It was peculiar.

Shroding moved, his tail twitching and ears shifting the only real clues that he was calming down from the tension my episode had caused. A moment ago he was like a feral beast ready to pounce and cut flesh; it wasn't in any of our best interest for Shroding to fly off the handle right now, not that he had a precedent for such behavior, but I still didn't want to take any risks.

"How can you be so calm?" I whispered to Asher, wishing to channel his peaceful aura. He out of everyone had been the most level-headed after Logan blindsided me.

"I have lived a lot longer than you, as you so eloquently alluded to. I might look like a child, and Callum might still act like one, but none of us are new to near-death experiences. Have some faith in us." His smile was reassuring and kind, reminding me again why I liked Asher—he was like Theo but with the calmness and kindness of Micah. Strangely enough he also reminded me a lot of Talie, in the way he spoke. I wondered briefly if she would worry when her letters to the farmhouse got returned.

"So," Callum interrupted, his hand on the hilt of his sword. "When are we doing this?"

CHAPTER 5
Confidence

"Tomorrow," Sir Martus resolved. "As much as I don't like it, Callum is correct. All we can do is rush things, not only because of the Nephesh Maveth, but Skithian's power is converging over Tyndale. We can all sense it, can we not?"

Asher tied a wrap over my hand and looked at each of us gravely. "I did not go to town just to get supplies, but to do recon on the state of things. Sir Martus is right." He settled his gaze on Shroding. "Grieving are moving up along the coast towards the palace. It is likely they will attack any day; we have less time than we thought."

"*Strings.*" Callum slammed his fist against his knee.

"We will need to complete the transformation tomorrow," Sir Martus affirmed again.

"Can you do it?" Callum demanded, leaning forward, his hands folding between his knees, gray eyes narrowed at me.

I shook my head. "It's not a matter of can. I *have* to, regardless of what happens to me."

Shroding growled, and I glanced at him. It was the first

input he had given since the interruption by Logan, perhaps because he knew it was what had to be done, no matter what his thoughts might be on the matter, or because he was still stewing over seeing me in pain.

"I made a promise," I said firmly. "Tomorrow, then," I agreed, waiting for the nerves to kick in, but surprisingly they didn't. Perhaps it was because this was what we had been working towards, or perhaps after everything I had been through I truly was okay with dying so long as it was for Shroding. I waited, but the fear didn't come. I had a million questions about how Sir Martus had found us, but again the more I knew, the more at risk everyone was. So I had to be content in obliviousness, trusting these men to handle everything, trusting them to keep us safe till our mission was complete.

Shroding prowled over to me, his head low, shoulders peaked. A low sound vibrated from his throat, not quite a growl but not a purr either. He stopped in front of me and sat, the tip of his tail sliding under the hem of my dress and touching my foot. The endless silence in my mind shattered as his thoughts tore through me.

"You do realize even if we try, it still might not work? Even if we can complete the transformation, you might still die?" His words were sharp, but also full of trepidation. He was worried that he would lose me.

"I know," I sighed, reaching to cup his furry cheek in my palm. I expected him to pull away, but instead he leaned ever so slightly into the touch, letting me brush my thumb along the curve of his nose, and though I wanted to tell him how I truly felt, I no longer had the privacy of our connection and did not want to say it in front of an audience. So instead I leaned down and kissed the tip of his nose; it was cold and wet, and for a moment I considered freeing him from the oath he'd sworn to me, because it was clear now that I would not survive and the oath he'd made would be pointless. But the foolish hope in my heart was too deeply rooted. Hope that somehow, someway, I would survive, and if I did, I still wanted that kiss even if he thought it was a bad idea. Even if it was selfish.

The men glanced at each other curiously after Shroding's and my exchange, but I could not tell if they were confused or disapproving.

Callum rose and cleared his throat. "Haya, may I speak with you?" He lifted a grape to his mouth, eyeing me with skepticism.

I stood, and he grabbed my wrist before hauling me out of the solar and back into the adorned blue hallway. I scrambled behind him, the hem of my gown catching and making my steps clumsy.

Callum glowered with displeasure as he shoved me into a kitchen. The floors were hard stone, a stove and chopping station set up in the middle of the room and five tall narrow windows lined the wall next to us. At the center, below the middle window, was a large porcelain sink. I tripped into the basin, using both hands on the rim to stay upright. Out the window I could see the ocean. The sky had cleared some, and the misty view gave way to the reds and oranges of sunset as they danced across the horizon. Distracted by the scene, I did not sense Callum's approach until he had reached around me, hands on either side of mine on the edge of the sink, his body pressing into my back.

My spine stiffened.

"Hold still, please." The vibration of his husky voice between my shoulders made my knees tremble. Slowly his arms came around my shoulders, his head resting atop mine as he just held me.

Callum leaned in close and whispered in my ear. "I will never forgive you, traitor." My heart dropped to the floor, as for a moment I thought he was talking to me before realization had my palms sweating for another reason. "I don't know what selfish ambition you are pursuing, or if it's just your childish hatred of Shroding that has you siding with Skithian, but just know this—" His breath was hot against my neck, and his calloused palms tightened over my shoulders, the rough pads making me shiver as they squeezed. "I will put an end to you."

Faintly, so faintly it was almost like a bird in flight, visible one second and gone the next, a part of my mind flickered, and I knew Logan had heard Callum. Had registered Callum's threat.

"He got it. Now, let me go," I seethed through clenched teeth, making sure he was aware just how unhappy I was with this little stunt. He could have just said it in front of everyone; he hadn't needed to drag me away, cage me in and then hold me.

He sighed, holding me tighter. "As for you, I expect you to hold up your end of the deal, bring Shroding back, save him one last time, and I'll make sure it is all worth it."

My brow furrowed, and I twisted in his hold, which was a terrible idea, as it brought me nose to chest with him, and I was forced to lift my eyes to see his face.

The sunset cast a pink pattern of light across one side of him, the other shadowed. It gave him the air of someone dangerous, which he was, but I hadn't considered he could be dangerous to me anymore. I was supposed to bring his precious prince back—he needed me alive; he needed me safe. And yet the look he was giving me as he leaned down, bringing us as close as we had been when we first arrived, did not exude a trace of protectiveness.

"What could you offer me?" I scowled, because there was nothing Callum had that I wanted. I didn't want a title; I didn't care about more power; he couldn't bring my family back, no one could, and the one person I wanted, cared for, had already rejected me. He couldn't change any of that. What else was there for me to care about? What else was there for me to want?

His hands slid down my shoulders, across my back, before settling on the small of my waist. "A home..." He squeezed my sides, pulling me into him. "A family..." His gray eyes moved over my face, and I couldn't deny how handsome he was. The sharp cut of his jaw, the imperious straight line of his nose, the knowing smirk that lifted one side of his face. "A chance to start over." His voice was laced with honey, and I melted into him, knees bending, back arching as if I were trying to reach up, to kiss him.

Strings, what was he doing to me? Wait. An errant thought, like a lost key sunken to the bottom of a lake, drifted in the back of my mind.

Orator.

Callum was an Orator, and as long as he was touching me, he could manipulate my emotions. His expression was clouded, and though seduction was heavy in his gaze, I could see his hesitation, a wariness like he knew what he was doing to me, and didn't like it.

Now that I was aware of what he was doing, I could feel his vibration working over me, like massaging out tight muscles.

"Close your eyes and relax?" he whispered, his breath light on my cheek.

Indignant, I clenched my jaw even though my body gave in to him, allowed him to move me, mold me into whatever shape he wanted. All the while my mind fought.

Callum was using me, luring me to him. Though I did not know why, I understood there was more going on that I was not privy to. I did know, however, that I had an advantage here. Callum was offering me whatever I wanted, and if I was so lucky that death did not steal me away tomorrow, I needed a reason to stay at Shroding's side. If it was up to Shroding, I supposed once he was human again, we would part ways in Romath. I would see him from time to time, as the king and subject we were. And even if induction to the court was granted, it did not mean I had to serve the royal family. I would be free to leave, go anywhere, do whatever I wanted, but the one thing I would want I could not have. Because as a nobody I would not be able to stay by Shroding's side, unless he wanted me there. Was it wrong to force myself into his life? To make it so we wouldn't be apart? Could I stand by and watch him fall for and love another? No, if and when it came to that, I would leave, for my own sanity. Until then, though, I did not want to be parted from him, at least not because of my status.

King Roark had never allowed titles to segregate classes; the only exception was for the military. As a soldier you were innately valued above others, even more so if you had the gift. That was the only class system that truly mattered in Shamar. If your parent had a high rank or role in the military, you were considered on par with that level, but only while serving. Of course that did not stop people from showing respect to those discharged.

I did not crave power, only the power to stay with Shroding as long as I could. So that was what I would ask for: a way to stay at his side.

Callum brushed my hair over my shoulder, fingers tracing the side of my neck that was unmarked. I reached up, stilling his hand.

"I know what I want," I breathed, the air in my lungs scant as he took up all the space in the room with his dominating presence, with the power of his Orator skill.

"Yes," he hummed, eyes closed and lips brushing the side of my face as if he was losing himself to his own ability. I knew consciously what he was doing, and though my emotions were giving in to him, my mind was clear.

"Train me as one of Shroding's personal guards—give me your job as his personal protector."

Callum froze, the one hand on my waist flexing for a fraction of a second before pulling back. I could almost hear his jaw grinding as he stepped out of the embrace. He watched me; the pink sunset that had illuminated his face was gone, the darkness winning dominion over his features. There was a coldness in his eyes that I recognized from when we first met weeks ago in the forest. The set of his jaw, however, told me he was just the tiniest bit impressed that I had not succumbed to his seduction.

"I suppose I can be persuaded."

"Thanks, Callum." I smiled softly, genuinely glad he was giving me this opportunity. It wouldn't be easy, training to be in the personal guard, but at least this would give me some motivation to live through tomorrow's ordeal, because now I knew I wouldn't be leaving Shroding's side anytime soon.

He looked down at me, his gaze curious. "I don't think you have ever thanked *me* before."

I hadn't? Even after all the times he had saved me? "Actually I did after you saved me from drowning." I smiled a bit too cheerfully, recalling all too vividly the steel of his blade at my throat.

"Doesn't count, you were under duress." He had the gall to smirk. "So this *is* the first time."

"Don't let it go to your head," I jested, knowing his head was already too big.

"I won't, this time, but next time I make no promises." He shrugged, crossing his arms, the stretch of his shoulders making his presence too imposing.

"What makes you think there will be a next time?" I crossed my arms, nowhere close to matching his haughtiness.

"Trust me, love—women are always gushing with gratitude towards me," he taunted me coyly, but I couldn't hear what he said next as the world fell away; as if my ears were full of cotton. At the word "love" my legs wobbled. The pricking of vibrations at my fingertips, coupled with a sharp pain in my neck, left me breathless. I slumped to the floor, gasps of pain ripping through me as I cried out.

Callum dropped to his knees in front of me, but I couldn't fathom his expression as Logan's voice split through my mind.

"And here I thought you were a loyal little pet to Shroding, but it seems like you might be keeping your options open." The goading clap of his voice sent shock waves of vibration through my torso, and with a cry I arched into Callum, one hand grabbing his shoulder, the other clamping over the mark on my neck. I squeezed my eyes shut against the agony, willing Logan to get out of my head.

Instead a vision burned behind my eyes. Fire marred the city below. The ink of night, a cover that allowed all the horrors of Golan to stretch their violent intent over the innocent people below. I watched from above, wings beating, chest searing from the unspent rage, waiting to be let out. On my back the soul of my master ordered and controlled the hordes. The city was ours, the first in a long line of battles to end the war and take Shamar. We had won. We had all we needed to keep moving forward; it would only be a matter of time.

Power flared, making me gasp as the vision faded. It was only after Callum's arms wrapped around me that Logan's voice receded, but not without one last jab.

"Try not to call my attention to you, love—as I said before, you won't like what you see."

Callum's face looked foreign, his normally cool gray eyes wide with panic as they slowly faded behind a screen of black.

"Haya," Callum's voice whispered gently. "You're okay, wake up."

I opened my eyes slowly, finding myself back in my room, lying upon the plush red covers of my bed, the softness odd against the stiffness of my body. "What happened?"

"You passed out." His hair looked more tousled than usual, as if he had been running his hands through it vigorously. "I should go get Asher so he can look you over."

"No! No, I'm okay." I pulled his arm lightly till he sat on the edge of the bed. "Please don't, I'm fine now." He looked unconvinced. "Really." I sat up and smiled anxiously. I didn't need him alarming everyone over nothing.

He nodded, though his expression was unconvinced.

"Thank you." I grinned.

His body seemed to relax, and I sighed with relief.

He smirked. "I told you, gushing with gratitude, but the

fainting thing is a first for me," he said cheekily. It took me a moment to recall our banter from before.

"Why did you call me that?"

"What?" His brow fell with confusion.

"L-Love..." I fumbled.

He looked unsettled, and then realization crossed his face. "Logan calls you that, doesn't he?" I nodded, unsure how he'd figured it out so quickly. It must have been the trigger that caused my mark to flare. "Logan was like a brother to me; we were all like family, having grown up together. The way people confused Asher and Shroding, well, they used to confuse me and Logan much the same."

"You don't look anything alike." Besides the blond hair and the pale eyes they were totally different. Callum was full, stocky. His features were what you would expect from a pretty boy and with the attitude to match. Logan was lanky, frail in a dangerous kind of way, like a malnourished lion, ready to kill without morals or remorse.

"I haven't seen him in a long time, but I'll take your word for it. We were very similar when we were young, but not just in looks—in mannerism, even in attitude. The biggest difference was Logan always challenged Shroding, whereas I wanted to protect him. I began to question his loyalty when we were young..." He trailed off. Shoulders slumped, he stood and walked to the arched windows looking out at the overgrown garden below.

To me Logan was a monster: he'd betrayed Shroding, poisoned me, and if the visions I was seeing were to be believed, then he was also very, very dangerous. Perhaps even beyond saving, but that didn't change who he was to those he'd grown up with. Callum still loved Logan, that much was clear, even if he'd threatened multiple times to kill him. Even at times Shroding seemed to have a softness towards Logan, though since the poisoning that appeared less frequently. "I will help you anyway I can, just like I am with Shroding. I might not have known you all for hundreds of years, but I see you as my friend." I wasn't sure I believed my words. I had been through hardship, but I did not want that to make me a hard or unforgiving person.

"You are either very stupid or brave. Asher and Shroding seem to think it's the latter, but I'm leaning towards stupid." Callum looked at me over his shoulder, a hopeful smirk lifting his cheek.

I shrugged, placing my feet on the floor. "Thanks for the vote of confidence."

"I should tell Shroding about this." Callum stood and turned to the still open door of my room.

I jumped and hurried to block his path. "No, don't. Promise you won't tell anyone—there is enough going on. Besides, it won't change anything; telling them does nothing." A plea filled my voice. I didn't want to burden anyone, especially Shroding. I knew him well enough to know he was already beating himself up for getting me involved to begin with, and besides, he already knew Logan was in my head; he didn't need to know how frequently. At least not yet.

Callum deliberated, then sighed. "I won't for now, but if it happens again, all bets are off."

I nodded. "Fine."

He crossed his arms. "As for our other conversation, I will only consider letting you be in the king's guard if you can best me in hand-to-hand combat."

CHAPTER 6

Fight

I skidded along the cold ground, the air whooshing from my lungs and the fabric of my shirt ripping along the side seam. Callum and I were outside in the garden, dead leaves crunching under our booted feet. Though I could not see the ocean, I could smell the salt in the air.

Callum pushed his gold hair out of his face. "Again," he ordered, breath a white puff in the dusk of night.

"It's too cold!" I whined, which if I was honest was not why I was mad. This was my fifth attempt to fight him, and all I ever seemed to accomplish was falling on my butt. The way Callum fought required years of body awareness and just plain skill. Skill I did not seem to have. So much for the king's power being "easy" to use like Shroding had said. But I supposed it was more difficult now with the taint from Logan.

"The cold has nothing to do with it. Just be glad I'm not making you fight in the snow." He pointed to the peaks Shroding and I had crossed what seemed like a lifetime ago.

I scowled. "The cold makes me all stiff, and I can't think about anything but the fact my toes are frozen."

"This is hopeless," Callum sighed, arms crossed just below the crest on his dark Krav uniform, posing like the commander he was. He had not been open or friendly to me since bringing me back to my room; in fact he was more closed off than he had been when he was suspicious of me. I wasn't sure what to make of it. "Shroding will just have to stay a cat, and you won't get to be his guard." He huffed and walked past me.

The basic movements weren't hard; it was moving and pulling my vibration gift out at the same time that I couldn't quite do anymore. Hence the landing on my butt.

Callum was trying to be gentle by only using enough of his power to knock me off balance, never doing lasting damage. Unless one counted the increasing number of purple bruises on my rear. Still I could feel Callum's growing impatience.

It wasn't like I failed on purpose. I wanted to learn, I just didn't understand what I was doing wrong. I threw my fist at the ground, feeling the cold earth crack slightly, the dry yellow grass scratching against my knuckles. Accessing the king's power was a lot harder with Logan's gift muddying things up.

"Wait," I called. With a deep breath I stood. I was behaving like I didn't want to bring Shroding back, which was not true. I had promised. I had to keep trying until I got it right. "Callum, wait," I said again louder. Callum stopped, glancing over his shoulder, one eyebrow raised. "We aren't finished." I leveled my gaze at him, his pale eyes reflecting the cold pale sky above. His lips twitched, and he stalked over to me. He moved like water, placid on the surface but with dangerous currents underneath. Though I was sure my toes were actually frozen, the cold didn't even seem to faze him. He moved like he was not the least bit chilled.

"Again," was all he said as he ran at me with fists raised. I tensed my muscles as if I could break off the cold surrounding them. I moved through Krav, starting with the basics, dodging, punching, crouching, kicking, until we were in an easy dance of swings and blocks. It got to the point when Callum always threw me on my butt, and I braced for the punch from his vibration.

It didn't come.

For a moment I thought I'd done something right, like I had used my gift and finally beat him.

"You aren't trying—you expect my blow and are simply waiting for it," Callum snapped, his voice close to my face. He had stopped his attack midmotion. His one arm was raised, blocking my swing, the palm of the other splayed out over my abdomen, the ripple of his vibration gift pressed against my stomach. His leg, which always made me fall on my butt, was wrapped around the back of mine. We held this awkward stance for a moment. "Try, Haya, you have to *try* to stop my attack."

"I don't know how," I groaned, moving to drop my arm and back away, but he grabbed my wrist, holding me in our tangled posture.

"You do. Pull the energy."

I remembered my breathing, like Shroding had taught me, and focused the power. It pricked at my fingertips for just a moment, before a gust of icy wind broke my concentration.

"What has Shroding been teaching you in the other dimension?" Callum antagonized me. "Or do you just spend all your time making out?"

My jaw dropped.

"No wonder you haven't gotten any better, too busy sleeping with the prince?" Callum continued as heat crept up my neck.

"He's a cat!" I nearly yelled, disgusted at the insinuation.

"He's not always a cat..." he goaded, leaning in, pulling my arm over his shoulder, still poised in the attack. Had Shroding told them about the spirit dimension, about our time together? Regardless, Shroding and I hadn't done anything since the last kiss, which, by Shroding's standards, had apparently been a mistake. So why was I so affronted by Callum's accusations? I grit my teeth, probably because I wished Shroding and I were doing the very things Callum insinuated.

"What's it matter to you what we do?" I growled, forgetting the cold and just wanting to get away from him. I pulled the power to my fingers and used my free hand to shove his away from my abdomen. We pushed and pulled in a new dance; the movements were the same, but this time his vibrations were not the only ones present.

"Did you forget he is a king? He will dump you like the nobody farm girl you are." Callum sneered, as he blocked another attack.

Strings, I knew Callum was a piece of work, but this taunting was cruel, and just when I'd thought we were starting to get along. I clenched my jaw, the bite of wind on my face.

"I can help pick up the pieces if you need a rebound." He slid his arm around my waist, chest pressed to mine, his warmth staving off the chill of the brisk night. He lifted me into a hold—an advanced move that told me what was coming next.

The bruise on my butt flared as I hit the ground with more force than usual. My power disappeared with the impact. There was a rush of heat in my chest as I stumbled upright and turned my back to Callum.

"Never fight angry," Callum instructed, his voice level.

"I'm not angry, I'm cold," I said too quickly, a tear escaping my eye.

"I only said those things to make you mad. They were not true." There was no sympathy in his voice, only fact.

"Of course, I know that." Still his words had stirred up the fears that lived freely in my heart. Fear that had only started growing stronger the closer we got to changing Shroding back.

"Please forget what I said. You did very well. Control your anger, and you will progress nicely," Callum advised. "It should be easier too, since you have done it in the cold."

My curiosity got the best of me, and I tilted my head to the side, my back still to him. "Why?"

"It's distracting, the cold; it makes it harder to concentrate. If you can learn to focus and fight in difficult environments, then when you are in less environmentally challenging conditions, fighting will be easier."

"I didn't beat you," I deadpanned, knowing the terms of our agreement had not been met.

"You can always try again." He shrugged and waved his hand over his shoulder, bidding me to follow him back inside. But his words still burned in my mind, and I didn't want to go inside to sit and stew alone. I needed to move, pace, something. The salty breeze blew across my face, and though it was freezing I desired to see the ocean more.

I followed the stone path out into the untamed gardens. Dried-up leaves and branches littered the path, crunching under my boots with each step. Rounding a large row of hedges, I took the path down to where the stones crumbled to white sand. To my left was a lookout that framed the rolling cattle hills and faintest buildings of the city beyond.

Pressure on my shoulder had me jumping and turning around. But I did not see the withered garden, only that the palace was ablaze. Screams of terror filled my ears. I backed away, hands covering my mouth to hold in my own scream as the vision before me shifted to a city of clay and stone crumbling.

"Seeing through my eyes, love?" Logan's voice shot through my veins like the poison his power was. Understanding filled me. These things were illusions from Logan's mind. He wanted me to see this destruction, like he had shown me the battlefield before.

"The sweet smell of victory and desolation."

"Nothing sweet about it," I hissed, teeth clenched tight as my stomach rolled, the stench of the horror too pungent, too real.

"If only you had the strength to stop me."

"I do," I warned, fists clenched so tight, my nails broke skin, as I watched the horrors before me. I did not recognize the city, but I could assume it was Erasmus, since the buildings were not like those in Tyndale or Romath and it was clear it was a major city.

An arm wrapped around my waist, pulling me back. Logan leaned down, resting his head on my shoulder, holding me against his chest. "Love, we are running out of time. I know you feel it too. This destruction is only the beginning."

I shivered in fear. The clenching in my abdomen made me dizzy with disdain.

"Get your hands off me."

"Of course, love." He stepped back, his hand trailing across my stomach and resting on my hip. "This is all in *your* mind after all. But soon enough, I will be holding you for real, and when I do you will know I have won."

The image before me shifted, and I was once again in the garden just down the path from the palace.

"Haya!" Callum shouted.

"Callum?" I gasped, rounding the hedges and taking the steps two at a time till I reached him on the landing.

He took in my appearance, my hair tousled and body shaking. His jaw clenched and unclenched a few times, his eyes unreadable.

"He is gone," Callum said, coming to my side. "Let's get you inside before you get pneumonia. A storm is coming through." The temperature had definitely dropped a lot, but it was hard to notice after what had just happened. "It's freezing out here; your fingers are purple," he chided, grabbing my hand and holding it up to my face. I blinked, preoccupied.

"We are running out of time," I whispered.

The cold air whipped around the side of the palace. Callum stepped in front of me, blocking the wind, and reached out to hold my shoulders.

"Don't do that," he scolded, and I looked up at him, confused. "Don't wander off on your own."

"I'm not a child." I smarted, thoughts still muddled, but finding his chiding tone just grating enough to allow me to think more clearly.

He worked his jaw.

"Come on," he said with forced pleasantness, and led me inside, his hand on the small of my back.

The door to my room creaked as he held it open; the walk back had been silent and tense.

"I'll let the others know you are resting." He placed his hands on my waist, whirled me around, and gave me a gentle push towards the bed. "Sleep," he ordered.

I nodded numbly, the ache in my bones pushing to the forefront of my thoughts. Maybe sleep was a good idea. I looked back at him but only saw the door closing.

Sighing, I collapsed onto the soft mattress.

Sometime later, a soft purring wrapped around my body, and Shroding's voice entered my mind.

"About tomorrow, I need you to promise me you will stop if it gets to be too much. If you can't do it."

I yawned sleepily, the embers of the fire giving the faintest glow to the room. "Do you think I can't do it?" I asked slowly, voice slurred with sleep.

"You can do anything," he said somberly. "I'm just concerned at what cost?"

"You are the king." I smiled, trying to make light of the topic. "More people than just me would give their life for you."

He growled. "I don't doubt you would push yourself to the brink of death to bring me back." I rolled into him, my eyes closing as I nuzzled, dreamily, into his side.

In place of his purr was a deep growl that almost had me sitting up and asking if he was okay, but in my sleep-addled mind I could not bring myself to care how upset he was.

"Romanticize it all you like, but you should not have to die so I can live." He touched his paw to my hand. "Promise me."

"I promised to bring you back," I answered, words drawn out and heavy. "I don't plan on dying tomorrow." I yawned again. I would not promise him, I could not promise what I could not control. Even if it gave us both peace of mind. It would be a lie. If I had to die, then I would die, but I would not be stupid about it. I would do my best to live.

"That's hardly a promise."

"That's as close as it's going to get."

CHAPTER 7

Ocean View

The sad song of a mockingbird stirred me awake. I opened my eyes, expecting to see the bright sun of day, but was greeted by the still dark night. Sitting up, I pat the blankets, looking for Shroding, brows knitting when I could not find him. I dropped my feet to the cold floor and padded around the room.

"Shroding?" I whisper-called, but the only sound was the chirping song of the bird. I walked over to the window, the edge of the closed curtain illuminated by silver light.

The moon shone brightly, and I scanned the horizon quickly, assessing that my room faced the back of the palace, a bedraggled garden below, and just beyond that was the sandy shore I had seen out the kitchen window. A lone speck sat on the white beach. In the silver light of the moon it was easy to figure out who was out there, as all around them the air glowed amethyst.

What was Shroding doing outside alone on the beach?

Not having a coat, I grabbed the robe from earlier and

wrapped it over my nightgown. I turned to leave, spotting a single pair of brown boots resting by the fire. After slipping them on, I maneuvered through the palace, looking to find my way to Shroding.

I wandered utterly lost for a while until I peered out a window and realized I was on the first floor. Giving up on finding a door, I heaved the latticed window open and climbed out onto the stone edging. It was not a far drop, but I would have to brace myself for the impact so I did not cause injury to my knees.

Using what I had already learned of Krav from Callum and Shroding, I landed on the ground and rolled; unfortunately I rolled right into a rose bush. I yelped as the thorns cut along my cheek and hands. The robe thankfully had protected the rest of my skin.

Shaking off my blunder, I walked through the ruined garden down to the shore below.

It was my first time ever seeing the ocean up close or setting foot on a beach. My boots sank heavily into the sand, and I shuffled awkwardly across the surface, having to lift my knees high in order to stay balanced. The fur-trimmed robe left a swirling trail in the sand behind me. Every few steps I had to lift it and shake it out as the sand kept piling up, making it harder to walk.

"Shroding." I cupped my mouth, calling for him but not yelling. The stillness of the night and crash of the waves were gentle warnings, asking not to be disturbed by anything other than birdsong. The mockingbird sang loudly; it must be perched somewhere in the garden behind us.

He turned, catching my call with his enhanced hearing.

Just like every other time I saw him in the moonlight, I

was drawn to him, that inexplicable hook tugging at my chest, needing me to get closer and closer to him.

Once I reached Shroding I sat down, resting my hands in the sand. It was freezing, and the sand, if not so grainy, might have been mistaken for snow. Shroding slid his tail to me, and laid it over my hand. Our connection was instant.

"You know," he began as if we had been in the middle of a conversation, "I still feel wary of the moonlight," he admitted softly. The moon sat imperiously overhead, looking down on us as if proud it had some power over the king. "As if it can still expose some secret about me that I want to keep hidden."

"Do you still have secrets to hide?" I probed, though we both knew he did. I wanted to know what secrets he kept. What things he did not want anyone else to know. I wanted him to tell me. I wanted to be his confidant for all things.

"Some habits will be harder to break than others, I suppose," he hedged with a sigh. "What are you doing awake?" he asked, turning his dark eyes fully on me.

"I think my sleep is all out of sorts. That and the mockingbird song woke me." I waved my hand back towards the gardens, to where the bird was still chirping away.

"It sings because it lost its mate," he said, watching the waves solemnly.

"How do you know?"

Shroding shrugged his shoulders. "It's one of the reasons they sing at night, but I suppose not the only reason."

"For a moment I thought you were going to say you can speak to animals."

He glanced out of the corner of his eye. "I would have mentioned that when we were making the pro/con list back at the shed."

I laughed. "Unless it was a secret," I teased, but he just shook his head. "What category would it have fallen into?"

"Con, definitely a con," he deadpanned, without missing a beat.

I snickered behind my hand and gazed up at the moon, its light fading behind wisps of gray. Storm clouds were rolling in, just as Callum had said.

The wind blew off the ocean, sending a freezing waft of salty air into my face. I pulled the robe tighter around me.

"It's definitely winter."

"The Celebration of Strings will be happening soon," he mused.

Nostalgia washed over me—memories of warm orange bread, my father's voice over a mug of hot cocoa, and Theo, Micah, and I tossing snow in the air.

"You're smiling," Shroding said softly.

"What did your family do for the Celebration of Strings each year?" I asked, subdued at having been caught smiling. I imagined Shroding's childhood filled with grand halls, glamorous people, and decadent food during the Celebrations.

"Well..." he began thoughtfully, "the castle always had a big party. The whole court would be there with their families. Many of the people from the surrounding cities would come to see the light show. The gardens in the city were lit up, and most years it snowed, so everything was covered in white."

"Like this." I sifted the silvery sand between my fingers, imagining it to be snow.

"Do you know why we celebrate every year?"

I thought hard about what my textbooks had said, but as

far as I knew, it was just a celebration of creation. I told him as much.

"When my father was young, shortly after the Seraphs returned from their journeys, he instituted a celebration to honor their sacrifice. The Seraphs were to be revered across the land, so we set a time in early fall for a festival. But at the intended party... Skithian sent a troupe of forces into the capital. The Seraphs were weak from their travels, and though they lacked the strength to fight, they rose up one last time to drive out his forces. We won that battle, but at the expense of their lives. A few months later my father decreed that the people would celebrate every year. That celebration was both remembrance and restitution—honoring the fallen Seraphs and the Creator who had gifted them to us in the first place."

"I never knew that was why we celebrated," I said, despondent at the dark turn the story had taken.

"Don't be sad. It is a celebration to honor them, not to mourn. We are supposed to drink and be merry." His comforting tone shifted to one of wistfulness as he continued. "I remember everything about those nights. At midnight, they set off fireworks."

"I've never seen fireworks," I admitted, wrapping my arms around my knees. "We didn't have them in Wycliff."

"You will. I'll make sure you do." He promised, and though we both knew the promise was likely an empty one, I smiled gratefully and nodded.

"Tell me about them?"

"The colors painted the pitch-black night. From the tower, it was easy to see them from every angle. They sparkled and glittered like pinwheels fluttering in the wind. Everyone gathered rejoiced, despite the ongoing war. It was the one night each year when we could truly let loose and live. My father took special precautions to ensure that Golan would never attack us on that night..." He sighed, gazing at the sky as though seeing something that wasn't there.

"Will there be a party this year?"

"I don't know. Perhaps?" His thoughts leaked through our connection, revealing his doubt. He hesitated to believe he would make a triumphant return to the court—that such a party could only happen if he came home as king. In just a few short hours we would know the answer.

If we survived.

The quiet peaceful night had me forgetting that we were about to attempt the near impossible. An impossible task I might not survive. Callum's words from the kitchen came back to me then. *I expect you to hold up your end of the deal, bring Shroding back, save him one last time, and I'll make sure it is all worth it.*

"Something strange happened earlier," I began. Shroding's ears twitched, turning towards me though his head remained forward. "Callum used his gift on me yesterday."

Shroding's head dipped, and his tail flicked away, breaking our connection. I was not sure why I had told him, but it didn't seem right to keep it from him either. Especially not after what Logan had implied. My heart was Shroding's, no one else's, and Callum could flirt all he wanted, but I would not be swayed.

"He must have taken a liking to you." Shroding's tail brushed along my hand, the connection fleeting as he whipped it away just as quickly.

"And you're okay with that?" I demanded, eyes narrowing, willing him to look at me. Of course he would be okay with it; he didn't feel that way for me. *He* was not jealous.

"Have you tried blocking Logan out?" he asked, changing the subject.

I thought about what Sir Martus and Asher had said, but between the weirdness with Callum and Logan's disruption I had not had a chance.

"No." I chewed my lip. "Should I try now?"

"Are you feeling up to it?" Shroding hedged.

I watched the waves rise and crash against the sand, their push and pull mirroring the struggle I felt every time I was in Shroding's presence. The clouds shifted, and moonlight spilled over the shore; Shroding's amethyst glow taunted and tested me, and I wished he would give me more than just his tail to connect to. But I understood his hesitation—our connection was at risk because of Logan, and only once Logan was gone would Shroding be comfortable around me again.

"Yes."

I closed my eyes, focusing on the power, working to bring it out. I thought of how I wanted to see Shroding, be with him in the pocket dimension again. How badly I wanted to save him. How badly I wanted Logan gone. Slowly, after what seemed like hours but was actually a few seconds, the power pricked at my fingers. Instead of the rush of power that used to flood my system at the slightest call, it was sluggish. Heavy as it moved through my body. I recalled the times I had shared power with Shroding, with the fire and when I sent him my childhood memory of Logan. How I'd threaded the power into him. How I'd created fire, the way I'd taken the strings of the king's power and linked it to the kindling. Willing the fire to spark. It was similar, but the focus I had this time was on dragging those strings of power back into myself. I pictured my body as a swirl of strings, the color of Shroding's gift since I did not actually know my own. I envisioned taking each thread and wrapping it around my neck. Until there were no more threads to grab. Then the glowing string at my neck pinched tighter and tighter till there was a line of vivid glowing bronze curved in a half moon over the bite. I imagined it in such great detail, as if I were watching it happen to someone else.

As quickly as it snapped into place in my mind, the faint whisper of Logan's presence vanished.

I had done it! I had focused the power, brought it to the bite mark and sealed it off.

The sound of voices forced me back to the present on the beach.

Asher, Callum and Sir Martus were around us in a defensive position.

"What's going on?" I glanced around to find the danger, as the world slowly came back into focus.

"The palace is surrounded," Asher informed wearily. Worry edged his pale features causing them to darken dangerously in the shadowed night.

"Surrounded?" I questioned from where I sat on the ground looking up at them. They all were crouched, poised for a fight. Shroding came to my side supporting me as I leaned into him. His ears and tail were lowered to the ground in tense vigilance.

"The Wraiths are here," he warned.

"It's not just Wraiths, but the Grieving as well." Callum pulled his sword from the scabbard at his hip.

"The Wraiths have possessed civilians from Tyndale," Sir Martus added.

"How many?" I asked, standing up.

"Too many," Shroding growled. Though I knew my life was close to forfeit, the way he said it sounded like it would be more than just me that would not come out of this alive.

"We need to get to the solar; there isn't much time." Asher cautioned.

The three men circled us as we ran for the palace. Though we could not yet see the Grieving, we could hear them—their moans of pain and anguish rallied through the night air.

"The Wraiths don't have much nighttime left," Asher encouraged us, sword raised and glinting in the moonlight. The rolling clouds caused the sky to be dark as pitch one second, and blinding with silver light the next.

"We just need to hold them off till sunrise," Callum snapped in agreement.

Sir Martus kept pace with us as we threaded the uneven ground. I bunched the bottom of my robe into my arms to keep up. I considered discarding it but it was the only thing staving off the winter night.

"Won't the palace be full of them already?" I pointed out, terrified we were walking into a trap.

"We barricaded the doors yesterday. The only one open is the one we came through."

Dread filled me. How could I have been so stupid? "No, there is another way."

Callum and Asher glanced towards me, but their questions died on their lips as we got to the steps leading to the garden.

We were greeted by a horde of Grieving that poured out from between the tall hedges. They were easily dispatched by the three men, but more rushed up from the beach behind us. The once white sand was blocked out by a mass of monsters, their decaying bodies crashing and slipping into one another. I swallowed a scream because this wasn't a small-scale attack; no, this was an army we would have to take down in order to survive. Panic fluttered the edges of my vision as more crept through the garden, blocking our path.

"We need to move now!" Callum yelled, slicing his sword through another head, the squelch of the flesh landing on the stones in front of me making nausea swim in my stomach. Callum sprinted forward, clearing a way to the palace as Asher and Sir Martus held back those funneling up from the beach.

I glanced down at Shroding. We were out of time. I would have to do the transformation now, or we were all done for. Closing my eyes, I reached for the king's power. We were far from safe, far from prepared, but what options were left to us? Before I could attempt to grab hold of the gift, a foul odor filled my nose, blocking out the salty air of the ocean.

When I opened my eyes, three Grieving had pushed through the overgrown shrubs and were bypassing our protectors.

"Shroding?" I hesitated, backing up the steps towards where Callum was fighting. Shroding saw them too and raised his hackles at their approach. Pieces of their flesh were torn away by the branches and dry foliage as they fixed their sunken eyes on us.

Glancing around the path, I searched frantically for a weapon. What I would give to have a sword like Callum and Asher.

I grabbed a stick a little longer than my forearm and held it aloft like a blade.

Shroding came close to my side, the grunts, howls, and

clash of metal ringing out around us as the freezing ocean breeze blew about like a specter watching the carnage.

"We got this," Shroding reassured me, a smug excitement shifting through his body, making him ready to pounce. I tightened my hold on the stick, the cut on my hand from yesterday bleeding though the bandage as I squeezed.

When the three Grieving were close enough I took on the one to the right. It had been a man at some point, but was little more than bones rattling together, flapping scraps of skin, red and oozing, clinging to what was left. It was then I realized most of the Grieving were severely decayed, already on the brink of death. I smashed the stick into its head, and it popped off, its bones disintegrating into dust at the neck joint. I gasped in surprise. The Grieving that had attacked the farm had been more robust. Still fragile and fleshy, but they had not decomposed. What did it mean that these monsters were so near death? Was it possible that they had been around for a long time, living in Shamar?

There was little time to dwell on these questions as Asher and Sir Martus were pushed back. Shroding ripped through the last two attackers, as my stick had snapped in half after taking down the one.

"Fall back to Callum," Asher ordered, his sword raised as he fought a possessed civilian. Glowing violet eyes peppered the faces in the army below. The Wraiths could be killed, but their supercharged abilities made getting close enough to light them on fire extremely difficult. I thought about the attack on Coinania and the Wraith I had defeated. It had only been a few short days since then, but so much had changed. The difference between now and then was that then I had been able to use the king's power. Now I would be lucky to survive.

"Let's go," Shroding yelled, before jumping up the stairs to where Callum was fighting a Wraith.

Fire shot through the possessed man, and Callum sliced through the black mass, killing the Wraith just as we drew closer.

"Inside now!" Callum bellowed, waving us through the open door as Asher and Sir Martus closed in on our tail.

Once inside, we shoved the door closed, barring it with Callum's blade. It would not hold for long, but it would buy us some time—that was unless the monsters had found the window I'd left open.

We were all sweating and panting despite the freezing cold.

"To the solar," Sir Martus huffed, moving ahead through the narrow servant's passage.

"Our priority is the king," Callum said with a hint of anguish. We knew what he meant. We were all expendable except for Shroding and by extension me.

"What do I need to do to complete the transformation?" I begged, steeling my voice and my resolve to see this through to whatever end.

"Water for life, fire for the spark that bids a heart to beat," Sir Martus explained as we went.

"I don't understand."

He stopped, turning to face me in the narrow space, and whispered.

A seed not watered dissolves back into dirt
In the midst of sorrow hope is a choice
For only by the breaking of bone and soul shall the power
revert

Up a wall of song and light one must hoist
The heat of flesh and spark of fire will make what was lost fill
with a greater power

73

"These are the king's words." Sir Martus placed his hands on my shoulder. "Only you can fulfill this prophecy. Only you can bring the king back."

CHAPTER 8

I Hold On

"How will I know I'm on the right track?" I nodded, ignoring the twinge in my neck as I turned to Sir Martus.

"You might not be able to connect as you once did"—Sir Martus gestured between Shroding and me—"but the king's power in you knows what to do. Trust him and trust yourself."

Still unsure, I backed up, letting Callum and Asher sandwich Shroding and me between them as we exited the passage and spilled out onto the plush blue carpet of the main hall. Except the hall was different; instead of blue fabric on the walls there was a pale yellow, and the double doors were a deep dark wood instead of the white ones that led to the solar.

"Where are we?" I breathed, and just then the skylights above rattled, the sound deafening in the arching hall, glass splintering. I threw my arms over my head, trying to protect myself from the falling glass. But no shards descended, and I peered up to see the glass had only cracked, and the once empty hall was filled with possessed villagers and Grieving.

"This is bad, we must have missed the turn," Asher hissed, lifting his sword. Callum and Sir Martus had no weapons to defend themselves with, and I was even more vulnerable. My hands shook with fear at the absolute mess we were in.

Shroding stood in front of me. His eyes flashed iridescent, and I instinctively dropped to the floor and wrapped my arms around his body, out of a need to be close to him and to protect him. I was scared, not just of the imminent attack but about the transformation. I had been so confident, but now everything was rushed, haphazard, and I worried I might fail him.

He rested his head on my shoulder and purred softly, reminding me of easier moments. I closed my eyes and breathed. Feeling safe even as danger surrounded us on all sides. Even if tonight I lost my life to save him.

"Haya." Shroding pulled back, eyes intense like he wanted to say more but couldn't.

"Get in the library," Asher ordered, running to the dark doors and shoving them open.

We sprinted inside. The library was massive; massive; two levels tall, with floor-to-ceiling books lining the almost rounded walls. Dark cherrywood cases of various heights stretched out in rows along the ornate gold and red carpet. The ceiling, like most of the ceilings in the palace, was made of glass.

Across from the large double-door entrance to the library was a bay window cut out between the bookshelves. The windows overlooked the gravel courtyard, the library centered above the main entrance to the palace.

Callum, Asher and Sir Martus moved books and shelves around quickly, creating a circle in the center of the room. They blocked off all the other doors, forcing the enemy to filter in through the main entrance.

"Shroding, get her somewhere out of the way," Callum ordered, and Shroding growled slightly, causing Callum to frown. "I mean we should put her somewhere safe from the fighting, Majesty." He amended.

Shroding brushed against the fabric of my robe, tail flicking in annoyance along my shin. "You could have left out the Majesty part," Shroding grumbled, and despite our circumstance I huffed a little laugh.

Still Callum was right, I needed a hiding spot. So I scanned the massive room for a place to go. Even though I could not fight like they could, I still wanted to help. We were severely outnumbered, I couldn't just sit back and do nothing.

An idea struck me. "Help me up there." I pointed to the top of a tall bookshelf filled with thick atlases. "I'll be out of the way." I promised.

Shroding glanced at Callum.

"Ohhkay." Callum drawled, catching on to my idea. "Now we are thinking." He ran over and knelt. "Hop on." I climbed onto his shoulders, and he lifted me onto the top of the shelf overlooking the circle they'd made of smaller shelves. He reached, steadying me at the waist until I straddled the case.

"Okay, I'm good."

Releasing me, he went back to building up a defense.

"Incoming!" Asher called as the sconces in the hall and around the grand room blasted to life, burning our eyes for a moment before snuffing out in a whoosh. Plunging us into darkness.

Every corner of the space was inked in black, as waves of vibration so abrasive stirred like a tornado through the towering shelves. Where were the vibrations coming from?

My hair whipped into my face as I squinted in the dark.

We all tried to shield ourselves from the thrashing vibrations in the air as the skylights above finally relented to the force, bursting outward towards the night sky.

Monsters scattered in like spiders from an open egg sac, scurrying inside from the broken windows and ceiling.

I pressed low against the shelf, ready to drop books on the heads of as many of the Grieving and possessed townsfolk as I could.

Callum charged forward, taking down one corpse after another with his bare hands. The smell of rotting flesh overpowered the musty scent of old books, making me gag.

Asher and Sir Martus stood back, ready to fight any that made it past Callum. Bodies passed under me, and I scooped stacks of books into my hands, leveling them at my targets before throwing them hard at the heads bouncing by. I focused my efforts on the ones with the glowing purple eyes.

One... four... seven... ten down. But more just kept on coming.

I glanced at Callum and Asher as they blocked and swung at the growing number of Grieving that poured in through the broken doors. They were back to back, covering each other from the senseless beasts around them.

I scooted further down the shelf to a section I could reach with huge encyclopedias. I counted as more enemies dropped unconscious from my blows. Slight guilt panged through me at the concussions these civilians would wake up with.

"Haya!" Callum yelled over the carnage.

My eyes did not go to where Callum shouted at me in warning. No, my gaze shot to the doors where *they* stood. The cold dread that clawed down my spine, brought on by night after night of the attacks in the other dimension, made it so there was no question who *they* were. The original wraiths.

They radiated a maliciousness like none of the other beings in the room. And their malaise was aimed directly at me. The four of them, their human bodies simply the shells to hold their incorporeal blackness, started towards me.

I could do nothing but cover my face as, in synchrony, threw a wave of vibration at the bookshelf under me, sending it, and me, flying into the air. The shelf toppled, and I watched in slow motion as the books crushed a handful of Grieving in its shadow.

I hit the wall, cushioned from the sharp stone by a thick tapestry embroidered with the landscape of Tyndale. Its lovely farms and rolling hills rippled like water at my impact. I rolled down, surprised at the screaming. Had I been screaming? With a hard thud I hit the floor, and blood dripped hot and sticky down my face.

Callum, Asher and Sir Martus moved the remaining shelves into a barricade blocking me from the battle.

"Haya, come on, we have an opening." Shroding appeared at my side. I shook my head to focus, and I crawled after him.

A small door was exposed; the painting that had covered it lay shredded on the ground.

"Where does this go?" I croaked.

"All over the palace. It's a secret passageway I used as a kid. This is our chance to get to the solar."

I stood on shaking legs and ran after him through the dark corridor.

The thud of our feet in the dark made my heart race. I imagined the creatures running behind us.

After a maze of turns I would never remember, I could hear the splash of rain against glass. Shroding rammed into the door ahead of us, breaking down whatever had been blocking the other side.

We stumbled through the broken door into the solar. The high glass ceiling sent a wave of relief through me. It hadn't broken.

"We made it," Shroding said, bounding forward.

The room was already prepared. The rug from the other day was rolled up against the stone wall, exposing the cracks in the wood floor. Candles dimly lit the room. The blue glass ceiling made the gray sky appear a deep cobalt shade I had not seen before. The panels curved up to the middle, where at the center a circular piece of glass had been removed, the cold air and rain of the day falling in.

I shivered and pulled my robe tightly over my shoulders.

The rain was falling steadily into a bucket. Shroding walked over and sat next to the water.

"What now?" I panted, holding the gash on my head. Shroding looked at my injury but said nothing. "Do I need to say something, like the poem Sir Martus told me?"

"This isn't magic, it's science. No mystical words needed," Shroding explained, more composed than I was, but I could hear the nerves in his tone. "I trust you will know what to do. Let the king's power inside guide you," he encouraged me.

"Sure, because that's not mystical sounding at all." I glowered.

"My father told me to surrender. He told me he would not be able to save me if I didn't give him control of my body willingly."

"Oh...?" I said mildly.

"I give you my body, willingly. You will have complete control."

I swallowed. "Right, okay. Let's do this." I nodded, mustering confidence I did not have.

"Haya, you were given that name for a reason—hold on to that," Shroding whispered. "I trust you."

Tears pricked at my eyes, so I closed them. There was no time for sentimentality.

I tested the hold I had put over Logan's taint and found the strings had begun to fray and loosen, so I focused again on tightening, wrapping and sealing him off. Once I was sure his presence was gone I attempted moving into the vibration dimension. It was painfully slow, but little flashes of color and sound began to filter into the darkness. I breathed in and out steadily, listening to the rain and letting the candles warm my exposed skin. My head was throbbing terribly, but then, when I was starting to lose hope, the vibration world stretched before me, colors and sounds dancing through my senses. I reached out for Shroding. The rain between us created a strange melody as it mingled with my vibration and his. I pushed my vibration out across the few feet till it met him. I pressed deeper, thinking about the prince trapped in the spirit dimension, in the pocket. I just knew I needed to link the vibration dimension and the pocket somehow. Taking a deep breath, I waited for the king's power to guide me. It belonged to Shroding and was moving its way back to him. I just needed to be patient. Shroding had said the power wanted to be used. I focused on the vibration, bronze and gold twisting around his form as behind my eyes the colors bled out, dissolving the blackness of the vibration dimension till it was bursting with light.

My eyes opened, the light too painful to keep looking at. I was under the rainfall with Shroding. The world was in a blue hue; swirling flashes of red and yellow shot through the air between us. I pressed my hands into the lights, expecting them to burn. And they did, but not like fire, not like the smoke of the Wraith. No, this pain was like thousands of jolts of electricity skating over my skin. I began to sweat from the heat born of the frictionless current. I screamed as my whole body dispersed into pieces. *This is what it must feel like using your own power against yourself.* I jerked back, vaguely aware that my robe had fallen off of my shoulders and onto the ground.

Don't give up! I told myself, and forced my hands back into the lights. My cries echoed like rolling thunder. Could Shroding see this too? Had I done something wrong? Was it supposed to hurt this much? My arms seared with pain where they lingered in the red and yellow flashes. I could sense my vibration in my arms as if I was holding a strange portal open. I blinked rapidly, trying to clear my vision. Tears of anguish poured down my cheeks. This was it. This was the spirit dimension—I was pressing into it from the physical, through the vibration dimension. I could still hear the strange melody, the sound of Shroding's vibration, the deep cello even amid screams and thunderous lights.

This was what I had to do. If I didn't push through this pain, no one would, and Shroding would be lost forever. I needed to fight. I needed to do what I'd come to do even if it meant death for me. Oh, how my body begged for me to give up, to let go. The electric current splintered my flesh. I thrust my arms deeper into the light, reaching Shroding's cat form on the other side. My hands were like dry ground cracking under the desert sun. I touched his fur with what was left of my hands, and then I sensed it. The vibrations of his skin, the vibrations of my own as the world around us swam in sharp colors I had never seen before. *I'm pulling him back.* I hadn't thought it would be a literal pulling, but it was. Out of the dimension and into our world. I gasped when his hand gripped mine, and for an instant I thought I saw him look at me, his dark gaze seeing me fully through our shared pain and chaos of colors. Gritting my teeth, I heaved with all my strength. I heard a defining pop that turned into a screech like a flute holding a long high note. Both our bodies dematerialized; the cracking sand sensation spread through my whole body, and all the strength slipped out of me.

The world turned fuzzy.

CHAPTER 9
Hide & Seek

THE RIP

Everything was dark. Too dark. Especially after all the light and colors. I blinked blearily.

There was a stillness to the air both familiar and jarring.

My pulse began to race, and terror all too familiar worked its way up my spine and settled into the back of my throat like the taste of something bitter. I was in the solar.

I stood, walking away from the hearth to the windows, seeing only a bloodred moon in the black night. Then it clicked; the haze of the dimension had me smiling with delight. I could call for Shroding, and he would come because it had worked! It had actually worked! I'd blocked Logan and used the king's power.

I'd moved dimensions, but something wasn't quite right. Why had I moved into the dimension instead of pulling Shroding out?

I turned. Where the red moon should have spread over the

floor, instead there were shadows, twisting and writhing. Another thought niggled at my mind—this was all wrong. I was inside the solar, not outside. Every other time I had moved dimensions, I appeared outside if I'd been inside a building. The barn at the farm and the shed in the forest were the only two exceptions to that.

"Shroding!" I called, my back pressing against the glass of the window, my every nerve ending warning me of danger.

"Haya." Shroding materialized across the room, as a dark mass of moving smoke barreled towards me. I closed my eyes, shielding my face, as I was sure I would be pushed from the window by the mass in a moment.

"Haya, move, please." Shroding grunted as if holding something very heavy. My eyes opened, and to my amazement he had a sword pressed against the dark mass. A light emanated from the hilt, preventing the vapors from getting any closer to me.

I scrambled away from the window and hurried to his side. "Where did you get a sword?"

"Not the time," he gritted out, shoving the Wraith back. "Here." He materialized another sword and handed it to me.

"I don't know how to use this!" I took it awkwardly, grateful for a weapon but also extremely confused by the fact we did not move to the pocket where it was safe. Why was Shroding here, in the place where the Wraiths could attack and kill us? It was just like the time when Logan had controlled my body and Shroding stabbed me. Was I unable to move to the pocket, where it was safe, because I was tainted by Logan?

"What has Callum been teaching you?"

He knew about my fight with Callum?

"Hand-to-hand combat," I answered in a panic because

the Wraith he was fighting looked as though it was getting bigger.

"Of course he is," he grumbled.

"Is now really the time?" I repeated his words back to him, but my mind was running with so many questions. Too many things were not adding up. Something had changed, but what was it?

"I suppose not." He exhaled, arms flexing as two more dark masses pressed against his sword.

"What do I do?"

"Just don't let them touch you. I'm sure you remember what that feels like."

I did, and I was not looking forward to being burned again. Especially after undergoing my body turning to sand in the physical dimension. I could only vaguely worry about that, as presently the Wraiths were triple in size and still growing.

Before I could ask Shroding why these Wraiths weren't vanishing like all the other times, more Wraiths were upon us, and I was swinging wildly at the stuff of real nightmares.

"Sheenagh, lend me your light," Shroding breathed like a prayer, and a burst of power forced the Wraith back off Shroding.

"Cut off their heads. The sword will do the rest," he yelled, slicing through the top of the mass in front of him.

Charging forward, I did the same, but not before getting burned on the leg and a few other spots. The pain was infinitely more brutal then I remembered.

Shroding moved with a grace and force I had not seen from him before. When we had trained together I could see his skill, but it wasn't like this; he hadn't been trying to kill anything. This time he was, and his power was undeniable; lethal. He crouched, lunged, flipped and sliced through Wraith after

Wraith like they were wisps of paper on the wind, impossible to hit for a normal person but easy for him.

As much as I wanted to watch him in awe I had my own monsters to contend with, and they were not even remotely easy for me to take down. What I knew of Krav helped, but the fear was real and nearly all consuming, making me slow and clumsy.

"Haya, I have an idea, but I need you to hold them off for a moment," Shroding shouted as he pressed a smoky mass back with his glowing sword.

"Okay," I panted, the blade shaking in my hands. I had no idea how to hold them off, and I had barely managed to stay standing with his help.

Shroding ran up the wall, taking long strides as he flipped up and gripped a sconce just under the curve of the dome. I had no time to watch what he would do next, as three new Wraiths appeared in front of me, forms easier to see, faces almost visible in the shadows, and their attention was fixed on me.

What followed was a blur. I raised my sword as the masses converged on me. I was sure I screamed, that I fought back, but all I knew was pain. Everywhere.

Then through the haze of black I could see the sun rising like a silent partner in the game of cat and mouse I had just lost. With its luminous arrival the Wraiths withered and disappeared, releasing their hold on my body in a gust.

I collapsed on the red and gold carpet. My nightgown burned in more places than I was comfortable exposing. I hadn't been able to avoid getting hurt. But at least I was still alive. I slumped to the floor.

Shroding dropped to my side, his sword vanishing as he

wrapped his arms around me. He took in my nightgown, his eyes flashing iridescent. "They burned you."

"I'll be fine." I sighed and hugged him back even though I hurt all over.

We'd never had to fight them like that before, so what had changed?

"Why didn't they vanish as soon as you appeared?" I whispered, eyes pinched as I forced myself to breathe in and out.

He pulled back, looking me over, taking in the marks along my neck and shoulder, across my torso and down my left side. My nightgown was hanging together by threads, but at least the important parts were covered. Mostly.

He bit his lip in thought. "If I had to guess, I would say it is because of Logan or something to do with the transformation. Does anything come to mind?"

My brow furrowed. "I blocked him—that's how I got here."

"True, but he is still there." Shroding's fingers traced the skin near the bite, but he was careful not to touch it. "Power like his could never enter the pocket dimension," he reasoned.

So we weren't in the pocket after all, but if the Wraiths were here then that means we were in the rip, the place Skithain had made to house the spirits of the Grieving. Something was still not adding up.

"They were different from regular Wraiths, right?"

"Some of them." He held me tightly, brushing my hair from my face. "They were the ones that attacked you back in the library, the ones that had tried killing you back on the farm."

"The original Wraiths?" I whispered, recalling what he had called them so long ago.

"Yes, better known as the Rephaim. They are the first four

men to join Skithian and taint themselves to become Grieving."

"And that makes them more powerful than other Wraiths?" A chill crawled down my spine at the thought of fighting more of them.

"Yes, think of them as being more powerful, like those in the King's Court are in comparison to the average person with the gift."

"You said four, but only three of them attacked us."

"I noticed that too. I am not sure where the other might be." He ran his fingers through his dark hair, concern evident from the crease between his brows.

I glanced at the spot where I had put down the sword, but it wasn't there. "Where did the swords come from?"

"The king insisted I have them when I transformed. Ever wondered why my back is silver?" He smirked.

"I thought it was symbolism, how it turned purple like a royal cape." I shrugged.

Shroding laughed, scooping me off the floor. I nestled into his chest, enjoying how close he was holding me. He carried me to the bay window but instead of placing me down like I expected, he took a seat himself, keeping me in his arms. I was deeply confused by his touch. Hadn't he drawn a line, said we were just friends? So why was he cuddling with me? I was sitting on his lap, his arm around my shoulders and the other draped across my knees. This did not seem like something friends did, but perhaps he was just trying to comfort me after what we had just survived. Strings know I was at a complete loss when it came to him.

He continued the conversation as if we were not sitting in front of a glorious sunset, holding each other in our arms.

"Perhaps, I never thought of that before. Actually, it's silver because that is where the weapons were when I changed."

"So why aren't they always visible?"

"I can materialize them as needed, and they dematerialize as well."

"That's handy," I breathed.

"Sure is. I didn't need to use them until now because I didn't have to fight any Wraiths." He sighed, gaze cataloging my injuries once again. Lingering on the very distinct holes in my gown. "You should sleep in fighting clothes." He glanced away, his cheeks a faint pink. "And you should learn some basic foils work once we get out of here."

"Foils?"

"Swordsmanship," he clarified.

"Ha, that's if we get out of here." I glowered, touching the side of my neck. "Logan's taint caused us to get stuck in the rip, but what do we do now? How do I finish the transformation?"

His hand reached out to touch the burn across my collarbone. I didn't flinch back at his touch, but I wished I could. Wished I could draw a line as easily as he had done. But when he did things like this, all I could do was hold my breath and wait. When he touched me all my love for him swelled to the point of bursting, and though I knew what he wanted, to stay friends, I couldn't understand the tenderness with which he did things like this. How was this not hurting him as much as it hurt me?

"Haya..." His voice was pained, and I wrestled with the desire to reach up and kiss him.

Why couldn't I just keep things platonic with him? Especially after the last kiss. After he clearly said no.

His fingers touched the side of my neck, feather light.

Could he see the pleading in my eyes? Pleading for just one more kiss. Just one.

"Did you enjoy my little detour, love?" Logan's voice shattered my mind, somehow infinitely more powerful in the rip than in the physical realm.

"Get out!" I yelled, pinching my eyes closed and reaching for the king's power, desperate to have it flood and overtake Logan again. The binds I had put on his vibration had vanished, and I could sense his taint seeping into every part of my body. "Ughh," I moaned through clenched teeth.

"But, love, I came to thank you." His wicked tone was littered with a minefield of lies and deception. "You opened a portal, and now all dimensions are synced together. You will be dead in mere moments in the physical world. Pity you won't get to say goodbye to your other lover, but I'll pay him a visit soon. He did promise to kill me on your behalf; surely he will avenge you once you're gone."

My eyes widened at the thought of Callum and Asher on the other side, fighting to protect us, to give us time to complete the ritual.

"No! Shroding will get out of this, and you will suffer for all you have done."

"Haya." Shroding squeezed my shoulders, and I lifted my gaze to his. Dark eyes, flecked with gold, stretched around me, filling every part Logan was working his way through.

"I heard everything he said"—Shroding scowled—"but this fight isn't over yet." He lifted me, holding me tightly to his chest as he turned around in the solar. "I can feel it, the king's power." Shroding breathed in deeply, eyes closing. "I can use it." His eyes opened wide, and the iridescence that was so prominent when he was Iri flashed in the dark depths. "There," he hummed, and a rush of power shot *through my body, pushing Logan out completely. For a moment my and Shroding's connection was back, in full force.*

"There you are," I sighed.

"Here I am." He grinned and leaned down, pressing his forehead against mine. A wave of emotion, similar to when Callum used his Orator skill on me, coursed through my very soul. But these emotions were not mine. I knew they were Shroding's, and the unbound burst of love coming from him had tears seeping from my eyes.

"Shroding." My voice cracked, and then the feeling was gone, the moment so fleeting I questioned if it had been real at all, because the next thing I knew Shroding was staring, a pensive look in his eyes.

"I think I can induct you into the court now."

He set me down, one hand on my waist until I was steady on my feet.

A golden gate of light and electricity ripped open in front of us. Was this the portal Logan had mentioned?

"We need to make you whole—we can deal with the induction later," I insisted, reaching for the gate.

"If you go through that gate now, you will be half-dead on the other side, if you're not dead already." His hair flopped messily across his forehead, the gate creating a cyclone in the room around us. "We have to do it now. I won't risk you going through the portal without the protection of the court."

He was so stubborn.

"I won't fight you, then. What do we need to do for you to induct me into the court?"

He turned his head towards the shattered window that faced the ocean. "We need water."

Then without a word I was in his arms again. "Hold on

tight." He jumped from the second-story window down to the gravelly dirt below.

Sprinting the short distance across the sand, Shroding had us at the ocean's edge within seconds. Was this what it was like when someone who knew how to wield the king's power had access to it?

"Using this much of the king's power here will draw Wraiths to us, so we need to be quick."

I had no idea what to do next, and not for the first time I wished I had asked more about what all the induction entailed instead of focusing so much on the transformation. The truth was I hadn't thought I would make it this far.

"This all seems too risky." I hesitated. "We should get you through the portal."

His jaw clenched as he set me down in the sand, the water's edge at our feet, and though it was winter in the physical dimension, the water did not give off any sensation of warmth or cold.

He cupped my cheek and leaned in. "I am not going through that portal until I know you are safe from Logan." The intensity in his gaze had me closing my mouth and pursing my lips.

"Fine," I acquiesced, glancing at the dark water beside us. The water was still, like a sheet of black stone. Nothing like the crashing deep blue and white it had been on the beach in the physical dimension. The stillness had foreboding inching down my spine like a cold finger over each vertebra. I swallowed the dryness from my throat and asked, "What do I do?"

Shroding's eyes glinted with mischief. "We're going for a swim."

CHAPTER 10

Induction

Though I knew it was water, it did not behave as water should. Which was not all that surprising, as very little functioned the way it ought to in this dimension. As I stepped onto the sheet of stagnant black, instead of rippling out around us, the water fractured like broken glass. The flat surface cracked in a million little fissures shooting out in all directions, my foot sinking to the bottom below. My mind told me I should hear the tink and shatter, but true to its nature it resonated with the deep sloughing of liquid in motion. We trudged through the dark water despite its strange behavior.

It was my first time in a body of water so vast, and though it was not the physical dimension I could sense the danger lurking below the surface. As if more than just the Wraiths made this rip their home. As a child there were stories of a sea beast off the coast of Tyndale. So on our one trip to the city when I was seven, I refused to go into the ocean for fear of the beast. The stories had been just as terrible as the tales of the Grieving, so it was no wonder I'd been scared. Ships snatched at sea were dragged to their watery graves by a massive eel, allegedly what Palace Moreh was named after, though the spelling difference made that theory unlikely. Though it would be impossible, I could not help but think of that sea beast now, lurking just below the plate of glass.

My nightgown clung to my legs, water absorbing into the fabric and making it heavy, as if weights were dragging around my calves and thighs the further we waded into the dark depths. I tried not to look too closely at the way the light fabric of my gown and Shroding's tunic turned flesh colored as they absorbed the water.

"Ready?" Shroding whispered. He had taken my hand back on the beach, bolstering my resolve, and still held it tightly as the water rose to my waist.

Peering up at him, I had no idea what I was preparing myself for, but I trusted him. He had always protected me, fought for me, and now with the king's power in his control I was even more assured there was nothing he could not do. It wasn't possible for him to be any more attractive in my eyes, but somehow his shoulders seemed broader, his face more assured. I wasn't skilled at sensing the gift in others, but with him I could. How power radiated off in waves, but instead of it being terrifying I was comforted. He was the kind of man who could and would lead a kingdom with authority and grace. The kind of man I'd follow into the darkest depths because I knew no matter what, he would protect me there.

He caught my stare, and when he met my eyes I could not help the unconscious way I licked my lips. He did not miss the motion, but as I stepped forward, my gown twisted, causing me to lose my footing.

Water splintered out around us as Shroding reached for me. His hand holding mine pulled up and back, spinning me.

The warmth of his arm wrapped around my waist as he caught me in a dip, derailing all logical thoughts when his face stopped inches from mine.

"Oh," I gasped, distracted by the teasing beads of water that peppered his cheeks.

"Are you okay?" His dark lashes stuck together where water must have splashed up in our spin. But more than just his lashes drew my attention. Though his question was in regards to my tripping, it was clear in his gaze that he was asking something else. Something I desperately wanted to believe as his breath tickled across my cheek. His arm flexed tightly around my back, arching me up to him. It was as if he meant to ask, "Is this okay," as if for the first time since we met, he was honestly letting himself imagine a future with me.

Maybe, just maybe what had been holding him back all this time wasn't his lack of love for me, but his uncertainty about the future. With us so close to achieving the goal of bringing him back, of saving us both, it seemed like he was finally allowing himself to feel.

"With you in this position, we might as well..." He trailed off, eyes tracing over my jaw, neck, then out to the side, a distant expression clouding his gaze as he focused on the water around us.

"Sorry?" I squeaked, my cheeks warming at his implication.

His eyes flicked back to mine, as if his thoughts had gone far away, but flashed back to the present and to his unfinished sentence. "Start the induction." He shook his head slightly, clearing whatever had distracted him. "Why did you apologize?"

I opened my mouth and then smiled tentatively. "What does this position have to do with the induction?"

Registering our dipped embrace, arms still holding me inches over the water, Shroding ducked his head as a faint pink dusted across his cheeks.

He cleared his throat, the knot bobbing as he swallowed. "I'll lean you back in the water and hold you under for a few seconds."

I nodded my agreement.

"Take a deep breath," he said as he slowly guided me into the water.

I looked up at Shroding, my heart still pounding from our embrace. He smiled assuringly, his eyes amused. Chewing my lip, I closed my eyes. The sound like waves crashing on the shore filled my ears as my head submerged. I opened my eyes and realized the water was all around me. I couldn't see anything in the black. There was no indication of the surface, and if not for Shroding's arm around my middle, I might have gotten completely turned around.

A zap of power ripped through my chest, punching the air from my lungs. Bubbles of precious air flounced from my lips as I tried to control my limbs. It wasn't painful, but it was strange, like something was moving through my body.

Jolts of electricity danced on my fingers, down my legs, across my chest, up my throat till I was full of the painless sparking sensation. It rushed across my body as if asking to be let in, and at the same time asking to burst out of me. It was everywhere. Pulsing against me.

In the dark, just like in the vibration dimension, an image formed. Shroding's vibration, the color and the sound of it permeated the water, skittering along my skin until all sensation was washed away except for his vibration. Except for the king's power.

This was not the vibration dimension, yet the dark water

made it seem so similar. Awash in the song of the king, my body relaxed, and then I was floating. The slight pressure of Shroding's arm holding me vanished, and I was buoyant in the sea of song and light.

Then I saw them. Beautiful apparitions I could only dream of, swirling out of the bronze strings till they took on their stocky forms, their shape so familiar, like coming home. Theo and my father floated before me. They held their arms open in an embrace. My father's face was gentle and knowing, while Theo's was smiling and proud.

I was not sure how with my body adrift in water, but I was able to run to them, and gripped them so tightly in my arms, the squeeze of our joint embraced pushing more air from my lungs. I did not care that none of this made sense. It was too good, too perfect to care. Like being terrified, just to find out everything was alright in the end. It was like being taken up high in the sky, then falling, only to land in the clouds. It was euphoric, it was addictive, it was dangerous.

Bubbles floated from my lips once more, and I opened my mouth to say the only words that mattered—"I love you, I miss you"—but my mind would not let me. A faint warning that I did not have any more air to lose kept my lips sealed tight. Self preservation burned in my chest, urging me to breathe. I needed air.

I refused to close my eyes, to miss a second of seeing my family once more. Theo chuckled, and my father ran his hand over my head.

"I will hold you again," my father promised as they drifted back. I gripped their hands in mine, unwilling to let them go. Logic whispered at the edges of my mind, reminding me this was not real, they were dead and gone. Whatever vision this was, it could not last.

"See you soon, Haybale"—Theo winked—"but not too soon."

Then suddenly, I was being lifted from the water.

Shroding's arms wrapped around my waist as he hoisted me out of the strange black depths and onto my feet. I stared at the surface of the splintered darkness as if they would still be there. But they were gone, and though my heart ached, it also was resigned, settled with the reality of their passing in a way I had not been before.

I took gulping breaths, coughing and sputtering water as Shroding held me tightly against him. I relished the feeling of his warm body holding mine. A dreamy, content smile lifted my cheeks as I leaned back to see him.

"Haya, repeat these words."

An oath, of course. I repeated after Shroding.

"I, Haya Golden, give my oath to the king of Shamar, for all my days, numerous may they be; I will protect, sustain, and do right unto the crown. I will never betray, harm or defame the king, the Creator or myself. This is my oath."

He let out a sigh, tension releasing from his shoulders. "It is done, then." He reached down, scooped his arms under my knees and around my back. I yelped slightly. But then I noticed how completely see-through my nightgown was now that it was entirely soaked, and I gripped him around the neck, leaning into him to hide myself, but that only served to press my wet chest completely against his.

"Was that usual?" I waved my hand towards the dark sea, my eyes heavy.

"Nothing about this"—he readjusted his hold—"is usual, Haya."

He carried me through the water, eyes focused ahead as I

peered up at him and yawned. Why was I so tired? Had all the adrenaline from our fight worn off?

"Is that why you look so..." I gestured to his face. "... like that?" My mind was too sluggish to find a good way to describe his expression.

"I knew you would react differently to the king's power..." He shook his head. "How do you feel?"

"Really happy, great even, like I could fly... but also so incredibly tired." I wanted to sing, dance, kiss Shroding—though that wasn't anything new. Somewhere in my mind I knew the rest was sorely out of place given our location.

"The state of euphoria is normal at least," Shroding noted with a slight chuckle. "While you're under, I give unfettered access to the king's power for only a moment before tapering it down to what your body can more easily tolerate." So that was what he had been doing with the water. "The influx can be a little..." He pondered for a word. "... overpowering," he deadpanned. "Water helps to moderate the vibrations, but because you have the king's power already in you, even tainted, it was drawn to you more vigorously. It was a lot harder to control with you." He bit his lip, embarrassed by the admission.

"So it's not supposed to feel like I'm being electrocuted?" I asked innocently.

His jaw ticked, and though he faced straight ahead, his eyes glanced down at me. "It isn't supposed to hurt."

I waved him off because it hadn't been painful, just strange. When we reached the shore I spoke. "So I'm a part of the court now?"

"Yes." His tone was clipped, my comment about being electrocuted clearly still bothering him.

"Did you see..." I trailed off, not sure how to explain the apparitions of my father and Theo.

"What you see when you get inducted is for your eyes alone, a gift from the Creator." He trudged forward, not setting me down as he traversed the sandy beach. "Except in this instance." He met my eyes. "Because of our connection, I saw them."

"It was real, then? Even the words they said?"

"Yes, it was."

Tears burned the corners of my eyes. I was so glad, so grateful I had been able to tell them goodbye, so grateful to have heard their voices.

He walked across the sand in silence, but with each step he took in this twisted dimension the joy of seeing my family faded and concern niggled its way in.

"Don't you think it's been a bit too quiet? I mean, we are in the rip; I would think more would be attacking us by now."

Shroding stopped walking, his gaze distant and unfocused again.

"Strings," Shroding snapped, and quickened his pace till we were moving in a blur. With a feat of strength beyond my understanding he leapt up, taking us both back through the open window to the solar. "The portal. How could I have been so dense?" he berated himself as he set me down. My legs were unsteady, and I gripped his arm for support.

"What?" I floundered, looking to see the portal was still there, still sparking and flashing with light; nothing amiss.

"If we can pass through, so can the creatures here." He glowered at the gate. "We have no time to waste. If the Wraiths came through this portal, they can't be killed by the means we used back in Coinania. If this portal is supposed to bind my

Nephesh to my body, then it might do the same for them. It might make them whole."

I shivered but pushed down the fear. There would be time to deal with the Wraiths later. Now I needed to finish what we'd started. Now it was time to pass through the portal and make sure he became human again.

My hand in his, we stepped up to the gate. The vibration and flashes of light tugged at my chest, calling me in, daring me to enter.

"Whatever happens, don't let go," he said. I squeezed his hand, relishing its warmth, its solid strength, and together we stepped in.

CHAPTER 11

Shroding

Light burst around us in a torrent, and though I tried to, I couldn't hold on to Shroding.

Violently I was ripped from him, my hand in his one second and not the next.

In the blinding light I watched through squinted eyes as a silver cat leapt into the open arms of the man; Shroding. They embraced, and purple light sliced out, cutting through the white glare.

Terror gripped me as I was thrown into the solar, spat out like poison from the thrashing golden gate. I slammed into the ground, bounded twice, feeling bones break with each impact before rolling limply to a stop.

I didn't think I could get any more afraid until I sensed them. Battered from the torrent, I don't know how I could be aware of anything apart from the shattered bones in my body, but their presence was undeniable and haunting.

The Rephaim. Three of the original Wraiths had come through the portal. My eyes opened, and though I knew my attention should be on the Wraiths, it was instead on the naked figure lying on the floor across the room. Each limb screamed with pain as I crawled, on hands and knees, to Shroding.

The gate crumpled in on itself, blinking out of existence with an earsplitting crack. Like thunder bursting directly in my eardrum. I grabbed my ears and closed my eyes for a second, but that was all it took for the Rephaim to turn their sights on Shroding. Billowing black robes, faces hollow and pale, with what looked like jewels inset in their foreheads. The Rephaim were real; flesh and bone.

"You will not touch him," I yelled, or at least I thought I had. My vision swam, and my voice sounded far away to my ears.

"We will enjoy finally killing you." They spoke in unison, the sound like a thousand knives scraping glass.

I cried out, my hands coming away from my ears bloody, whether from the gate or their voices I didn't know. My knees buckled, and I dropped to the ground. When had I even gotten to my feet?

Then they were speaking in my head. A mix of noise, one like a whisper in the dark. Another like the screeching of bats. The next like the wailing of cicadas in the summertime. The sounds overwhelmed me.

I panted, trying to bring power to my palms, but I was so drained. The fatigue made me weak. I threw what I could at one of them, making it flinch but nothing else.

Tears burned my eyes.

This was it.

I hoped Shroding would escape. I didn't even know if I had succeeded. If he was alive. I tried to stand but was thrown down as the three of them pounded me with vibrations. My body broke apart. Hot and sweating all over, my skin tore against my bones. Vomit lodged in my throat, choking me. The sensation from before I entered the gate was back, my skin sloughing off like sand. At the slightest breeze I would simply blow away, like dust, even as sweat dripped from my brow, affirming my solidity.

My voice was hoarse; I couldn't cry out anymore. I couldn't do anything. Shadows wrapped around inside me like a seal over my heart; the smoky darkness filled what empty space there was in my lungs. I tried to hold on to consciousness, but the world danced in and out of focus.

Then all at once it stopped. The Rephaim were gone, but I couldn't move. I couldn't feel anything.

It was better. Numb. The pain was far away.

Blearily, I watched Callum charge in with a group of Golan fighters from Coinania.

Mama Meod moved through the battle towards me.

I realized numbly that I had stopped breathing. I could tell as the world seemed to stand still. After so much noise— the song, the thunder—the quiet was almost painful.

Slowly the vague pulse of my heartbeat and rain pattering the floor reached me.

At first it was just Callum's mouth moving, making shapes, then sound boomed in my ears. "Shroding! My prince," Callum's voice thundered, his tone a mix of fear and amazement.

"She's not breathing," Asher whispered close by.

Boots hit the ground, the drumming making my whole body shake.

Had I succeeded? Was he alive? I squinted through the chaos and saw him. Shroding. He was lying in his human form a few feet from me, Callum at his side.

"She is still not breathing!" Asher's alarmed voice hurt my ears.

Shroding lifted onto his forearms. Callum took the robe I had lost during the transformation and wrapped it around Shroding's exposed body.

"Shroding." Callum's voice shook as he was finally reunited with his prince. His king.

Tears left my eyes. I had done it. He was alive. Safe. Callum would protect him.

I wanted to be happy, to smile, but my body was cold; all the warmth that would have come from celebrating our victory was too far out of reach.

"Callum, help me!" Asher panicked.

I wanted to tell them it was okay. This was what had to happen. I'd been made to save him, and save him I had. He would now save the world, and I had fulfilled my promise. Callum's eyes finally left Shroding to look over at me.

But my gaze did not meet stormy gray eyes, but onyx flecked with gold. Shroding's gaze was unfocused. He blinked a few times, and then he *saw* me, his eyes widening with recognition. I wished I could smile at him. The muscles to do so were no longer under my control. I wanted to tell him it was alright, that I was content.

I wished I could have kissed him one last time. I wished I had told him how much I had grown to care for him instead of my weak attempts at a confession. I wished I had been bolder. I thought I finally knew the answer to my questions. I'd stopped doubting the love I had for him; my prince, my hero, my friend. I would always love him and watch over him even if I could not live out my life with him.

His hand reached out to me. "Haya." His voice spoke my name, this time not in my head. His lips moved, and my name... my name was on them. The first word he'd spoken in nearly two hundred years. I mused at how it had sounded so different, yet the same, in my head. Still I liked this voice better, much better. The timbre was soft, like the brush of silk on bare skin, but also deep and warm like swallowing a hot drink on a cold day, its warmth spreading through my chest. It was more than I'd imagined it would be. I wanted to tell him, but I had no air with which to say, "Your voice is beautiful, coming from your lips."

Like peace, and strength.

Everything he would bring to Shamar.

I closed my eyes, and through the connection that was no longer there I told him all that was in my heart.

"I'd give my life for you. To make you human again. I would sacrifice it all, watch my home burn. I'd follow you into the cold, ice, and snow. I would drown in freezing water. Pining for the chance to see you, touch you one more time. I would endure the bite of power and the loss of my will, all so you could be saved, all so you could live. All so I could love you a little bit longer. All so I could stay by your side. Even if you didn't want me. Even after you rejected my affection. I would do it all again, and again and again. Because you are that important, and I am just a passing memory for you to overcome and save the world."

"Haya, don't give up, my dear, don't lose heart. I give you my life. This time I want you to live for you, not just for him."

Mama Meod's words stoked a fire in me. Light shattered my every thought. Broke down my every self-sacrificing ideal.

My chest rose, air funneling into my lungs like a balloon being filled near to bursting.

I would live.

No, I *was* alive.

"That's the most I can do for you, child. Despair no more, for you have overcome death itself."

The world snapped into focus like a kaleidoscope cracking and focusing on one thing instead of a million fractured pieces.

"She's alive."

"She's gone."

CHAPTER 12

Seeing

The rustle of fabric swirled around me. I was lying on something silken, my body deliciously warm, content.

"Haya?" a deep voice whispered, the sound so tender, so soft I curled into it. As if the voice were something tangible, something I could hold in my hands. When my hands connected with skin my brow furrowed.

Who— My eyes opened slowly, lashes sticky and lids heavy. When the world came into focus the first thing I saw were my hands wrapped around a tan bicep, the muscle thick and taut. My gaze followed the arm up over a linen-clad shoulder, roamed across sharp collarbones, the open V of the vest allowing my eyes to drink in more tan skin, then finally up to a face I knew better than my own.

Shroding sat at the edge of the bed I lay in, firelight warming his face. He held perfectly still as if somehow, in my freshly awakened state, my hold on him had the power to paralyze him. His lips parted, dark hair falling over his cheekbones, shadowing his flint eyes. Eyes so intensely focused on me that I flushed.

Something was off, though, yet I could not place what it might be. I must be back in the spirit dimension. I had to be.

I slid my hands down his arm to the covers and pushed myself up, wincing with the effort. Shroding scooted closer, reaching his arm around my back to steady me. I was grateful for the support, as the room teetered left and right before affixing itself in the correct position. Strings, my head ached. My mouth was tacky and dry, and each time I blinked, the scrape of crusties along my lashes irritated my eyes. I tried to rub them away, embarrassed Shroding had seen them. I leaned back into his arm, needing the support more than I'd realized, and with a sigh I took in the room, glad it had finally stopped tipping back and forth.

The pocket dimension was different, though; where I expected to see fuzzy frayed edges around the hearth, along the red leather chair next to it, I saw none. The deep blue rug and stone walls were jarringly crisp. I blinked a few more times, waiting for my eyes to correct the errors. When they didn't and the fact that the hearth was lit and we were inside registered, I looked up at Shroding. He was smirking, amused.

He watched as understanding bloomed over my face. Neither one of us spoke. I knew we both wanted to, but something about this moment was wonderfully fragile. Neither one of us wanted to break it.

We were both *here*. Human. Together. For the first time.

And on some level we knew speaking would ruin this inexplicable joy. Both of us had words to say, itching on the tips of our tongues, but we held them in and just looked at each other. As if the first words that we'd share would have a deeper meaning than any other words we had spoken to each other so far.

I shifted closer till our hips were touching, my hand on his over the knit cream coverlet.

Where my expression was hesitant, his was awestruck and a little bemused, like at any moment he would begin to laugh. I realized then that he was seeing me for the first time, in color. Colors he had not seen for two hundred years. I was embarrassed. I didn't know what my hair looked like, if my skin was dry or oily. I didn't know if I smelled bad, but I could guess I did. Yet the way he looked at me, none of it seemed to matter.

With shaking hands I touched the dark hair dusting his cheek. It did not shimmer like his fur had; it was just human hair, and the mundaneness of it brought tears of joy to my eyes. His fingers wrapped around my wrist, steadying my hand with his strong, unwavering grip. He tilted his face into my touch. His cheek was so very warm.

We had done it. We had brought him back. He was really, truly alive. He was really sitting here with me.

Tears pooled in my eyes. My prince was saved. I had fulfilled my promise.

"Shroding." My voice cracked.

"Haya," he whispered, tears of his own glossing his dark lashes. The bed protested as he rose. "Come with me," he urged. His hand around my wrist glided until my hand rested in his.

I would follow him anywhere; surely he knew that by now.

Slowly I stood, and he wrapped the oversized fur robe

around me. It hung off my shoulder and pooled at my feet. My legs shook, and he lifted me into his arms. He had been strong in the other dimension. I had never thought him weak or unable to protect me, but the way he held me now was infinitely more solid, more secure than any of the times before. He was unmovable, a rock of a man. I nestled into his hold, comforted and still reeling from the truth that we had done it.

He carried me through the halls of Palace Moreh, my arms wrapped around his neck. Through the glass ceiling I could see the sky was gray, only just being touched by the morning sun. We moved silently down to the first floor and out into the patio of the garden in the back. A cold wind whipped around the stone exterior, but not even the frigid chill of the snowcapped mountains could faze me while in his arms. Not even the terrifying memories of the Grieving circling and attacking us in this very spot. It was as if all we had suffered through was a distant nightmare far removed from the incandescent reality we found ourselves in now.

Before I knew it we were stopping on the shore, the rocking of the waves a soft symphony in the early dawn. Birds chirped their morning songs as the water, a pale dusty blue, bled into the horizon line. As if the seemingly endless expanse before us was the Creator of Strings saying this was a new beginning, not just the start of a new day.

I rested my chin on his shoulder. The sun moved like a cat, its rays stretching lazily over top the mountains behind the palace. Gold and bronze lit the sky to a pale yellow that turned the mountains a strange purple blue. I dropped my chin and nestled my forehead into the side of Shroding's neck, and within moments the ocean's color deepened to a pristine cerulean, the horizon catching the yellow haze from the sun behind us.

Shroding sat in the sand, cradling me in his lap. Then he broke the silence, the rumble of his chest against my ear.

"I had imagined this for the last two hundred years. I had thought the one thing I wanted to see more than anything else was a sunrise. A sunrise from this very spot I had sat at as a child hundreds of times." He sighed wistfully, and my chest pinched, grateful that he would share such a tender memory with me. "I tried so hard to remember the colors, to remember the warmth. The way the newness of the day cast hope with the touch of the sun's first rays. As if the sun was breathing life over the land. This was the one thing I had thought I wanted to see again. Until..." His intense gaze, directed at the ocean, shifted till it bore down on me. I met his eyes, and a shiver not from the cold tickled across my arms. "I had thought..." he continued, "but that day on the dandelion hill and every day after..." He tipped his head, the sun highlighting along his jaw. To my surprise his eyes flashed iridescent in the sunlight, and on instinct I reached for him, my thumb brushing the skin under his eyes.

Leaning into my touch, he continued, "The only thing I wanted to see in color, to remember in detail"—his hand lifted to my cheek—"was you." His thumb mimicked the motion of mine, caressing the skin along my cheekbone. "Your green eyes." He slid his hand back into the mess of my hair at the nape of my neck, pulled a few strands around and lifted them between us. "The exact golden hue of your hair." He pressed the hair to his lips, and my breath hitched in anticipation. Everything about this moment was perfect, and was exactly what I had wanted with him. All I needed now was for him to lean down and kiss me. Put an end to my questioning. I wanted to confess with fervor and be confessed to with the same conviction. All his secrets and mine laid bare.

His eyes fell to my lips, and the breath rushed out of me with that simple glance. His onyx eyes were soft, his thick lashes giving them the heavy sleepy look of the cat he had once been. My hair fluttered down, and pain flashed across his features. He took a shaky breath, fingertips tracing the side of my neck where Logan had bitten me.

I waited for the pain, Logan's voice, anything to prove he was still with us at this moment, but nothing happened. So why did Shroding look so forlorn?

"Haya." The way he said my name was pure electricity. The oath hung between us. A kiss still not given as payment. He smiled, but it did not reach his eyes. My brow knit in uncertainty. It could all be different now. I had accomplished what we'd set out to do, but I was still just a farm girl from the north. I could never be with the prince, the soon-to-be king.

"I am—" he began.

"Are you—" We stopped and locked eyes. Time stood still as we both tried to read each other.

"Ladies first.."

"No, Your... Majesty." The word was thick on my tongue. "Royalty first." I swallowed, kicking myself for how squirmy the words made me. He was a prince, after all. A king. I should get used to this.

He smirked, shaking his head slightly, trying not to laugh.

"Haya, please I insist." Was that an order? I would just take it as one since this was so awkward I just wanted to get it over with. My palms were sweating.

"Are you okay?" I asked lamely, glancing down at where

his hand still lingered on my neck. He could tell that was not what I wanted to ask. He waited instead of answering. "Uh, well, I was thinking. We have come really far, and I know I completed the task of changing you back, but I think... uh... if I go home—I mean, I don't want to go home, but if I did—there is nothing there." Strings, how could I say what I wanted when he was looking at me so tenderly. "So instead I want to fight. I think I could still have use in this battle." I dropped my head, not able to bear seeing the unending patience in his gaze. "Please, Your Majesty." Urgency filled my voice though my tone stayed low. "I want to stay and fight— I..." I stopped myself from adding that I wanted to stay with him. It was not appropriate since I did not know where we stood anymore. I did not dare meet his eyes. He knew I cared for him. I had already told him that. It was his move.

"You seem to have this amazing ability to keep me alive," he sighed, his words surprising me.

"It's hardly anything I have done. It was the king's power in me."

"No, it's because *you* had the king's power. If it had been anyone else, I don't think I would be sitting here."

He lifted my chin, a soft smile spreading across his features. "Haya," he breathed, uncertainty gone from his face, "stay with me." My heart fluttered. "Stay with me if that is what you want."

His words melted the very essence of my soul, and I opened myself to the kiss that burned between us. Just a breath away, and it would be done. His palm cupped my neck, holding me firmly in place.

The pain was back in his eyes, but there was desire too, longing I had only glimpsed a few times before.

"In three days, members of the steward's court are set to arrive, and we will head to the capital."

The moment shattered, as reality set in, heavy and important.

"How long have I been unconscious for?"

"Five days. The Rephaim escaped. We don't know how many Wraiths were able to pass through the gate."

I looked out at the water; flashes of the portal and subsequent moments littered my mind, like scraps of paper I needed to piece together.

"Is Logan...?" I tapped the side of my head. Shroding pulled back and smiled out at the ocean.

"Your soul is free. Mama Meod took the taint of the Nephesh Maveth from you." His relieved smile warmed my heart. "There is a lot we don't know about what she did, and since the mark still remains, there could be lingering effects, but Asher and Sir Martus seem to think you will be able to live a normal, healthy life."

"So he doesn't see..." *everything happening*, I wanted to say, but Shroding's open smile answered my unfinished question.

"He cannot."

I exhaled, my shoulders rolling with relief, and my hand dropped to my ribs. "I was hurt, the gate, I-I..." My head throbbed as I tried to remember.

"We had a plan, one you couldn't know because of Logan, but she and some fighters from Coinania were camped on the edges of the mountain to come to our aid in the event of an attack. It was the only way we could catch Logan by surprise and the only way we won that battle."

"Mama Meod..." I whispered as her words drifted back to me. *This time I want you to live for you, not just for him.*

Despair no more, for you have overcome death itself. "I died."

Shroding closed his eyes and squeezed me tightly. "You died, but Mama Meod..." He clenched his jaw in a mix of sorrow and gratitude, his dark brows cinching together. "She gave her life to you, taking Skithian's taint in the process."

I nodded numbly a few times, accepting what she had done for me, what she'd asked of me. To live for me? There was no life I wanted to live apart from him, however there *was* something I wanted aside from Shroding. I wanted to get stronger. My agreement with Callum settled strength into my bones. With Logan blocked would I be able to fight at full strength?

"I understand," I said with finality, and though some tears did escape for the loss of Mama Meod, I knew she would not want me to mourn her. She would not want me wrestling with whether I deserved her sacrifice, because she would not have given her life if she did not believe I was worth dying for. And though my ego wanted to remind me I was just a nobody and she was a leader of an entire clan, I could not deny that what she had done was the reversal of what I had been willing to do for Shroding. That thought dried my tears and filled me with gratitude instead of sorrow, because I could finally hear Shroding's words clearly now.

"Romanticize it all you like, but you should not have to die so I can live."

Daylight poured across the sand, glittering across the water before us, and though my body was sore, healed of wounds but still aching, I shifted off Shroding's lap to kneel in the sand. Slowly, on unsteady feet, I rose. The sagging robe did little to help my clumsy, weak state, but if I had any hopes of becoming someone who could protect the people I loved, then I needed to start right away, as soon as possible, to get stronger.

"Where are the others?" I asked, chin lifted, gaze fixed across the water at a distant point, a new dream taking shape on the dawn horizon.

When the time came, Shroding would not be fighting Skithian alone.

CHAPTER 14

Dissolution

Shroding walked me back to his room, where I had woken before our beach excursion. He told me to rest while he gathered everyone in the library, which was apparently in better shape than the solar.

Light streamed in from the large arching window. He had been gone for some time, the sun high overhead.

I stepped out of his room into the bright hallway. The winged lion carved above the doorframe stared down at me, reminding me once again that Shroding was royalty and I needed to know my place. I glanced around the hall. Would it be okay to just go to the library instead of waiting? I chewed my lip, looking up at the lion carving, its authority bearing down on me. Was waiting for Shroding to return an order? If I left, would I be disobeying him?

The hallway was chillier than Shroding's room, and with a shiver I wrapped my arms around my waist. The inappropriately thin fabric of my nightgown gave me pause. Apparently Lev had been with the group from Coinania and had changed me out of my ruined nightgown into a fresh one.

She had stayed for a few days before heading back to her village deep in the mountains. I had been unconscious the whole time. Hesitating, I glanced back at the door to Shroding's room, contemplating going back in to get the robe.

A voice snickered behind me, one I was not familiar with. "What a precarious position to be in. Are you sneaking in or perhaps sneaking out?" a smooth, languorous voice breathed as if just beside me, but when I whirled around no one was there.

The corridor was brightly lit, skylights above letting in the gleam of day. There was nowhere for someone to hide. Still I could feel their eyes on me like a cold finger down my spine, making my skin prickle. My fight or flight instinct kicked in, and I readied myself to run. Something told me I wouldn't make it far, though. There was a predatoriness to the voice. It didn't seem wise to connect myself to Shroding's room.

Before I could say anything, footsteps cut through the rising tension. The sound of Asher's and Callum's voices filled me with relief. I did not look in the direction of their voices; once they were close enough I would tell them about this intruder. The two men came around at the other end of the hall, Shroding following a few steps behind.

Callum and Asher did not skip a beat when they saw me.

"Haya, how did you sleep?" Asher smiled down at me, coming to my side. His eyes were knowing, as if trying to tell me some secret.

Callum stripped his jacket and draped it around my shoulders. He wrapped his arm around me and pulled me along with them as they continued down the hall. I marveled at the smooth but intentional actions. They had not even been surprised to see me standing in the hall. My feet fumbled with uncertainty beside Callum. Callum squeezed my shoulder.

"I slept great!" I chirped, the crack in my voice exposing my obvious discomfort. Why was Callum still holding on to me?

The three men glanced at me and burst into laughter at my expense.

I gave them a questioning look but eventually chuckled too.

We made it a few more paces down the hall when Asher turned and stopped. "I'm afraid Shroding and I are needed for some business. Please excuse us." He ushered me towards the door on my right.

It had a rabbit carved into the doorframe. I gave Shroding a quizzical look but he simply nodded and turned to leave with Asher.

I was about to ask what was going on when Callum unceremoniously shoved me towards the door. I glanced back at Shroding as he rounded the hall corner. For a brief second our eyes met, but I could not understand what he was trying to tell me, and even though Logan's taint was gone, it seemed like my and Shroding's connection was gone for good.

Callum, impatiently and a bit harshly, yanked me into the room, jerking me out of my lingering stare. I stumbled into his chest, hitting my nose. "Ouch," I winced, and righted my footing. "What is going on?" I snapped, rubbing my nose as he shut the door.

I took in the room. The bed was white linen, and in front of us sprawled one tall window that poured in the bright afternoon sun. The large hearth was unlit, making the tile of the floor freezing against my bare feet. The whole room had a chill, and I crossed my arms over my chest, grateful for

Callum's jacket hiding my state of undress. I should have been more uncomfortable, being so lightly clothed in front of Callum. Oddly enough I wasn't.

"What do you mean?" Callum shrugged while walking around me. "Ah, your clothes." He tapped on the bedpost, signaling me to the garments that lay there. "Food is ready. Just head down the hall and make a left, right—" I cut him off, as I already knew how to get to the kitchen and dining area.

"What is going on?" I repeated, standing in front of him, forcing him to look at me. "No offense, but, why are you here and not..." I hesitated, my cheeks warming. "Shroding?"

He crossed his arms, copying my stance. "The prince can't tend to you all the time." His answer was stern, like a father chastising their child.

"I know that!" I retorted, then sighed. "I guess this is how it will be from now on," I muttered.

"Don't worry, Haya." Callum placed his hand on my head, making me feel the gravity of our height difference. "We will take care of you." He smiled down at me; his pale eyes shining like gray pearls in the light. I could not help but smile back, though he still had not answered my question.

"Take care of me? I'm still waiting for an apology for the last few days."

He frowned, aggravated.

"I'm sorry," he said lamely.

I scoffed at how forced the apology was.

"Yeah, well, me too," I said with heavy sarcasm, the taste of it foreign to my tongue. I hadn't been sarcastic since Theo left. Before my thoughts could get trapped by that realization I quickly changed the subject. "What was that maneuver earlier?" Did they already know about the intruder? Were they just trying to get me away from whatever had been in the hall with me?

"I don't know what you mean?" He shrugged again, looking past me at the door. *Looking for an easy escape,* I thought grimly. I wouldn't get answers from him, but Shroding would explain it to me, so I would drop it for now.

"Fine," I clipped, moving aside to let him pass. He nodded, ready to leave, accepting my dismissal, then paused.

"Congratulations on bringing him back, and surviving."

I narrowed my eyes, remembering why I had wanted to meet with him on the beach earlier. I wanted to fight Callum again.. Something in me told me this time would be different, that maybe I could best him and secure my spot in the guard. "Spar with me," I demanded, stepping around him to block his path again.

"Now?" He looked incredulous.

"Yes, now."

"Okay, meet me in the courtyard in ten."

I nodded. "Thank you for your jacket." I shifted, starting to take it off in order to give it back. Callum glanced at me and cleared his throat, quickly averting his gaze. Cheeks heating, I shrugged the jacket back on, covering what I had forgotten was my near see-through gown.

He brushed past me. "Just bring it with you and maybe change first." He waved his hand over his shoulder to the clothes on the bed, then disappeared through the door.

I really needed to start sleeping in my training clothes like Shroding had suggested.

———

Callum stumbled back.

The ground was cold and slippery as mist from the ocean created a haze in the air much as it had the day we arrived at Moreh.

"Good move, Hay—" I didn't let him finish. The hard black leather Krav suit I had put on was infinitely easier to fight in than any of my previous clothing. How, with its near stonelike exterior, was a feat of fashion I did not understand.

I came in close, my movements sure, no longer hesitant as they had been the last time we fought. Perhaps it was living through dying, or maybe it was that Logan wasn't weighing me down, but I *was* stronger. Sturdy in a way I hadn't been before. Though the king's power was back with its rightful owner, a piece of it, a small segment remained with me, allowing me to call upon it in a fight.

I threw a powered punch at Callum's face, not even a little afraid I would hurt him. He lifted his hands, blocking it, but grunted as the vibrations I had pumped into my knuckles threatened to send him flying. He twisted, grabbing my arm in a swift motion that made me crash into his side. He held me to him.

"You're feistier than usual today," he noted a smirk on his lips. "You actually pose a little challenge."

"Little?" I sneered, thrusting my head forward, making him flinch. Instead of hitting him I shifted my hips and swung my leg out and up, the movement one Shroding had taught me in the other dimension. Charging power on to the top of my foot, I targeted his torso, but missed by a mere inch. I was sure if my foot had connected, his ribs would have broken.

He dropped my arm, springing away from me so quickly I stumbled and exposed my back to him. His palm came down, slapping hard between my shoulder blades. "Want to tell me what's wrong?"

I winced as I rolled forward and swiftly righted myself. I didn't answer as I twisted into a crouch, swinging my leg at his knees, my hands pressing into the damp ground. He grabbed my kick, wrenching my leg painfully. "What?" he asked innocently. "Cat got your tongue?"

My teeth ground together at the pain, but I held in my anger, letting it simmer just below the surface to give me momentum but not distract me.I tested his hold on my leg—it was tight enough to anchor me as I pushed up from the ground, the vibration of my gift giving me extra lift over his head. I hurdled over him, keeping my free leg tucked until I was behind him. I corked in the air and kicked between his shoulder blades, catching his surprised look for only a moment before I crashed facedown in the grass. I turned my head to see he too was down, his hands having braced his fall, the same as mine.

He coughed.

I shuffled to my feet, out of breath and shaking slightly with adrenaline. "Do you yield?" I panted, unsure if this counted as a win against him.

He rolled over, lying on the cold ground, gaze fixed on the clouds overhead. "Are you sure this is what you want?"

"I am."

"You know we were surprised when we could still sense the vibration gift in you. Shroding told us you did not manifest at fifteen." He sighed. "I was going to void our deal, but since you can still fight..." He trailed off.

I came to hover over him, hands on my hips and brows raised expectantly.

"Very well, I will train you to be in his personal guard."

"Good."

"Shroding won't like this." He shook his head from side to side.

"He will adapt."

"You're stubborn, but Shroding's stubborn too." He winced like he knew very well from experience.

I shook my head, thinking back to the girl from the farm, the girl who'd accepted things as they were. She had accepted far too much without really fighting back. I was different, I had to be different now.

"No, Callum. I'm obstinate."

He threw his arm over his eyes and chuckled. "I won't go easy on you," he warned, and though I was prepared for it, my stomach still dipped with nerves. "Not even a little bit."

"I expect nothing less." Then I turned and walked inside, leaving my new boss to stew in the grass alone, his jacket next to him where I'd tossed it as I walked away.

The fight had taken more out of me than I had expected, and once inside I collapsed on my bed, fading into sleep without a single thought about the ramifications of what I had just done.

CHAPTER 14

Dissolution

When I woke a few hours later I was on my back, the covers tangled around my legs, and a note on the end table.

Callum and I have stepped out, Asher is here if you need anything. I already set up the bath so the water will be hot for you. I will see you when I get back. Stay warm. - Shroding

Next to it was a carafe of warm tea. I got out of bed to bathe, bringing the warm drink with me. The palace still held the chill of winter, but the fire in the hearth helped mitigate the worst of it. The daylight had wavered into dusk, and though I lamented letting so much of the day pass, I was proud I had done the one thing I had set out to do. I was a member of the royal guard, Shroding's personal guard. He definitely would not like it, but it ensured I could keep him safe a bit longer. Shroding had said himself I had an uncanny knack for keeping him alive—I just hoped that would continue to be the case.

My mind drifted to the morning, replaying it over and over and over again as I soaked in the glorious tub. Shroding had *longed* to see me. He had basically implied that I was more wonderful than a sunrise. I didn't know how to take that admittance, especially when the moment had been so perfect, begging for a kiss to seal the deal. So why hadn't he?

When I climbed out of the bath my whole body hummed like a light bulb getting too much power. Giddy excitement at seeing him had me changing quickly into a different Krav suit. It wasn't as battle ready as the last one—the hard leather had been like armor across my skin—but this one was a buttery cotton, and hugged every curve in a less secure way. Also unlike the other it was not black but instead a deep green enhancing my eyes. Hair braided down my back I ventured out to find the men.

Following Asher's voice, I found him in the library, talking with Sir Martus.

"They are doing a sweep of the perimeter?" the older man asked.

They had not heard me come in. The library was still in shambles; books and shelves were stacked up against the wall, a torn, broken mess of them piled up at the doors, which could no longer close, the hinges bent at odd angles from the force of the attack almost a week ago.

"Making sure our guest from earlier has not returned..." Asher added, and I hesitated to make my presence known. So they were aware of the intruder? Who had the voice been in the hall?

"We will need to be careful who we let into the palace with the Rephaim having bodies again—they can easily blend into crowds." Sir Martus huffed, clearly upset by our blunder. We should have gone straight through the portal, but if we had, I might not be alive at all even with Mama Meod's sacrifice.

"It will be a pain, cleaning up the palace without extra help," Asher grumbled.

Had they hired cleaning crews from the town to help restore the palace after the attack? Was that how the intruder had gotten in? Was that voice one of the Wraiths? Gooseflesh patterned my skin at the idea that a Wraith had been watching me.

Footsteps approached from a passageway on the other side of the room. I ducked deeper into my hiding spot.

"Shroding, you need to take it easy. You are going to make yourself sick," Asher warned. "What were you thinking, having him run all over in this storm?"

"We were on the intruder's trail and would have caught up if not for the weather." Callum huffed grumpily.

"Asher, please, I'm fine," Shroding assured him, but his voice was tired, making me worry. Had he been outside this whole time? It was late, but I didn't know the time to be sure.

"Are the members of the steward's court coming?" Asher asked, his voice less irritated but still worried.

"Yes, but just three of them. They should be here in two days," Sir Martus relayed.

"Good, good." Asher sounded relieved.

"How did things go here?" Shroding's voice was soft, tentative.

"She slept the whole time. After fighting Callum I'm not surprised, but from what I could tell she does indeed have the gift. However she lacks the ability to move to any of the dimensions. I don't know if it is a skill she can retrain or if it is permanently gone for good. Time will tell," Asher explained.

"I see." Shroding's voice held a mix of relief and disappointment.

"Well, don't look so glum—we were expecting her to not have the gift at all." Callum's voice was steady and unsympathetic. There was a pause.

"Shroding, did you talk to her about leaving?" Sir Martus inquired.

There was another pause. "She won't leave, then?" Asher sighed.

Shroding's low whispered voice resumed speaking, but I couldn't hear anything.

"*Strings*, Shroding. It doesn't sound like a little crush to me," Callum snapped.

"I never said it was little," Shroding bit out, his voice rising, "and for the record I said I would give her the choice. In the end I will do what is best for her, to keep her safe. So back off," Shroding finished defensively.

"Calm down, we aren't blaming you. She is pretty, and you spent a lot of time together after being isolated for two hundred years. It is only natural you might develop... something... for each other," Asher reasoned diplomatically.

It bothered me tremendously that they could talk so carelessly about my feelings. Just this morning Shroding had said he wanted to see me. Me. Not them, not the court. Me. *So why should I go away?* My internal bravado faltered as my insecurities poked out from their dark depths. Shroding had over four hundred years of relationship with them and only a mere two months with me. What right did I have to come between them? I had done what I came here to do. I didn't want to be the reason a wedge formed between them. Maybe I should go home? The thought hurt so much I had to lean against the wall for support.

"Shroding, I have always supported you. Always. But her role here is finished. She has no part in what is to come. She would be safer back home, back with her family." Callum's voice held a finality that stilled my heart. He had just agreed to train me—had that been a lie?

"We should let Shroding sleep. It's been a long day for all of us," Asher mentioned, above the scrape of a chair on stone. For a moment I panicked. I hadn't intended to eavesdrop. I needed to leave.

"She does not have a home to go back to." I froze, Shroding's voice nailing me in place. "You know she lost her brother, her father. Her home literally burned to the ground before her eyes. She didn't tell you, but she *had* a proposal. She lost everything because of me. Because she chose to help me. Do not tell me she isn't a part of this. I have watched her suffer for months. I have been the cause of that pain, and I can't..." His voice trailed off.

The hallway took on a warped look, making me feel like my head was going to pop. Pity? Pity. Guilt. Shroding didn't love me, he felt *responsible* for me... just like Micah had.

The room was silent for a long time. My feet unsteady under me. I didn't want to hear any more. I didn't want to know any more.

"If she chooses to stay and you let her, we will understand, but that choice will not free her from the pain she has gone through. It will, however, seal the fate for more pain to come." Callum's voice was tender and knowing. It made me sick.

"I have already asked her to stay, and she is welcome to for as long as she wishes to," Shroding finished with the authority of a king silencing all others in the room.

My heart hurt as I backed away, and once in the hall I ran

to my room. I closed my door silently. I had been strong. I had changed him. I had survived death. I had power. I had strength. I wasn't useless, I wasn't weak... not again. I was not helpless... I didn't need anyone to be responsible for me.

I walked heavily to the tall windows and pressed my head against the cold glass, easing the headache that rocked behind my eyes. I wanted to pretend I hadn't heard any of their conversation. I wanted the airy, warm, happy feeling from this morning back. The way Shroding had told me he'd wanted to see me, my eyes, my hair. They weren't just pretty words, right? They had meant more, hadn't they? But if that was true, then surely he would have told his closest friends that I was staying because he loved me, wanted me, that I was more than a character playing a role in his story.

CHAPTER 15

Armory

When I woke I was lying in my bed. A tan arm was draped across my hip.

I pushed up, finding the arm belonged to a sleeping Shroding, who lay next to me, his dark hair spilling over the pillow. His long lashes dusted the curve of his cheeks. My heart squeezed while my mind flustered. He had stood up for me last night, but I was still angry. I couldn't figure him out. What he wanted. He was here with me again, but he had told me he wanted to be friends. He had warned me things would change. He had warned me he would hurt me. Then he had told me with such tenderness that I was all he had longed to see. What did it all mean?

"Shroding?" I nudged his shoulder. His eyes fluttered but didn't open. Rolling from his side to stomach, he leaned forward, stretching his arms out like a cat, and despite myself I smiled, recalling too many moments like this with Iri. I shouldn't be letting my guard down, and yet Iri was the fastest way to disarm me.

He smiled, his eyes still closed. "Morning. Sorry I was gone yesterday." The apology alone ebbed my anger.

"What are you doing here?" I raised an eyebrow, keeping my voice as level as possible.

His eyes opened fully, and he sat up, hanging one leg off the side of the bed. He wasn't under the covers; he had been lying on top of them like he always had as a cat. Sleepily he rubbed the back of his head. "As weird as it sounds, I have gotten used to sleeping next to you." My cheeks heated. "Is it very weird?"

"Erm." I coughed. "It's a little weird now that you are human," I mumbled, embarrassed.

The hearth had fizzled out in the night, and the chill of early morning raised the hairs on my arms. I kicked myself for wearing my nightgown to bed instead of the Krav suit. Crossing my arms, I fumbled to my feet and grabbed a robe, then wrapped it around me. "Uh." I fidgeted. "Won't they be looking for you?" I poked my thumb at the door.

"Oh." He leaned back in bed with an amused smirk on his face. "I'm sure they can find me if they need to. Vibrations and what not." I had forgotten he gave off a vibration now. Once he'd gotten his body back his vibration gift could be sensed by someone with the gift. "You're bothered by what you heard last night?" he asked knowingly.

"You knew I was there?" I balked.

"I always know where you are," he murmured, turning his face away from me. Was he blushing, or was the redness in his cheeks from anger?

"Are you angry at me for eavesdropping?"

"No, but I am sorry you heard it." He looked back at me, and all traces of amusement were gone. "What Asher said about your gift, how it's not the same, does it make you sad?"

"I'm not sure," I whispered, uncomfortable with the topic. I was sad. So sad words could not convey it. I was sad that I would never be able to move dimensions, that I had lost my connection to Shroding and that it seemed his friends thought I should leave.

Shroding watched me, his dark stare questioning. I stared back, unsure what to do. Shroding lay on the bed like he owned the place, but then again he did. He was somehow more self assured now than he ever had been in the spirit dimension, and it was a bit intimidating if I was honest.

I needed to change the topic.

"Is it strange to walk on two legs again?" I probed, leaning my shoulder against the bedpost, trying for but probably missing nonchalance.

His cheek lifted in a smirk, amusement glittering in his eyes again. Had he made this expression a lot when he was a cat but I just couldn't see it?

"It's less strange than learning to walk on four," he quipped, accepting the subject change. "It's like being on sea legs, I feel... off balance." I nodded, sort of understanding.

A loud bang made us both jump and look at the door.

Callum strode into the room, a sword slung over his shoulder. "Well, Shroding, time to break you in." I glanced back at Shroding, confused.

"What—" I began, but I was cut off by Callum swinging the heavy sword. I gasped, tripping backwards into the mantel, as Shroding fumbled to get off the bed.

The sword ripped through the duvet. Feathers filled the air as Callum vaulted the bed to where Shroding stood with a small wooden stool raised in front of him like a shield.

"Callum, you could do this without giving the girl a heart attack!" Shroding chided.

"Now where's the fun in that?" he bantered coyly but turned to look at me. "Don't worry, Haya, I'm just trying to scare the sea legs out of him." He hefted the great sword over his head and grunted, "Ya know, get him back on his two feet and ready to fight!" He took another swing at Shroding, who dodged again, this time bumping into the dresser, causing the lamp to fall off and break.

Callum had overheard us—had he been eavesdropping? I didn't know what bothered me more: him swinging a sword around, destroying my room, or the fact he'd eavesdropped. Then again I had also been doing my fair share of snooping, so who was I to judge.

Callum let out a booming laugh that I couldn't help but smile at even though I was concerned for Shroding. He had seemed fine yesterday, carrying me across the sand, but perhaps he was recovering just as slowly as I was.

"Okay okay, you hothead, can we take this to the armory before anything else breaks?" Shroding implored, and used the stool to leap over the bed and next to me.

"I will see you later." He gave me a boyish smile and leaned in. I could feel his breath on my lips, the proximity making me freeze. "Heh, sorry..." He smirked, leaning back a little. "... about the blanket." And then he hurried out of the room.

I slumped onto the mattress, feathers puffing up as I touched my lips. What the heck had just happened? Had Shroding really almost kissed me?

I remembered Callum was still in the room, and I peered at him uncertainly.

Face impassive, he wasn't looking at me but at Shroding's retreat. After a moment he followed Shroding. Glancing back, he said, "Be a dear, Haya, and clean this up." He gestured to the room with a shrug, heaving the sword over his shoulder and disappearing.

Okay, what in the Strings had just happened? *I think I was almost kissed.* I flopped back; a feather floated down to land on my nose. After what I'd heard last night and witnessed this morning I really had no idea what was going through Shroding's head. Another feather floated down onto my lips, reminding me of the last kiss we shared in the spirit dimension. He had said it was a mistake, but now, now I didn't know what he thought. I grimaced and set to work picking up the scattered down.

Once the room was tidy and I'd changed into the supple Krav suit, I searched for the armory. The palace was still a maze, and though I was not sure where most things were, I had a pretty good sense it might be underground. Similar to how it was set up at the Citadel in Wycliff.

I was correct.

Weapons lined the walls; axes, spears, and swords. The room was circular with a large sandy floor. Light streamed in from long, narrow windows around the perimeter of the room. I found a spot on some crates and watched the boys spar. Both Asher and Callum showed no mercy to Shroding as they sparred. Though, there was still a fair share of goofing around. I made them take breaks to eat and hydrate just as my mother had done for my father and brother when they worked the farm for long hours. Shroding expressed his gratitude by saying at least *I* was going easy on him.

Shroding not only had to access the vibration dimension but fight at the same time. He was amazing. Though he was struggling, he still managed to look graceful. I observed his movements so I could practice them later. Though, there were parts of the sparring I could not see at all—they moved at a speed so much faster than I could follow.

As I watched I realized I would not be able to keep up with Shroding. I had never been able to to begin with. Shroding had always been on a path, a mission, and I'd just gotten to come along for part of that ride. I was never supposed to stay until the completion.

The one thing I feared happening was; I was getting left behind. Again. With every flawless kick and dodge the chasm grew. No matter how hard I worked I couldn't catch up to him.

Yet I needed to be useful to Shroding so I wouldn't be sent away like Callum and Asher wanted. I didn't really blame them for wanting me to go. Shroding did need to focus, and I was a distraction, especially if he was always worrying about me. I needed to give him a reason to think I could take care of myself. I needed to prove I could protect myself. I wasn't going to let my fears stop me this time. I wouldn't let fear be the reason I did anything anymore. Sure, the thought of joining the king's guard had started with not wanting to be apart from him, but now it was personal.

He hadn't told me he loved me; he hadn't tried to commit to me the way Micah had been willing to.

I had always thought wanting more was a bad thing, but I understood now that contentment was the absence of growth, and I had finally started to grow. I finally believed in myself enough to be more than just a farmhand. More than a tool for the king's power thrust upon me to save Shroding. This realization, spurred on by the king's power, made me want to fight back against the darkness in this world. Beyond just bringing Shroding back. Beyond loving him.

I had something to offer, and somehow that was enough to make me realize I was good enough. I could want more, not because I had the king's power but because, with or without it, I was still enough.

I recalled the first time Shroding and I had kissed, the way I had just gone for it. Foolish and brazen. That was the kind of person Shroding had helped me become. Someone who could just go for it, even if it was scary, or a little silly, or really very stupid. I had gotten to experience more of life because of him. My world had expanded, and in turn I had too. My mind had opened to a life beyond the mountains that encased my existence in Wycliff, and I no longer believed I would want to go back even if I could.

I had understood even then, kissing him, that if I fell for him, I would never be the same, and those words were never more true than they were now. I was not little Haybale. I was Haya Golden; descendant of Armond Golden, general to the late King Roark. I had greatness in me, not just thrust upon me. Shroding saw it, and pulled it out of me. That was the kind of person he was. I could see it in the way Callum and Asher looked at him as well. He had pulled greatness out of them too. He had helped them become more.

I loved him for that. I loved him. I'd never told him in so many words, but it was true. With every breath I loved him more and more. It was like the ever expanding universe. The dimensions and worlds out there, the endless depth of the vibration gift. That was my love, ever growing, ever changing, but completely for him. Just like growing pains, it hurt as much as it was beautiful. I couldn't stop it now even if I tried.

I had let fear dictate so much of my life without even realizing it. I had feared getting the gift as a child but also not getting it. I had feared the idea of the war and having to fight in it. I had chosen to accept things, thinking that would make the fear easier to handle. I had feared Micah's feelings for me, doubting if I could love him, when I knew I had, and we could have been happy. I feared being useless, so I always tried to be useful. I feared what I did not understand, which was a lot, I had realized these last few weeks. The whole time I'd been scared. I had feared losing more people I loved, so that even now I had to question if I was choosing to fight out of fear. After watching Shroding move and dodge and hit, taking Asher down even in his weak state, I just wanted to be as cool as him. He never gave up, even after two hundred years of isolation he kept going. He kept living life. Against all odds.

Callum pushed Shroding and stumbled back, sand crunching under Shroding's weight as he dropped to the ground with a thud, ripping me from my ruminations back to the present. It wasn't the first time Shroding had fallen down, but this time he didn't seem to be getting up.

"Shroding," I whispered. *Get up.* Asher stood off to the side, having gotten too worn out. They had been at it for hours.

"Callum, give him a minute," Asher cautioned.

Shroding swung his sword at Callum's legs, pushing him back a little. Callum's eyes narrowed at me. Challenging, as if saying, "Are you strong enough to guard him, to be his protector?" He raised his sword to strike at Shroding again, but his eyes remained on me.

"Callum!" Shroding scowled up at his friend in alarm, then raised his sword. Their swords hit together with a boom that could have only been vibration gifts hitting each other. I knew they had been using their gifts to strengthen the blows or push each other back, but this sounded different. What was Callum doing? I looked to Asher, who shook his head and turned away to leave the room. What the heck was going on?

Shroding was tired. I could see it in the way his shoulders shook, holding Callum back. He tried to push himself up. "Callum?" Shroding demanded through clenched teeth.

"Logan won't go easy on you—he is not the same anymore," Callum said, his voice low. Shroding looked up at Callum, surprised, and then glanced at me. Callum took the distraction and threw Shroding back so hard he broke the divider that separated the arena in half.

"Shroding!" I cried, running to him, when Callum slammed into me, knocking me to my side on the ground. "What are you doing?" I thrashed, trying to crawl out from under him to get to Shroding.

"Proving my point." I froze as the blade of his sword touched my throat. He straddled me, his hulking weight triple what I could lift on a good day at the farm. My wide eyes stared up at the commander, chest heaving.

"Callum, I order you to stop this!" Shroding yelled, climbing out of the rubble. "You are scaring her needlessly."

"This isn't about her. She makes *you* weak because she is weak." Callum glared at Shroding, the first time I had ever seen him look hostile towards his king. Anger burned in me like acid in my stomach. Before they could realize what I was doing, I called the little bit of power I had, forcing the blade from Callum's hands and flinging it with my gift as far across the room as possible. I pushed up, kneeing him in the groin just as he tried to shove me back down. I knew I didn't look cool, not like Shroding had; I was sure I was flailing about wildly, but I had done it. Callum toppled over, a low groan escaping his lips. I rocketed to my feet and backed away, my heart pounding into my head. I wanted to say something snappy, but my shock at kneeing him was greater than my capacity to be witty.

"Haya..." Shroding's voice was tremulous. I knew it hurt to get hit there, but the way Callum seemed to go deadly still, moans so low and pained, I was afraid for a moment that I had done something worse.

"I didn't mean... I knew it hurt to— but I just— didn't know... Is he going to die?" I panicked, voice rising. A low laugh came from Callum between whines of pain. Shroding's clear laugh rang out, making me jump slightly.

"You are absolutely *incredible*," he said between deep belly laughs. He walked over to me, but I could see he was struggling. I hurried over to support him and took his arm over my shoulder. "He learned his lesson—he won't be calling you weak again. Future generations won't forget either."

"Oh," was all I could manage.

Asher came back in with an ice pack. "I told him this was a bad idea. It turned out better than I thought, though." Asher winked walking past me and Shroding to Callum. He tossed him the ice pack but looked back at me. "How are you feeling, Haya?"

"I'm fine," I said, impish, looking at Shroding. He was grinning from ear to ear.

"Let's get cleaned up—I think we have had enough of 'curing my sea legs' for the day." He chortled again. "Don't you agree, Callum?" Callum said nothing but waved his hand over his head dismissively. Shroding unwound his arm, took my hand and led me back to our rooms. I was covered in sand

and liked the idea of a bath, but I wasn't half as bad as the boys, who were covered in blood and sweat.

"What was he thinking?" I asked incredulously.

"You will have to ask him that," Shroding said softly, as if he didn't want to talk about it.

I nodded, intending to do just that.

CHAPTER 16

Stay

I changed into a simple dress of burnished yellow, and flats so soft they were more like slippers on my aching feet. I wandered through the halls, looking for the other men in the palace, but when I could not find anyone I headed towards Shroding's room.

"Callum knows he needs to apologize." Asher's voice carried through the ajar door.

I smiled, knowing they were talking about me. He did need to apologize, but I also was a bit in the wrong. I really shouldn't have attacked his manhood. I owed him an apology but settled that I would only give it when he owned up to his mistake first.

I knocked on the door.

"Sorry to intrude, I just..." I trailed off, mouth hanging open helplessly as my eyes widened, taking in the sight before me.

Shroding sat in the high-back red leather chair, his freshly washed dark hair damp in the firelight. He was shirtless, his tan chest exposed, broad shoulders and biceps glistening with faint water droplets. A pattern of purple and green bruises adorned his torso and arms, no doubt from sparring. His head was tipped back, hands curved over the armrests, ankle over his knee, stretching the cream cotton pants over his legs. He was tired. I could see it in the faint discoloration under his dark eyes, but when I walked in he immediately sat straighter, lifting his head to look at me.

I should have met his gaze, but my eyes were fixed on the way his abs flexed with his movement. I swallowed thickly, the room easily fifteen degrees hotter than any other room in the whole palace.

"Please leave us," he said softly. I blinked, alarmed, and turned to leave, but instead Callum and Asher stood from their chairs and brushed past me to the door. They nodded to Shroding and inclined their head to me in acknowledgment. Callum's eyes lingered on me for a second longer before both men were gone and I was left alone with a half-naked Shroding.

I was nervous. The air in the room was heavy with something I had no name for. I pulled tentatively on the end of my braid. Had Callum and Asher finally convinced Shroding to make me leave? Was this the moment he told me to go? I had already fulfilled my use. I knew he didn't need me anymore, but I hoped he still wanted me. Maybe he had pursued me to get to this point but would discard me now? It was irrational, Shroding was not like that, but I doubted myself and I doubted us. *He's not the man in my dreams anymore; he is a prince and the man to lead us to freedom in this war.* I wrestled with these thoughts, unsure how Shroding really saw me now that he was human again. His actions were so confusing, but after the morning on the beach when he told me to stay, I had begun to believe it was what he wanted too.

He rose from his chair and stepped to me until his bare chest was level with my face. Strings, this was wholly unfair. A drop of water curved over his pec, down one, two, three abs before absorbing into the cotton of his trousers. He was perfect, and I was already in far too deep.

His hand closed over mine, stopping me from mutilating the ends of my hair any further. His touch quickened my pulse. Heat filled the narrow space between our bodies, and I cleared my throat, lifting my eyes to him.

"Sorry I have been so detained as of late." His dark gaze locked with mine, and as if he had not seen me an hour ago, he perused my face, drinking me in, searching me, and when a small smile played at his lips my heart melted. His hand took mine and drew me over to his bed. Hands curving over both my shoulders, he sat me down, and my knees, which were wobbling, slackened with relief.

The room was spinning; every sensation he caused in me made me more lost for words and sense. I was grateful to be sitting, but why had he not put me in a chair? That would have been more proper. I glanced at the door to his room, having not heard the click of the latch when Callum and Asher left. The door was closed, and I sucked in a sharp breath.

"Haya." He spoke gently, carefully, his hand resting over mine on the duvet as he knelt before me. His dark hair curled around his ear and fell back from his face as he looked up at me, eyes flashing in the dimming firelight. "Stay with me tonight?"

I nearly slid off the bed in shock.

Stay with him, in his room? In his bed? I eyed the plush

mattress, my whole body burning with something akin to a fever. We hadn't even kissed since he became human, but he wanted to... to... I swallowed audibly. With wide eyes, I fisted the coverlet, mouth agape.

His brow furrowed for a moment before his eyes widened as well. "Oh Strings." He slapped a hand over his mouth. "That is not what I meant." He looked up at the ceiling and ran his hand through his hair, and I could only imagine the torrent of thoughts that hammered through his mind because of the misunderstanding. "I mean..." He sighed, frazzled. "I am used to you being near." He walked over to his chair and leaned his forearm on the high back. "Why would you think I meant..." He stopped himself as he peered down, hand splaying across his bare torso. Had he not realized he was shirtless? Then he looked at me on his bed, and the flush on his face deepened. His throat bobbed as he swallowed.

I wanted to save him from his mortification, but I was too lost in my own.

"Strings," he muttered again, striding over to the adjoining washroom and returning wearing a loose tunic.

"I'm really not used to this. It's like I remember decorum, but with you I think I'm still..." He tapped the side of his head before waving his hand out in a swirling gesture.

"A cat," I finished for him.

"I'll do better, when we get to Romath I really won't be able to see you like we do now. I think I've become very selfish in my time as a cat..."

"What do you mean?" He was the most selfless person I knew.

"I know I should take you back to your room, do what *is* proper. I know it, and yet, the only time I've been able to sleep these last few weeks has been when I'm next to you," he finished, sheepishly turning his gaze to the floor. "I know you said it's weird, but just for tonight, do you mind?"

I thought of his arm across my hips this morning. No. Nope. I absolutely did not mind. I wanted to say as much and throw myself on him, but I refrained. "Well, it is late," I hedged, trying hard to hide the growing grin on my face.

"Very late." He smirked. My acquiescence was all the invitation he needed to wrap his arms around my waist and pull me onto his lap, his head leaning on the headboard of the bed. I nearly jumped out of my skin with nervous excitement. He rested my back against his chest. I fit perfectly against his body and relaxed into him. His arms wrapped around my torso, his cheek against the side of my head. We were still on top of the blankets, and for me that was a line I was not ready to cross until I knew for sure how he felt about me.

"So," I began conversationally. "Are your sea legs improving?"

"Better everyday, but some things are not quite what they used to be." He inhaled and sighed.

"Like what?" I turned my head to peek up at him but could only see his jaw.

"I kept some of the traits I had as a cat."

"Wait, what?" I twisted to the side, reaching for his cheek, needing to check his features for anything odd. Anything I might have missed. Whiskers, pointy ears. Perhaps he had a tail, though I didn't recall seeing anything peculiar since the transformation. "It's my fault. I must have made a mistake." I drew my legs around to sit on my heels in front of him to get a better look.

"Whoa." He scooted back, pressing as far as possible against the headboard. "Watch where you're swinging those knees." He eyed the body parts in question, which were between his legs. Flashes of my knee connecting with Callum earlier made me blush.

"Oh my." I jumped back, falling to my butt on the end of bed, my foot kicking him in the chest. "I'm sorry," I gasped at my clumsiness. Pulling my knees to my chest, I wrapped my arms around them and held them tight to do no more harm.

He laughed softly, rubbing the spot on his chest I had hit. "How are you so cute?"

I flushed, then I winced. Cute? Cute was what I'd thought of him when he was Iri. I'd had no idea how offensive that could sound when you liked someone. I didn't want to be cute, I wanted to be irresistible. "Come here." He reached out to pull me to him again. This time we were facing each other. I unfolded my legs to the side and laid my head on his shoulder. The hard muscle underneath twitched as he squeezed me tightly into him. He definitely was more human than cat now. That I could be sure of.

"You did nothing wrong," he assured me. "I think because half my life was spent as a cat, these traits carried over. Sir Martus thinks in time they will fade, the longer I'm human."

"What traits?"

"Well, for one I can see and smell just like I could when I was a cat."

So I hadn't imagined the iridescent flash. "Before, your eyes flashed like they did when you were a cat."

"Yeah, weird, right? I scared myself the other night when I went to the bathroom with the lights off and my eyes reflected in the mirror." He chuckled, his chest rumbling against my cheek. "I can see at night, and though I couldn't see well up close as a cat, I can see fine now, and of course I can see in color." He unwound his arm from my shoulder and pushed up his hair, showing his ear. "Then there is this." His ear looked normal, but then he turned his head slightly and I saw it. The tuft of silver hair behind his ear. I reached up and rubbed it between my fingers. In the dim light I couldn't tell if it sparkled the way his fur had, but I was willing to bet it would in the sunlight.

"It's like something out of a storybook," I mumbled.

"You think so?"

"It was always hard to imagine you as a human when you were a cat, even though I knew you were," I confessed, still holding the silver strands. "It's the same now. You were a cat, but even though it's only been a few days it feels like a long time has passed. This"—I pulled gently on the silver patch—"is like a permanent reminder of everything we went through. What we overcame together," I whispered softly, the words in their truth making me reverent in their wake. He too fell silent. Gently he maneuvered us, sliding down, till he was lying on his back. His chin resting on my head, arms wrapped tightly around me.

"You are beautiful," he whispered softly into my hair. I sighed. It wasn't a confession, or dedication of a future together, but somehow it was so much more. It was affirmation that he thought of me. He didn't want to be parted from me as much as I didn't want to be parted from him.

Tentatively I splayed my hand over his chest, burrowing deeper into his side.

We fell asleep in each other's arms.

CHAPTER 17
Weapons

The rush of water running for a bath had me blinking my eyes open. The yellow dress I wore was rumpled, my legs twisted in the fabric as I sat up leaning on my forearm.

"Good morning," Shroding whispered from the red chair he sat in, a cup of tea in his hand, while the other held a sheaf of parchment.

"Hi," I breathed, rubbing my eyes.

He tipped his cup in the direction of the bath. "Clean up and dress in a Krav suit."

"Are we training?"

"Yes, I'll sleep better at night if I know you can defend yourself with more than your fists." He said "fists," but his eyes dropped to my knees, and I had to hold back a chuckle.

"I thought you slept just fine next to me?" I teased, throwing his words from last night at him.

Expecting him to tease me back, I was surprised when instead he stood, his cup of tea forgotten and the papers he had been reading were crunched in his hand. "Last night was the last time; it won't be happening again," he clipped briskly, and grabbed the sheathed sword that had been leaning against the hearth.

I wanted to ask why, why last night had to be the last time, but I already knew the answer. The king couldn't be seen in Castle Judahall canoodling with a farm girl, a subject of little consequence. Even if I was successful in being a part of the king's guard, I would not be anything more than an employee of the king. So instead I asked, "Is that the sword from the other dimension, the one you pulled from your back?"

"Sheenagh. My father's sword, or better known as the Creator blade. "

"Foils training?" I enquired, recalling his comment in the other dimension about learning to wield a sword and not just my fist.

He nodded once.

"I'll be ready in five," I chirped excitedly. Learning to use a sword would be instrumental in me being a good guard for Shroding, and even if it hurt, I would do everything I could to get stronger.

In record speed I was dressed in the thick black Krav suit and standing in the armory with Shroding. His sword was pointed down into the sand, hand absently twirling the hilt, making a distinct hole amid the grains.

Shroding's dark eyes reflected the amber lights as he looked over at me. I watched as the wheels in his mind turned as if trying to figure out how to explain to me what his hundreds of years of skill and knowledge could easily comprehend.

"I only have a half hour—Asher and Callum took over the perimeter watch, but I should switch out with them soon."

Though they had not directly talked to me about the intruder or about the fact the intruder was probably one of the Rephaim, they were taking turns monitoring the palace to ensure it had not come back.

He pulled a sword from a rack behind him and held it out to me.

"I don't think I should be handling a real sword just yet." I paled at the sharp way the blade glittered beneath the sconced lights. The small narrow windows high on the stone walls only let in a little bit of sun, keeping the space dark and dangerous.

He sighed. "You won't hit me. If you get close, I'll use my gift to stop the blade. You should do the same. Learn how to protect yourself," he said, seeming more annoyed than I thought necessary. "Half hour," he said impatiently, holding out the blade. "Time is ticking."

I huffed and grabbed the hilt, more concerned about cutting myself than him.

He walked over and adjusted my grip on the blade. "Hold it like this." His fingers slid over mine in an intimate way that made my brain foggy. As if sensing my distraction, he tapped his boots against my feet. "This foot here, the other here." His breath tickled the hair braided loosely at my neck. "Hold that stance, just like in Krav. Lower your center of gravity," he advised, his hands moving to my hips and forcing my knees to bend. I swallowed loudly and tried to focus on his words and not his actions. He wasn't doing this intentionally, was he? "You will need to account for the weight of the sword," he explained, releasing me and walking to stand across from me.

I did as I was told, trying hard not to take his blunt way of teaching personally. He had been in a mood since I woke up.

What had changed his attitude so suddenly from the open sweetness of the last few days to whatever this was?

We started slow, simple parries and thrusts. It was very similar to Krav. The main thing to account for was the weight of the weapon, which had my arms burning terribly within a few minutes.

"That's a solid stance. Your grip is good too." Shroding mirrored me.

"How did you continue to develop Krav and foils while trapped?"

"Books mainly. I would read them as a cat and practice them in the pocket. It was complicated at first, but with enough practice anything can become second nature."

He lunged forward, his sword movements clean and direct. I met him blow for blow till we were both breathing heavy. Naturally I knew he was going easy on me, slowing his attacks to make them simpler to block and dodge.

Shroding jabbed his sword forward while ducking to avoid the blade I swung at his head. His fast thinking took me off guard, and I sidestepped his blade, losing my balance. My foot caught awkwardly in the sand, and I stumbled, losing my grip on the sword.

Shroding smiled, seeing an easy win, and swung Sheenagh in a fluid arc before leveling it with my chest.

I willed the gift into my feet. The sensation of speeding up my body was nauseating as I shifted faster than my mind could keep up with. Using a Krav skill I had learned with Callum, I kicked my leg up and twirled around. My boot connected with Sheenagh's hilt as I blurred behind Shroding, grabbing my sword from the sand and lifting it to his back. The fabric of his tunic caught on the tip and slipped up to reveal his toned, muscular torso. His dark pants hung low, exposing two very attractive divots in his lower back.

I swallowed, my cheeks burning, ready to explain it was an accident. That I hadn't meant to lift his shirt, but my heart hammered so hard it drowned out the apology in my head.

"Enjoying the view?" Shroding smirked over his shoulder and lifted his hands in surrender. "I severely underestimated your tactics, but we can play dirty if you want."

"You were going easy on me," I accused, still holding the sword and his shirt up.

Shroding laughed, the sound dizzying with levity. "Then should I make it harder?" he purred smoothly, and in a movement faster than mine had been, he dropped to the floor and grabbed his sword while swinging his leg, knocking me off balance again. At the same time he sent a burst of vibration through the room, making the lights flicker. Distracted, I glanced up at the sconces. When my eyes fell back to him he was low to the ground, his shirt gone.

My eyes widened.

The divots on his back were nothing compared to the V that cut into his lower abs. The planes of his chest seemed to dance in the flickering lights, the shadows enhancing the curves of his muscular chest and arms. Sure, I had seen his bare chest yesterday, but that had been unintentional—this was definitely not. The teasing glint and smirk on his face told me everything I needed to know. He knew exactly what he was doing and exactly how to distract me because he knew I was attracted to him; a part of me, a small quiet part, whispered that he'd always known, that he could smell it on me since the very first time we kissed in the other dimension.

I stood there dumbstruck. My palms began to sweat, making the sword in my hands hard to hold.

"Haya?" he purred, his dark eyes glittering dangerously.

I shifted into a crouch, trying to follow his next move, but my eyes were entranced, following instead the flexing of his biceps. A faint competitive voice in my head whispered that this was wholly unfair, but I doubted very much that fairness mattered right now to the prince.

Shroding, still low to the ground, launched himself up, Sheenagh arcing overhead. I lifted my blade, stopping his downward arc. We began again sharing blow for blow. His blows were charged with vibrations, making my whole body tremble at the contact of his blade. I too charged my moves, thinking quickly on how I could stop his onslaught. Shroding would never hurt me, but he definitely wasn't going easy anymore. His moves were stronger and more calculated than before.

He shifted to a new stance, and I spotted an opening, my mind forming a plan. Shroding raised his sword in both hands, and I took the opportunity, planning to use the Krav move Callum favored, the one that had put me on my rear a few times.

I smirked as I flipped the hilt of my sword so the blade pointed away from Shroding. Pumping vibrations into both my hands, I slipped into the gap. My left arm reached up to block his sword arm while my right moved in to punch his perfect abs. And just like Callum had always done, I slipped my foot behind Shroding's, a little too excited to see him fall on his perfect butt.

My enhanced punch stopped well before I hit Shroding, as if something had grabbed my arm, preventing me from moving.

"What—" I panted, looking up at Shroding, who stepped around my foot, his bare chest inches from my nose. He leaned in till I could feel the warmth of his cheek against mine.

"Who do you think taught Callum that move?" Shroding whispered as his warm breath brushed the shell of my ear.

For a second we were so close it was almost like we were dancing. Moving in a far more dangerous game than either of us were aware of. Or perhaps we were aware, and that was part of the appeal?

My heart would have stopped beating altogether if it wasn't for the rush of adrenaline feeding my competitive side. He released the vibration holding my arm, and I looped around him in a swift flow.

A few things happened then. I was behind Shroding, my right arm hooked around his sword arm as I turned my blade in my left hand so it pointed at his side.

"Got you," I said, triumphant.

He laughed slightly, and I realized the point of Sheenagh rested under my chin. Confused, I glared up to see that Sheenagh had flipped and the point was now coming out the other side of the hilt.

"Not every opening will lead to your victory." He twisted out of my hold, knocking my sword from my hand, his foot tripping mine as we tumbled to the sand.

He pinned me easily, his hold too fast for me to follow. My eyes roamed his sculpted chest hovering over me.

We were just friends, just friends. Friends. But did friends practice swordplay half-naked? No, no they did not.

I groaned internally. "That has to be cheating," I whined, gesturing with my chin to his exposed physique.

"No matter how your enemy may try to tempt you, never become distracted from your objective," he reprimanded sardonically. "Especially if they use seduction as a tactic."

He laughed, standing, and held out his hand to me. I took it and stood next to him, chewing my lip, telling myself I was flushed from the activity and not his nearness. Ha. who was I kidding. I wasn't fooling either of us.

The lights regulated, filling the room with a warm humming as if giving tangibility to the energy we both had expended.

"That has to have been the most fun I've had in two hundred years." He grinned widely, his dark eyes delighted and no longer smoldering, to my great relief.

I cleared my throat and glanced at the swords on the floor. "How did you do that with Sheenagh?" I pointed to the hilt carved in an ornate pattern, different from the smooth metal of the generic sword Shroding had given me.

"Ah." He knelt and picked up his weapon with triumph on his face. "This beauty is the only one of its kind. A sliding blade." He held out his hand, the long sword extended out to the right. I felt him send a jolt of vibration through the hilt, and the silver metal slid through the hilt, appearing on the left side in a swift movement. The sound was like a sword being drawn from its sheath.

He flipped the blade and spun it into the scabbard at his hip. He sheathed the sword I had been using and said, "The blade is yours. I recommend wearing it at all times. Even if you are a novice."

"Right," I agreed, a little breathless from the display.

Asher burst through the armory doors. "Shroding! They are here."

I turned, about to ask who, when Callum strode up beside Asher. "The Court arrived early."

CHAPTER 18

Traitor

Asher hurried to the courtyard after quickly explaining the plan. We would meet in the throne room—not the official throne room like in Castle Judahall, but a greeting space where the king had met guests in the past during his stays at the palace. Since the solar was still in shambles it was the next best place. Asher would bring the guests inside and then wait outside with Shroding. Callum and Sir Martus would talk first and signal them when it was deemed safe for Shroding to enter. I was to stay next to Callum the whole time. A silent presence no more noticeable than the light fixtures on the wall, were Callum's exact words. Apparently that too was a precaution. I didn't have the time to question their plan, as we were all on the move.

I gaped at the throne room, swallowed by its massive columns and ornate arches.

I hadn't known this room even existed in the palace. Shroding explained it was mostly used for parties and not often for kingdom business.

"Please refrain from talking to them," Callum said

dismissively as he brushed past me to stand next to the small raised platform across the room. The platform had a seating area, and the left wall was made entirely of windows. The sky was gray and misty, but in the distance the lights of Tyndale twinkled across the rolling plains. "If they speak to you directly, you may respond, but I will try to avoid that. They already know as much as they need to about you; whatever Sir Liam told them is sufficient. Shroding doesn't need you to be any more of a distraction."

What was that supposed to mean? I pushed my anger down. To Callum, I knew I was the biggest burden of all. It was as if he thought I was in the way of the king's grand purpose. Other than having been the gate by which Shroding would be human again, I didn't see how else I could be holding him back.

I sensed Asher's power along with the others coming down the hall. Something was strangely off about the others' vibrations. I shifted uncomfortably, unsure what that meant and if the Callum, Asher and Shroding noticed it too.

"Just this way—I will bring the king in shortly." Asher's voice drew closer, and I hurried to stand out of the way against the far wall next to Callum.

One man and one woman entered the room with Sir Martus as Asher left to get Shroding.

The woman was young, only a few years older than myself. Where was Sir Liam? The kind older man who had delivered such heart-wrenching news to me only a few short weeks ago. Had he not come? Who was the other man, then?

They wore long green robes similar to what Sir Martus had worn the first time I met him. They had the same look in their eyes that I had observed in Shroding and later in Callum and Asher. Eyes that had seen more than most. Eyes that had lived long. Unlike Shroding and his friends, these eyes looked hardened. Like eyes that had digested all the simplicities of life—little movements, gestures, and tedium—in so many numerous ways that those little simplicities lost all meaning.

The girl had her dark hair plaited above her ear. The other man had a long tawny braid down his back.

Callum walked forward, assisting the woman up the steps to the couch. When they were all seated they began to talk.

"Sir Liam briefed us on the situation." The tawny braided man spoke loudly. "I'd always suspected a prince's existence, but I had no proof. It is a great relief to all of us that the king had a son. A great relief indeed." He looked around, eyes passing briefly over me before moving on. "Where is the child?"

I winced at the use of the word child in relation to Shroding. He was nearly four hundred years old, hardly a child. As if the room hadn't made me feel small enough, the older man's words and fleeting glance told me I was nothing more than dust along the baseboards.

"Sir Henry," Callum began. "We were under the impression that you would be coming alone, with Sir Liam."

"Ah yes, indeed. As a court member I had to receive permission from the steward to leave Castle Judahall, as you know. The steward desired I also bring Lady Sadia to accompany me. Sir Liam, regretfully, had to attend to business elsewhere," Sir Henry explained, a tension passing between him and Callum that had my stomach twisting in knots. Sir Martus barely looked at his companions; instead his gaze was fiercely trying to communicate something to

Callum. I wondered if Callum knew Sir Martus well enough to understand whatever he was trying to convey.

Callum beckoned to the door, drawing our attention to the two men entering.

Shroding lifted his head, Asher trailing a few steps behind the prince. Shroding sauntered forward; in place of the dark pants and tunic he had worn in training, he was dressed in a red brocade double-breasted vest, matching pants and knee-high black boots. Sheenagh hung strapped at his hip, and his loose hair brushed the high collar of his vest. He looked every bit the king he was.

"This is Prince Shroding." Callum gestured and stepped back down to stand in front of me. I was sorely underdressed for the occasion.

"It is an honor to meet you." Shroding spoke, authority radiating off him in waves. "But, Sir Martus, I am a little confused—only your face is familiar to me." He glanced at the other two guests.

"Your Majesty"—Sir Martus shook his head sadly—"I am one of the last of your father's chosen court."

"What?" Shroding looked at Asher and Callum for confirmation that what he said was true. Callum nodded grimly, and I wondered why they had not prepared Shroding for this news. "What happened to the rest of the court? By the end of my father's reign the court numbered over fifty."

"Most in your father's court perished on the battlefield fifty years ago; others passed due to ailments and age. The steward did choose to replace those lost, but without the king's power no one could be granted the full rights to the court." Without the king the court could not be given the gift of long life. Only the king's power could do that. "Back in Romath there are seven others who were chosen by the steward. Most are the great-great-grandchildren of those who served your father. Like Sadia, here." He gestured to her, and she gave a small sad smile. She was like me, a descendant of someone great, and brought into that greatness. "Your Majesty, with you the court can rise again." Sir Martus's voice was hopeful. Did he hope Shroding would induct those the steward had chosen into the court?

Shroding looked at Sir Martus and nodded. I frowned. It did not seem like a wise thing to agree to so easily. Shroding did not know those men and women or where their real loyalties might lie.

The meeting continued on for a while, and I grew weary as night settled outside the windows. I remained a silent observer until Callum asked me to bring food for the guests. A tray I hadn't noticed had been organized on a long table under an ornate tapestry of the rolling green lands of Tyndale. All eyes shifted to me as I brought over the tray and set it down on the round table in the center of the seating area. Still no one asked anything about me, so I continued to be silent, moving back to stand in my corner.

"Our prince, we have forgotten something—before we can talk of anything else we need to have your agreement..." Sir Henry spoke gleefully.

"Agreement?" Asher narrowed his brilliant blue eyes, the chill in them apparent to everyone. It was clear Callum was Shroding's brawn while Asher was his strategist.

"We come with a condition from the steward," Henry justified firmly, glaring at Asher's tone.

Callum raised his eyebrow, skeptical, glancing at Sir Martus, but judging from the perplexed look on Sir Martus's face he had no idea what Sir Henry was going on about, or what condition the steward might have set. "What else could the steward want than to have the rightful king on the throne at this dire time?"

Sir Henry spoke again. "The court and the steward request that Prince Shroding be crowned at the Celebration of Strings in a week's time."

Asher and Callum exchanged a look but said nothing. I chewed my lip. I had forgotten about the Celebration, a whimsical and cheery time of year I had looked forward to and enjoyed as a child, but the last few weeks had stripped away most memories of such times. Now they flooded back, and I had to put a mental stopper on the line of thoughts before I burst into tears in front of these important people, embarrassing myself. Had it really only been a few weeks since Micah and I had talked about the celebration on our date? How had so much happened and yet so little time had passed? It was confounding.

Sir Henry continued, "At his coronation we ask that the prince also marry."

Up until this point I had done perfectly, being as silent as the ornate carvings etched into the sconces, but at this I gasped aloud.

Sir Henry, however, did not stop. "This will be done to win over the people and give them something to rally behind. A celebration of not just a king but a continuing monarchy so we do not suffer as we have the last two hundred years. The hope this will give the people will change everything. And hope is a tool we must use to win this war. Morale has been low, and this news can turn a fading people into warriors again. They will fight for a royal family they love, as they loved King Roark and Queen Elina," he finished, eyes narrowing with grim seriousness.

My stomach dropped, and without consciously choosing

to use it, my gift danced at my fingertips, out of my control, roaring with the emotions inside me. All eyes turned to me, alarmed by the wash of power that flooded the room. In an attempt to control myself I wrapped my arms around my middle, pressing my palms against my sides to hide my shaking hands.

Shroding sat perfectly still, dark eyes pinned to me, unreadable, but not alarmed like everyone else. They were steady, knowing.

"I'm sorry," I whispered weakly. "I'll just—" I shifted from foot to foot, wanting to leave, desperate for air.

Shroding watched my movements, studying me in a critical way strangely similar to how Iri would observe me on the farm. I supposed I should not have been surprised by that —they were the same person after all.

"Very well, then," Shroding muttered, rising to his feet, "I agree to these conditions. Should I perish, there would be no one left to carry on the king's power, and such an event would spell ruin for every kingdom."

"Wonderful." Sir Henry grinned, eyes sliding to Sadia, who tucked her chin demurely, fluttering her lashes in Shroding's direction.

Then it clicked. Sadia had been *picked* to marry Shroding. My heart slammed against my ribs. Had Shroding guessed that was why they'd brought Sadia here? I turned, not caring if it was rude, to stare at Shroding. But he wasn't looking at me; instead he glared at Callum, whose own face was etched with distrust. My heart raced for a different reason then. Shroding didn't like the idea? He didn't want to agree? Or had he just not been expecting to marry so soon after becoming king? It wasn't my place to get involved in political affairs, and yet...

"Wonderful indeed," Sir Martus tutted, an almost diabolical gleam in his brown eyes. "All there is left to do is find a suitable match." He shifted in his seat, facing me. "Miss Haya, child, could you see yourself queen of Shamar?"

The silence in the room was deafening as all eyes fell on me again. I stared blankly, unsure I had heard him correctly.

"S-Sir?" I stammered, my mind skipping over itself to make sense of his words.

"It's a simple question, dear."

"You can't be serious." Sir Henry stood, enraged, his braid coming loose with his outburst. "We all agreed Sadia was perfect."

"Sir Henry, calm down," Martus said dismissively, his attention still on me as he said, "You are of worthy blood, and age is merely a number." He huffed. "Look at me." He chuckled, but he was the only one laughing. "It's settled. Haya, will you be Shroding's match?"

"I—" I wanted to say, *yes, of course, that's all I want,* but the words wouldn't come because everything about this was wrong. Something else was going on here.

"Haya..." Shroding rose slowly from his chair, hand settling on Sheenagh's hilt. "I'm sorry"—he didn't look sorry, he looked angry, displeased with the turn of the conversation —"but I need to talk to the court in private." He flicked his gaze to Asher, then to me.

Asher took the hint and, arm around my shoulders, led me to the door. Confused, I did not resist. "Give us a few moments," he whispered in my ear as he deposited me outside the throne room.

I stood there stunned.

As the door closed I heard Sir Henry snarl, "I beg your pardon!"

Yelling followed, voices running over one another, but it was the sharp metallic ring of swords being drawn that made my blood go cold.

I reached for my blade at my hip, ready to help, but the doors would not open. I slammed my body violently against them. The clash of swords intensified. I needed to get through the door, but it would not budge. Calling on the gift, I powered my fist to break down the wood when a hand grabbed my arm.

My head snapped to the side, following the trail of ebony skin up to a man I had only seen once before; the memory of that moment flooded my senses and almost took my legs out from under me.

"Sir Liam?"

"Allow me." His firm but kind pat to my shoulder had me stepping back. His salt-and-pepper dreads were disheveled, cuts and scrapes patterned his forearms, and where he had worn metal adornments last I saw him, this time he wore none, his Krav suit tattered as if he had fought an army to get here. He crouched low, one leg back, arms in a running pose. He held the stance, blood dripping on the floor. Then he rose tall; in a blur of vibrations and raw power he lifted his booted foot and kicked down the five-inch-thick door, but when it hit the ground it did not crash with the boom I expected—it shattered into thousands of tiny flecks of wood and metal. I would have asked how he had done it if I were not horrified by what I saw on the throne room floor.

CHAPTER 19
Maddening

The seating area was decimated, cushion fluff and fabric littering the hard floors. Tapestries hung ripped and askew, and the stone of the walls crumbled to sand in patches across one section. Sadia and Henry lay on the ground, blood seeping from stab wounds in their chests. Their faces were gaunt, vacant of life, eyes still open, gazing unseeingly.

I choked on the bile in my throat and covered my mouth unconsciously to smother my scream.

Callum held a sword to Sir Martus's throat.

At our entrance Asher turned around. "Haya," he warned, moving to push me back outside the doors, but when he saw Sir Liam, he raised his sword.

I ran around Sir Liam, slapping Asher's blade by the hilt, knocking it out of his hands; it clattered to the floor, its silver metal gleaming unblemished with blood. "Stop! Stop this!" I yelled frantically.

Shroding had his back to me and did not turn. "Asher, get her out of here. I don't want her to see this."

"My king," Sir Liam called, causing Shroding to stiffen and turn. "I see you have dealt swiftly with the traitors. I come bearing more news."

Asher grabbed me from behind, his hold enhanced, and though I struggled I could not break free. I needed to stop Callum from killing Sir Martus.

"Did you come to tell me Skithian's followers have infiltrated the court? Because it's a little too late for that," Shroding snapped.

"I have come to tell you as much and more, Your Majesty." Sir Liam approached but stopped when Shroding's hand reached for Sheenagh's hilt at his hip. "You may take my head if you so wish, but let me tell you first what has happened."

"Proceed." Shroding's voice was cold, detached. This was a side of him I did not know, had not seen outside of when the marauders had attacked us on the mountain. It chilled me to the bone.

"On my way here, through the woods to the south I was intercepted by two Wraiths who accompanied these two." He gestured to the bodies on the ground, which were decaying at an unnaturally rapid rate. "The Wraiths had bodies, even though it was daytime." He shook his head, laughing slightly when none of us balked at his revelation. "I see you are already aware of such anomalies." He cleared his throat. "It took me by surprise. They intended to detain me, for torture later, but when I fought back they sought to kill me to prevent my coming here."

"Why did they not want you to come, aside from the obvious?" Shroding clipped, inpatient as he stepped down from the platform, hand tightening on Sheenagh's hilt. His face was smooth apart from the divot between his brows.

"Erasmus is under siege." Sir Liam bowed his head, somber, eyes to the ground as Shroding continued his approach. "The attack began almost three months ago, but Skithian's forces prevented word from getting to Claw and Wing or the castle; the steward is unaware. He is also unaware that Henry and Sadia came here. They came at the order of Logan to marry you off to Sadia with the intent that she would slit your throat on your wedding night."

"Skithian has grown very bold," Callum growled.

"Multiple plans, each one overlapping each other. Backups upon backups to ensure Shroding's death," Asher murmured to himself behind me. His grip slacked, and I shoved free of his hold, sprinting past Shroding to Callum. Drawing my sword, though I was not really sure what I planned to do with it. I couldn't take Callum on with a blade, and I was pretty sure I had only won our Krav fight by sheer luck.

"Sir Martus is not one of them. He helped us bring Shroding back." My hand shook as I held the blade aloft.

Callum glared at me, the knife at Sir Martus's throat pressing in. "You said you followed the king's star, but is that really how you came to know Shroding had returned?" Callum demanded, eyes on me though his question was directed at the wrinkled man kneeling at his feet.

"As I told you, I knew about the star from the journal King Roark had given me," Sir Martus explained, his tone serious but free of fear despite his situation. "I've had my doubts about Henry and Sadia for a long time, hence why I proposed Miss Haya as the bride in the hopes of exposing any nefarious plan. There was truth to what they said, which made it harder to be sure of their loyalty."

"What truth?" I asked.

"The steward did say that if the true king ever came to the throne, he would need to marry and secure an heir as quickly as possible."

"The steward would never demand such a thing!" Callum gritted out, hand flexing on the hilt.

"When the steward said this, did you see his eyes?" I asked, breathing heavily, lifting my sword to Callum, my pathetic attempt at a threat not even warranting a glance from Callum.

Sir Martus attempted to look my way. "No."

"Couldn't the steward have been possessed?" I reasoned desperately, looking at Asher and Shroding, who were staring at me as if I was crazy for drawing a blade on Callum. I ignored their shocked expressions and continued. "Was it at night?" I demanded, my attention back on Sir Martus.

"Those in the court can't be possessed," Callum snarled, unconvinced.

"That is true..." Shroding whispered, voice low with worry. "But what if Haya is not the only one Logan has infected with the Nephesh Maveth?"

Callum met Shroding's eyes, a forlorn expression stretching his features so flat and vacant I worried he was about to pass out.

I dropped my sword—I was no threat to Callum anyway. If he had wanted, he could have knocked the blade from my hand with a simple vibration. Any of them could have.

Slowly Callum drew back his knife, and he stumbled away, looking like he really was about to collapse. I reached out, steadying him, but when his eyes met mine they blinked at me unseeingly. In a blur I was slammed to the ground, the air knocked out of me as my back cracked on the stone.

Callum hovered over me, his face twisted in rage.

"Connect with him." He shook my shoulders. "Connect with him! I know you can. Now do it!" The force with which he shook me had my head hitting the floor, making me dizzy. "I'm going to kill him!" he hollered in my face, and I realized Callum wanted me to link with Logan.

"I don't know h-how," I stammered, reaching for my gift to stabilize my body from the jostling.

"Callum!" Shroding yelled, his cold face splashed with a red rage of his own. "Let. Her. Go."

Callum froze, eyes focusing as he realized what he had done. "Strings," he swore, helping me to stand. "I'm..."

I blinked a few times, waiting for the wave of dizziness to pass. When it did I walked over to Sir Martus, who still knelt on the floor. I would deal with Callum later; right now we needed to know who was truly loyal to the king.

"Swear this oath to me. That you have never and will never betray the king," I said slowly. "It is the only way we can trust you."

"If I swear that oath and I was possessed at any point prior and betrayed him, even against my will, it will count. Having lived as long as I have, losing the court now will cause my immediate death."

"I know," I said gently, hating that this was what the Kingdom of Shamar had fallen to. Threatening those you should trust most. But what choice did we have? We had to know if Sir Martus was with us or not.

With a deep breath Sir Martus pressed his fist to his chest and repeated the oath.

The grand room held its breath as we waited.

After a few moments passed I smiled, satisfied, and the room filled with palpable relief.

"Haya, I don't know if what you just did was brilliant," Asher began.

"Or unbelievably stupid," Callum finished, but I was not looking at him or any of them. I had my own anger stewing in me at them choosing to shut me out. If I was to be on Shroding's guard, I could not be sent away anytime something dangerous or difficult needed to be done. I was still not a part of their inner circle. Even though I had brought Shroding back, even though I could still fight, even though I was part of the king's court.

I stood slowly, intentionally keeping my back to the bodies on the floor. I didn't think I would be able to manage seeing them again without throwing up.

"If Erasmus is under attack, we have no time to waste here—we must go to the capital. As commander, I need to rally the troops," Callum said matter-of-factly as he sheathed his sword, which he had wiped clean on his pant leg. A horrible crimson streak across the tan fabric taunted me with the violent actions he had taken only moments before. Callum owed me a lot of apologies after what he'd just pulled.

I did not notice Shroding's approach until he was right next to me, his fingers gently touching the back of my head. "Are you okay?"

I grabbed his hand and dropped it at his side, stepping away. My mind reeled from everything that had happened, and as much as I wanted to embrace him and cry with relief that we were all okay, I couldn't. Not with the nagging voice that whispered, *He didn't like Sir Martus's suggestion. He doesn't want to marry you.*

Sir Liam, who had been quiet, finally rose and grabbed Shroding in a bear hug. Shroding's eyes went wide.

"Let me hug you just this once, my king," the older man said gruffly. "I have been waiting a very, very long time for you."

The heartfelt devotion and longing in Sir Liam's tone reminded me again exactly who Shroding was. Sure, I knew it, but without the amethyst glow that had called to my very soul, it had gotten easy to just think of him as a man. But this outward expression of pure adoration and delight reminded me that Shroding was more than just a man: he was a symbol, a light in the darkest night, and he would change the world no matter who stood in his way.

It would take two days by train to reach the capital. Sir Liam went on ahead to Erasmus to assess the situation there and report back, while the rest of us were to continue on to Castle Judahall. While we were gone, Palace Moreh was to be cleaned and repaired for future visits—not that we would be returning anytime soon.

We were to get on the next train, which left in two hours. Sir Martus secured us a private car where we could travel discreetly, along with cloaks that could mask our vibrations, allowing us to go undetected during the trip.

I had returned to my bathroom, hoping to wash away the horrible events of the night. Absently I watched the soapy clouds swirl at my feet like an endless storm, only to get sucked up by a black hole and disappear. I found myself wishing I could drain away the hurricane inside me along with the one looming on the horizon outside. A winter storm was brewing off the coast.

I climbed out of the tub, wrapping the oversized robe

around me one last time as I sank to the floor and leaned my cheek against the rim. I fought the images in my mind. The bodies of Henry and Sadia, the blood. So much blood. I had seen a lot since this journey had begun, but never dead bodies. The Grieving were one thing, but this was different. The Grieving weren't human anymore—they didn't even look human—and dead animals were normal on a farm, but people, never had I thought I would see murder. I didn't even know how to process what I'd seen. To know that Callum could kill so coolly, so swiftly. All of them had been so calm about the whole thing. It was chilling. Would I need to become that way too? In order to be on Shroding's guard, I probably did need to be willing to take a life. I probably did need to accept I would see death again and again and also be the one to deliver it.

I shook my head, trying not to think any more about the events of the night, but Sir Martus's request that I marry Shroding forced its way into my mind. I squeezed my eyes shut, demanding my thoughts to stop. Even the right thing at the wrong time could be the wrong thing, my father had often said, and I found myself wishing those words to not be true now.

My fingers deftly twisted my long locks into a braid.

A knock at the washroom door pulled my attention away from the dismal track of my thoughts.

"Haya?" Shroding called, and I walked slowly over to the door, holding the robe tightly to conceal my naked skin underneath.

I opened the door. He was freshly washed, in a simple tunic and pants once more, dark hair dripping onto his clean shirt. He took in my robed appearance, and a faint pink warmed his cheeks. "I wanted to see how you were doing after"—he shifted uncomfortably—"what you saw. It was your first time."

I understood Sadia and Henry had been spies. I understood they'd wanted to kill Shroding. But they were still... people. "One minute they were alive and we were welcoming them, and the next they were dead"—my voice was hollow—"murdered by your one-man army." There was bitterness in my tone, but I was not sure why it was so venomous. I brushed past Shroding into my room, looked in the dresser for a clean Krav suit and unfortunately found none. Perhaps traveling in a Krav uniform would draw more attention, so instead I pulled out the yellow dress I had worn in Shroding's room only the night before.

"Callum saw a threat and neutralized it. It is not how I would have handled things, but both he and Asher are different. There are two hundreds years' worth of differences I'm still having to reconcile and get used to. Not to mention how easily the court has been infiltrated." I turned around to see him run his fingers through his hair, the silver patch catching the firelight. "Shamar is not the kingdom it once was, and Claw and Wing at present is the only organization I trust, but that was tested tonight. If the steward isn't safe from Skithian's reach, no one is. There's no excuse for killing them, but I hope you can forgive us. I am sorry it had to happen this way." He faced the hearth and rested his arm on the mantel, staring at the flames.

I frowned seeing his dismay over what had happened. This wasn't the kind of kingdom he wanted to build. I thought of the way he had gazed down at the town of Coinania, longing to live in a world made of compassion and unity. He would have a lot to face ahead of him in order to create the kind of kingdom he dreamed of. Even though it was Callum's quick action that had taken their lives, I could hear how Shroding took their deaths onto himself. Asking for forgiveness, as if he had been the one with the blade in his hands, when he hadn't even drawn his sword. He would take whatever punishment Callum deserved onto himself, because that was the kind of king he would be. A just but sacrificial one.

I laid the dress on my bed and reached out to him, turning and lifting his chin.

"We have been over this—you have nothing to be sorry for."

"No, I do. More than just what happened today." He peered down at me, his dark eyes big and full of secrets. "There is so much I want to say to you. So much, but the words..." He cupped my cheek. "I've been human for a little over a week, and"—his thumb brushed under my bottom lip, making my mouth part for him—"I want to and will tell you everything, but could you extend your patience just a little longer?"

I was not sure what he was referring to, but from the flash of desire in his dark gaze, could he be asking me to wait for the kiss? The oath he had given to me was still unfulfilled between us. How long would he have to fulfill it before it put his life at risk?

"You said when we get to Romath, things will be different," I reminded him, lifting on to my toes to get closer to him. The robe slipped as my hands gripped the tops of his shoulders to steady myself. His gaze raked over my exposed collarbone, the skin of my shoulder, back up the column of my neck, till our eyes met.

"Haya." His tone was a flimsy warning. One tiny push

and he would give in, I could see it in his eyes; he would finally fulfill his oath to me.

"Shroding," I teased, "before everything changes, will you not finally repay me for everything I have done?"

He swallowed, eyes glassy in the firelight. "If you had asked for anything else... I would have given it to you ten times over already." But his lips were angling to mine, his arm wrapping around my waist, causing me to step fully into him, our bodies flush. He closed his eyes, and right before our lips met, he turned his face, burying it in the exposed curve of my neck. It was not the touch I had been expecting, but somehow it was just as tantalizing. I gasped as his lips skimmed my clavicle, his nose tracing the line of my throat. But still he did not kiss me.

My breath stuttered, and he chuckled against my skin, sending warm shivers through my whole body.

"These next two days, trapped in a train car with you and my brothers, might actually be the death of me. Wanting to be this close to you, having you sleeping a bunk away but not within my reach, might ruin me completely," he murmured, forehead resting on my shoulder. "I shouldn't want to touch you so badly—I shouldn't be even doing this, you're in shock from tonight, you died only three days ago—and yet, every minute I'm away from you feels like the years I was trapped as a cat, perilous and empty." I waited, hearing these truths for the first time, my heart skipping wildly in my chest. "Asher and Callum wanted me to send you away, wanted me to focus on being a king, and I know they are right." I stiffened, but he only squeezed me tighter. "With Erasmus, the Wraiths, my coronation, Logan and Skithian, my attention should not be so divided, but..." He shifted his head, mouth coming to my ear, and I squeaked when his teeth nipped at my earlobe. "You are everywhere, and it's maddening. How could you do this to me?" he panted, his breath warming my skin, his words making me come apart.

"I don't understand." Because I truly didn't—what had I done to him, other than protect, save and fight for him? I loved him, he knew that by now, knew that all I wanted was him, but why did he make it sound like such a terrible thing? He clearly wanted me too, so why was he fighting it so hard?

Slowly he set me down and stepped back with a sad smile as he brushed the baby hairs out of my face.

"Don't entertain what Sir Martus said earlier." He curled the hair around my face. I was about to demand why not, when he spoke again. "I'm going on ahead with Callum. I will see you on the train." Then in a blur of enhanced speed he was gone.

I shuddered, bereft and cold, wishing I knew how to gather more patience for this impossible man.

CHAPTER 20

Trains

The train lurched as we set off. The rattle and steady thrum of wheels over the tracks was a perfect lullaby.

We'd boarded the train twenty minutes ago after taking the short wagon ride into town to the station. Asher and Sir Martus had cleared the station of bystanders, not willing to take the chance that civilians could be possessed. When we boarded the train car, I observed just how cramped the next two days would actually be. It was small, two narrow bunk beds on one side, with a small shared bathroom, which thankfully had a door. At the entrance of the car was a booth-style seating area and table. Four large windows were on either side of the car, but the darkness of night gave no indication of what the world was like outside.

Callum swiftly drew the curtains closed and dimmed the lanterns. "We need to be as inconspicuous as possible," mumbled. "The enemy will be expecting us to go to Romath."

"But they will be expecting us to take the fastest route."

Asher sighed, sliding into the booth across from Sir Martus. I glanced at the four beds and the five of us uneasily.

In the tight car it was hard to move around four hulking bodies. So when Shroding came up behind me I was not surprised his body brushed mine.

The tickle of his breath over my ear as he spoke did give me a start. "One of us will be on watch at all times, so we will be sleeping in shifts."

"Makes sense," I murmured, walking over to a bottom bunk, overwhelmed by the mess of the day. I just need to lie down. The rocking of the train did nothing to keep me alert and awake either.

"Get some sleep," Shroding encouraged me, sliding the curtain to my bunk closed once I was tucked in.

I listened for a moment to the hushed voices of the men talking, but it quickly faded.

In the morning the scent of fresh bread and something tangy and bitter filled the air.

"You're awake," Shroding sighed, and I opened my eyes to his face inches from mine, where he knelt next to my bunk. The bright midmorning sun seeped past the edges of the drawn curtains. I untangled my legs from the blankets. "My turn to sleep." He grinned, helping me to my feet and guiding me to where Callum sat at the booth. I took the seat across from him. Shroding set food and a dark liquid in front of me that was giving off the bitter smell. "Play nice, you two." He pointed at Callum and me before swiftly sliding into the bunk I had just vacated.

"Morning." I yawned.

"Good morning," Callum said tentatively, watching me rub sleep from my eyes, and once they were clear I noticed the staggeringly large bruise forming on his right cheek.

Seeing my stare, he turned his face, taking a sip of his own bitter liquid. "I deserved it."

"Is that because of yesterday?"

He set down his cup, the clink on the saucer nearly drowned out by the snoring of what sounded like Sir Martus on the other bottom bunk. "I owe you multiple apologies."

I raised a brow in expectation, tearing a piece of the bread and popping it into my mouth.

"I didn't hurt you, did I?"

"If I say no, will that assuage your guilt?" I goaded.

"No."

"Then what does it matter?" I shrugged and chewed another bite.

"I let my anger get the best of me, I..." He clenched his fist on the table, and I narrowed my eyes on it. He immediately relaxed. "I'm not handling Logan's betrayal very well."

"I don't know how to link back to him, and honestly I hope I never do again. It's horribly unpleasant."

He nodded. "I'm sorry."

I sighed.

"I'm also sorry for fighting you in the arena, but I'm pretty sure I already got my punishment for that." He winced a little, recalling my knee in his groin.

I looked away, my face heating with embarrassment. "It's forgiven, but did Shroding really do that?" I pointed to his cheek.

"No." He tapped the side of the table. "Not intentionally. We had words, and he pushed me, and I slipped on Sir Martus's robes. Face landed here." He pointed to the end of the table. "I've had way worse; I don't really even feel it. He should have beat me senseless for attacking a civilian."

"I'm not a civilian, though—I'm part of the guard," I clarified, and he had the gall to look sheepish. I narrowed my eyes. "Did you let me win our fight that day?"

"Why do you ask?"

"Because I get the feeling you don't want me here with Shroding."

He moved the curtain to the side and peered out the window at the passing scenery. "You *are* a liability to him."

"So why did you let me win? Why let me join the guard?"

He sighed, running his hand through his hair and then slumping his cheek into his palm, elbow on the table. "Because I wanted you to train under me."

"Why?" I asked even more incredulously; I had not expected him to say that.

"I hoped to help you get a bit stronger before..."

Anger rose in me. "Before *what*?"

"Before we reunited you with your mother and sent you home," he mumbled quickly.

"But we had a deal," I emphasized through gritted teeth.

"No, we didn't. To truly be in the guard you have to give an oath, and Shroding would never let that happen. You don't belong here."

It was as if he had slapped me and a bruise was forming, but instead of on my face it was in my heart. Of course I wanted to be reunited with my mother, but I did not want to leave Shroding. I couldn't.

"I saved Shroding once—I know you thanked me for it, but in payment I am going to ask you for something, and I hope you will give it to me as thanks for what I did years ago." Callum stiffened. I knew it was a low blow, drawing on his honor as Shroding's protector. It wasn't fair, but I wasn't playing fair anymore. I needed Callum's help if I was going to get Shroding to let me fight. "Let me join the royal guard. Let me serve under you. Let me give *you* my oath."

"No," he snapped. I flinched at how quickly he denied me. "If you give your oath as part of the king's court, you will be bound to serve the king. Bound by orders."

I clenched my jaw. "That's *what* I want."

"Is it?" He leaned in, questioning. "Would you give up your free will just to be close to him?"

"I wouldn't be losing anything. He would never take my choices from me. I know him."

"Don't you think by binding yourself to the king's guard, to him, you are taking away his choice? Hm?"

I glowered, but he was not finished.

"It's manipulation, and I won't have any part in it."

"I'm not doing it to manipulate him." I fisted my hands on the table. "I can't lose anyone else. I just don't know what else to do. I don't have anything but my life to risk and—"

"You would risk the life Shroding is doing everything in his power to protect?" Callum stood and hovered over me, the streak of light from the open curtain cutting across his face. "You are so selfish and immature—you have no idea what is going on, and you think you can still help?" He bit out a bitter laugh.

Anger of my own, fresh and sour, roiled in my chest. "Then tell me! Tell me what is going on! I am going to help, and I can do a better job if everyone would stop protecting me and start including me in what is happening! Who was that intruder, hmm? Start there. Tell me, Callum!" I was on the verge of screaming.

"You already know it was a Rephaim."

"Exactly, and you know who figured that out? I did, on

my own. I know more than you might think about what's going on here."

"And they call me a hothead," Callum teased, his angry mood diffused slightly. "He will never take your oath; he does not want to control you."

I closed my eyes, defeated. I would get sent away, then.

"So in his stead I will receive your oath."

"What?" I gasped, as he loomed over me.

"Your oath, I will take it." He leaned in, our noses almost touching. "I will give you this inch." His fingers held up between our faces indicated just how small that inch was. "I will give you this inch, and you will slink quietly back to that bunk"—he pointed to the one above Shroding—"your tail between your pretty legs, and tomorrow when we arrive in Romath I will teach you what it means to be in the king's guard." My stomach dropped and seized like after eating something rotten. I scrambled to register the meaning in his words. The pretty legs comment would have made me blush if it wasn't laced with a threat. A threat. Definitely a threat. I had gotten what I wanted, but somehow it seemed like I'd lost something else.

Shakily I put my fist over my heart as the others had demonstrated when they gave their oaths. "I give my oath to serve in the king's guard."

"Under whose command?"

"T-The commander's," I hedged. Placing his hands on the table and seat back, he leaned in, bringing his lips close to my ear so our cheeks touched. I tilted my cheek away, his breath on my ear.

"Say it."

I swallowed. "Under Commander Callum McClain," I whispered. A rush of power pulsed out of me as if my vibration strings sprang from my body, detaching and sinking into Callum's. It was then I noticed something I had not before: a thread, like a bronze string, trickled out of my gift and flowed to Callum, but not only to him; three other strings fluttered out to the sleeping men on each bunk. Were these the oaths I had been given? Only now that I was in the court could I sense them?

What had I just agreed to? If I denied Callum's orders going forward, I would be giving up my connection to the king's court, and though I had been saved by Mama Meod, I didn't know how losing the power of the king's court might affect me.

"It's done." He leaned back and smiled unsympathetically. "Now scurry along, lass." He stepped aside, thumb jerking towards the bed behind him. "That's an order." A strange compulsion had me on my feet and climbing the ladder to the top bunk above Shroding in seconds. This was not what I had expected.

What had I done?

CHAPTER 21

Romath

Flashes of a memory, of fire and dragon wings and death, of watching a city burn and crumble, had me bolting upright, slamming my head on the metal ceiling, which was far closer than I had anticipated. I yelped in pain, grabbing my forehead.

Not a memory. Logan's vision.

Shroding was there, moving the curtain. "Haya?" Concern laced his features.

The connection with Logan was blocked, but the vision... Why was I remembering it now? Could Logan be the one destroying the city of Erasmus? The buildings were definitely like the ones I had seen in my studies. Had I glimpsed Logan's plan? Had he intended to show me the destruction he was wreaking?

I needed air. I needed the cold air of winter to fill my lungs and assure me that the fire was not real.

"Air," I croaked, and before I could say more, Shroding was lifting me easily down from the bed and over to the booth, where he eased in next to me, reaching across to crack the window open. He did not move away but rubbed my back as I gasped in the icy winter air. It made my eyes water, but I refused to close them. I took in the coastline speckled with trees; leafless in the dead of winter. I sighed, relieved.

"Everything okay?" Asher slid in across from us.

I sank against the worn leather seat; the cold air whipping my face made my skin stipple. I shivered, my hand rubbing the side of my neck. I closed my eyes and tried not to recall how Logan had cornered and bit me back in Coinania. The memory was quickly blotted out by another set of lips that had been there only a few hours ago. Shroding's soft voice, the hum of his words against my skin.

My face heated. I didn't want to think about that right now either.

The thunk of the window being shut had me opening my eyes. "Are you okay?" Shroding's voice was soft and gentle.

"Just a bad dream."

Shroding did not look convinced but nodded, accepting my answer.

"We are almost at the city's border," Asher assured us before going to wake up Callum and Sir Martus.

"Do you want to talk about it?" Shroding asked, lifting my chin, forcing my eyes to meet his. I dropped my hand from the faded bite on my neck.

"I think when Logan and I were linked, I saw his plans to destroy Erasmus."

"You didn't say anything about him showing you things?" Shroding frowned.

"There were bigger things to concern myself with," I said in my defense, referring to making him human again. But I went ahead and told him everything, from the fainting spells to the armies clashing and the dragon's fire.

Shroding tilted my face to the side, his fingers brushing my cheek. He was so close, and despite the company in the car with us, my eyes fluttered closed at his touch.

"I fall asleep to you two making kissy faces, then wake up to see you're at it again. Please, please spare us," Callum groaned, dropping into the booth in front of us.

Shroding removed his hold on me. I turned to face the men. "Callum," Shroding said coolly, his voice like honey. "Talk back while you can, but once we're in the castle you better hold your tongue." It was a warning, yet a smile tugged at his lips. Callum held his hands up in surrender, but then his eyes grew shrewd.

"And what about you, Your Majesty, will you hold your tongue?"

Shroding glared, but Callum was unrelenting. A war was occurring before my eyes, one I had no idea the end goal of.

We were all quiet for a beat before I interjected, "What's the plan for when we arrive?"

"Well, I'm not meeting anyone until I've had a shower..." Shroding sighed, leaning back, crossing his arms, and for a moment he looked like the overindulged prince I'd expected him to be. Something about it made me want to tease him.

"Please tell me you still lick yourself?" I poked at his chest, recalling the way Iri had groomed himself as a cat.

Shroding gave me a side eye, a smirk playing at his full lips. "Not when I can help it."

"Ugh, that is all kinds of weird and wrong." Callum gagged.

"I was a cat, and being dirty..." Shroding shivered. "Well,

it's a compulsive thing." Shroding tilted his head back, looking up wistfully. "Hours and hours, I'm sure I spent at least half my two hundred years as a cat cleaning my fur, time I'll never get back," he groaned dramatically. I considered how matted his fur had still been, even with the time spent grooming—not to mention the fleas.

"You really used your own spit?" Asher asked incredulously.

"Can we not talk about this? I swear, I'll never be able to look at him the same," Callum begged.

"I'll miss it." I grinned, recalling how the sound had been peaceful. Lulling even.

"You will?" Shroding peered at me through dark lashes, one eyebrow lifted.

"It was soothing, rhythmic. It could put me right to sleep." I shrugged, only mildly embarrassed.

"I will never understand how you could enjoy seeing our king live as an animal." Callum scooted over, letting Sir Martus join us in the booth while Asher puttered around, getting food and drinks for us.

I didn't say anything; I didn't want to say how easy it had been to forget he was a king when he was just a ball of fur, when he was just Iri. The name I had given him before I knew he was the prince of Shamar.

The train whistled, and Asher peered outside, pulling back the curtain so we could all see. "Well, look at that. There is really something to be said about coming home."

Outside, the late afternoon sun was edging its way to the horizon, the ocean to the left as we passed over a massive bridge. The train turned, the view unblocked by the forest below as the city spread out before us. All our eyes fixed on the spire growing out of the city center like a beacon of light.

Castle Judahall caught the sun, and just as everyone had said, it refracted the sunlight, making it glitter and shine the way Shroding's fur had. Prisms of light leapt from the sides onto the buildings below. The white stone sparkled every color. The tower was not perfect in its cylindrical shape; it had angles and edges, balconies jutting out on all levels. Where the palace in Tyndale had been glass and elegance, this castle was sharp and dazzling. The white stones that made up the castle were piled high on what looked to be a mountain, growing in stature at our approach. Once across the bridge we dropped into a valley, passing between tall white walls where the forest pressed into the stones, roots tangled and growing along the white facade. The city gate was ornate golden metal and opened for the train to pass though.

We slipped though the lower part of town, turning and weaving though the busy streets.

I had never seen Romath before, but the stories did little to illuminate the impression I was forming. The city was glowing, not just from the abundance of technology but from the jewels catching the sun.

"Most people don't know this, but the castle was built on a mine. All around Romath are mines full of precious gems. The largest is in the foundation of Castle Judahall. Of course, now it's empty of all the jewels, as they were used to decorate the city," Asher gushed, clearly relishing having someone to share this information with since everyone else in the car already knew.

"What happened to the cave below?" I wondered.

"It was remodeled," Shroding answered vaguely.

I marveled at the great white walls surrounding the city; they were so tall I could still see where they wrapped around behind the castle. My mother was here, somewhere within these white walls, and that thought was infinitely relieving.

"Remodeled into what?" I asked, but no one answered as the train slowed to a stop in the main station.

The men bustled about, and before I knew it we were cloaked and climbing off. Instead of exiting the station with the rest of the passengers, Callum ushered us to a side door in the brick walls of the station.

"We can take the elevator up to the castle from here," Asher assured us, and led the way to an elevator. I had only ever heard of such a contraption, and though the men seemed comfortable with the idea of getting on, I was a bit hesitant. Not wanting to show it, though, I stepped inside the metal box, which shook with the added weight.

When Sir Martus pushed the buttons on the right panel and the elevator groaned but began to move, I grabbed on to Shroding's arm. Seeing the distress in my eyes, he smoothly wrapped his arm over my shoulder, his smile reassuring. I would have been embarrassed, but I was too preoccupied with the fact he was holding me. Taking advantage, I leaned into him, and a small voice in me told me to relish this, to not hold back my affection for him. My gut was saying this would be the last time Shroding would reach for me like this. So I curled my arms around his waist and hugged his side, pressing my face into his tunic and closing my eyes. He still smelled of mint and cedar, and I breathed him in, my whole heart aching with the fear of what would happen once we exited these doors.

The ride was long as we went up and up and up. No one looked at our embrace or told me to step away. As we passed each floor the tension in the group built. Callum crossed and uncrossed his arm easily six times, while Asher's hand gripped the hilt of his sword, knuckles nearly white from the pressure. Then there was Sir Martus, who looked the most anxious of all. He ran his hand over his braided beard, twisting the end similarly to how I play with my own hair when I'm nervous.

Only the quickening pace of Shroding's heartbeat against my ears told me he was uneasy too.

CHAPTER 22

Obligations

I was not prepared for what my eyes beheld when the elevator opened. We filed out into a grand room with shiny ebony columns that rose high up to the ceiling, creating arches that glittered like the stars in the night sky. The rest of the room was glass, like the palace in Tyndale, but the whole hall was accented with bronze and gold fixtures that sparkled with rubies, sapphires, and emeralds. The floor moved like water, and I realized, intrigued, that it was water moving under a floor of clear glass. I walked forward, noticing the liquid also poured down the sides of the black columns, giving them their shine. I touched the water; it was cold.

"Welcome home, my king," Callum said to Shroding behind me. Words passed between them, but I didn't hear it as I continued into the hall, gazing up at the glass ceiling.

Asher was beside me. "Spectacular, isn't it?"

"I've never seen a room so beautiful." I had marveled at the solar and throne room in Tyndale, but this was unreal. How they had the water pouring over the columns and under the floor, making the space glitter and shine, was sheer magic.

"Come on, I'll show you to the rooms," Asher said pleasantly, a hint of something in his blue eyes; excitement, maybe? Asher seemed to know the castle better than Callum did, which for some reason I found odd. Callum was all about "royalty" all the time; it seemed strange he didn't know the floors well. Had he spent most of his time outside the castle?

Glancing at Shroding, I wanted to ask how it felt to be home, but the moment quickly passed as Asher whisked us out of the columned room into an expansive hallway. If Moreh was a palace of blues, golds and plush things, then Judahall was a castle of hard, angular colored gems. The corridor had red tiles in a dizzying circular pattern across the floor. One wall was paneled in dark wood while the other was lined with arched glass windows. From the windows I could see the city below. We were high, very high.

It had always seemed odd to me that Castle Judahall was the spire in the city center. It was very conspicuous. Like broadcasting to Golan to come attack the sparkly tower in the middle of the city.

Asher had us turning down a side hall and stopped in front of a somewhat nondescript door.

"This is your room, Haya," Asher said politely. "We will send someone to get you shortly for dinner. I believe clothes and other things are already provided for you inside."

"Get someone to send for her mother," Shroding ordered a guard who had begun following us sometime after we had left the ebony room.

"Of course." The man nodded, his golden helmet clinking against his shoulder plates as he bowed. Unease twisted in me. Who was trustworthy in the castle? Were we really safe? Glancing at Callum and Shroding, I looked for any sign I should be worried but saw nothing of note on either of their faces. In fact they appeared more relaxed and composed than they had in the elevator. What had changed?

Asher pushed the door open, and like in Moreh the rooms had animals carved above the casing. Mine, to my astonishment, was a cat, big and fierce, carved of a smooth black stone.

"Thought this would be a fitting room for you," Shroding whispered close to my ear but not so close as to be inappropriate.

"I do love cats," I teased a little coyly.

A gaggle of maids shuffled by, and their giggles and pink cheeks were unquestionably directed to the four men accompanying me, but when I turned, Asher, Callum and Sir Martus were gone.

"A friend of mine will come to get you when it's time to eat. Your mom should arrive soon; wherever she is in the city we will find her," Shroding promised, and I nodded. "I should warn you, dinner will be a large affair with the steward. Everyone who needs to know what is going on will be there, but don't be intimidated—Callum and Asher will be with you the whole time." He said the last part with a tone that was distant, formal, almost unfeeling. Without another word he gave a curt nod and disappeared down the corridor.

I watched him go, but after a few moments I chalked up his dismissiveness as nerves over the dinner, and went inside.

The linens were a crisp white, and the black floor flowed with the same water as in the first room. Above the four-poster bed was a massive painting spanning the expanse of the ceiling. My hand covered my mouth as I gasped.

A large silver cat sat on a grassy hill, and all around the animal was a sunset of rich purples, pinks and reds. Flashes of the moment I'd met Shroding for the first time, on the dandelion hill, filled my mind.

Still gazing at the mural, I twirled around the bed and over to the far wall. Though the layout was virtually the same as Palace Moreh, there was one major difference. In place of a window that went from floor to ceiling, there was a bay window and seat. The cushion was a muted green, and I sat down and peered out onto a circular garden below that, despite the cold, still bloomed with colorful flowers. How would I get down there? I would need to ask Asher or Shroding later.

The en suite was a simple white-on-white space that held a shower and bath that didn't need any fancy twists and turns to start the hot water, to my great relief. After my skin was scrubbed clean, I washed my long hair. The thick mane was still slightly damp when I twisted it down my back in a long braid, tying off the end with a tie I found on the bathroom vanity. I turned to look over my shoulder in the mirror, watching my braid settle along my back. The pearl-crested hair tie was much more elegant than the utilitarian ones I had back at the farm.

Scanning through the wardrobe, I was unnerved to find not a single Krav suit. Dresses of bright pinks and yellows bombarded my eyes, with fabrics and textiles I had never seen before. I thumbed through till I found one that appeared the least loud. A simple blue wrap dress without any embellishment. It had long sleeves and was more formfitting than it had appeared on the hanger. It pooled on the ground, and the neckline scooped low across my shoulders, making every inch of my sharp collarbones visible. I shut my eyes, trying and failing not to remember the feel of Shroding's nose and mouth tracing the skin there.

"Hello?" a woman's voice called from the bedroom. "Miss?" the voice called again.

I hurried out of the bathroom. "Yes?" I responded, a bit breathless.

The woman looked surprised and then relaxed. But my mouth was ajar as I took in the striking woman before me. She appeared about my age; short curls of white blonde hair framed an elegant narrow face, high cheekbones, full lips, and eyes the color of the sky before a snowstorm. She was pale like the fair ladies in old paintings. An ivory goddess draped in gray gossamer that made her eyes unnaturally stormy. I was incomparably plain next to this otherworldly being. Her voice was as light as wind chimes and had the same soothing effect. "Hello, I'm Natalie." She held out a slender hand. I took it gently, nervous the calluses on my fingers would disgust her. Her pink lips parted, showing a pretty smile. I smiled back hesitantly.

"Haya."

"Oh yes, I know, the girl who saved Shroding." Her eyes sparkled at his name, and my gut twinged with possessiveness. Who was she to say his name like that? "*A friend of mine will come get you.*" Shroding's words flowed through my mind. He had never mentioned having a friend like her. What little hope I had in my relationship with Shroding dwindled. I did not compare to this ethereal creature.

Dragging me from my thoughts she said, "Everyone is waiting. Time to go." Then she linked her arm though mine and led me gracefully from the room and down the corridor I had come through with the others. She took us up a flight of stairs and through two more halls. I didn't bother to ask where we were going or indicate how uncomfortable I was with her arm in mine. The last thing I needed was for us to walk in together, an easy comparison to anyone with eyes.

The doors to the reception hall were open, and like with everything in this castle I had to hold in my gasp. The walls to my left and right were glass windows, some clear and others stained glass of ethereal images. One of a forest at twilight, another a mountain at golden hour, another of golden sand and leaves overlooking the ocean. Each one took my breath away, but there was more splendor than I could comprehend in every part of the room. A long table stretched out before us was adorned with flowers and candles and tiered dishes of fruit, meat and bread. Most of the seats were full, guests chattering among themselves. The room smelled of lavender and decadence. A latticework hung across the whole ceiling, spilling beautiful purple flowers in various hues. The white floor was so polished I could see the reflection of the flowers below my feet.

Natalie dropped my arm and gestured for me to have a seat. I searched the room for Shroding and found him at the head of the long table with an older man, who I assumed to be the steward, next to him.

"This is new—you're doing, Natalie?" Asher came up behind me, scooping up my braid and holding the pearl band out between us. To my surprise Natalie visibly tensed.

"No, that was all her." Her voice was still angelic, but in her eyes I could see the same possessiveness I had felt when she mentioned Shroding.

Asher released my hair and reached out to her, brushing the sleeve of her dress as if he was about to take her hand.

"You look lovely as always, Natalie." His eyes blinked slowly like a lazy cat, and the mannerism was so like Shroding that my heart fluttered of its own accord. They held each other's gaze, and my presence was quickly forgotten. I started to back away from them, not wanting to intrude on whatever moment they were having, when the heel of my shoe came down on someone's toes.

"Sorr—" I turned to see Callum, who braced his palms against my exposed shoulders, steadying me. His hands were warm, solid, and heat crept over my cheeks.

"Touching every girl in sight, Asher? That's supposed to be my thing," Callum teased, breaking the little moment Natalie and Asher were having. Natalie glared at Callum, but even the glare made her face look pretty. Both men were smiling knowingly, and it was as if I was interrupting some special reunion. Did they all know each other? Why had no one ever mentioned Natalie?

"Please come, sit and eat!" called the elderly man who sat next to Shroding. He had a long white braid that arched over each of his ears, the rest of his hair cut short. His skin was wrinkled, and he wore long white robes similar to the ones Sir Martus wore where he sat a few seats away. It was only when I saw the bronze pendant of the king's crest hanging around the man's neck that I confirmed my suspicion he was the steward.

"Yes, Father," Callum and Natalie said in unison.

Callum's palms were still pressed against my shoulders, holding me, and suddenly I was very grateful for them. Without them I was sure I would have fallen over in shock. Callum and Natalie were brother and sister? Not only that, but they were the children of the steward? I looked between their faces, only now seeing the similarity in their eyes, the wide set almond shape and pale color nearly identical.

Numbly I let Callum lead me to a seat. Once I was sitting I noticed Shroding's eyes on me. His expression was unreadable, but his dark gaze bored into me as if trying to dig some secret truth out of my expression. It was moments like this I wished we still had our connection. The quiet in my mind was nice most days, but I missed our secret moments, secret conversations.

Callum sat next to me, Asher and Natalie a few seats down from us.

The steward bid us to eat and celebrate the return of the king. For a while it seemed like all that would happen at the gathering was eating. The food was indulgent, far more expensive and lavish than the food we'd had at Moreh or anywhere else in my life. I ate slowly, though, not sure if all the rich flavors would settle as well in my stomach as they did on my palate.

"So this is the sister you mentioned?" I said conversationally to Callum.

"It is," he answered, reaching across my personal space to grab a roll stuffed with some kind of orange jam. "Is there something bothering you?" he whispered, face so close I could see each of his blond-tipped lashes.

"It's unexpected," I admitted, eyes dropping to my plate, needing a distraction. Picking up and taking a bite of something peachy, creamy and deliciously sweet, I waited for him to settle in his seat.

"Why, because she is as delicate as an orchid plant and I'm a carnivorous one?"

"Well, you said it, I didn't." I smiled, amused by his comparison.

"Asher, Shroding, and Natalie. They are my family. I love them as much as I love myself." He winked, elbow nudging my arm, and I knew he was downplaying the truth of the situation. He was the steward's son, in line for the throne, and that changed everything about the dynamic of our relationship. Yet he was actively trying to tell me he wanted nothing to be different between us.

"Wow, that must be a lot." I rolled my eyes dramatically and chuckled. "Your ego is as fathomless as the ocean."

He smirked sardonically, his strong jaw shifting. "You said it, lass, I didn't." I found my cheeks warming ever so slightly at our banter.

Sir Martus stood then, the movement catching my attention as everyone else mingled unaware. His face was grave, making my smile falter. He looked over at me, catching my stare. He shook his head once, glancing at the steward before storming out of the room.

Nerves twisted in my stomach, making the pastry want to find its way back up.

Shroding, who had been eating and chatting moments ago, was now slumped, his hand covering his face. His dark hair fell over his hand, obscuring him even further from my scrutiny.

What had happened?

CHAPTER 23

Politics

The steward rose, tapping his glass to get everyone's attention, which was pointless because the moment he'd stood everyone went deadly quiet.

"As I said before, we are so glad the king has returned, myself more than anyone." Shroding watched the display; his crumpled appearance from moments ago was gone, and in its place was an air of authority befitting a king. Shoulders back, chin lifted, eyes unwavering, as if the moment of despair had been my imagination. "A son lost to me, found," the steward continued, a genuine grin lifting his wrinkled cheeks. "It is my pleasure to announce him finally becoming my son, not just figuratively but legally." Callum tensed beside me, and the sinking in my gut worsened. "The late king and I had many great hopes for the world we would build together, a world inherited by his son, Shroding, and my daughter, Natalie. We long anticipated such a glorious day as when we could unite our two families." He raised his glass, and everyone at the table did as well. I reached for my drink with shaking hands but couldn't reach it in time for the steward's next words. "They are to be married at the Celebration of Strings this coming Friday, securing the line of the king for future generations." The room clamored with surprise and joy.

My hand slipped against the glass, the thin flute tipping and shattering as it cracked the edge of my plate. No one noticed, and my eyes weren't on the mess I'd made, but on Shroding. I saw the moment he sensed my gaze on him. He flinched, eyes narrowing, but he held his head straight, refusing to look at me. Had Shroding agreed to this? When, how... why?

My gaze bounced around the unfamiliar faces till it anchored on one that mirrored my shock and alarm back to me. Asher sat perfectly still, his hand held out with a raised glass, but it trembled, the red liquid shifting from side to side. He looked sickly white, as sick as I felt. My eyes skimmed over the girl and fell on Callum, who was watching me, his expression impassive. It was then the tears burned my eyes. Callum held my eyes for a moment, flinching almost imperceptibly as my tears pooled and spilled over.

The steward had stopped talking, and I took the moment, while everyone else driveled senselessly about the news, to stand and run out of the room. I didn't care if anyone actually noticed. I just couldn't be here anymore. I couldn't listen. Once in the corridor I pressed my face against the cold glass window, the lights of the city below twinkling up at me. Once my problems had been so small; I had been among those below who did not carry the pain on their shoulders that I now did. I closed my eyes, remembering how Micah had been safe, a safe love. How the farm had been a warm and simple place, unlike this glittering world I found myself in.

Still all that safety had been a lie in the end; this was my life, and there was no going back. Theo, my father, Micah, were all becoming distant memories, and it scared me. There was no safety net to catch me anymore. And I was falling, falling so fast and hard through the pain and horrors of the last few months, and somewhere in the back of my mind I was still expecting those around me to catch me as my father and Theo always had.

I was plummeting further down, and each time I was sure I'd hit the bottom, I only met more air, more empty air, nothing catching me, nothing stopping my descent. I had been falling for so long now that if I finally did hit the bottom of my grief, I was sure it would shatter every single bone Mama Meod had given her life to mend.

A small voice whispered that I should catch myself, that I needed to be my own safety net. But even as the voice implored it of me, I hoped Shroding would come through the doors, hold me in his arms and tell me it was not true. That I would never lose him. That I was who he wanted.

The door opened behind me, and hope sprang in me like a million stinging bees in my gut. I turned to see golden hair and stormy gray eyes.

"Haya."

"Callum," I breathed, not hiding my disappointment. I slumped against the window, numbly staring at the city below. "Is this why you got so angry? Why you demanded to speak with Logan through me, because the steward is your father and you didn't want him to have been afflicted like me?" I waved at my neck.

"I spoke with my father—he is not tainted by Logan. He remembered the conversation with Henry and Sir Martus. But he was referring to the agreement he made with King

Roark about Natalie. He never intended to have Sadia be Shroding's match."

"Is that supposed to make me feel better?" My voice was hollow to my own ears.

He turned my head away from the glass and stared down at me, brows knit in concern. "None of this is easy."

"Not easy for whom? You? You're the son of the steward, soon to be the brother to the king." I slapped his hand away. "Yeah, you have it so hard." I had meant for my words to be biting, but instead they were just words, my voice holding no inflection, none of the venom I was feeling.

He had the gall to look chagrined. "I won't lie, I have wanted this. I wanted to be his brother not just in name but legally for a long time. But not like this, not this way."

His expression clouded, but I didn't care to know what was concerning him. My anger was too big for my body as I snapped. "What other way, unless you have another sister I don't know about?"

Callum pursed his lips, pale eyes scanning my face and seeing all the anguish I was unable to hide. "It isn't personal, don't make it that way."

"Not personal? What's not personal about it? Marriage *is* a personal thing. Don't try to tell me this is a political marriage." The word "marriage" came out a little breathy, as if it had the power to take my breath away completely if I was not careful in how I said it. "It should never be political." But what did I know of politics? What did I know about marriage and royalty? A few weeks ago I'd been just a girl on a farm, with no plans to be anything else.

"Haya—"

"No!" I whirled on him, newfound anger roiling under

my skin. I did not know about royalty or about being a king, but I wanted to believe love still mattered, even in the court, even to Shroding. "Do you think King Roark, who loved Queen Elina, would want his son forced into a loveless marriage?"

Callum glared at me, his pale eyes like shards of ice stabbing into me. "What makes you so sure it's loveless?" His words chilled me to the bone.

Why *had* I assumed it was loveless? Because I had hoped Shroding loved me? Because after the way he treated me the last few weeks he had to love me? He couldn't love someone else? Each time he had come close to showing me love, it came with a but, a not now, not yet, not... *me*. He had never told me he loved me, never expressed the desire to be with me permanently, at least not in a romantic way.

"She grew up with us. She is as old as Shroding—don't make assumptions about people you don't know," he continued, defensive, and my heart recoiled as if slapped but not just by his words. My heart broke a little knowing Theo would have been like this, would have stood up for me like Callum just had for Natalie. The heartache of losing my brother tore through me anew, but I fought it, refusing to show my pain, refusing to pity myself for the loss.

"Fine." My fists clenched with unexpressed anger. I didn't want to fight for someone who did not love me, who loved another. Still, there was an attraction, and I knew we both felt it, both wanted it. But I was not the kind of girl to steal another's man. I would keep the line Shroding had made; I would be his guard, nothing more, nothing less, because that was how it had to be now that he was an engaged man.

Callum grabbed my upper arm and dragged me down the hall with him as if I were a child. "Come on, you need to blow off some steam, and I have a promise to uphold."

"What promise?" I glowered, but my curiosity had me going along with him.

"I said I would show you what it means to be in the king's guard."

I followed him through the maze that was the castle. He was infinitely more sure footed as he led the way to the guard's quarters and training rooms. It was probably the only area of the castle he actually frequented when he was visiting.

Did he opt to stay here instead of on our floor with the rest of us? No, I doubted he would let himself be that far from Shroding.

The halls changed from rich red with gold adornments to simpler pale walls and wood floors; the doors were ornately carved with a strange writing, but aside from that there was nothing all that different from the homes and taverns back in Wycliff.

At the end of the hall was a set of double doors. He pushed them open onto a handful of men sparring in a matted arena.

When they saw Callum they immediately straightened and formed a line, bowing their heads.

"Commander!" the men announced in unison.

"At ease." Callum sighed and strode over to the wall of weapons. His sword was strapped to his hip as usual, but mine was back in my room. I hadn't thought it appropriate to wear to a dinner with the steward—perhaps I had been wrong?

The men relaxed and carried on with their training; a few

glanced my way and murmured what I could only assume were questions as to why I was here.

I glanced down at my blue dress, the way it rippled around my feet, and frowned.

"I'm not exactly in clothes made for training," I whispered to Callum, coming up behind him.

He kept his face forward, finger under his chin in thought, but his eyes peered at me. "No, lass, you most certainly are not," he muttered, gaze drifting over the curve of my collarbones. I raised a brow, and his eyes snapped forward, followed by his hand reaching out to pluck a long narrow sword from the wall. It was similar to the blade Shroding had given me, but in place of a straight flat tip, it was needle pointed and very, very sharp. "All the more reason to train as you are. You never know when an attack might happen, and it's best to be able to fight—"

"In any condition." I cut him off, taking the weapon, having learned this lesson from him well enough, before.

He took off his high-collared charcoal vest, revealing a black tunic underneath, tucked into his light gray trousers. He also did not look dressed for a fight.

"You are a fast learner," he praised, walking onto the mat.

As soon as he approached, the other men scattered, gathering their weapons and wiping sweat off their brows with towels. I was not comfortable fighting in front of these men, and a large part of me wanted them to leave so I would not embarrass myself in front of any other people in the castle guard.

"So are you commander over the mobilized army, king's guard and castle guard?" I wondered, following him to the mat and bending into a Krav position.

"I am." He twirled his blade around his finger and thumb

in an overly cocky display of skill. "Though Asher oversees the castle guard when I'm not around."

"And the king's guard?" I asked, blood pumping a little faster as I readied myself for a fight.

"I *am* the king's guard; there hasn't been anyone aside from me until now." He lunged forward, sword cutting between us in a blur I was only able to track with the gift. Our conversation was cut short as we parried and attacked, careful to avoid cutting skin. When his blade got a little too close for comfort, I sensed him using his vibration to pull his blade back just enough to avoid nicking me. My dress however steadily became riddled with tiny tears.

It took extra concentration to factor in how my dress would slow down my strides. It tangled around my feet and made moves I had all but mastered look sloppy and novice.

When I fumbled a very simple Krav move thanks to the dragging hem, Callum grunted with annoyance.

"I could have taken your head off." He scowled. "If you were in real danger—no, if Shroding were in real danger—what would you do about that problem?" He waved his hand at my flowing skirt.

My brow furrowed, and I understood what he meant for me to do. The dress was already ruined, but it seemed so wrong to destroy one of the only dresses in my wardrobe that didn't have me grimacing in distaste. Sighing, I bunched up the hem and sliced through the fabric at my knees. It tore so easily I almost laughed, remembering the thick leather Krav suit at Moreh and wishing I were wearing that instead.

A few gasps had me glancing up. The other men had stayed to watch our match and were now whispering and smirking at my exposed legs. One of them whistled, and my face heated.

What was their problem? Hadn't they seen legs before? I ripped the blue gown the rest of the way around the backs of my knees, but an unexpected tear had begun to travel up my thigh. Was this why the men were whistling?

Callum glowered and turned to the men. "And what do you think you're doing in the presence of your commander?"

CHAPTER 24

Lessons

The men startled, looking sheepish. One who had not whispered or made any lewd gestures stepped forward.

"Commander, this is highly irregular. A woman in the training room, and to be in such a state of undress, is highly improper."

Callum's jaw worked. "And, soldier..." He stepped forward, tipping his blade in the direction of the man. "If you saw this display occurring under any other circumstance, would you allow your men to catcall and whistle at a woman in distress?" I was hardly in distress, but I bit my lip, unsure what exactly was going on and what I should do, if anything at all.

"C-Commander?"

The blade was now at the man's throat, but to his credit the man did not flinch or back away.

"If anyone else were goading a woman into a vulnerable position like this, would you stand back and. Let. It. Happen?" His last words were cutting, sharp, a clear threat.

"No, Commander." The man straightened, and those in his charge followed suit, grabbing their weapons. In a blur Callum was fighting against six men, and within moments it was over. The group who had been training so diligently were crumpled to the floor, some bloody but mostly just bruised. I did not envy the sores they would have as I thought back to the nasty bruise that had been plastered on my rear from my fight with Callum.

Callum knelt and lifted the soldier he had spoken to off the floor by his shirt collar.

"I expect to hear word of you and your men's chivalrous acts in the coming days, or we might need to have a repeat lesson," he growled low and testily. The man nodded vigorously. "Good. Now leave us."

The group shuffled out with murmured apologies to me, and I almost felt sorry for them.

"What was that?" I asked after they were gone.

"Natalie told me some guards were harassing the maids of late. We have very strict policies as part of the guard. They just so happen to be some of the offenders. Word will spread, and the issue should be resolved quickly. Castle guards are held to a higher standard than the army soldiers."

"Does that mean the army gets away with such behavior?" I asked, curious.

He laughed. "They get to commingle with the opposite sex, yes, but we take assault and harassment very seriously regardless of station."

"Wait, are you saying to be in the castle guard you can't... um..." I trailed off, not really wanting to talk about such things with Callum but infinitely too curious for my own good.

"While stationed in the castle they are expected to remain celibate, to ensure their focus is not elsewhere."

My eyes widened in surprise. "Then are you—" I stopped myself, having not meant for those words to come out.

His stormy eyes cut to me, trailed over my shoulders, down to my legs and back up. "I follow the rules my men do," he said easily, but his voice was anything but relaxed. Tensions pulled like a cord between us, and despite wanting to keep my thoughts and dangerous questions to myself, I could not help the need for answers.

"Why did you use your Orator skill on me back at Moreh?" The words were unintentionally breathy. "Why did you try to kiss me the day we arrived at the palace?"

Though the room was brightly lit, it was unsettling how his eyes shifted from gray clouds to inky black as his pupils stretched like a warning between us.

"Those are difficult questions to answer."

I swallowed, waiting. When he could tell I was not backing down or shying away, he sauntered forward. He did not touch me, but he stood so close I had to tilt my head to look up at him.

"Shroding asked me to pursue you, in order to confuse Logan. He knew if Logan suspected you and he were together, then he would target you in other ways, not just mentally but..." He trailed off with the unspoken threat I understood all too well. Shroding had promised to protect me, to keep me safe from such lustful attacks. I shivered imagining the havoc Logan could have wreaked in my mind had he tried hurting me in those ways.

"So it was all just an act," I breathed, relieved and a bit unsettled at how well Callum could pretend that way with someone.

He stared down at me, lips in a thin firm line. "Is that what you want it to be?"

My brows pinched at his question. "Are you saying it wasn't?" The words were so soft, so unsure, I immediately regretted them. Callum was definitely the kind of guy who was not lacking in dalliances with the fairer sex, so it was nearly impossible for me to read the sincerity in his words. He was too good at being smooth, too practiced, in a way Shroding wasn't. Sure, Shroding said things that made me weak in the knees and confused the heck out of me, but I did not question that his emotions were genuinely his. When he had asked me to stay, I knew he meant it, wholly, completely. When he told me he'd wanted to see me in color more than the sunrise he had missed for two hundred years, I did not wonder if it was a line.

"Haya..." His expression changed, as if saying I caused more problems than I was worth. "I'll take you back to your room."

We walked in silence back through the halls, a strange weight between us.

"What are these markings?" I asked as we passed the soldiers' quarters and the strange carvings around the doors.

"They are Old Golan, wards to keep us safe from anyone tainted with Skithian's power."

I blinked a few times, stopping to trace the letters. I clenched my hand to my chest as a sharp pain lanced up my arm, burning at the side of my neck.

"Strings, Haya! Don't touch it—you have Skithian's taint, thanks to Logan. These wards could kill you."

"They ward off Wraiths and Grieving?" I panted, blisters forming across my fingertips.

"Yes, it ensures no one from the guard is corrupted.

There are warded rooms all throughout the castle. It's how we know my father is not tainted the way you are. He would have turned into a pillar of ash by now if he were."

I scoffed. "That's stupid—why wouldn't they just ward the whole castle, making the whole place safe, not just a few rooms?"

Callum looked displeased with my observation. "It was that way for a very long time, but Shroding sent word ahead of us through Sir Liam that the wards that covered the castle as a whole should be taken down before our arrival."

I balked. "Why in Creation would he do that?"

"Because we did not know how they would affect you, if you would die instantly or if the king's power would protect you."

I recalled the way everyone had been nervous on the elevator; I had chalked it up to them being anxious to be back at the castle, but had they been worried about me? Worried the wards would somehow still kill me even though they'd been taken down?

"That's just..." I searched for a word that fit how absolutely ludicrous Shroding's decision had been, but the best I could come up with was, "stupid." He was putting himself and everyone else in the castle at risk, all so I could be close to him?

"He does a lot of recklessly stupid things for you," Callum murmured, mostly to himself. Shroding had asked me to stay with him and had done everything in his power to ensure I could, even putting the castle in danger. So why was he going through with getting married to someone else? Why do all that to keep me close, just to run into the arms of another woman? It didn't make any sense. Stewing in silence, we continued our walk.

"How's your hand?" he asked, a bitter edge to his voice.

"It's fine." I shook it out slightly, the faint tingling still pricking at my neck. Like an itchy bug bite. We turned into the corridor that led to my room.

A door was ajar a few steps ahead, and heated voices could be heard within. I couldn't make out what they were saying, but as we passed the door I hesitated, then peeked in. Natalie was saying something, her expression pinched with worry, her small frame shaking. Her pale blonde hair brushed her shoulders as she gazed up at Asher. His blue eyes narrowed, and abruptly he clutched her small waist, pulling her into him, and kissed her. My eyes went wide, and I blushed. I should have been more surprised, but for some reason I wasn't. The way they had looked at each other, how they sat together... I think I had already suspected there was something going on there, but what did that mean for Shroding? Did he know his fiancée was kissing one of his best friends?

Callum grunted, yanking my upper arm as he had done earlier and hauling me the rest of the way to my room. I let him, too confused by what I had just witnessed to protest.

He opened the door to my room and pushed me inside.

"It's not proper for me to come in." He didn't meet my eyes. I considered how many times he had come into my room back in Moreh. Things really were different in the castle. "Someone will bring you breakfast in the morning." He nodded and turned away.

"Wait," I gasped, reaching out. I grabbed his arm and pulled him inside. He caught the doorframe, holding himself awkwardly over the threshold. "Just wait a minute." My mind was reeling. He didn't move from where he'd caught himself in the doorway. "W-What is going on between Asher and Natalie?" I demanded, releasing my hold on his arm.

He put his head on his forearm, which rested on the frame. Sighing, he closed his eyes. "They have been together for ten years." He paused, letting that sink in. "Half of which he has spent with me, looking for Shroding. They would have married long ago, but Asher said he wouldn't, not until he found Shroding. It was an oath he had made to his father before he passed." He rubbed his closed eyes. Slowly he opened them, his pale eyes boring into mine. "Asher is taking the engagement harder than you. He had planned to propose when we returned from Tyndale."

I backed up, sinking down on the edge of the bed. "How could Shroding do this to Asher?" To all of us? How could he agree to this? Why?

Callum shook his head, his golden hair falling into his eyes. "Haya, you have other things to worry about. In three days it will be over. They will be married. But you..." He walked over to me in the dark room, all pretense of decorum forgotten.

The dim glow from the garden lights filtered in through the window, painting streaks across the floor. The water caught the glow like a river sparkling in the moonlight. I waited for him to turn the lights on, but he didn't. Instead he knelt in front of me, brushing my braid over my shoulder, the pearls of the tie tinking together as it fell down my back. Slowly his fingers returned to my shoulder, and trailed up the column of my neck. I flinched as his fingers skimmed Logan's mark.

"You have this to think about. Your future, without him. Start thinking about yourself a little bit. Are you sure you truly want to be on the king's guard? Because I will release you from your oath if that is what you wish."

228

CHAPTER 25

Petals

I eased out of his hold, my mind trying to catch up. Callum had snapped at me earlier, saying Shroding loved Natalie, but then he'd admitted Asher and she were together. Not only that, but Shroding had risked the safety of the castle so I could be here with him. Nothing was adding up.

I needed to clear my head; I needed air. In a few quick steps I was opening the bay window overlooking the garden. The air was cold but not as frigid as in Tyndale. Under a lantern's light, a dark-haired figure sat on a bench under a massive tree.

Shroding.

"How do I get down there?" I pointed to the garden below, looking at Callum over my shoulder.

Callum was on his feet, watching me, but I knew from where he stood he could not see Shroding sitting outside. Though he frowned at my request, he turned and led the way. "You need to be careful not to wander the palace alone.

Not all the doors that are warded are marked as plainly as the guard's quarters."

When we stepped outside onto the brick path, Callum paused, letting me walk out ahead of him. Shroding was at the end of the path, elbows on his knees and face in his hands. Small pink flowers covered the tree above him, and a few petals fluttered down with the breeze.

The wind was cold, and I momentarily wished I had changed into something not riddled with holes and tattered at my knees.

"Good night, Haya," Callum whispered, and then before I could even turn around he was gone, leaving Shroding and me to talk.

Cautiously I made my way down the path to him. Roses bushes, hedges and what looked like fruit trees peppered the sides of the walkway. Whimsical white flowers covered the ground, obscuring the dirt and grass. There were only a few lanterns sprinkled around the garden, leaving spots pitched completely in darkness. It gave a sense of mystery to the quiet place. It was odd how silent it actually was with a massive bustling city just below. It was so silent that the soft pat of my flats on the pavers echoed, alerting Shroding to my approach.

Dark eyes met mine, and my heart squeezed painfully in my chest. In the light I could see the smooth planes of his cheeks; his cupid's bow, nose and brow were highlighted, making him into a painting of light and shadow. His dark hair twisted down the sides of his face. Why was he in the garden? Had he come to see me? Was he waiting to explain what had happened earlier at dinner? Had he come to tell me it was all a lie?

I stopped in front of him. "I didn't expect to see you again today." Or much at all now that he was gearing up to take the throne and deal with all the endless issues that would entail.

He stood, his formal attire for dinner was replaced with a plain tan tunic and brown pants. His shirt hung open, the sleeves billowing in the breeze. I shivered, goose bumps breaking out across my exposed skin.

"What happened to you?" he breathed, reaching out to touch my bare shoulders.

"You're getting married," I blurted out, stepping out of his reach. Perhaps because we were in a romantic garden, alone, at night, and he was looking at me like the one thing he could never have, and it made me angry. Angry that he could say and do these things as if there were no consequences. Regardless of what Natalie did with Asher, I couldn't let my heart straddle the edge anymore.

He tensed, and I immediately regretted bringing it up.

"I—" He hesitated, running his hand through his hair. "You have to know—" he began again but stopped, giving me his profile before slamming his fist down hard against his thigh. I watched him struggle, my heart wrestling my mind, demanding I stay silent and let him work it out, all while I desperately wanted to reach out to comfort him.

"I had forgotten about my father's promise with the steward." He gripped the back of the bench, his knuckles turning white from the force.

"Do you love her?" I didn't want to know. I *really* didn't want to know, and yet the words exited my mouth as if there was nowhere else they could possibly go.

"Would knowing make you feel better or worse?" He hung his head, voice cracking on the last word.

I didn't know. What could I say? So I said nothing and let him decide.

"I love her," he said simply, no elaboration or justifications. Just love. Simple, uncomplicated. Easy. Something my love for him never seemed to be. The words fell around me like a cage numbing me to all sensation. Shroding's eyes flickered in the dim light, the only sign Iri was still there, still in the strange man before me. "Now let me walk you back to your room, before you freeze." But I couldn't feel the cold anymore.

"Did you ever love me?" My throat was dry, the question slipping out like a whisper through a grapevine. A secret that would only ever be murmured in hushed social circles, a hidden truth, a rumor, something and someone to pity.

Nausea rolled through my stomach as my knees shook. Strings, I needed to breathe. I would not pass out.

"Haya." A breeze blew again, petals of pink falling between us as he stared at me, concern etched on his features as he looked me up and down. A war was raging in his eyes, and I wasn't sure which side would win, but I needed the side that would hold me, tell me it would all be okay, that would swoop in and save me now. "What happened to you?" he asked again, eyes roaming my disheveled state.

"I was sparring with Callum."

His whole demeanor changed, his shoulders dropping in defeat, the tension moving to his brow. He stepped forward, and I let him get close, closer than Callum had been on the training mat. I sucked in a breath as he took my chin between his fingers.

"What did you and Callum talk about on the train?"

For a moment I was lost; I struggled to recall the day before, but when I did I paled. "What do you mean?" Did he somehow know about the oath?

He bent down, pulling me into him, and at the contact

my body melted into his. His warmth steamed away the cold shell that had solidified across my skin.

"I have the king's power. I can feel the creation of an oath given or taken by anyone in the court." As if to prove his point, a pulse of power rippled through me. The sensation was peculiar, though I only had a moment to register it before I became distracted by the heat of his hand at the small of my back.

Callum's words stuck in my mind. "Shroding would never let you take an oath." Would he be angry that I had joined the king's guard under Callum?

"I'm sure I don't need to remind you that oaths are dangerous and should not be given on a whim. They should be fulfilled with haste to avoid anything untoward occurring," Shroding murmured.

Though he had intended to warn me, it had the opposite effect, and I soured at his words. "What about your oath? Is there a reason you have not fulfilled the one you made to me?"

His dark eyes refracted the light, the outer corners pinching as he registered my question. I could see too many emotions, too many thoughts still warring inside him. Desire, longing and a touch of anger, maybe even jealousy? He'd had so many opportunities to resolve the oath made between us, but he had stubbornly refused to kiss me, and now it was too late. He was engaged to another.

"Would you be satisfied if it happened now, here?" he challenged, angling his head in such a way as to bring his mouth inches closer to mine. "Would fulfilling the oath finally free us?" he murmured, and an unsettled feeling bubbled in my stomach. When I had given my oath to Callum and he commanded me, I'd had no control over my body, I'd had to do what he said all because of the oath. Was it the same for Shroding? Did we keep finding ourselves in these desperately needy situations all because of the oath I had made him take? Did he want to send me away but couldn't because the oath was not fulfilled? Each time he approached me, pulled me in, almost kissed me, was it because of the oath and not because he *wanted* to? I was drawn to him because I was in love with him, but was he drawn to me because of a stupid vow? One he'd warned would hurt me in the end. But I hadn't cared. I hadn't cared how it hurt me because I had just wanted to be with him. Was I manipulating him, like Callum said?

"Why did you not make me leave all those times? Did the oath force you to keep me close, even though you wanted me gone?" I whispered back, the intensity of our conversation fading everything else to shadows around us.

"Even when I knew I should send you away... Even when I tried, the words always came out the opposite. After everything we have been through, I don't want you to be far from me. It makes me anxious that something might happen to you and I wouldn't be there. Even now, knowing that in three days everything will change again, I can't do what I know I should."

"And what is that?"

"Kiss you," he breathed, his eyes dropping to my mouth, "and end this compulsion."

Tears pricked in my eyes. The way his gaze lingered on my lips, I knew he was fighting that very compulsion now.

"Is that all this is?" I wavered. "A compulsion?" It was so much more to me. So much more I could barely breathe when his hand moved from my chin, across the skin of my shoulder, down the curve of my waist. His warm hands burned through the fabric of the dress until they stopped at my hip. His fingers pressing into the fabric made me shiver for reasons unrelated to the cold.

"You will get better at wording oaths, how to be exact in your request and vague when it is needed. The oath you requested of me has no timeline for completion. So every time we are together I *feel* it. The pull." He mirrored his words, pulling me flush against him. "But when I don't follow through, nothing bad happens because I just have to kiss you at some point while I'm human. And though that could be fifty years from now, it sure does make it difficult to be around you, anytime. All the time," he confessed.

This wasn't what I wanted, wasn't what I needed from him. How could I have been so foolish?

"Do you..." I swallowed the words but tried again. I needed to get this out. "Do you have feelings for me?"

He blinked, pulling back a fraction of an inch, eyes glassy and full of desire. He cupped a hand behind my ear. "Such a loaded question... " he whispered gently, eyes fixated on my lips, and the shame of what I had done ruined any delight in having him look at me with such longing and desire.

His eyes closed, his breath on my lips. For a moment my resolve faltered as it always did when he had me in his arms, but I rallied, because I had to, because I would not kiss him now. Not when he could so freely say he loved another but not me.

I pulled back, breaking his hold completely. "I release you from your oath." The string I had noticed on the train quivered and snapped between us. A faint tickle of power sizzled in my hands.

Shroding's eyes flashed open. He was surprised but composed himself, hiding it behind a wary frown. "Why?"

"I have already taken one kiss from you. I don't want any more unless it is something you want to give…"

He winced, shuffling back a step, and I instantly mourned the loss of him. For only a moment there was genuine hurt in his dark eyes, but why, I couldn't understand.

"Then the oath is broken, the deal is off." His voice was steady, but he was leaning on the back of the bench as if he needed the support of the worn wood. "So you're leaving, then?" His tone was smooth, guarded.

My brows knit; he did not understand my reason for releasing the oath. Not at all, because I was not leaving, even if he finally could tell me to go. He knew I loved him, and he just assumed I would leave now that he was marrying someone else? I may have to give him up, but I wouldn't let him fight Skithian alone.

I knelt to the ground.

"What are you doing?" Alarm was evident in his voice.

"My king, I pledge to you my life." I fisted my hand over my heart. "I, Haya Golden, very great-granddaughter of General Armond Golden, offer you my service as the newest member of the king's guard. I will live my whole life protecting you under the guidance of Commander Callum McClain. This is my oath to you."

Shroding backed away from me, and I tried not to let that sting. I forced my head to remain straight, to hold my position no matter what he chose to do next.

"Why do you do things that only serve to hurt you in the end?" I kept my eyes down even though his tone beseeched me to look up at him, to meet his eyes. But I knew what I would see there, and I couldn't bear it.

"My king," I repeated,I repeated, asserting the line he'd drawn between us the last time we kissed.

"Do as you wish," he whispered so faintly it was hard to hear even in the silence of the garden.

I had done it, I had owned up to the oath I had made with Callum and was able to give it to the person I had intended to make it with from the start. I forced the thoughts about how I would manage to guard him once he was married to another far from my mind.

I expected him to walk away, but instead he held out his hand to me. With a deep breath I let him pull me to my feet, a new current flowing between us at the creation of the oath.

"Let me take you back to your room."

I followed him quietly down the corridors, and too soon we were in front of my door.

"I should thank you." He dropped my hand and faced me. "The blankets my father had made..." He hesitated, and I recalled the blanket Theo had given me the day he left to fight. The one Shroding had curled up on when he was a cat. The three-starred blanket that had gotten destroyed in the fire at the farm, and the one in this palace, which I'd promised Shroding would see again. "I got to see it today, thanks to you." His eyes were full of gratitude and something akin to admiration.

"Glad I'm fulfilling all my promises to you, and in record time." I forced a smile, though I wished he would say something, anything about the oath I had made.

He looked past me at the door. "It's late. Good night, Haya." He tipped his chin towards the door.

I waited for him to walk away. He didn't.

I chewed my lip, taking it as an opportunity to ask, "The cat, in the painting, is that why you picked this room?" I asked in the stillness of the corridor. I could see the lights of the city below, bright and unknowing of how the kingdom would change in just a few short days.

"This was my room growing up," said softly. My eyes flashed back to his, though his were distant, seeing past the door, remembering a childhood long before I was ever born. "I wanted you to have some part of me, even if it could only be the cat."

My breath caught in my chest, and heartache of the acutest kind rocketed through me, making me wish to take back my question.

"G-Good night." I yanked the door open and threw myself inside, positive he saw the tears in my eyes as the door closed. I sank to the floor and sobbed. Iri was the only part of him I was allowed to keep. This Shroding, the king, was beyond my reach. If he did not reach out for me, there was no way I could hold on to him.

CHAPTER 26
Haybale

A knock on my door woke me. At some point I had crawled into bed and fallen asleep from exhaustion. I kicked my legs free of the thick white comforter and stumbled to the door. I was still in the blue dress, and my hair was tangled down my back. I would need another shower.

I opened the door, and an older man pushed a cart into the room. He had short dark hair; he wore what appeared to me a butler suit. "Hello, miss. This is your breakfast." He kept his eyes to the floor, his head turned away from me. "The king has requested your meals be brought to you and that you stay inside for the day to rest." He pushed the cart further into the room. "Should you need anything, please call the staff using this." He bowed slightly, pointing to the wall next to the door. A gold panel was affixed to the wall with a clear call button and speaker I hadn't noticed before.

"Thank you," I mumbled. Did Shroding really not want me leaving this room?

"If that will be all." He backed out of the room slowly. I sank to the edge of the mattress and rubbed my still tired eyes. Shower then food, I decided, but the sensation of someone watching me crawled over my skin, and I glanced towards the door. The man was long gone, and there was nothing out of the ordinary in the rest of the room, so I set to work cleaning, washing, and finding another inconspicuous dress.

The food was simple, eggs and fruit, but its simplicity was comforting after the extravagance of yesterday's meal. I sat for a while looking out at the garden, recalling the events of yesterday and that Shroding would be married in a few short days. Though this hurt to think about, I couldn't seem to stop myself. It rolled around in my mind, lighting a match to every kind word he had ever said to me. "*I love her.*" As if it was the easiest thing to say, but I supposed when you knew you loved someone, it would be easy.

Sometime later another knock sounded at my door. I pushed the fluffy fabric of my gown to the side so I could walk and open the door. The dress was a pale pink and was the only other gown that had long sleeves. It had a high neck with a diamond cutout over my chest. The skirts were needlessly voluminous, but aside from that it was the least jeweled garment in the bunch.

"Callum."

He stood in his Krav uniform, face solemn, but when he caught sight of my dress he began to snicker.

I put my hands on my hips. "What?"

"You look like a cupcake."

I shoved past him into the hall, which only made him laugh harder.

"Where are you going?" He followed me.

"To train. I'm assuming that's why you came to fetch me." I glowered.

"The arena is that way." He pointed down the hall I'd just passed. I took a deep breath, fighting my annoyance. "But that's not why I came to get you."

Intrigued, I stopped walking. "What, then?"

"Haybale!" Micah shouted down the corridor; the smile of my friend warmed every cold and broken part of my heart. Micah looked the same; tall, lean, light hair a bit longer than when I saw him last. His skin was tanned and smooth.

Shroding, Asher and Natalie followed him as Micah bounded towards me at a full sprint. I didn't care what they would say as I yanked up my dumb skirts, ran to him, and threw my arms over his shoulders. He swung me round and around as the others looked on.

"Glad to see you survived saving the world." Tears streaked my cheek as he set me on my feet and bent to kiss my forehead. I could not help but blush. He was like home, and my heart pulsed as if it could burst with joy. I was grinning from ear to ear, the biggest smile I had worn in weeks. It was foreign but good. So, so good. I squeezed my arms around him.

"The world is hardly saved, yet," I teased, looking up at him, his signature smile shining a light over all the shadows in my mind. "I'm so sorry to have left you like that; are the kids—"

"They are perfect, and they miss you," he said quickly. "But I was freaking out the *whole* time. Especially when Etienne came back bloody and dirty." He shook his head, clearing the image. "I was sure you had died." He said it jokingly, but I could see the terror in his eyes at the memory.

"I will never leave you like that again," I said solemnly, holding his gaze.

"Is that an oath? I hear they are pretty serious business around here," he whispered conspiratorially.

"Yeah, I've learned that lesson." I nudged him, and he smiled, taking me in his arms again.

"I missed you."

When he pulled back we looked at each other for a long moment, and I could see he was assessing what had changed between us. If there was a way to go back. Back to that moment at the wagon where he could have kissed me. I knew there was no going back—my heart belonged to another, even if he didn't want it. Still, I would always love Micah.

"Micah, I..."

"Shhh, it's okay, I know, I know," he soothed, rubbing his hands along my arm. I held back my tears, but then my eyes filled and brimmed over anyway.

"I love you so much," I whispered thickly.

"I love you too—nothing will *ever* change that." He held me a few moments longer.

"Ahem." Callum cleared his throat, and we broke apart. I had completely forgotten we had an audience. I held on to Micah's hand, needing his support as Shroding had seen the entire interaction and my petty self hoped it bothered him. From the blank look on his face, it definitely had not.

"I don't believe we have met," Callum said. "I'm Commander Callum McClain."

"Micah Ilsan, I'm Haybale's, I mean Haya's, childhood best friend."

"Haybale?" Callum gave a funny look at the name and moved closer to my side till our group was in an odd-shaped circle.

Callum draped his arm over my shoulder, giving me a squeeze. Though this action would have otherwise produced a frown from me, the joy of seeing Micah alive and well could not be diminished. By Callum or Shroding, even by Natalie, whose arm was linked onto Shroding's, their sides from shoulder to hip touching. Asher was intentionally not looking at either of them.

Micah glanced from Callum to me. "No, no, sorry, I'm the only one who can call her that." In good humor he lifted Callum's arm from my shoulder.

"I'm sorry, but that is simply not true." Natalie's buttery soft voice broke in. We turned to look at her. Her delicate features were bright with surprise. "Haybale?" She tested the word softly.

"Natalie?" Shroding asked, confused as she dropped his arm.

She floated right up to me and wrapped her slender frame around me, effectively removing me from both Micah and Callum. I froze, my whole body rigid. I looked helplessly at Micah, Asher, Callum and Shroding.

Shroding reacted first, pulling her off me.

"Natalie, what are you doing?" Shroding demanded, brows knitting. She brushed him away with a wave of her hand, treating him with a coldness I was surprisingly jealous of. I wished I could brush him off so easily.

"Haybale?" She checked, and I nodded numbly. "From Wycliff?" She beamed, lifting my hands in hers as my brows cinched. "I never thought in a million years that I would meet you like this. How cruel is our fate. It's me, Talie. Your pen pal for the last six years."

I stared at her blankly, as if it was some kind of joke. My pen pal was the daughter of the steward? Sister to Callum?

How in the world had I not learned this or figured it out in the last six years?

She smiled so tenderly I could not remember why I'd vowed not to like her. Oh right—she was marrying Shroding. "It makes sense now why I have not received a letter from you in four months, a lot has happened to you." Her face darkened, and she turned to Callum. "The brother you mentioned..." Callum must have told her about Theo. "The one who died..." She looked back at me. "That was Theo?"

My mouth hung open.

"Can someone please explain to me what is going on?" Shroding demanded, an edge to his voice that bordered on my own panic.

"Haya and I have been pen pals since her sixth-grade year. You know how I volunteer for the program that helps kids write, but we didn't stop after the year was over. We have written for years. We did not sign our full names, so I only knew her as Haybale, and she only knew me as Talie. She has been my only friend while I have been tucked away in this castle alone. While the rest of you *left* me." Her voice was soft but accusing on the last part.

For a moment we all stood there silent, registering. Registering our relationships and how in less than five minutes they had all shifted.

All the letters I had ever received from Talie flowed through my head as I tried to find any indication she was the daughter to the steward, that she was the closest thing our world had to a princess. There was nothing from her first letter to her most recent; she had always been elegant, kind and open about her life. We'd never asked about who each other's parents were, and we'd never told each other. They were simply parents in our letters. We had shared our feelings and deepest thoughts, but neither one of us had ever let our family define us. She may be the daughter of the steward and the sister to Callum, but she'd been and still was Talie, my friend. A girl who knew some of the deepest parts of me, things I couldn't even tell Theo.

I was first to find my voice. "Then the brother, Cal, you mentioned in your letters, was Callum?" I clarified weakly. This girl had been my confidant and companion for six years. Talie had been my big sister, a voice of reason when I had fights with Theo or my mom. My alter ego when I wanted to feel cool and classy, because that was who she was to me. The levelheaded, classy big sister I had imagined sharing clothes with and meeting one day in Romath. Like I was doing right now.

"You wrote to Haya about me?" Callum looked incredulous.

"What a small world we live in," Shroding whispered, stepping out of our circle. He shook his head, looking at all of us, his expression apprehensive. "Please excuse me." He gave a curt nod and strode away down the hall. Callum hesitated but gave a quick nod as well, running after him.

I stared uncertainly at Talie. I had resolved to dislike Natalie immensely, but how was I to do that when she had just, most inexplicably, become one of the people I cherished?

"We should probably talk," Talie sighed, watching her brother run after her fiancé.

"Yes, we probably should," I agreed.

"I'll just excuse myself." Micah turned to me. "Haya, I'll see you later. I'm in the fox room two doors down from yours." I was surprised to hear he would be staying in the castle, but I was grateful he would be close by. Micah said goodbye and left with Asher.

"Would you like to come to my room?" Talie offered her arm, and we stared at each other for an awkward moment before I slipped my hand through.

CHAPTER 27

Openhearted

Natalie's room was light and elegant just like her. She was soft and proper just like her letters had always been but with an undercurrent of sadness I could never place. She really was the same girl.

"Please sit, Haya." I sat on the curvy white chaise. "You have grown up so very much. How beautiful you are—no wonder he likes you." I wanted to ask her who, but figured she was referring to the exchange she'd seen with Micah. I hadn't written to her about the proposal, but she knew well enough that there had been something between him and me.

She placed a small plate of cookies on the table in front of us and held one out to me. I took it, and murmured an awkward thanks, but her eyes were on my hand. Though the pain of the burn from the ward was nearly gone, the blisters were still there across my fingertips.

"What happened?" she asked, her bright eyes wide.

"Callum showed me the wards, and I was careless." I shrugged. "They probably told you what... Logan did," I hinted, hoping not to have to explain it myself.

Her light brows cinched in worry.

"I can heal this." She cupped her hands around mine. Her gift was warm against my skin.

"What do you mean? You can heal—" I blinked, surprised.

"Yes, well, but I was never very good at using it, but I've gotten better recently."

"Whoa," I gasped, the skin on my hand smoothing out, the blisters dissolving.

"They don't know," she said softly. "Cal, Asher and Shroding. No one knows I can use my gift to heal. Very few people are able to." She sighed. "I was alone for so long. I didn't have anyone but books, research my father was doing in other cities. I learned about people who were healers, and it turned out I had an affinity for it as well. I thought it would make me useful in the eyes of my brother and Asher." I listened to her explain, hearing the sadness that had always plagued this beautiful girl in her letters to me.

"So why don't they know?" I asked, genuinely confused. If she'd learned this skill to help them, then why had she not told them already?

"If I tell them, I worry it will make them more reckless. That if they knew I could patch them up anytime, they would be more aggressive in training. Less careful on the battlefield." I nodded, understanding.

"Why tell me?" I asked.

"You're Haybale." She smiled, her eyes brimming with tenderness.

"Talie." I tested the name, feeling it adjust to the person in front of me. "I'm so happy to finally meet you, to see my friend... but to be honest, I had resolved to dislike *you*."

"Yes, I can understand that." She nodded sagely. "I can

see you have feelings for Shroding. But you and I were friends first. Besides, you must know I don't want to marry him. Even when we were children, I never liked him like that." She scrunched her nose in disgust.

I flinched, surprised and confused. Shroding had said he loved her. Did she not know?

"He says he loves you. In your letters you spoke about someone you liked." Was it Asher or Shroding? My heart was too fragile to believe anyone's words so easily. "You never spoke about living in a castle," I criticized.

"I couldn't."

"It feels like my whole life has been one big lie." I marveled at how true the statement really was.

"No one has intentionally lied to you; everyone was missing information along the way," she defended gently. "We can't hold what people don't know against them." She ran her fingers over my braid in a soothing motion.

"Does Shroding know you don't love him, that you love Asher?" I probed, seeking clarification.

"Oh yes, he does. I told him I did not want to marry, but I don't have a say in it."

I blanched. "So he is *forcing* you?"

"No!" she said, horrified. "Shroding would never; his hands are tied just like mine. Shroding is against it as much as I am, but the people need this, or so the court says. Something about stability for the kingdom since the steward will be stepping down. The steward has me and Callum should something happen to him, but Shroding has no one. If we marry, then Callum would still be in line for the throne, and the people already trust Cal immensely."

"I guess it makes sense." So it really was all political. The room shrunk in on me, the air thinning. They might not love each other romantically now, but they would need an heir, and at some point they would kiss and be together intimately. It might take time, but eventually Shroding might come to desire *her*, and the thought made me sick.

"I was so excited to meet you—when I heard a girl was coming with the boys, I was hoping for a friend." She fell to the floor in front of me. "Haya? Is there anything I can do? I can tell you love him so much. "

"I think I need a few minutes," I gasped. "Thank you again for healing me. I won't tell anyone." I stood and ran from her room. I wasn't sure which way would lead me outside, but I needed air. I needed to get out of these walls.

Asher was waiting outside Natalie's room when I came out. "Your mother is here. I'm taking you to her." He reached for my arm to lead me. Swallowing my panic, I nodded and let him guide me to the garden.

It was bright, the late afternoon sun warming the space like a greenhouse, though it had no encasing. I wondered how in the winter these flowers could bloom, how the space could be so warm. Rich red and yellow flowers lined the brick pathway through the garden. My mother sat on a bench under a cherry blossom tree, the pink buds vibrant against the greenery all around.

"Mom!" She looked up, but I was already running to her, my arms wide. Tears filled my eyes. Her light hair was twisted up, her freckled skin paler than when she left. She wore simple work pants and a sweater, not all that different from the clothes she'd worn back at the farm.

Her arms wrapped around me. "My Haya, my Haya," she cried over and over, running the length of my hair through her hands, alternating the motion like she had when I was a small girl.

"Mom..." I breathed into her shoulder absently. I never wanted to leave her arms, but the questions I had been longing to ask her burned the back of my throat, ready to burst out. "What happened?" I pulled away, wiping my tears with the back of my hand. "Why did you not send for me?"

She gently drew me to sit, holding my hands firmly in hers.

"It's hard to explain." She squeezed my hands, rubbing her thumb over my knuckles.

"When you got to Erasmus...?" I trailed off, not sure what I needed to know, not sure if Father and Theo had been dead from the start. Not sure I wanted to know everything.

"When I arrived they both were going to be okay." Her green eyes searched mine, heavy with tears of her own. She blinked, looking away over my shoulder. "They were healing well, and after a few days passed I decided to send you a letter to let you know." Her voice gained strength. "Theo was having terrible nightmares and kept wanting to leave the hospital. It was so hard to watch." She closed her eyes, taking a few deep breaths. "Before I could mail you the letter something happened." A tear escaped her eyes. "The hospital was attacked, by Grieving, and what I now know to be Wraiths—"

"I know what they are," I interrupted, not wanting her to explain any more; it was clearly too painful for her to say, too painful for me to hear.

Her eyes were wide, seeing horrendous things I wished I could take from her memories. "They locked down the hospital, but it did nothing but make us easy targets. Your father and Theo, they helped me get out but... died in the process. I hid for a few days at the army base before word was sent requesting I identify their bodies. I did, and I think it was the shock of everything, but I got sick." She buried her hands in her face. "I didn't want to leave them." I wrapped my arms around her and told her it was okay. "Losing your father and brother like that..." She shook her head. "I kept telling myself you were safer at the farm." Her voice was hollow, far away, lost in the memory of saying goodbye to her only son, and the man she loved.

"We are okay and together now. Nothing else matters," I assured her, though I could not stop my own tears from falling. I might have gone through a lot the last few weeks, but so had my mother. She was as broken as myself, in so many ways similar, but completely different. I had only seen my mother cry once when she got the news of my grandparents' death when I was twelve. It had been unnerving then, to see her tears. My mother was controlled, strong and capable. I had expected to be as unsettled as I was then, but I wasn't. She was still strong, capable, but I saw her for who she was; a person just like me. Someone who could hurt and cry.

"My distant cousin gave me a place to stay and helped me with the funeral preparations. Theo and your father are buried here. Micah told me the farm was destroyed."

"Do you want to go back?" I asked, unsure if she would want me to go with her. Unsure if going back to Wycliff, to the farm, was what I wanted.

"What is there to go back for now? You are here." She looked into my eyes, pushing my hair from my face. "The town will get another family to take up the farmland. Micah's mother found jobs at the Citadel for the children. I have more support here than back in Wycliff."

Though what she said was true, she still trembled, fresh

tears falling. We were both letting go of the life we used to have.

I nodded, not trusting my voice. We held each other and let the tears flow freely, letting all the pain and acceptance of everything that had happened wash over us like a submersion and rebirth.

When we had regained some composure I told her about my journey and what had happened to me in the weeks we were apart. While I talked she idly gathered my hair, braiding it loosely over my shoulder till it stayed in the twist without a tie.

"I wonder why the Wraiths and creatures didn't go after Father like they did Theo and me."

"Honestly I don't know. Maybe we will get answers someday, maybe not this side of life."

"Did you know about the king's power?"

"I didn't know your father was involved in all this; he only told me that you and Theo would be special, that he was special. I thought it was his ego talking—every parent thinks their kid is special." She was thoughtful for a moment. "Still, I think in the back of my mind I always knew there was something dangerous about the stories he would tell you two. I never liked when he talked about the war, or the armies of Golan. I suppose that was his way of preparing you while keeping it a secret. I think when neither of you got the gift it really threw him."

"I remember that, when I didn't get the gift, he acted so strange for a few weeks. Panicky—we all thought it had to do with the harvest."

"I think he was afraid the prince had died and that was why the power didn't manifest." She smiled grimly.

"Are you mad he never told you?"

She sighed. "I don't think I would have believed him if he had. You know him, always embellishing his war stories, though now it makes me wonder if they were embellishments after all." She shrugged sadly. "Guess we won't know." I frowned, looking down at the grass. I toed the dirt, pushing my cream flat hard into the earth, making half moons on the ground.

"So will you stay with your cousin's family?" I asked tentatively.

"I-I don't want to live alone." She wavered, nothing like the composed woman she'd beens the day she left the farm. It would take time, but I was sure she would find her way back to the controlled and confident woman she had always been in my childhood.

"Mom, you aren't alone. I'm here. We can live together," I assured her, but I was not entirely sure that was what I wanted.

"I want more than anything to be with you, but do you want to leave here?" She gestured to the castle, seeing through my offer.

Did I want to leave? Shroding was getting married to another—did I want to stay and see that? *No, no I really didn't.* Still, the idea of leaving him despite our romantic, or lack thereof, relationship hurt me. I couldn't go, not with the way things were; I wanted to part as friends at least. I would leave when I could say goodbye thinking only of him as Iri, my dear friend. Once I helped him defeat Skithian and was released from all the oaths. Then I would fade from his life, as a pleasant memory.

"That's what I thought." My mom interrupted my musings with a knowing smile. "I can tell you are needed here and at least here I know you are safe. We can still see each other whenever, and the minute you want to leave I will be waiting."

I nodded. "If you are sure?" I added, not liking the idea of parting.

"Yes, honey." She tugged the loose braid she had made of my hair, the way father had when I was growing up. "That is from your father. He wanted me to tell you not to worry, or be afraid. You are stronger than you think you are." She smiled, her green eyes sparkling from all the tears she'd shed. "You gave him new strength the day you were born. He adored you, and was so *very* proud of you." She touched my cheek gently. "Theo wanted me to tell you he was sorry. He never wanted to have the power pass to you. I didn't know at the time what he meant, but he said you would understand. He loved you so very much." I nodded, fighting back tears, surprised I had any left to shed.

A light flickered above us, and I looked up, noticing for the first time that the sky had grown dark and the garden lights were turning on. "It's night," I whispered.

"I should go, but I would like to take you to see your father and brother. For you to say goodbye."

My chest tightened at the idea of visiting their graves. Did I have the strength to do that? "Yes, after the coronation."

"I'm glad you are okay." She leaned down and kissed me on the forehead. I smiled up at her. "Someone is waiting to lead me out." She dropped my hands still clasped in hers. "Good night."

"Good night, Mom." I watched her leave the garden the way I had come in.

CHAPTER 28

Suffocation

I wandered the garden for a while, not quite ready to go back to my room. Curving around a new part of the path, I spotted Callum leaning against the stone wall beside a different door than the one I had entered through.

"Were you waiting for me?" I asked, and he nodded, opening the door. Silently I followed him up the stairs and down a hall I was unfamiliar with. His hair was damp with sweat—had he just come from training? Was he taking me back to the arena? I was in no mood to spar right now. I just wanted to go back to my room and sleep.

"Have you thought more about my offer?" he whispered warily, as if he didn't actually want to know my answer. I had already made up my mind to stay with Shroding no matter what, and as long as the king's guard was the way to do that, then I would not change my mind.

Before I could answer, voices rose a few doors down from where we walked. Ignoring Callum's protests, I sprinted past him towards the argument, Shroding's voice mixed with a handful of others.

"You can't call us here and demand this," an angry man yelled, his voice echoing down the corridor. The murmur of many unintelligible complaints wafted out to where I peeked through the sliver of the open door. I reached for the handle, wanting to enter, to make sure Shroding was alright, but Callum closed his hand over mine, preventing me.

"Please." His jaw clenched. "Don't make this harder than it already is, lass."

Shroding's calm voice reverberated through me. "Remember your place. Remember *your* cause. Hate will not win this war, and senseless distractions will do little to afford victory," Shroding appealed. He stood tall at the edge of a round table in what appeared to be a study or— judging from the maps, covered in makers and tokens—a war room. A thick crown rested heavily on his brow; the circlet was woven of silver and gold vining, coming to a crest between his brows that dipped down, a red gem in the center. His clothes were a pristine white with adornments of all manner of colorful gems. He looked every bit the king he was, and as such more out of my reach than ever before. Gone was the secretive, simple tunic-clad prince I had bared my soul to.

"Before the Celebration of Strings you will be tested for your loyalty, and I will not induct you into the court if you are found wanting, as were Sadia and Henry. You will be tried as traitors to the crown. You have been chosen by the steward, but under my rule you will need to prove yourselves to no one else but me." Shroding's voice carried over the room, an authority in his tone that tempted me to draw nearer, just as his amethyst fur had always called to me. "As for the other matter, the steward and I resolved it already—your opinions on the matter can be kept to yourselves."

Callum tensed behind me, and I turned at the same time

he slowly, silently closed the door, muffling the voices. I furrowed my brow, annoyed that I couldn't keep listening. What had the steward and Shroding resolved? Did it have to do with the wedding?

But my questions faded as Callum held the handle behind me, angling himself till my back pressed into the detailed trim work on the large doors. He said nothing, but the look in his gaze rang all my warning bells. I knew that expression. He was staring at my mouth, and he didn't need to touch me for me to know his emotions. He did not use his Orator skill on me to bend me to his will as he had done in the kitchen at Moreh. Instead he flicked his gaze from my mouth to my eyes, the question clear.

"Please, Callum, don't..." I breathed. I didn't know why he wanted to kiss me, but I didn't need anything else confusing me right now.

A throat cleared, and a guard approached us, the moment broken.

"This came from Sir Liam—it is urgent." The guard held out a letter, and Callum stepped back, taking it. He read the contents and scowled.

"What is it?" Had Erasmus fallen? Were we out of time to stop the attacks Logan had shown me?

"Take Miss Haya back to her room," Callum clipped, fisting the letter in his hand. He stormed away without a glance back at me. I watched him go.

"Miss?" the man asked, but before we could begin walking, another guard ran around the corner.

"All guards are needed—there's a breach at the southwest gate!"

"What?" the man Callum had assigned to me gasped.

Though I couldn't see his face because of their helmets, I could imagine his shock.

"A hoard of Grieving showed up. Some of the civilians outside the city walls have been possessed. We are needed now!" the other guard snapped.

"I will escort Miss Haya to her room." The man who had brought me breakfast this morning appeared next to us, his butler suit primly pressed as he waited unalarmed by the news of an attack.

"Thank you." The guards nodded and sprinted away.

I wondered if I should go with them; I was part of the guard too, but... I was the king's guard, not a castle guard. My job was to protect the king. If we were under attack, then I needed to get my sword from my room and protect Shroding.

"Lead the way," I huffed, ready to get out of this fluff of a dress and into anything I could fight in.

We moved through the hall, silence dragging between us.

Had it always taken this long to get back to my room? Perhaps the man was lost, or maybe I was turned around. The man did not seem to notice my distress and kept walking. Every few paces, however, he would peer behind him to make sure I was still there. I glanced around. Had all the guards normally posted in the corridors been called to fight? From what I could tell there were always at least two soldiers on each floor, but so far I had seen none, and we had been walking for a few minutes. Unease yawned inside me.

"Where are we going?" I probed.

"Back to your room, miss," he said again, but there was an edge to his voice, something I had not caught before. Disgust? Anger? Vengeance?

I stopped dead in my tracks. I knew nothing about who managed the staff at the castle. Just because we'd concluded the steward wasn't corrupted didn't mean others weren't. Wasn't that why Shroding was testing the loyalty of the court? He believed there was corruption in the ranks, that Henry and Sadia had not been the only ones.

The hall we were in was far from the opulence of the red and gold one that held my room. Why had I just followed this man so blindly?

"Who are you?" I paled, wishing I had strapped my sword to the fluffy pink dress. What good did it do me if I wasn't wearing it all the time? But there wasn't time to berate myself further for my error, as the man stopped and turned.

A rush of vibration tossed me into the stone wall. I protected my head with my arms, feeling them buckle under the force. I cried out once, short and low. I would not give him the satisfaction of hearing me cry for help. I could fight back; my training to become a guard was not for nothing. I rebounded so quickly I was able to land a blow to his face and side before the slice of a blade connected with my upper leg. It cut through the voluminous fabric, finding my skin beneath.

I recoiled, rolling along the floor and creating distance between me and my attacker. The blade was short and thin, reminding me of the meat skewers my father used to make on hot summer days. I definitely did not want to get stabbed by that. I leapt to the side as he charged, desperately searching for an opening past the blade. I lunged forward, throwing a weak wave of vibration at his knife hand.

It gave me the opening I was looking for, and I aimed for his head to knock him out. Maybe it was my dress slowing me down, or the lack of consistent training since Shroding's transformation, but he was too fast, impossibly so. He rammed into my side, and I smashed into the wall, stones pressing into my front, digging painfully into my cheek. He grabbed the back of my head, holding it roughly against the stone.

I gasped, my head throbbing from the force. If I could see anything, I would probably be seeing double, but at this angle all that was visible were the gray rocks of the wall.

Why was no one coming down this hallway? Could I even call for help with my airways so pinched?

I wheezed in my attempt, and the man laughed. My arms were pinned between me and the wall. I concentrated my power there, willing as much as I could to break me free.

"Do you remember a certain old lady?" the man asked, the knife at my back cutting into the dress along my spine. His breath was hot on my neck, making me shiver. "Miles?" I flinched as the buttons of my dress were cut open. "Your 'cat' broke his ribs and killed him." My eyes widened. The last I had seen of Miles was his possessed decaying form chasing me down.

"Vibration sickness killed him." I coughed.

"It would have if not for the broken ribs." Shroding had thrown himself into Miles to get him off me, the crack of his ribs so evident I couldn't deny it was possible. "Move," the man said, grabbing the back of my neck and steering me towards a door with a boar carving, its tusks looking as sharp as the blade at my back. The power I had been building in my arms dissipated as we entered the room, my body becoming heavy and sluggish. What was happening to me?

Like a doll he tossed me to the wood floor. My dress ripped, the last of the buttons at the back coming undone. I rolled to face him, ready to fight, but my limbs were leaden.

"I will let you die as he did. I'll just break a few of your ribs, puncture your lung"—he waved the blade around arrogantly—"and let the internal bleeding fill your airways until you drown in your own blood."

"What does Miles have to do with you?" I lifted my head just enough to glare at him.

He laughed, a sick delighted sound. "Have you not figured it out? I am the Wraith who possessed him. I was there when he died, and though I don't care that he's dead"— he waved off Miles's existence—"I must say watching him die that way stirred a longing in me. What a delicious way to go, so slowly, so painfully, so fully aware of your *suffering*. The way he struggled for that last breath." The man licked his lips as if tasting something delectable.

"You're a Rephaim," I panted, the gash on my leg pulsing painfully.

"It is lovely to have a body again, I must thank you for that." He knelt and lifted me by the bodice of my dress; the stiff fabric bowed, only held on by my arms in the long sleeves. He bent his face to my neck, and sniffed the pale bite mark. "Oh, Logan." He *tsk*ed. "I do wonder if he will be mad that I got to you first. He did, very much, like playing with you." He dropped me, my head cracking against the floorboards. I tried to fight back, but my gift refused to come to me. Was this some kind of drug? He flipped me onto my chest, then sat down on my legs, his weight pinning me easily to the ground.

"Get off of—" I hissed, my breath catching as his fist slammed into my ribs. Pain exploded across my torso, my whole body lurching from the force. He slammed his fist a second time, into the same spot, and I saw stars.

"Just a few more is all you need." Again his fist cracked into my side, and I heard more than felt the shattering of bones. Shroding had hit Miles once, the force enough to break ribs, and though the Rephaim over me now had the power to do the same, he was intentionally drawing it out, making it hurt more. "I've watched you closely since you arrived. The commander tried so hard to woo you, to throw us off, but your dear prince only has eyes for you and you for him. He will be so distraught when he finds you. I trust he will act out of anger just like the king did, when we took his queen."

Another punch to my side, then something warm and wet pooled under me.

Blood. My blood. I was going to die, again, and this time there was no benevolent grandma to save me.

Everything was growing fuzzy. My lungs struggled to fill with air.

I didn't even notice his weight was off me until I was being kicked onto my back by the toe of his polished black shoes.

"There, now I can watch your pretty face take that last rattled breath." He caressed my cheek as he squatted beside me. "There, there, take those last easy breaths," he cooed, but none of my breaths were easy now. I coughed up blood, my jagged inhales making it apparent I was not getting enough air.

Shroding... Was this how it would always be? If by some miracle I lived through this, would this just happen again? Would I ever be strong enough to protect him, to protect myself?

Thunder shook the wooden floors, and I vaguely wondered if there was a storm outside, but I could no longer see the empty room; my vision was shadowed. Maybe it was because I'd faced death before, but it no longer scared me. No longer made me afraid. I would get to see Father and Theo again.

Arms wrapped around me, the motion, oddly enough, allowed air to fill my lungs. I coughed, eyes focusing for a moment.

"Shroding?"

"Don't you dare give up. I will always come for you, so don't you dare give up." Tears spilled out of the corners of his dark eyes, and I tried to smile.

"The blade had serum on it."

"Strings."

"He got away."

The snap of voices shuddered around me: Asher, Callum and others I didn't recognize. All I wanted to see, to hear was right before me.

"I've got you," Shroding assured me, scooping me up and carrying me as he had only a few nights ago.

CHAPTER 29
Healer

I shifted uncomfortably under the thick blankets. Kicking my foot free, I rolled and groaned in pain. Why did my whole body ache?

"You're awake." Talie's honey voice drifted through the room.

Above me was a familiar mural of a cat. I was back in my room.

"How long was I asleep?"

"Not long, a little over an hour. How are you feeling?"

"Confused. How did I get—" Shroding, he had found me, save me from the Rephiam.

"I healed the puncture wound in your lungs when they weren't paying attention. It was the most I could do; they had already seen the cut on your leg and your broken ribs. The doctor set the rest and wrapped your leg," she explained in a rush, and I struggled to follow her words. "But once they all left for the meeting, I worked on mending everything else. Of course the discomfort will linger, but you won't have a scar." She pat my hand, which she held between hers. I hadn't considered how a scar would matter much when I was dying. I already had scars inside and out. What would a few more matter? My skin wasn't perfect like Talie's. I had worked on a farm, after all, and been through too many battles to still be unblemished, but her words were oddly like a balm. Just because I had scars didn't mean I wanted more.

"Thank you," I croaked. "I'm actually really glad to hear that."

She laughed lightly, brushing my wet hair over my shoulder as she helped me sit up. "I gave you a bath to wash the blood off." I fingered my damp hair; it takes forever to dry even if it's loose. Idly I began to braid the strands but stopped when my ribs screamed their protest.

"The blankets will get all wet if I leave it loose."

"The blankets are already wet, but here..." She reached for the comb on the nightstand. It was the one I had stolen from Callum. I guess he'd finally given it to her. "Allow me," she offered, and slowly set to work.

I closed my eyes, breathing through the discomfort sitting upright was causing.

"I told the doctor I would care for and clean your wounds, so no one should suspect I've healed you. But you will need to keep it from them, please," she begged, her voice small, as if she was ashamed to even ask it of me.

"Talie, I understand. Tell them when you are ready."

We were silent for a while as she finished with my hair.

"Not that I expected the group to be sitting here waiting for me to wake up, but where is everyone?" I'd at least expected Micah to be close by.

"They are in a meeting," she sighed. "We think the attack at the southwest gate was a setup so the Rephaim could get to you. Shroding had already planned to vet the men and women my father appointed to the court, but he has expedited the interrogations."

"Interrogations?" I frowned.

She shrugged uneasily.

"Why aren't you in the meeting?"

"I wanted to stay with you. We haven't gotten to talk much since you arrived, and it seems like you might still hold it against me, what happened with Shroding." Her voice was hushed on the last part, and though she still held herself with confidence I could see her brow furrow in the dim light.

"I don't. I... understand the situation..." And I really did. But she was right. I was holding something against her, all of them actually. "I know I'm new to this, the court, castle, to life lived for hundreds of years, but I'm trying. I guess I'm jealous of how you all are together. The way you can read each other, pass messages... connect. I see it, and I feel like I'm always missing something. A step behind. Like I don't belong here."

"Haya, we grew up together; sometimes we forget that the people around us didn't. It's hard when you have lived so many years. I'm sure you have seen it. The lifelessness that can overtake someone, the way we lose what it means to be alive." She brushed her hands over my bandaged arm and took my hand in hers. I closed my eyes, relishing the gesture of friendship, of confidence. She was right—I had seen the dead look in the eyes of Sir Martus, Callum, Asher, and even Shroding at times. Even Talie's letters at first had carried the lifelessness she spoke of.

"You have changed that. You have given energy to the king and in doing so revitalized this monarchy; Shamar. When Callum called me from Tyndale I heard it in his voice for the first time in nearly fifty years. *Hope.* You gave him that." I recalled the look on Asher's face when he held up the silver fur to the moonlight so many weeks ago. The way his whole body had lit up.

"It was the king's power in me," I corrected.

"You gave us all hope. The funny thing is, you were my hope long before you had the king's power. When we started writing, at first it was a way to pass the time. A way to live outside these walls. Then I came to see you as a person, an outlet, a friend. After Asher and Callum left the castle I had no one who could understand the sadness in my heart. But you did, you listened and you were there. I thought to myself that if there were people like you still in this world, then Shamar still had a reason to fight. When you live as long as I have, you begin to see bodies instead of people. You helped me to see people again."

I smiled, giving her hand a squeeze. "You were the big sister I never had. The farm and my family were great, but sometimes I felt so alone. I felt like no one else thought like me, felt like me. Talking to you made me feel less lonely."

"Now that you are in the court, we can be together for a long, long time." She touched my cheek. "I will be here for you always. Living a long time has its cons." I knew what she meant. She was talking about when I would lose my mother, and Micah, when they aged and died but I would live on. Looking back, if I had known, I would have made Shroding appoint my mother to the court so she would live as long as me. So I would never lose her. I would have chosen that as the oath he gave me instead of a stupid kiss. But I hadn't known then; I hadn't understood what path I had taken by helping Shroding. I was a lovestruck child. How my life had changed over the last few months was unnerving. How much I had mentally unraveled and despaired alarmed me.

"I'm sorry I was not there for you with Theo and your father." A tear rolled down her cheek, and I struggled to sit up.

"No, no, don't cry." I wrapped my arms around her, ignoring the pain.

"Haya, I love you. I'm so very sorry."

"Shhh, please... please don't do that, don't blame yourself." I tasted salt on my lips as my own tears rolled down my cheeks.

"Nothing about this path will be easy, has been easy, but you will always have me. I promise." Talie pulled away, wiping her eyes and mine. She kissed my cheek and helped me lie back down. "Rest now."

"No." I resisted her help. "I want to know what's going on. Will you take me to the meeting?"

She knit her beautiful brows, pale blonde hair falling around her face. "Are you sure you want to go?"

"Yes."

She helped me out of bed and wrapped me in a thick red robe. I leaned on her arm as we moved through the halls. To my surprise four guards were posted at my door and followed silently behind us as we went.

"The individual who oversaw staffing was indeed responsible for letting the Rephaim in," Asher announced as we entered the meeting space. It was the same room from the first night, the dinner with the steward, except there was no splendor. Instead the table was bare; the court officials were not dressed in finery but in their sleep attire, expressions as rumpled as their clothes, as if they had all been dragged from bed.

Outside the massive glass windows the city was dark. It must be very late. Had my mom left the castle safely? Had it really only been a few hours since I spoke with her? My head spun from how much had happened today.

"Haya." Shroding stood and walked over to me. He was still in the white and gold coat that made him look so much like a king, but now it was marred with blotches of deep crimson. My blood. He had not cleaned up. "How are your wounds? Did you open your stitches?" He turned his gaze to Natalie. "She should be resting."

"No, I-I'm fine." I held up my hands, stepping between them. "I insisted I come."

"Haya, I have spent enough time with you to realize when you are lying to me. You're terrible at it." His hand stretched, fingers grazing the robe's fabric along my side. "Are you in a lot of pain?"

"It's manageable." Thanks to Natalie's gift, but I didn't say that last part aloud.

Eyes narrowed, he glanced skeptically at me, but did not press me any further. Instead he waved at a guard, who brought over two chairs for Natalie and me. I expected him to return to his spot at the front of the table, but he merely grabbed his chair and plopped it next to mine. Without looking at me, he sat, reached over and took my hand in his before resting our joint hands on his thigh. Mine was not the only surprised expression in the room.

"As we were saying, the traitor in our midst has been dealt with, but I'm fairly certain they were not working alone."

———

The meeting dragged on well into the early hours of the morning. Each court member was taken to another room and interrogated; some returned, while others did not. Shroding eventually left my side, and Micah took his place. He said nothing, but the worry in his gaze was evident.

Eventually when my eyes began to droop, Micah brought me back to my room to sleep.

"The castle is funny about the whole entering people's room thing," I murmured sleepily against Micah's shoulder as he tucked me into bed.

"It's because the maids love to gossip," he whispered conspiratorially, brushing hair off my forehead. "But I'm not afraid of a little gossip," he assured me.

And I knew he meant it because it was his face I saw when I woke the next morning. His clothes from the night before rumpled and askew in his sleepy state. He had stayed the night with me and though I knew it should concern me, it didn't.

The next day was uneventful. The only person besides Micah who I saw was Natalie, under the guise of checking my wounds. Meals were brought to Micah and me, so I knew it was no secret Micah had spent the night.

We talked the whole day, played board games in bed and laughed as much as my ribs would allow me to. I told him everything that had happened from the moment the dreams had begun to Shroding's transformation and my induction. He listened as I'd known he would, taking it all in with the tender ear of a lifelong friend. We cried, we laughed and most of all we mourned together. The loss of my naivete; my loss of self. At the point of the story when I needed it most, he held me, tapping my shoulder once, pausing, twice, pausing, and then a quick one-one, signaling the phrase "I'm here" from our childhood game. It was a day of peace in the midst of chaos. It was *home.*

I knew the sweet spell would only last for a day, as the next was the coronation and wedding.

"You love him, don't you?" Micah asked sometime after Natalie left. The room darkened to twilight as the world outside grew quiet and ready for sleep, a silent prayer that the monsters would not come out tonight.

"Is it that obvious?"

"I suspected when you jumped into a fire to save him. I could see it was more than loyalty to king and country."

I chewed my lip, resting my head on the headboard. Micah sat next to me, leaning his head back as well. We stared at the hearth in front of us, the fire's warmth filling the space.

"Shroding left a message for me back in Wycliff, to come to the castle for the Celebration of Strings. His message said, 'Haya will need what family she has left.' How he anticipated you would be here by this point is beyond me, but I am glad he had the forethought," Micah explained.

Heat burned the backs of my eyes. Seeing Micah again was a balm to my soul that I needed. Only Shroding could have known how badly I would need to see him and my mother.

"I promised my father I would protect you, and I've done a spectacularly terrible job at that."

I folded his hand into mine between our hips. "Don't say that."

"It's true, but even if I have been remiss in my duty to your physical welfare, I won't be to your heart."

Tilting my head, I looked at him. I searched his profile, but he did not turn even though I knew he could feel my stare.

"He loves you," Micah breathed. "He is completely stupid for you."

"No," I laughed. "That's not true."

He turned his head, facing me. "Come on, Haybale. I *know*."

My brows pinched.

"The stunt he pulled in front of the court, that was a blatant slap to their faces. Sitting next to you, taking your hand." He held up our joint hands, giving them a little shake. "He was telling them to back off, that you are his. It was a threat and a challenge."

"No, it was..." I didn't know what it was.

"Even if he hadn't done that, I *know* the look he gives you."

"What look?" I asked, but I already knew, because I had seen it too, so many times.

"It's the same look I gave you countless times but you never seemed to notice."

"Micah..."

"No, no, it's okay. I missed my shot with you. I see that, I've accepted it." He flashed me his signature grin. "I can be the big brother I've always been to you; that is more than enough." He squeezed my hand.

I didn't know what to say, so I just looked down at our hands. Grateful he was here with me.

"So this is me protecting your heart, okay," he warned seriously, making me look up again. "He is a king, he has to protect an entire kingdom. He can't only protect you, even if it's what he wants to do, even if he is willing to sacrifice everyone for you, you can't let him. You have to be stronger than his desire to burn the world down for you. You have to keep him grounded, keep yourself safe, so he can keep everyone else safe. Do you understand?"

His words slammed into me like arrows, words so similar to things Asher, Callum and Shroding had said but not so succinctly, not so pointedly.

I sat up, tucking my knees under me. "I understand." I nodded, and for the first time I did. I may have known this information before, but I had been jealous and petty about it, but now... Now I understood what Mama Meod had asked of me. Living for myself, protecting myself, fighting for me, was the same thing as fighting for him, as protecting him. Because he could not keep everyone else safe if he was too busy saving me.

CHAPTER 30
Dance

A rapping at my door startled me awake.

Micah lay next to me, his flaxen hair hanging over the foot of the bed. The card game we had fallen asleep playing was a discarded mess between us.

"Who is it?" Micah groaned.

"I don't know." I scrunched my face, rubbing my eyes as I climbed out of bed.

"Let me get it." Micah yawned, rolling out of the bed faster than me and wobbling over to the door.

Figuring it was probably Natalie or breakfast, I turned to my wardrobe. I needed to get dressed anyway, and thankfully I had expressed my lack of enthusiasm for the clothes in my closet to Natalie, who had come by yesterday with at least three dresses passable by my simple standards.

"Shroding, I mean, Your Majes—"

I froze facing the mirror, but there he was, standing in the doorway, reflected back to me, looking perfect in a deep purple vest. His face an inscrutable mask, hair tousled like he hadn't had time to brush it in a while.

"Micah," he interrupted in a flat, almost disapproving tone. In the reflection I watched his eyes flick to the rumpled bed, then to me.

Micah stepped aside to allow Shroding in, his sheepish expression saying everything my shocked one was not.

Shroding had heard, no doubt from the maids, that Micah had not left my room for over a day.

He made no move to enter; instead he continued. "Micah, we received word from your mother that she needs you back at home." He relayed the message with formality, but I could hear the tight control in his words. "Now that the trains are running again, we can get you on the next train to Wycliff this morning"—he spoke clearly, and though his words were for Micah, his eyes did not stray from mine in the mirror—"unless you have a reason to stay." I couldn't help but flinch at the implication.

In that moment I missed our connection, missed finding him in the other dimension the most. But even when I could, I still had not been able to figure out what was going on in his head. Not really. If what Micah said was true, and he loved me and had basically said that to the court through his actions the other night, then why, why was he still engaged to Natalie? Despite the fact she didn't love him. Would he share his secrets with her? All the secrets I wanted him to pour out to me? All the parts of him I still yearned to know?

Micah laughed, startling us both.

"Shroding, may I call you that?" His easy grin was back as he pat Shroding with brotherly affection on the shoulder. "Whatever you think happened here, absolutely, one hundred percent, did *not*. My sister and I fell asleep playing cards," he explained, and I glanced at Micah's reflection, startled. *Sister?* Micah had always been family to me, but with my crush, back on the farm, I hadn't wanted to consider him as a brother. Now, things were different; I had just spent two nights with him and there was no appeal, no longing to kiss, no longing for *more*. Micah was truly like a brother to me now, and it was a comfort and balm to my splintered heart that he saw me as his sister. My chest squeezed, and I blinked away the burning in my eyes.

Though Shroding's shoulders relaxed a fraction he was not ready to let it slide. He stepped into the room, closing the door with a defining click.

"Tell me, Micah," Shroding began, a taunting ring to his words, "is making out against a doorframe something a brother would do with his sister?"

Micah paled slightly, recalling how Shroding, in cat form, had interrupted us kissing outside my room back at the farm. Micah peered at me for help, but Shroding stepped to the side, blocking his view of me, effectively cornering Micah against the door.

I couldn't see Micah's face, but his next words were as taunting as Shroding's had been. "Tell *me*, is making out against a tree, then telling the girl it was a mistake, a very princely thing to do?"

Silence followed, and for a beat no one moved. I barely breathed.

It was Micah who broke the silence first. "I would recommend the prince make things right before his wedding tonight."

"There isn't going to be a wedding," Shroding whispered, and I was not sure I heard him correctly, but when he faced me and repeated, "I'm not marrying Natalie," I knew I'd heard right.

I didn't know how to explain what happened in my body

next, but it was as if I couldn't breathe but was somehow filled up with more air than possible. Euphoria, exultation expanded my heart to near bursting. All of it was happening inside my chest, but outwardly I just stood there in shock.

"That's my cue." Micah smirked, giving Shroding a little shove in my direction before walking out and leaving us alone.

Somehow the mirror had detracted from Shroding's opulence. He was blindingly attractive. Not seeing him for one whole day had made me weak for his good looks all over again. As if the endurance I had built up against him had crumbled back down to nothing and I was seeing him for the first time in the pocket dimension all over again.

"You aren't—" I began, hands folding over my stomach as butterflies ravaged my insides.

"I'm not—" he said at the same time.

We paused awkwardly. He stepped forward, tapping the post of my bed.

"The steward and I have come to an agreement that it would be better to announce to the world my return and focus on the war efforts without a bride," he explained. The hesitant, almost tentative look in his eyes was dizzying.

He wasn't getting married.

"How did you get them to agree?" I doubted, too flustered by his admission. "The court was so set on you getting married."

He took one single step towards me, and my breathing hitched, eyes dropping to his booted foot and back up. My legs were so firmly rooted in place, I could have just been a tree in the garden outside my window. "It doesn't matter. I am their king—it's not for me to earn their trust but for them to earn mine." He stared over my shoulder, eyes distant as he spoke. "My father reigned nearly his whole four thousand years without a queen. I, too, can reign without one for a while."

I held perfectly still, the distance between us slight but somehow greater than any space we had before.

"Did you come to tell me this?" Was that why he'd shown up at the break of dawn?

He took in my nightgown as if seeing it for the first time. It was thicker than the one in Moreh, at least, but with the sunrise backlighting me I knew the outline of my body was visible.

I could pinpoint the moment he saw it too. His hand flexed at his side as if holding himself back from reaching for me.

"You should get dressed." He turned his face to the side, a dust of pink coloring his cheeks. The room filled with a different tension, and I grabbed the first dress I saw and dipped into the bathroom.

Donning a sweetheart teal gown, I rebraided my hair, tried and failed to avoid looking at the mark on my neck. It was faded, barely there, but still visible to my eyes. I clenched my jaw as I recalled how the Rephaim had sniffed it. Logan's scent. My skin crawled at the idea that I smelled anything like that monster. Could Shroding smell it? The night we boarded the train he had been so close, and with his cat sense of smell had he been able to pick up on it?

Disgust rolled through my stomach.

"I heard you need someone to teach you how to dance for tonight's celebration," Shroding said through the door to the bathroom.

Natalie had mentioned yesterday that I would need to dance and there were specific group dances I needed to know, but I had waved her off. I had no plans to dance; my foray into the dancing scene had started and ended on my single date with Micah at Club Jubilee.

"I don't think I should be dancing in my condition." I glowered.

"The event will be broadcast to every major city." His tone was matter-o'-fact. "People congregate in the cities' conference halls to watch and celebrate," he reminded me.

I knew about the events in other cities. The Celebration of Strings was a big deal even without the announcement of the rightful king.

Wycliff had been too small, so many people traveled to be with family or friends in the big three: Tyndale, Romath or Erasmus.

"I guess I could use a little guidance."

"They are prepping for the party all over the castle. Your room is a bit too small." He looked around, then slid his hand into mine and leaned in. "Follow me, I know a better spot." He grinned, leading the way.

Wordlessly I followed him, my steps wooden as we moved up to the floor above my room. I stood awkwardly in the doorway as Shroding stepped though into the king's chambers. A massive bronze crest of the king was plastered above the standing-height hearth. A fire blazed inside, and though the heat was comforting against my chilled skin, it also seemed dangerous, stifling. I wasn't sure my heart would be safe, alone with the king, in his room. Even if his room was four of mine put together.

Shroding sat on the couch in front of the fire, his eyes flashing iridescent in the light.

"Sit with me?" he asked, and for a second he appeared

every bit the nineteen his face depicted. Unsure, hesitant, hopeful.

I swallowed and stepped inside, but I couldn't bring myself to go to him, not yet.

"Why did you break off the engagement? Was it for her?" It shouldn't matter, but it did. "Because she loves Asher?" I whispered as if the question was never meant to be said aloud, let alone heard.

He exhaled sharply. "I did it for you." The force of the words settled between us, and my heart raced at the implication. "You have lost so much because of me," he continued, his voice rough, edged with something I couldn't place. "As soon as I found out she was your friend, I couldn't go through with it, knowing it would change things between you two, that you might lose someone else."

My breath caught. He had done it for me. He had changed the steward's and the court's minds, gone against his father's wishes, for me. I had been the reason after all.

"Do you hate me for making that oath to be in your guard?" I asked, surprised when the words left my lips.

His eyes softened, and he approached me. His hands on my arms made my heart leap. Slowly he reached past me, pulling the handle of the door and closing it with a soft click.

He was so close. His mint and cedar scent wrapped around me, muddling all logical thought. He did not step away, and my heart ran off with my sanity, and I found myself hoping he would kiss me.

"I see nothing to hate." He caressed my cheek, and this time when he touched me I knew it was not because of the compulsion of the oath. He glanced at my mouth, but instead of moving in he stepped back, hand finding mine, his other sliding around my waist. "Shall we?" he hedged, pulling me deeper into the room.

On instinct I lifted my hand to his shoulder and let him spin me around. We glided along the red carpeted floor, and though his bed, fit for a king, was far off in the corner, my eyes kept drifting to it. The purple blanket with three stars appeared to wink at me from across the room.

When his hand slid from my waist to my hip I stumbled.

"S-Sorry, it's the shoes." I flushed, and he leaned in to whisper, even though there was no one to overhear us.

"Sure, blame the shoes." He chuckled softly, and my whole body warmed.

"It is the shoes," I muttered weakly, but he was already spinning me out and pulling me back in.

"After what you went through the other day, I did not expect you to be able to dance this well."

Stopping the dance, he slid his hands softly around either side of my ribs. If I didn't know he was checking for my injuries, I might have flushed harder from the sensation of his hands caressing up and down the curve of my waist.

I frantically shoved his hands away, wrapping my arms around myself.

"You aren't wearing bindings." His eyes narrowed intently on the lack of material under my dress. I had forgotten to wrap my ribs in my haste to get dressed. "You aren't even limping from the gash on your leg."

Before I could protest he scooped me into his arms and set me on the couch. He knelt on the floor, pushing the fabric of my dress up over my knee, the feel of his hand on my calf almost distracting me from what he had discovered.

In place of the gash were just some fading bruises.

"Haya, what is this—"

My mouth opened and closed, unable to form words.

He reached for my waist and the zipper that held the dress together at my side.

"Shroding?" I yelped as his fingers pinched the zipper. His eyes snapped to mine, and as if realizing what he had been about to do, he dropped to his haunches, grabbing the hem of my dress and pulling it over my exposed legs.

"Strings, Haya. I'm sorry." He blinked a few times, perplexed. "Do you have the healing gift?" He looked flummoxed, knowing that logic made no sense at all. Then as if seeing something he hadn't before, he said, "Natalie. It's Natalie, isn't it?"

I didn't know if I should even bother playing dumb—there was no way he would believe me. As he had said the other day he had spent enough time with me to know when I was lying, so instead I redirected. "I'm okay—isn't that all that matters?"

CHAPTER 31

Vows

We found Asher, Natalie and Callum on a terrace, having what looked like brunch. My stomach growled, but I ignored my hunger cues, concerned with what Shroding was going to do. I was not sure why it was such a big deal. Yes, the healing gift was exceptionally rare, but Shroding seemed angry, and I didn't know why.

Natalie glanced up, her glowing smile faltering as she took in his expression. She set down her teacup and rose to her feet.

"Did you two know and decide not to tell me?" Shroding demanded, pointing between Callum and Asher.

"Shroding?" Callum asked, standing as well. He looked at me for help, but I didn't know what was wrong.

"Sir Liam sent you word that he fought another Rephaim while on his way to Erasmus, which was gravely injured but escaped." Shroding pointed at Callum. "We agreed that a healer must have helped the Rephaim in the castle, but our healer was sent to the front line weeks ago." His jaw clenched.

Understanding dawned. *He must think Natalie is a traitor, helping heal a wraith and also helping him get to me in the castle.* "No!" I panicked. "She doesn't heal anyone, she keeps it a secret."

Asher's and Callum's eyes snapped to Natalie, who looked down guiltily at her hands.

Shroding strode up to her, breathing through his nose to try and calm down. "Tell me that is true, Natalie. Tell me you didn't heal the Rephaim who *tortured* Haya."

This was bad.

"I used to disguise myself and walk through the city, healing those who might not make it with just medical care," she whispered, and Asher collapsed into the chair, horror in his brilliant blue eyes. "I have not done it for many years now, since things have gotten so bad. But a servant told me of a butler who had been attacked just outside the castle after taking holiday to visit his family." Tears pricked her eyes. "I asked to see him to get him medical help. When she took me to him he was already very far gone; still I had her fetch a doctor. While she was gone I healed him."

"How did you not know he was a *Wraith?*" Callum sneered with disgust.

"I didn't know Wraiths could have bodies that weren't part of a possession. He was unconscious, and I didn't see any memories from him. It was all a blank—I had thought it was odd at the time, but I don't know, I assumed it was a fluke."

"Talie, you have had the healing gift all these years?" Callum's voice broke, sorrow in his gray eyes.

"I wanted to tell you."

"You should have told us," Shroding snapped.

Tears spilled over as she dropped to her knees. "I'm sorry, Shroding. Haya." Her tears stained her cheeks as she lifted her eyes to mine. I stepped forward to defend her, but Asher beat me to it.

He shoved Shroding back. "She was clearly afraid too."

"Why?" Shroding scrunched up his nose with irritation.

"Because in this world if you're a healer, you are sold off into slavery; you become a tool," Asher snarled.

Shroding looked surprised. "It was never like that. Slavery has been abolished for as long as I can remember."

"You have a lot to learn about the world you left two hundred years ago," Asher hissed, helping Natalie to her feet. Shroding's jaw clenched.

"That's not fair—you know it wasn't his choice," Callum interjected.

"Yes, you're right," Asher amended. "But we were left behind all this time to manage the pieces of a world without him." There was anger, pain and something else in Asher's words.

"No, I do have a lot to learn, to catch up on." Shroding balled his fists at his sides. "Natalie, I'm sorry you felt the need to hide this from us. I would never have let anything happen to you." Shroding softened, resting a hand on her shoulder.

"You are my sister—how could you not even tell me?" Callum asked, hurt.

"You were gone, all of you were gone for so long... What was I supposed to do? I was left here with a shady court and a father who didn't have time for me. I couldn't trust anyone to protect me. I planned to tell you, eventually, since we all came back together, but I didn't want to become a tool to you. Just a piece of equipment to whip out whenever someone was hurt. I—" Asher hugged her then, stopping her words, but angled his head at Shroding, his eyes vivid and burning like blue fire. Shroding's eyes flashed at the challenge.

I had never seen Asher so angry, and it unnerved me more than anything else I had seen lately. He was always calm, collected, and self-assured.

"You can't just come back and treat us like this." Asher's chin jutted in my direction. "She has become like a sister to me." I softened at his words; they had become family to me too. He jammed his finger into Shroding's chest. "When we told you to make her leave— When we begged you, you refused." He threw his arm out, gesturing to me.

"Don't bring Haya into this," Shroding said with just as much force.

Callum stood then. "Asher, please calm down." Surprising all of us with the role reversal.

"She is as much in this as we are. You were the one who told us that, don't you remember?" Asher glowered.

"You are way out of line," Shroding warned, his tone firm, eyes sharp. "Be honest and get angry about what is really bothering you."

"I waited for you!" Asher bellowed. "I waited for my king. I put my life, the things I wanted"—he squeezed Natalie tightly to his chest—"on hold all so I could chase after you." His anger subsided, but the pain was there, the lost time, the shame of admitting it aloud.

Shroding closed his eyes, taking a deep breath and letting it out slowly. "Asher, I never asked you to put your life on hold for me." Asher looked about to protest, but Shroding held up his hand. "I never asked you to stop pursuing the things you love. You made that choice on your own. You made that decision. So unmake it," Shroding finished with a gentleness that didn't quite fit the harsh reality of his words.

Asher nodded, resolve in his striking blue eyes. He stepped back from Natalie, holding her delicately by the shoulders.

"This is not the romantic moment I had hoped to give you, but..." He knelt, pulling a small pouch from his pocket. "I've been carrying this around for a decade. Please tell me I can finally put this on your finger. Please be my wife."

Natalie threw herself on top of him, knocking him to the pavers in the most aggressive display I had seen from her.

Somewhere in the laughter and tears was a sloppy yes.

Shroding smiled sadly and turned on his heel, leaving the terrace and the happy couple. I glanced at Callum, who looked at me with an expression I could not comprehend.

Shroding was at the door to his room when I caught up to him. I panted, trying to catch my breath from my short sprint. I would need to find a place to run laps and build up my stamina if I hoped to be on par with Callum and Shroding one day.

He opened his door, and I followed him back inside.

Dropping onto the couch, he put his head into his hands in the same gesture as in the garden. I hadn't seen it then, the brokenness in the motion, but I saw it now.

"I only ever seem to hurt you, while all you do is save me."

I knelt between his knees, cupping either side of his face. He had just gotten into a fight with a friend, and I wanted to comfort him even if I didn't agree with his statement.

"You have saved me too."

His flint eyes searched my face. Whatever he saw in my expression gave him the answer he was seeking, because then he was suddenly lifting me, like I weighed no more than a feather. His arms wrapped tight around my waist as he repositioned us, the faint rip of fabric easily ignored, lost as I was in his onyx eyes. Pulling me over top of him, he buried his face in my neck on the side opposite the mark. He leaned his back on the armrest, settling me against him, my hands braced against his chest, fingers gripping the tops of his broad shoulders. My knees straddled one of his legs, the other planted on the floor, a scrap of fabric limp under his boot. The torn hem of my teal dress spilled out beside us, a rumpled display of his urgency.

"Haya." His lips brushed my collarbone, and I shivered. The sharp edges of his vest dug into my arms. He lifted his head till it was level with mine. Our lips a breath away. There was no oath, no reason for him to lean in, but he did. His fingers slid down to my hips slowly, intentionally. My breath hitched as his hands fisted the fabric. He closed his eyes and took a deep breath. "I didn't mean for..." he tried to explain, but I already knew. The betrayal he had suffered at the hands of Logan still haunted him, such that even the inkling of another friend turning on him sent him spiraling.

"I know, but it's okay." I smoothed his hair back, finding the silver strands and rubbing them between my fingers.

"Strings, Haya." He tipped his head to the side, leaning into my touch, and I swear if he could still purr, he would have. Pulling my hips against his, he hissed out a low, low groan.

"I need to get dressed for the coronation." But he made no move to do just that.

"Shroding, I—" But all logical thought was gone, and I didn't even know what I wanted to say, because I wanted to kiss him so badly it hurt. Everything in me was hung up on that one word. Kiss.

His lips moved, slowly, tantalizing, along my cheekbone, his breath warming the skin until there was nowhere else for him to go.

Dark eyes found mine, and I gave his hair a gentle tug, just as he had done to me the last time we kissed. The faint flecks of gold winked out as his pupils grew, his lips parting.

"Oath or not," he breathed, "I wanted to do this, to feel this, with you. Just you."

Then his mouth was on mine, and it was everything I'd known it would be. I bent into him, our bodies not close enough. His hands roamed over my sides, pushing and pulling me to the rhythm of his mouth. I stretched my arms over his shoulder, gripping the edge of the couch for stability as his tongue licked across my lips before meeting mine. He pulled me deeper into the kiss, and I melted against him. Gasping as his hands dropped to my thighs. The room was sweltering, but the fire of the hearth was nothing compared to the heat of his hands kneading the backs of my legs. He broke the kiss, both of us panting. When he focused his attention on a soft spot between my neck and shoulder, I sighed. I wasn't prepared for the shock having his mouth there would cause to my system, but the embarrassing sound that escaped my lips told us both I was very into what he was doing.

I wanted more, needed more, but even I knew we were moving too fast. All the pent-up longing and tension was making it impossible to pull away, impossible to let this moment end.

"Those sounds..." He nipped at my lips before kissing me again, and I shuddered, my relief palpable. He was not pulling away, not retreating, not telling me this was wrong or a mistake. He just kept kissing me like it was all he had to do for the rest of the day, when we both knew it wasn't.

He sat up, and in a movement faster than I could sense, he laid me down on my back. His body hovered over me for a beat before I wrapped my arms around him, pulling him down on me. The weight of him had me arching. He slipped his hand under my back, supporting me as his mouth took mine again. When his tongue found mine, another embarrassing noise was ripped from the back of my throat.

His responding chuckle sent shivers down my spine.

Slowly, as if the power were buried under mounds of sand, my gift sparked between us. A building momentum of electricity that, once I acknowledged it, seemed to only grow stronger. With our bodies touching, it was no question that the other vibration in the room was his. It rolled off him and crashed into me like the waves meeting the shore in Tyndale. I was reminded how beautiful his power was. How it shone golden bronze and sounded like the hum of a cello. Was he seeing my soul now? Seeing its color and sound? Was he realizing how woven my power was to his, how it thrummed with the need to be wholly his?

"Strings, Haya, give an inch and you take a mile," he groaned, breaking the connection. He pulled back, letting me see his glassy eyes and smirk. "I can't say I don't like that about you, though." He tucked a loose strand behind my ear. I waited for him to tell me it was wrong, for words that would derail my heart and send me running, but they didn't come.

He noticed my confused expression and helped me to a sitting position. "Did I hurt you?" he asked, brows knitting as he searched my face.

I blinked back the tears of relief. "No," I whispered, "you didn't."

CHAPTER 32

King

Natalie had a whole beautification team waiting in my room for me after I left Shroding. I had wanted to stay with him, but Sir Martus had knocked, warning Shroding not to be late to his own coronation, so we'd parted with one last toe-curling kiss.

When I was scrubbed and polished from a bath, Natalie beamed encouragingly.

"Just let them work their magic—when they are through, you will be adorned in finery fit for a queen," her lyrical voice assured me. She flitted out of the room, the glow of love radiating off her, as the ring Asher had given her shimmered in the fading sunlight. It seemed like finally everything was falling into place.

Natalie was right, the emerald green gown that hung across my body amplified every asset of mine to a degree I was not used to. Its long velvet shape clung to me like a second skin. The V of the neckline was just a few inches higher in the front than in the back. Though my back was exposed, the long sleeves brushed just past my knuckles, keeping me a bit warmer on the cold winter night. The hair at the crown of my head was elegantly curled back in an elaborate twist as the rest of my hair tumbled down to my waist in gentle waves. I was beautiful, and as I stepped into the ballroom, the space glowing with audacious gowns and long coattails of vibrant blues, reds, and golds, I knew I belonged. The whole hall glimmered like the jewels outside the palace at sunset. It was as if the jewels were all brought inside just for this one night. The ceiling was strung with lights and ribbons of gold. It was everything and so much more than Shroding had described.

Natalie came to stand at my side, the epitome of elegance in an aqua gown that twisted to one side in a flurry of lace and gossamer. She sparkled just like the rest of them.

I scanned the room, looking for the familiar faces of my friends, when I saw him far off in the crowd.

Shroding's shirt was black but to my surprise held the same iridescence as his eyes. His long vest was emerald velvet, the same as my dress, but brandished bronze detailing fit for a king.

His onyx eyes were on me, gaze tracking my even movement across the ballroom. Even surrounded by many faces of the court who were clearly talking to him, his attention was not deterred. For a moment it was as if we were back together in the other dimension, just him and me; everything else distant and unfocused. My heart raced, eager to meet him on the dance floor, waiting for him to ask me to dance.

"May I have this dance?" The moment was broken as I turned to the voice next to me, finding Callum standing in a rich red and gold suit that brought out a hint of pink in his cheeks. He looked dashing too.

"Are you blushing?" I teased.

"It's warm in here; lots of people." He gestured to the throng of bodies around us, smirking.

I took his outstretched hand, drawling, "Suuure."

Callum stepped into rhythm with the other dancers, gliding me along with him. Talie had been swept to the dance floor by Asher, whose smile was blinding as he twirled her in his arms. They were unquestionably the most handsome pair in the room.

"You look... incredible," Callum murmured, bringing my attention to him.

"Thank you." The crushed velvet of my dress reflected the lights above as we moved, and I grinned contentedly up at him. I did look incredible.

Callum continued talking about the guests and the events of the night, but my eyes had drifted across the ballroom. Natalie had switched partners and was now swaying with Shroding, their path leading to me.

Flint eyes held mine, and I itched to run towards him.

Callum's lips tickled my ear, surprising me. "It's rude to stare at someone else when your dance partner is talking to you." I stiffened as if caught doing something wrong. I lifted my face, but Callum's breath on my cheek gave me pause. He was a lot closer than I'd thought he was. "I'm leaving for Erasmus in the morning." My brows knit. How was he supposed to train me if he was gone? "I'm trusting you to keep each other safe." He pressed his hand into the curve of my back, his fingers touching the skin there as he drew me closer. "Also, I release you from your oath." A sizzle of power sparked across my skin as the oath I had made him snapped between us.

"W-Why?" I breathed uneasily. What did his leaving mean?

He straightened, his storm gray eyes tender as he spun me out and let go. His hands found Natalie's, and strong steady arms wrapped around my waist from behind.

I gasped as Shroding spun and then lifted me up by the hips, following the motion of the other dancers. Above the crowd with a sea of other women lifted by their partners, I could see the full expanse of the room. The ballroom was a massive oval spanning the circumference of the spire. Tall windows and doors curved along the perimeter. Heavy chenille curtains in jeweled tones were tied back by thick gold cords, allowing the night sky to twinkle through the glass. A few doors led to balconies, where partygoers retreated for relief from the heated space. The night was cold, and bits of frost clung to the edges of the glass outside. The far wall was solid, a backdrop to the raised platform where the court and Shroding would sit for the announcement.

I peered down at the king holding me aloft. His face came into view as he slowly lowered me. My body sliding along his as my arm wrapped around his neck, noses nearly touching as he held me a foot from the ground. His lips parted, and I knew he was thinking of the kisses we'd shared only a short while ago.

"Shroding..." I whispered, my mouth inching towards his. The muscles of his strong body held me tight to him.

His smirk was playful as he set me down, then dipped me over his knee. "I'm glad to see you getting along so well with my friends." His voice was smooth but had a hint of something. Jealousy? I had to admit it was rather nice to see him show any kind of possessiveness over me, first with Micah and now with Callum.

"You are lucky to have such loyal friends." I winked, letting him know with my coy smile that there was no one else I'd rather be with. His expression softened.

"If only all my friends could be as loyal as them..." A hint of a shadow passed over his features, and I knew he was thinking of Logan. But the shadow passed quickly, and he leaned in to whisper, "As loyal as you." My chest swelled with pride. I would always be loyal to this man. To this kingdom. But more assuredly to my heart, which beat for him.

I was hyperaware of the tips of his fingers brushing the skin of my back as he lifted and then spun me. When he brought me in, it was not as before, but it was enough to make my skin heat and lips part. His effect on me was implicit. The effect he had always had on me, from the beginning. He could see it too, because his eyes grew a fraction darker, his hands squeezing a bit tighter. We were inching past what was a prudent space between partners, but neither of us seemed to care.

"Go to the southwest terrace when the bell rings the third time; just before the fireworks."

"Okay." I nodded, eager to have time alone with him.

"Good girl." I shivered in anticipation as he spun me out of his arms again. The music finally drew to a stop, and it was time for Shroding to give a speech before the people, before the bells chimed and the fireworks would fill the night sky.

"Time for me to be a king," he said solemnly.

I brought him close before he could walk away. He looked surprised but leaned into my invitation. I whispered with passion, "I wish I could send you off with some grand words, some wisdom, but you have lived longer and are far wiser, so instead let me assure you this. No matter what the people think, or the court; no matter what happens in this war, you will always be Iri, my friend." I reached up, touching my hand to his face. "I might not have known your father, but I know you will be an even greater king than he was." His eyes bounced between mine, with a softness that melted my soul. The first bell rang out, and murmurs spread through the crowd for the announcement. I let him go, his smile never faltering as he ascended the stairs to the throne.

The steward stood, arms raised. "Esteemed guests and friends, it is with great joy on this fateful day that I step down as your steward." Gasps spread through the crowd like thunder on the wind. Only the reporters from every major news outlet in every city and town remained vigilant. They all visibly inched closer, ready to take in the news of the century. "My king, and dear friend Roark, may he finally rest in peace, had hid our deliverance for many years, in the hopes that one day we would be deserving of it. A prophecy stated the son of Elina and Roark would wipe this land clean of Skithian and his scourge. Today I announce that deliverance. A son was indeed born to our most beloved royalty. May I present Prince Shroding, son of King Roark, the rightful king of Shamar!" Shocked yelps and hoots of joy rang out through the room. The faces of partygoers were painted with a mix of elation and wonderment at the startling news.

Shroding slowly stepped forward to stand beside the steward. The shouts around me grew louder. Some saying how much like the king he looked, others saying it was a lie, while yet others used their own vibration gift to sense the king's power.

Slowly I backed through the crowd until I successfully

pressed against the wall where I'd stashed my sword, a better vantage point to spot threats. So far I did not see anything amiss.

"I know many of you might have your doubts, but I can assure you the same power, the same blood that ran through King Roark's veins flows through mine. My father protected me for such a time as this, and now I will take his place, restore the court, and free our world from the enslavement of Skithian!"

The room flashed with a bright light that at first I thought was an attack of some kind but quickly realized was coming from Shroding. He was letting everyone see his vibration, the color, the sound; somehow he merged the vibration dimension and this one for a moment to prove his heritage. Prove he was the true king.

Everyone fell silent, in awe of his beauty. I fought back tears. I had thought I would never see it again, but here it was, the bronze glow twisting over his skin, around his face, reflecting back in his eyes, making them like thick honey. His gaze fell upon me, and he watched as the tears rolled down my cheeks. I did not know if he did this for them or me, but either way my heart swelled with delight.

The room erupted with shouts of joy, laughter, cheering and singing. I chuckled softly, wiping my tears. The reporters vigorously recounted the events, announcing the news to every corner of Shamar. In two short days the whole kingdom would have reports of the new king.

Sir Martus came forward and placed the crown from the other night onto Shroding's head, making it official.

"My friends, the king!" Asher stepped forward, gesturing to Shroding.

The crowd whooped and hollered, chanting, "King Shroding of Shamar!"

The steward was the first to fall to one knee, the whole audience following suit; like a wave crashing to shore, everyone descended to one knee. When the wave reached me in the back of the room, I caught Shroding's eyes again. I smiled, lifting my dress to go down, but he shook his head, and I hesitated. Everyone's faces were downcast, so no one saw when Shroding placed his fist over his heart and bowed his head to me. Lifting his head, he mouthed the words "thank you" across the great hall.

I bit my lip, fighting tears. Against so many odds we had brought him back—he was home, he was king.

The second bell chimed, and the crowd rose.

"My people, my first act as your king will be the restoration of the court."

A handful of men and women from the other night ascended the dais. Callum placed a pin of the king's crest to each chest, their names read off one by one. I recognized a few from the interrogation Shroding had held the night the Rephaim had attacked. Everyone clapped dutifully. Then Asher and Callum were also announced as Shroding's advisors, earning another great roar from the crowd. The servers brought out flutes glasses and tankards of all manner of ale, the masses downing drink after drink, raving with merriment.

The third bell rang out clear and bright in the hall, inviting everyone to the west terrace to watch the fireworks. I wanted to go to watch them as well, but Shroding's request had me slipping out to the southwest terrace.

The terrace was empty save for a lounge and table. It was much smaller than the west terrace, which was more of a platform that jutted over the garden below, its massive size designed for large groups. This terrace, however, was much more narrow and faced the city. The wind whipped violently the closer I got to the banister.

Footsteps on the stone bid me to turn and meet familiar iridescent eyes.

CHAPTER 33

Dragon

"Your Majesty." I bowed dramatically, lifting my skirt to one side in a curtsy.

He huffed a laugh through his nose as he sauntered forward, the doors to the terrace closing behind him; the lock thrust into place, making my heart skip. Had he used his vibrations to do that?

A tickle of power waved off him as the knot tying back the heavy curtains was cut loose, and the lights inside the ballroom disappeared. For a moment we were pitched into the darkness of night, but then fire sparked to life around the space as candles and lanterns glowed. I gasped, taking in the man before me, all lean lines and broad shoulders. Shroding was not one to use his power needlessly, but his little display now had me a bit weak in the knees. I knew the king's power was strong—it wasn't that that was surprising. It was the ease with which he could wield it; not even breaking stride, he had caused a cascade of events with his gaze intent on me.

He paused a foot away, a devious grin on his lips.

"It is incredibly improper that I am here, alone with you,

but it's nothing we haven't done before, I suppose." His voice thrummed in my ears, and I could feel its vibration as he leaned in, linking my arm with his, and guided me to the lounge. After pressing me into the seat, he sat down facing me, cupping my cheek in his hand. I leaned into the touch.

"Is it okay for you to be here right now?" I looked around dramatically.

"Trust me, we are fine. Callum is around the corner; no one will come looking for me." He smirked.

"You have been the king for all of what? Five minutes, and you're already looking to get away," I teased.

"I made a promise to show you the fireworks. I'm a king, and a king should keep his promises," he explained sagely, making me chuckle.

"You were great up th—" I began, but his thumb, pressed into my lips, stopped my words of praise.

The jovial glint in his eyes faded as he spoke. "I asked you here so I could talk to you; the fireworks don't start till midnight, so we have some time. As much as you are going to want to respond, I need you to stay silent, otherwise I'm not going to get all this out." He glanced at my mouth under his thumb. "I should have said all this before I kissed you, but better late than never, isn't that what they say?"

I huffed a small laugh.

His thumb smoothed over my lips, and I could sense how badly he wanted to kiss me, because I wanted it too. Whatever he wanted to say could wait, couldn't it?

"Don't look at me like that," he warned, a groan of pain sliding out between his teeth. "If I kiss you now, I won't end up saying any of it."

I took a deep breath, folding my hands in my lap as if to say, "I'll be good," and nodded, telling myself to be patient.

He reached around me, pulling a blanket from the arm of the lounge. "I have been a fool," he began, and wrapped the warm fur over my shoulders. "I have been a complete fool, thinking I could keep away, keep my distance. It wasn't fair to you. I confused you and myself, all this time. I thought I knew what I was doing. I thought I could predict how this was going to go, but..." He paused, folding the blanket over my shoulders. "Do you remember when we met, how I got so angry when you kissed me?" I frowned, not really thrilled with the reminder. "Of course you do." He ran a hand through his hair. "When you asked me to kiss you, to prove I was real, I didn't know if you were pretending to not know me or if you were using me. But Strings know I wanted to kiss you even then. I fought my feelings for you for so long. At that time I genuinely believed I would never be human again. I had lived without hope for half my life, and I didn't want to give you hope for something that could never be."

I opened my mouth but quickly shut it, waiting.

"Later when I kissed you, I knew it was too late." He dropped his hand from the blanket and turned to stare at the expansive night sky. "That despite my poor efforts to keep us platonic, you had already developed an unhealthy interest in me, and I had come to want you too much. My kissing you then was *completely* selfish. You had nearly drowned in that lake, and the relief that you were there, in front of me, was all consuming. I wanted all of you at that moment and didn't care about the consequences. I didn't care about all the reasons I had to keep my distance. Even if I lived the rest of my days locked in the other dimension and only had your nights, I was delusional enough to believe I could live with that. That it would be enough for me to have you, as a man in the spirit dimension and as a cat in the real world. But when you asked for the oath..."

He turned towards me, and I flushed at my brazen behavior.

"After everything you had suffered because of me, I knew I had to stop because you would endure worse—loving someone who could never give you a future? A family? I began to doubt I was the best thing for you, that I could even *protect* you. In Coinania, the Nephesh Maveth—it was all because of me. Logan targeted you because of me." His voice cracked, and I squeezed his hand. Dark eyes met mine, and the pain there was unmatched, yet he pressed on, needing me to understand. "So I tried to keep away from you, to keep a line between us. But your sincerity made my rebuffs futile. In Tyndale, Callum and Asher told me to send you away; they *begged* me." He threaded his free hand through my loose hair, twisting it absently around his pointer finger. "For your sake, they told me it was for the best, but again I was selfish. I *never* wanted to send you away. When I became human again, I thought maybe it was a chance for us. I wanted it to be," he exhaled in a rush, the longing so clear in his voice. "I wanted to kiss you that morning on the beach, but you were so weak. I thought I would be taking advantage of you in that state, so I waited, but it was just an excuse. I waited because I was afraid. I didn't know after everything I'd put you through, after *dying* for me... if you— if you would still want me."

I was restless, desperate to interrupt, but he only took a short breath, and I knew he was not finished.

"And then you took an oath to protect me as part of my guard... I didn't deserve your blind devotion. I was the reason you were in danger time and again. The best thing for you was to stay away from me, away from everything in my life. I was sure you would leave with your mom as soon as we arrived in Romath. It was part of why I didn't fight the wedding at first. I foolishly hoped it would push you to leave on your own. When you didn't and the Rephaim attacked—" He took a shaky breath. "I wanted to be close to you, to hold on to you. But Micah was there, and I thought perhaps you'd taken him up on the proposal from so long ago."

Butterflies slammed into my stomach at his words.

"I was gutted at the idea that he would have you the rest of his life, and I realized how much it must have hurt you to hear I was marrying Natalie. I've not properly apologized for putting you through that." He searched my eyes. "I'm so sorry I hurt you with my stubbornness and my failed attempts at protecting your heart. I'm sorry."

"Shhh." I placed my hand on his cheek. "I understand. But where is this going?" The hope in my voice burned like a fire ready to destroy me again if this turned out to be a buildup to him pushing me away.

"Haya." He whispered my name, and it cracked like broken glass from his lips. As if my name were dangerous to him. "I have given up trying to know what's best for you. So if you want me, I am yours." He lifted his hands, palms splayed out as an offering. "I am done being trapped in a turmoil of my own making."

I slipped my hands over his and smiled, but before I could say anything, the clamor of explosions blanketed the sky. We stood and he tucked me against his chest, wrapping his arms around me from behind.

The fireworks burst in colors bright against the night sky. Rich reds, gold, blue and purple danced, shimmered and sparkled above. I was so enraptured, the boom resonating in my chest as they popped. It reminded me of the vibration dimension. The way the colors were vivid and alive. The crackle of the fireworks whistling one after another like a song. It was beautiful.

When they lulled, Shroding leaned down to my ear.

"My father and mother used to watch the fireworks from here. My father wrote in his journal that when I found someone who amazes me in every way, that I should show her these fireworks." I tipped my chin, turning to look up at him. "This part is the finale." His fingers wrapped around my waist. He was warm, and though I wanted to give him my attention, the thunderous explosions of light drew me away again. The last firework that went up split into two, twisting and swirling up around each other into the dark like two people dancing across a black sea. Then it was silent. I waited, but the burst didn't come.

Slightly disappointed, I asked, "What happened to the last one? It didn't finish."

"That one is special, wait for it." He gently tilted my face high to the sky. Higher up than any of the others had gone. We waited. The night sky was quiet, and in the stillness I could feel every movement Shroding made behind me. He shifted from one leg to the other, as if uncomfortable. His breath was shallow, as if he had been running a race. His hand pressed firmly into my waist as if I were a rock he could use to hold himself up.

Light flashed through the sky, illuminating both of us in a gold glow. Like the sun had risen early for just a second and the darkness was blotted out in favor of the light. I jumped, startled by the delayed explosion.

"Wow," I breathed, watching the twinkling lights flutter down like streamers to the city below.

"It's called the King and Queen." His voice was heavy

with emotion. "They stopped making them when my mother died. This one was made special for tonight."

"For your return?"

"No." His tone was tender. "For you. I wanted *you* to see it. To see what the king and queen mean to Shamar. What it would mean for you..." I twisted in his arms till we were chest to chest. His dark eyes watched me so intensely I was lost to them. "If you married me..." he finished, and just like that he unraveled me. Every part of my heart and soul unfurled its protective hold to let him in. "As royalty you are expected to disappear, to become a tool for the kingdom, and when you are needed most you are expected to shine the brightest. That is what it would mean for you to stand by me. It would be the same as losing your freedom. You have lost too much already because of me. I don't want to be the reason you lose anything else... "

But didn't he see that even if I had lost, I would have gained something better? I would have gained him. His love, his devotion, his heart. Could I really lose myself when I would have gained so much more? *I'm still so young,* I thought bitterly. Did I even understand what it meant to love with my whole heart, selfless and unhindered by my own fears and insecurities? But I knew with him, I could figure it out. I could overcome those shortcomings.

"You have to know, I am a king first. I'm not practiced at this." He brushed my hair over my shoulder. "I haven't been with anyone romantically. I'm not like Callum, if that is what you are hoping for. I don't have the words like he would."

"I don't want Callum," I said firmly, removing the lingering doubt in his eyes. "This is new for me too, but we can figure it out together."

He lifted my chin higher and pressed his lips to mine in a

soft, sweet kiss. A seal and a promise. He stayed close, holding me to him as he murmured, "I made you wait; I'm sorry for that."

I reached up, wrapping my arms around his neck, and kissed him. "Shroding, you are worth waiting for." *I would do it again,* I wanted to add, but knew he wouldn't like hearing that right now. Maybe someday in the future we would come to see one another through each other's eyes. Maybe then all the pining and longing would make sense to the other person, but for now this was enough. He wasn't running or hiding anymore and neither was I.

"Is there anything else you are still keeping from me, anything else I should know?" I asked between kisses.

He pulled back, cupping my face. "Yes, there is."

My brows lifted with anticipation.

"So there is no question or doubt left in your mind." He skimmed his nose over my cheek and kissed just below my ear. I fought the whimper threatening to escape as he moved. Trailing kisses along my jaw until he found my mouth once more. Kissing me deeply one more time before he pulled back and met my eyes. "I love you, Haya Golden. I don't know if there was a moment since we met where I wasn't falling in love with you."

A scream interrupted the moment, and Shroding instinctively tucked me to his side, turning to look over his shoulder towards the sound.

"Fire! Fire!" the muffled voice of a man hollered, the thud of his feet carrying him past our terrace.

"What's happening?" I asked, trying to look past Shroding.

"It's fine, it happened once when I was a kid—the fireworks must have caught something on fire. The guards are equipped for this," Shroding assured me, letting me out of his arms. He smiled calmly. "Don't worry," he assured me again, but his smile wavered as a thick stench whipped across the terrace with the wind.

"What's that smell?" I gagged, nose catching the horrible stink of rotting eggs.

"Sulfur?" Shroding muttered, perplexed.

"Shroding, we have to go, now!" Callum burst through the doorway; the curtain and rod ripped from the wall above and clattered to the floor behind him. His sword was drawn and eyes crazed in a way I had never seen before. Not even when Coinania was under attack, or when we were overrun at Palace Moreh.

"Callum? What is it?"

"A dragon."

My brain stalled. A *dragon?*

And flashes of the visions Logan had shared with me sliced through my thoughts.

Shroding met my eyes, his expression saying he was thinking the same thing.

"We don't have time for this." Callum came out onto the terrace and pulled Shroding away from me at the same time I caught something shiny out of the corner of my eye. An impossibly large white wing rounded the side of the castle. Its black claws cracked stone and shattered the jeweled facade as it gripped a lip for support. I only took in its yellow eyes for a second before I twisted, readying to sprint to Shroding but already knowing it was too late.

Shroding was yelling, struggling, as his commander dragged him inside. I couldn't hear him, but I didn't need to because the terror in Callum's eyes told me enough.

Light erupted around me as a sound so ear piercing and

beastly rattled my eardrums to the point I was sure they had to be bleeding. The ghastly clamor made the screech of the Rephaim seem tame. Senses overloaded, I couldn't tell that the ground was shaking and collapsing under my feet. The stone of the terrace split down the middle, with me on the side plummeting to the city below.

THE STORY WILL CONTINUE IN...
From Ruby Sands

Shroding's POV
Taken Back

"Shroding!" Callum called, but my legs were already moving. I was nearly sprinting down the hall to the steward's rooms. "Stop!" He called again, but I ignored my friend and kept going. "Don't make me use my gift," Callum threatened, and I glared at him over my shoulder. "I mean it." He jogged up to me, and I whipped around on my heel to face him, reeling from the truth of the situation.

"I can't marry her." My tone was final, no discussion necessary. It was clear Haya had had no idea who Natalie was, and Natalie hadn't mentioned it either. Perhaps she hadn't known until Micah called Haya by the shared nickname? Now that *I knew*, there was no way I could marry Natalie. I refused to be the reason Haya lost connection to anyone else from her past.

Strings, what a mess. I raked my fingers roughly through my hair.

"Then don't," Callum said simply, but I could hear what those words cost him to say. I knew what it meant to him to have me become his brother, legally. It meant as much to me as well. In my eyes, we have been brothers since the trial King's Challenge when we were eight. We were groomed to be the future leaders of the kingdom, but he was not just my comrade, but someone I looked up to. A year older than me and he'd had such control with a sword even as a child. I'd been impressed and idolized him. He was fiery and fierce in a way that, as a child, I hadn't been. I'd had to be hidden, a secret, and that pressure had kept me from expressing my full range of emotions; but Callum got it. He could see the emotions I did not convey and conveyed them for me. He made me better, brighter, and challenged me to get stronger. I had accepted my lot of becoming the next king. I had accepted the prophecy that would decide the fate of the kingdoms, but my shoulders ached from the pressure. Then Asher and Callum had taken some of that burden and lumped it on themselves. I'd cried the first night I had met them. Cried tears of relief and joy. I wasn't alone. Not anymore, not with them on my side. I would not have to endure the future alone; because somewhere in my mind, even as a child, I knew my parents would not be there to see me become king. They would not survive the endless war. They would not escape Skithian's evil.

Callum's gray eyes narrowed on me. "Nothing changes for me if you do this, but it does for *them*." He put his hand on my shoulder, and I nodded.

Natalie was more like a sister to me. I had never harbored romantic feelings for her, and though I would have honored my father's arrangement, had circumstances not changed, I was not sure I would have been able to give her what she had with Asher. I didn't even want to try. So what did that say? What did it say that the only lips I wanted to kiss, the only eyes I could get seemingly lost in, were those of a woman not my betrothed.

Strings, this was a *ridiculous* situation.

"I will speak with the steward, and resolve this issue promptly." My jaw clenched in annoyance. "Don't follow me," I warned, pivoting, and continued to the steward's chambers.

I should have rejected this plan from the start. Selfishly I'd thought I could force Haya's hand, that seeing me engaged would make her leave, would cause her to go, and save her the heartache. Deep down I don't think I ever really planned to marry Natalie. If Haya had left, I would have ended things with Natalie shortly after.

Stubborn, impossible, resilient Haya had sworn an oath to me instead, throwing my plans, my resolve, clean off the highest rampart of the castle.

I passed a window that framed the garden from last night, like a painting. The pink tree curled over the bench, and I closed my eyes. The memories from last night crashed through my mind, unwelcome in their fervor, forcing me to remember every excruciating detail.

The air was cold, its bite curling across my chest where my tunic hung loose. This garden was the last thing my mother had curated in this castle before her death. It had once been a training arena, as it was connected to the guards' quarters on the far west side. She'd wanted me to have a place to play outside when I could not leave the castle, so she'd designed and commissioned it on my behalf. It was filled with happy memories, but in the last two hundred years it had changed. The upkeep kept it in good condition, but the trees had been saplings, the shrubs coming to my calves, then. Now it was a true garden, stately and bursting with life. I dropped my head into my hands, sitting on the bench under the blooming flowers. Some petals fell free and littered the brick at my feet like snow. She would have loved it.

My mind wandered back to the dinner, the steward's announcement and the look on Haya's beautiful face. Strings, it did not matter how many times I looked upon her, since getting color back in my vision, she took my breath away every time. At dinner it had been no different. She'd walked in wearing that tight blue dress, her shoulders and neck on full display. The tug to kiss the skin there had me ripping my eyes away from her. The night we'd left Moreh, the compulsion to kiss her had been near torture. Her soft gasps, the way her body crested into mine, would have had the resolve of weaker men crumbling; nearly had mine digging its way into the ground when her scent overpowered Logan's taint, masking his smell on her skin. I had almost believed he was truly gone, his mark eradicated by our passion, but I had opened my eyes and the bite was still there. My resolve had solidified once more, and I'd stopped because I could wait, would wait, had decided to wait and give her a kiss that would ruin her for all others, but... but that plan was ash now. Because of that dinner, because of the steward's announcement, which he had blindsided me with only minutes before he announced it. Decorum and politics, drilled into me as a child, had prevented me from standing and rejecting his claim then and there. How could I denounce my father's and the steward's plans while the court cheered, delighted by my betrothal to Natalie? I couldn't, and that was why I hadn't.

When I heard the glass shatter, saw Haya's eyes water, smelled her soft sweet scent dissipate from the room, I'd broken as easily as the fluted glass had in her hand. I'd sent

Callum after her in my stead while acid burned in my stomach. I'd known I had to speak with her, explain how I could go from holding her, touching her, nearly kissing her, to engaged to another in a matter of hours. She deserved an explanation, but what could I say? None of the words were right. None of the reasons made sense. Just when I had begun to believe we could be together. Just when I had accepted I was really, truly a man again and not an animal, not trapped, the cage bars had slid right back into place. Obligation, kingship, propriety, responsibility, rulership, oaths, prophecies, war... *Strings!* It was unbearable when all I wanted was her.

As if summoned by my longing, there she'd been. Walking towards me on the brick path. I had been so lost in my thoughts I hadn't even heard her approach until she was right there, in front of me. I sank into the memory.

Her dress was torn, legs exposed. She must be cold. Then I saw the slit up to her thigh, and my blood thrummed a bit faster and a bit harder through my veins. Who had done this to her? Was she hurt? My eyes zeroed in on the tiny nicks in her dress, no bigger than my fingernail but peppering her blue gown as if someone had had the chance to stab her hundreds of times but chose not to draw blood.

"I didn't expect to see you again today," she whispered, her soft eyes so open, so understanding, I wanted to become the dirt wedged between the pavers. I had been given the love of a woman I did not deserve. Her love was so pure, so earnest, and I had destroyed her life because of it. Would there ever be a day I did not loathe myself for the horror I had inflicted on her life? Everything I had taken from her weighed down the scale of my feelings, till I was not sure there was any other option but to send her way. She needed to *leave*, not just the garden, but the castle, my life; entirely. But those were words I could not bring myself to say to her. A vague thought took shape in my mind, not quite solid but growing with clarity.

I got to my feet, anger simmering under my skin. I swallowed thickly when Callum's scent mixed with hers on the wind. She had been with him? Of course, I had sent him after her. Of course they'd been together. I kept forcing them together, even back at Moreh, like a fool. I had no right to be jealous that he could touch her, no right to be angry that he had. Still my hand reached for her.

"What happened to you?" I did my best to hide the hurt when she pulled away, not letting me touch her.

"You're getting married." She looked as though she wanted to cover her mouth with her hands to prevent the outburst, but was too late.

"I—" Strings, the words were impossible to say. Running my hand through my hair, I gave myself a moment to think. "You have to know—" I tried again, but those words were not right either. *I'm a fool. I want you. I changed my mind. Consider what Sir Martus said in Moreh and be my queen. I love you.* But those thoughts were drowned out by the new idea solidifying in my mind. If I married Natalie, Haya *would* leave. She would go with her mother tomorrow if I made it clear I was really going through with the marriage. Asher and Callum were right—I should have sent her away after the transformation. I should have been strong enough to let her go. Now I would be. For her sake and for mine. If I was the cause of her losing someone else, getting hurt, I might never recover. Saying goodbye would hurt us both, but it had to be this way. It was for the best. *I can't think of the kingdom when my mind is so tightly wound up by her. Her breath, her smile, the way she fidgets with the end of her braid.* The idiosyncrasies I had noticed long before I recognized my feelings for what they were.

I grabbed the edge of the bench, lead filling my stomach, making it hard to stand, as I prepared to say what I must. "I had forgotten about my father's promise with the steward."

"Do you love her?" Her voice trembled. The surprise at her question took my breath from me. Why would she ask me this? Of course she would want to know—she was honorable, she wanted me to be happy, and would give me up only if she knew I was in love. Because she was good and true. I forced air into my lungs.

"Would knowing make you feel better or worse?" Worse, we would both be worse off if I told her the truth. If I told Haya that I loved her more than I could stand. That the love I had for Natalie was a candle compared to the raging volcano of affection I had for Haya.

"I love her." I closed my eyes as I said it, voice flat and clear. When I opened my eyes she was shivering, and the lead weight in my stomach nearly buckled my knees. Strings, I needed to hold her, to pull her close; that oath sparked and jolted between us, but I ignored the compulsion to kiss her till we were both senseless. I wished I had my jacket from dinner so I could at least offer that. Instead I clipped, "Now let me walk you back to your room, before you freeze."

"Did you ever love me?" she asked, her body swaying slightly. Did she realize she was crying?

I was gutted by her tears, everything in me wanting to reach out to her. My hands flexed at my side as I restrained myself.

"Haya." A breeze blew again, petals of pink falling between us as I stared at her. Her tears were not just from my confession, right? She must be injured somewhere? There were enough rips in the fabric to indicate more was going on, but even as I thought the lies, I knew she was not suffering from any physical pain. "What happened to you?" I pressed, needing to know what had occurred with her and Callum. The oath that had clicked into place between them on the train had jolted me awake for an instant, long enough for me to hear Callum's last words to her before she climbed into bed.

"It's done. Now scurry along, lass. That's an order."

Whatever oath they had made, it gave him control over her. It sickened me to know he had agreed to such an oath, and it only served to deepen my fears that Callum had begun to look at Haya as a conquest.

"I was sparring with Callum," she offered, but I already knew that much. What I didn't know was what had transpired between them on the train. Was it only an oath, or was there more promised between them? Asher had shared with me enough about Callum's reputation over the last two hundred years, and though I knew some of it was probably embellished, I could not help the unease it caused me. Callum was charming, even without his Orator ability, but with it he was irresistible. Had I pushed them into something more?

Against my better judgment I stepped forward, and to my surprise she let me close. Let me slide my hand under her chin and lift it.

Her mossy-green eyes fluttered, pupils inking out the color I had become so fond of. Did she know this attraction was part of the oath we had made? No, she couldn't know that this implicit need, which formed the moment we'd first touched, was amplified by the oath.

"What did you and Callum talk about on the train?"

"What do you mean?" Her lips parted, and for a moment all I could see was the desire in her gaze. The weight in my stomach shifted as if magnetized to her. I leaned down, and all it took was a single finger to her spine and she was pressing into me. Her chilled body drawn to my warmth, like a moth to a flame.

"I have the king's power. I can feel when an oath is given and taken by anyone in the court." Oaths were dangerous—I had thought I had made that clear. To accentuate my point I plucked at the string binding us together. A pulse of power rippled through me. It had been a mistake to touch the oath; as if prompted by the contact, the urge to kiss her intensified, and my hand splayed firmly across the small of her back. She was so fragile in my arms, soft and breakable. "I'm sure I don't need to remind you that oaths are dangerous and should not be given on a whim. They should be fulfilled with haste to avoid anything untoward occurring." The heat in my voice only made the burn to kiss her stronger. Her wide green eyes were no longer filled with tears but instead indignation. That was most unexpected.

"What about your oath? Is there a reason you have not fulfilled the one you made to me?"

Strings, was she asking me to do it now? To kiss her? Because I would, if only to end the burn, which was becoming excruciating the longer I held her and did not act. It would be so simple to give in, to taste her once more. She had been so enraptured the last time, her tongue sliding along mine, her sighs of contentment swelling my pride a bit too much. How would I ever let her leave if I kissed her again?

"Would you be satisfied if it happened now, here?" I demanded, my body ready to move in the last inch should she give me the go-ahead. "Would fulfilling the oath finally free us?" I murmured, losing myself to the moment, to her breath on my lips, the curve of her body anchored to mine as if she had washed up on my shore and needed no other solid ground but what I had given her.

"Why did you not make me leave all those times? Did the oath force you to keep me close, even though you wanted me gone?"

I pulled back slightly, sensing there was more going on but unable to grasp it. Her words were not enough to cut through the haze that had clouded my mind. I would have admitted anything to her, just to end the need, the hunger driving me to desperation.

"Even when I knew I should send you away... Even when I tried, the words always came out the opposite," I confessed. "After everything we have been through, I don't want you to be far from me. It makes me anxious that something might happen to you and I wouldn't be there. Even now, knowing that in three days everything will change again, I can't do what I know I should."

"And what is that?"

"Kiss you," I whispered. Her breath hitched when my fingertips pressed more firmly into her spine, arching her more. She must be on her tippy toes by now, but I wanted her not just needing to reach me but wild with the same hunger that had possessed me. "And end this compulsion."

I was hanging on by a thread, having let my own fears get in the way of stopping this before it got out of hand. I would not slam my mouth over hers the way my mind clawed at me to do. The way the oath pleaded for. I would not take the sweet mews I knew she would make, as much as I wanted to hear them. No, she would have to be the one to close the gap, take from me first before I let this desire devour us both.

"Is that all this is?" Her eyes glistened. "A compulsion?"

So much of what was happening right now *was* the compulsion. But not all of it. Not the way I moved my hand down her neck, skimmed her delicate shoulders, skipped down to the curve of her waist. Not the way I found her hip and pulled, the tips of my fingers finding the top of the slit in her dress. *Strings, stop there,* I demanded of myself, knowing any further and I would succumb fully to the oath.

"You will get better at wording oaths, how to be exact in your request and vague when it is needed. The oath you requested of me has no timeline for completion. So every time we are together I *feel* it. The pull." I bunched the fabric of her dress in my hands, stepping into her and pressing us together, her eyes fluttering closed for a moment. "But when I don't follow through, nothing bad happens because I just have to kiss you at some point while I'm human. And though that could be fifty years from now, it sure does make it difficult to be around you, anytime. All the time," I admitted, needing her to know and yet also using it as an excuse. The solidified plan to use my engagement as a way to end things with Haya, to save her, *whir*red in the back of my mind. Past the haze of lust and love. My chatter had allowed reason to take root in my thoughts again. I had an iota of control over myself and needed to use it. But her next words had me falling into the rose-colored haze once more.

"Do you..." She swallowed. "Do you have feelings for me?" She was so naive. How could she still not realize everything I did was for her? Because I wanted her more than the air I was breathing. Because I loved her too much to ruin any more of her life. I might be prophesied to save the kingdoms, but in this moment I would save them all just so she could live in a world of peace instead of death and pain and loss.

I slipped my hand from her hip and cupped her cheek. "Such a loaded question..." I whispered gently, knowing if I kissed her, it would be goodbye. It would be done. I had drawn it out long enough. Closing my eyes, I resolved to do what I must to protect her even if it hurt her for a short, fleeting time.

Cold air slammed into my torso, which had been delighting in her warmth for far too long.

"I release you from your oath." A faint tickle of power sizzled in my empty hands, hands, shock widening my eyes. She had released me?

"Why?"

"I have already taken one kiss from you. I don't want any more unless it is something you want to give..."

The jarring shift not only in my body temperature, but in the burning knot that had coiled in my chest, was gone. The compulsion eradicated even if the desire to kiss her still lingered everywhere across my skin. I'd known I would still want her after the oath was resolved, known it would hurt to be parted from her, but I had not expected this emptiness at having her depart from me so abruptly. *Strings*, I still wanted to hold her. Perhaps the compulsion had been so strong because my feelings for her were already all consuming?

"Then the oath is broken, the deal is off." I grabbed the bench for support, holding it instead of her, grounding myself to it. "So you're leaving, then?" She'd broken our oath. My plan had worked, if differently than intended—she planned to leave just as I had anticipated.

As Callum, Asher and I had planned before we left

Moreh; of course I had planned for her departure to be tied to her reunion with her mother, but this worked just as well. Yes, this was fine.

Her blue dress bunched as she knelt to the ground, the slit letting her whole thigh glimmer in the moonlight as she settled on one knee.

"What are you doing?"

Her face was downturned in shadow. The silver glow of the moon crowned her bowed head. She looked like an ethereal knight about to vow her life to her king. The lead weight returned to my stomach with a force that had me shaking. No, no, this couldn't be happening, but the words were already leaving her mouth.

"My king, I pledge to you my life." She fisted her hand over her heart. "I, Haya Golden, the very great-granddaughter of General Armond Golden, offer you my service as the newest member of the king's guard. I will live my whole life protecting you under the guidance of Commander Callum McClain. This is my oath to you."

I took two steps back as the oath locked into place between us.

"Why do you do things that only serve to hurt you in the end?" I snapped helplessly, because I could release her this instant, and reject her oath, but in order to safely release an oath there was a cooling-off period of seventy-two hours, at least, otherwise it was the same as the oath being broken. The consequences would be the same as failure. She would lose the court if I released her now, and so I swallowed my anger and fear. She could not leave now with her mother. We had to suffer through another few days, where she would watch me wed, and endure the heartache it would both cause us.

"My king."

If a heart could shatter, mine would have at the finality in her tone. I would be her king and nothing else, when in my heart I wanted to be her partner, her lover, her friend. Those dreams died as readily as the petals falling from the tree above us.

"Do as you wish," I exhaled, because what other option did I have? I would never control her, never order her. She was bound to me in a way wholly different than I wanted—but she was bound nonetheless.

She accepted my proffered hand, and I lifted her off the cold ground. "Let me take you back to your room."

I had never failed so badly at something before, and though I would not hear the end of it from Callum or Asher, at least one person would be glad for the arrangement. Sir Martus, probably the only person in the court who realized from the moment he met us that I was completely in love with Haya. Sir Martus had always been good at reading me. His attention to me as a child was one of an attentive teacher but now was beginning to seem more like that of a caring father. He'd been distraught by my engagement announcement, more so than I had been. Sure, I had been angry, blindsided and sad, but I had not cried. Sir Martus, on the other hand, had shed tears while pleading with me to reconsider. As if he were crying the tears he knew I could not shed. It did not matter how much I wanted to be with her, I would do what was best for the kingdom even if that was not what was best for me. A small voice whispered that, more than the kingdom, I would do what was best for her, and being with me had already caused her too much turmoil.

"I should thank you." I stepped ahead of her in the corridor that led to her room. Needing to distract us from the conversation in the garden and embrace the reality before us. I would marry Natalie, and Haya would be forced to stand by my side and watch, all because of her oath to protect me. To *guard* me. She had been doing that from the beginning. Why didn't she see that an oath was never needed for her to protect me? To save me. She already had more times than I could bear to count. The most recent being when I stepped into my father's room, now mine, and saw the purple blanket embroidered with the three stars. She had promised I would see it again, and though I had thought her promise sweet then, when it was fulfilled earlier today I shed tears. She had brought me home, while I had decimated hers. "The blankets my father had made..." I hesitated, stopping at her room. "I got to see it today, thanks to you."

"Glad I'm fulfilling all my promises to you, and in record time." Her smile was forced, and I averted my gaze.

"It's late. Good night, Haya." I tipped my chin towards the door and waited for her to go inside. She didn't move. I needed her to get inside before I said and did something else foolish.

"The cat in the painting, is that why you picked this room?"

The painting, of course she would ask about it. It was why I had selected this room for her to stay in, but it wasn't the only reason. My mother had painted it herself after having a vision, and I supposed she must have known all along what would become of me, since she saw it while I was in the womb. I never considered it before but what else had she seen? Had she known I would meet Haya on that hill? That I would fall in love with her?

"This was my room growing up," I confided, having

chosen this room to share more about myself with her. I had decided this before we had arrived and had hoped to tell her stories of my childhood, deepening our relationship more. I had wanted to tell her everything about me, open up completely, and my childhood, as wrought with turmoil as it was, had seemed like a good place to start. That was before the disaster today turned out to be. So instead I relayed my new reason, which was infinitely worse. "I wanted you to have some part of me, even if it could only be the cat." Because Iri was in fact all she would ever have of me. Those fleeting months that would live in my mind for all time, reminding me, long after she was gone, that a love that is all encompassing, all consuming, did in fact exist in my lifetime. With her.

"G-Good night," she whispered, green eyes glittering as she opened and shut the door.

I bit the inside of my cheek, fighting back the words I wanted to say. *I'm sorry, I love you.* But they served no purpose, as they changed nothing. I gripped the doorframe, nails nearly splitting the wood with the force of holding myself back from barging in after her and wiping the tears from her eyes. I could feel the vibration of her sobs through the thick wood, and anguish fractured through me as my other hand covered my face.

When I finally stepped away, determined to leave, my hand came away wet with my own tears.

"Your mother loved watching you play, in the garden, from that very spot," the steward said, standing before me in the hallway where I had gotten lost in the memory of the previous night. The sunlight streamed across the floor between me and my best friend's father.

Callum had left me alone with my thoughts after our argument about calling off the wedding. I swallowed thickly, shaking my thoughts back to the present.

My resolve returned as the steward stood before me. His flowing robes and open smile, though wrinkled with age, reminded me this man was on my side. He would not force me to do something I did not wish to do.

And I did *not* wish to marry Natalie.

"We need to talk about the wedding."

———

"Haya!" I hollered, watching the white wing of the dragon disappear around the edge of the castle. Callum wrestled me inside, away from the broken, crumbling balcony. The traces of Haya, and my rendezvous, fell to the city below.

"Have the guard search the rubble!" Callum ordered a soldier to his right, his grip on me still firm.

Air wouldn't fill my lungs as my thoughts fought the worst cases. She could be dead in the debris below, body mangled and broken. Or had the beast taken her? With a blast of power I freed myself from my friend and ran to the opposite side of the celebration hall, towards where the dragon had flown. Broken glasses, plaster and discarded items from the party littered the floor. Lost shoes and scraps of torn dresses added to the horrific scene, underscoring the panicked way the guests had fled the attack.

Without touching the balcony doors across the room, I shattered them with my power, stride not breaking as I ran to the edge of the balcony. In a fluid motion I leapt onto the railing and narrowed my gaze on the horizon. The icy wind cut sharply across my face, but my enhanced eyesight told me what I needed to know. They would not find her in the wreckage.

The dragon's white wings flapped higher into the sky. The faint glow of the blue volcano was barely visible in the dark night. Moonlight glinted off the white feathers as the beast roared a chilling cry into the darkness. It echoed off the stone and gems around me, painful to my enhanced ears though the beast was already quite far away. Ignoring the pain, I fixed my gaze on the flutter of gold trailing behind the monster's claw.

"Haya," I growled, anger and frustration making her name a vow. I hadn't been quick enough. If I hadn't let Callum pull me away from her. If I hadn't let her go. She would still be here. Fists clenching at my sides, I shook with power and rage. I had *failed* her. *Again.*

"Shroding, come down!" Callum shouted, but I didn't react, couldn't react. A building fire was growing inside me; the power thrashed and roiled, becoming far too tangled with my emotions for me to think clearly. When four hands grabbed my arms to drag me off the banister I answered the dragon cry with a bellowing threat of my own.

The sound was like none I had ever made before, and I imagined I would never make again. It ripped from some primal, soul-deep place I had never known was inside me. Callum and Asher, who had hauled me down, backed away from me as vibrations burned across my skin, the friction so hot, steam lifted into the freezing air.

"Shroding!" Callum yelled as my cries of anguish brought me to my knees, head bowed and hands limp at my sides.

"Callum, use your gift now!" Asher's voice whipped around me, but it was distant, unfocused, as the night burst behind my eyes like flaming stars. What was happening to me? What was this? I needed to calm down. I needed to think rationally. She wasn't dead. She could be saved.

I would save her.

Yet my power was raging wild and unchecked, and I had no desire to control it. No desire to tame it or quell its roar.

"He will take down the castle," Asher warned.

"I know!" Callum shouted.

That's not good, a small rational voice in my mind whispered, but it was quickly quieted by the anger, the fury of having Haya ripped from my arms.

Enough. It was enough. We had suffered *enough*. She had endured enough.

Callum reached through the scalding steam and touched the back of my neck. His hand was ice on my skin; it did not only cool my flesh, but it did what I could not—it quelled the rage. The power quickly retracted as my emotions twisted from a tempest to a still lake. Calm. Like floating. The serenity had me lifting my head and tilting it back. Then I was falling into my commander's arms.

"Shroding?" Asher appeared next to Callum, brows knit in concern.

"I'm alright," I grunted, closing my eyes for a beat before opening them again. Taking deep even breaths that oxygenated me down to my toes, I sat up. When I was sure my clarity of mind was stronger than the anger, I shook off Callum's touch. "I can manage."

Asher and Callum shared a look of uncertainty. They were still in shock over what they had witnessed, and, if I was honest with myself, I was too. The king's power had never been so riled up before. I shrugged off their worries and rose to my feet.

"We need to do damage control." Asher glanced around, and I took in what was concerning him. The glass of the balcony doors blanketed the ground in little glinting mirrors that reflected the moon's glow. Like millions of tiny moonlit tears. I clenched my jaw, mind shifting right back to Haya. How much pain would she have to endure? How many tears would she cry? I had taken her tears onto myself. Owning each one of them since the moment I had found her on the dandelion hill. Tears I had caused should be mine to claim, mine to carry for all time. My burden and privilege. How many would I miss collecting? Anger simmered under my skin once more. I turned on my heel and entered the ruined celebration hall.

Stepping over the party's remains, I recalled her words of encouragement as I'd taken to the dais, her faith in me to be a great king. Not even an hour later, I'd failed her.

When I strode over the dance floor, I could almost feel her hands in mine, soft and pliant as they had been when we danced. The slide of her curves against my body. Her openness and trust in me. Even in the empty space her scent lingered, my nose able to parse hers out from hundreds. Unconsciously I brushed my thumb over my lip. Strings know I would have kissed her, while we danced, if I hadn't intended to speak with her so soon after. Each thought, each memory, slammed into me like a physical punch.

I would save her, but it was the crunch of boots entering the vacant hall that saved me from my own ruinous thoughts.

"Where is she?" Micah stormed in, and for a moment it did not make sense that he was here. He was supposed to have left already. Sir Martus's words, before the party, flicked through my mind.

"Micah wishes to rejoin the court. He wants Haya to

believe he has left but would like to keep watch over her in the shadows, if you can agree."

I was supposed to induct him in the morning, but all those plans were a million miles away, forgotten the instant she was torn from my arms.

"We are still look—" Asher began, but I cut him off.

"The dragon took her."

"It was flying southeast," Callum noted. "Towards Golan."

"A dragon?!" Micah scoffed in disbelief, then after taking in our downcast expressions he amended. "Is that what caused this?" He gestured around himself at the chaos. At the broken and wrecked return of the king. Not only had I failed to protect the woman I loved, but I'd failed to keep my people safe. Failed the very night I was announced as having returned. The people, much like Haya, had trusted me, cheered and celebrated me, and I had done nothing when the dragon attacked. I'd been so caught up in her I hadn't even thought of the civilians, the homes damaged by the falling debris.

"In part," Callum hedged, answering Micah's question.

"We don't have time for this," I snarled, striding past all of them and into the hallway. I continued to the strategy room. A domed room three doors down from the king's chambers, my chambers, where earlier today I had kissed and held the most precious person in the world to me. The ache that settled into my chest was cavernous, growing each second she was apart from me. Yawning wider and wider. At what point would the emptiness become so dark and deep that I couldn't find my way out of it?

Shaking those thoughts, I moved the maps and markers around, looking for the information I needed.

I did not need to check if the three men had followed me; I knew they had. "Get the team in Firna on recon." I shuffled a few more papers. "Send scouts to the members of Claw and Wing stationed here"—I pointed to the villages sandwiched between Romath and Erasmus—"and here. I want to know every single flap of that beast's wings. I want to know every place it lands, where it eats, what it eats, and even if it stops to take a piss. I want this information by the end of day tomorrow," I snapped, anger sliding along each word.

"Consider it done." Asher bowed and disappeared, but not before I caught the look he shared with Callum. A hard, measuring stare, edged with warning, as if they were communicating the shared awareness, taut as a drawn bowstring, that I was not well.

I knew what the look meant, and though I was put off by him needing to make that face to my commander, I couldn't blame him for doing it. I was not myself. Even I could tell that much. When we were children, I was never one to get angry and lose control. I was level headed, like Asher, and rarely impassioned about anything. There was no question about the fervor radiating off me now, though.

"So you're going after her, yourself?" Micah asked, glancing between me and Callum.

"After the plan is in motion, Callum, you go and fulfill your duty. Save Erasmus." I lifted my eyes from the notes littering the table. Callum's blond hair was mussed, his hand blistered from trying to hold on to me while I raged. Shame was a fleeting emotion, coming and going in a second as I narrowed my gaze at him, awaiting his response to my command.

"You are the king—you can't go where I think you are

intending to." Callum strode up to the table, gaze narrowing in kind.

"*I am* the king, and I will go wherever I please," I answered levelly even though the tempest was rising in me again, threatening to blow this room into pieces. "Will you disobey your king?" My jaw clicked as I ground my molars.

"I am your guard."

"Asher will accompany me. Micah"—I cut my eyes to the young man standing uncertainly by the table—"is joining the court tonight. I will send for Sir Martus and call for a team to be assembled across the border."

"Shroding, you can't be—" Callum began, but my fist came down onto the table, snapping it in half, the impact startling us all.

"I will dig through every grain of sand and ash in that forsaken place if that's what it takes to bring her back." My shoulders shook, the vibration strumming against my skin again as I growled my promise low and sharp, leaving no room for any more denials or refusals. "Do as you are ordered, Commander."

Callum's throat bobbed as he nodded, eyes unsure as if seeing me for the first time.

Sir Martus entered the room a moment later, surveying the damage. After Micah explained what had happened, so I did not have to, we readied the induction pool. I tried to regulate myself enough to do my job and give Haya's best friend the court, but my emotions were too volatile. I struggled to release the power to him. It was as if the power was thrashing, desperate to be free but also refusing to part from me, as if I were in mortal danger if it did.

"*Strings*," I snapped when the fourth attempt failed.

"Maybe we should wait a day, until we have news of her

and you are a bit more... settled," Sir Martus offered, and my shoulders heaved, breaths ragged in frustration and exhaustion. Micah stepped back in the narrow pool as if I might lose control at any second.

"Callum," I snapped, lifting my eyes to my friend, who looked on silently. I knew he was concerned for Haya as well. He had come to care for her enough that he had begged me to rescind my order that he should flirt with her to throw Logan off.

Haya had been fast asleep beside me when I proposed said scheme.

Lev's tent in Coinania was warm and lit by a steady fire in the center of the room. The smell of herbs and medicine permeated the air, making my sensitive nose itch uncomfortably. I was stretched out alongside an unconscious Haya, who was recovering from Logan's attack in the chief's tent. Asher, Callum and I circled the fire as we waited for Mama Meod's return.

Haya's fever finally broke, and she was going to be okay, at least for now.

Mama Meod had explained that the Nephesh Maveth was fatal. However it could be removed by the person who'd inflicted it, either by choice or by death. If that wasn't possible, then it could be delayed, but only if I inducted Haya into the court, which I could not do as a cat. Our only hope was to act quickly and while in the middle of the transformation I would have to find a way to have her join the court.

"We don't know if Logan targeted her because of the king's power or because she is Shroding's companion." Asher spoke, rubbing his chin in thought where he sat cross-legged on the other side of the firepit.

I could guess it was a bit of both, but now that I knew Logan would have access to her thoughts, I worried he might be drawn to her for other reasons. I had done my best not to be overly expressive in my feelings towards her, but Logan might be able to tell she had become more important to me than was prudent.

Callum poked the wood with a long stick. "We just need her to bring Shroding back," he said flatly. I narrowed my cat eyes on him.

"You heard what Mama Meod said—now that Logan has tainted her, he will be able to hear everything and know what she knows." Asher stated the very thing concerning me. "He might find something to use against her, or us, or Shroding."

"Is there stuff to *know* about you two?" Callum queried in my direction with raised brows.

I tilted my head away and slowly moved the letters around on the board I had been using to communicate with them. "We kissed... twice."

"Ugh, as a cat?" Callum grimaced, sticking out his tongue. My tail flicked hard to the ground in annoyance.

"I'm not always a cat," I wrote messily with the wooden pieces.

Callum's eyes grew wide, and he nodded, rubbing his chin. "Oh really?"

"Enough teasing him," Asher interrupted, glancing over the board and following our conversation. "What concerns you, Shroding?" Asher inquired gently.

"If he knows about us, he may hurt her worse than he already has. I need one of you to be a decoy, throw Logan off our scent." It took a while for me to spell out all I wanted to say on the board, having to shuffle the letters carefully. As I did not have too many multiples of the same letters I had to spell out two or three words at a time, allowing Asher to write down the completed sentence once it was finished. Time consuming but necessary. They were both patient, choosing to hold off speaking until my thought was complete. My sharp shoulders moved awkwardly in a shrug, and Asher stifled a smile at what I could guess was a bizarre-looking gesture.

"I'm spoken for." Asher held up his hands and scrunched his nose.

"I don't think this is a good idea," Callum hedged. "I haven't been the nicest to her; we wouldn't be very convincing."

"You already have rapport with her. Plus you flirted with her at camp, that first night you met, in the woods," I pointed out. Callum, from the little bit Asher had already shared with me, was quite the ladies' man.

"Sure, I flirt." He waved at her sleeping form beside me, and I bared my teeth. "She's not even my type."

All the better, if she wasn't his type. Though the memory of him keeping her warm, tucked against his chest after the lake incident, warned me he might be lying. He had looked like he wanted to kiss her then—had I misread the situation?

"Please don't order me to do this." He scowled.

I hadn't thought I would *need* to order him. What had been a request was quickly becoming a command, and I was not sure how we'd gotten to this point.

"Be nicer to her," I shrugged my shoulders again, "flirt a bit more than usual. I'm not asking you to marry her, just to keep her safe," I reasoned, hoping I would not regret asking this of him.

Callum glanced at her sleeping form again, and his gray eyes softened. "Alright. To keep her safe." He cleared his throat and looked at his nails with interest. "I can force myself to flirt, a little," he drawled long-sufferingly. "If it's for my king." He sighed.

I rolled my eyes and rested my head on my paws, ending the conversion.

"My king," Callum said solemnly, stepping forward to receive my command and bring me back to the present. The induction pool lapped at my thighs as I recalled the reason I needed to ask Callum for a favor once again.

If I could not manage my emotions, then I would need to borrow Callum's Orator ability, at least for a short time. Once I got traction on finding Haya, I was sure I would be better, that I would be able to think more clearly.

"I need your help." I extended my hand to him, and he instantly understood. The wash of calm that hit me was prompt. I took a full, deep breath. Callum flinched a little, and my brows knit. "What is it?" I asked, perplexed.

"I've not experienced this before." Callum shuddered, and I ripped my hand away.

"Is it hurting you?"

Callum swallowed. "I thought it was just the heat of the king's power, before." He lifted his burnt hand, and though the one I had been holding seconds ago was not marred, he flexed it as if it were in pain. "An Orator's abilities should not pick up on the other person's pain. We have a sense for it, sure, but we, I have never felt it before." Callum looked at Sir Martus for answers. "Has this ever happened in history?"

Sir Martus closed his eyes, pondering as he rubbed the braid in his beard. "Once. I read once about it occurring if the emotion experienced by the Orator and the Oratee is connected somehow."

Callum raised a brow, stepping forward, defensive. "What do you mean?"

"You are suffering as well, now that she is gone, are you not?" Sir Martus tilted his head, stare probing.

"We are all concerned for Haya." Callum's eyes shifted as if caught. I watched his thumb and forefinger scrape together, his tell, and the yawning hole in my chest grew bigger, a seed that had been adrift taking root. A well of dread I had ignored—thinking it wholly in my head, fueled by my own jealousy—was swelling inside me.

"You love her," I accused, the words sharp and pointed, as if I had any right to be angry about it, when I had forced him to be close to her. To pursue her, make Logan *believe* they were together. Disgust at myself dripped into the dread, and I feared it would poison everything till I was bitter, distrusting and covetous.

"If he does and tried to remedy your anger and sorrow over her, it is reasonable that he would experience acute pain, as his own emotions are in line with yours." Sir Martus cut through my thoughts, his words solidifying what Callum would not utter. I could see in his stormy eyes that he would never own it; for my sake, he would leave it unsaid, ambiguous, and I didn't know whether that made me pity him or envy his restraint.

Micah stepped forward, the water sloshing around his hips. "That would mean you must love her as much as the rest of us. So if you tried to calm my anger, you would also experience pain." He lifted his hand, and Callum shook his head, stepping back. His expression was guarded; the walls I had seen him use as a child to keep his family safe were being laid, mortar and stone heaving up and up till I could no longer read his expression at all.

"It would be a good test to confirm the theory," Sir Martus reasoned, glancing between us all. I did not miss the mischievous glint in his wise old eyes.

"Fine." Callum took Micah's hand, and Micah gasped at the sudden shift in his emotions. Callum closed his eyes, the creases at the edges conveying what he dared not say. He jerked his hand back. "Happy?" He glowered at Sir Martus. "Meddlesome old man," He muttered under his breath, words no one but I could hear.

"It would seem we have an answer, then," he confirmed.

"I don't *love* her." Callum held up his hands as if bored by the whole conversation. "I've just grown fond of her, the tiniest bit." He shrugged, crossing his arms.

Before I could push Callum, force him to recognize the feelings we all could see, Asher returned, panting slightly.

Instantly on alert we all braced ourselves. "The first report indicates the dragon did stay the course southeast, however it went above the cloud cover somewhere east of Senmal." A small town on the hill just outside the city.

"*Strings*," I huffed, returning my attention to Micah's induction. I might not be able to save Haya at this moment, but I could protect her best friend and first love. I would protect any and everyone who mattered to her as long as I drew breath. Even if she didn't. I nearly lost control again at the thought, but I forced myself to focus and remain calm. Haya was tough. Tougher than most gave her credit for. She would stay alive until I got to her.

She had to.

When Micah broke the surface of the water, coming out as the newest member of the court, I changed the oath that would bind him to the court. He was different from the rest.

He was not joining to protect me but to protect Haya. His oath needed to signify that.

"I vow to protect Haya Golden, to never harm her," he said, head bowed.

"Breaking the oath will not kill you, nor remove you from the court. Instead it will temporarily paralyze you for exactly one hour," I explained, making sure the oath was clear and exact.

He placed his fist over his heart, accepting the oath and letting it snap into place between us. It was a comfort to know Haya would always have someone watching out for her in the shadows, in addition to me, of course.

"I would like to make a second oath," Micah pressed, and my brow furrowed.

"Why?"

"Because harm is too vague." He shook his head. "I promised my father I would protect her. I've done a poor job of that so far, and if I don't have an oath with a binding consequence, I fear I may let her down again. Fail in my promise to my father."

I nodded, understanding but also unsure. He wanted a death oath? His commitment was deeper than I'd ever thought. How had Haya ever thought this man's love was purely out of responsibility? A part of me was jealous, but a greater part of me respected him. She drew allegiance to her like the moon draws the tides. "Give whatever oath you deem fit," I offered, and he placed his hand over his chest once more.

"I swear this to the Creator above, should she lose a single drop of blood at my hand, may I lose all mine in red recompense."

Callum, Asher and Sir Martus balked at the declaration.

There was nothing I could do as the second oath snapped into place beside the first.

His oath was unnecessarily harsh; however it was not my place to dissuade him from such a commitment. Especially when I knew what he meant by it. He would give his life for her, and though it was a bit too close to giving one's life as part of the Nephesh Berit, I also understood I had taken the woman he loved from him. Whisked her away into a life of adventure and danger that had already gotten her killed once and nearly a few other times. I would not nitpick his oaths. They were his to bind himself with. My power was merely the executor of such bonds.

For Haya's sake I hoped the consequences of these oaths would never come to light.

———

Days turned into weeks, and despite knowing it caused him physical pain, I could not lead the kingdom without Callum's gift clearing my head on a daily basis. I had never become so dependent on another's gift before, but when news of the dragon grew thin, my despair was like a living thing hanging over my back. I had met with Haya's mother in a desperate attempt to feel close to her. It went as well as one could expect when her daughter was taken on my watch.

I waited for the numbness to set in, for the grief, as it had when my parents died, when I became a cat. I waited for it to become a dull ache instead of an unmovable vise over my thoughts, but relief would not come. Leading a kingdom at war while the only person I wanted at my side was Strings know where, subject to what the Creator only knows, did not provide any reprieve from my heartache. Still I forced myself to eat, bathe and give orders, file papers, sign and lead because that was what the kingdom demanded of me. It was only when I was knee deep in tasks or under Callum's gift that I had relief. But my time with Callum had drawn to a close, as he was needed to lead the army in the battle to win back Erasmus. With him gone the next weeks that followed were soul crippling, even as I poured everything into my work, my kingdom I could sense my ardent need for Haya might overtake all rational thoughts. Could overtake my duty to the kingdoms.

I wasn't one to have nightmares, but when they began I knew time was running out. I saw her screaming in pain, sobbing, her brilliant green eyes—ones I had teased her about, but were actually infinitely more vivid than she had led on—pinched in anguish. She spoke to me, whispered pleas to save her, to find her. The nights where she was in my arms, hitting my chest and saying, "Where were you, where were you," over and over and over again, were the worst. If I knew where she was, I would be there in a heartbeat, forsaking the throne just to bring her home to me.

When we finally received word from Sir Liam, who had tracked Haya down using his gift, I was arguing with the court about trade routes and the failed wheat crop this year. The envelope shook as I tried and failed to listen to the middle-aged man give his report on the wheat blight. The whoosh of blood pounded in my ears as I saw the scrawl of Sir Liam across the top and tore into the envelope. I scanned the words.

Kidrisol. Head to basecamp, I will have a team waiting for you there. Do not ascend without them.

The scrawl changed to Callum's hand, and what it said had me rising from my seat, shredding the letter.

Logan is the dragon.

I had a place and an enemy. There was nothing in all creation that would stop me from going to her, so when the court protested my leaving, I threatened to have them all thrown out of the castle for treason. They may not know it yet, but they were preventing the rescue of their future queen, and I did not care if I seemed like a tyrant in that moment because I would not leave her in the hands of Logan a moment longer.

Asher smoothed things over with the court while I readied the horses and left the castle behind.

Sir Martus stopped me at the white gates. His long flowing robes flapped in the wind, his hands steepled at his chest.

I pulled the horse I'd borrowed from the soldiers' stables to a stop. "Do not dare ask me to stay." I glared at the man I had come to respect as much as my father.

"She will be queen someday, I could tell the moment I met her. I would never stand in the way of that, however I do caution you. This battle is the precursor to your fight with Skithian. It would serve you well to make allies along your travels."

I nodded numbly, itching to get on the road, to take action, to get to her. Asher rode up behind me, and I frowned. "I need you here."

"I go where the king goes, that is the promise I made to Callum when he left." Asher stretched his arms in front of him and grinned. "Besides, you have never crossed the border; I have. I know what we need." He tossed me a cloak and smirked. "Bundle up, my king, you're in for a wild ride."

I wrapped the cloak over my shoulders and tightened the strap of Sheenagh on my hip.

Sir Martus bowed his head. "Since you did not complete the king's challenge when you came of age, this will be yours. The court agrees, and should you return with Haya, then the challenge will be complete."

I clenched my jaw, dipping my chin in acknowledgment and urging the horse to run.

This was a challenge I would not fail...

I'm coming, Haya.

CASSANDRA CIELO

FROM Ruby Sands

THE TOWER, THE DRAGON
BOOK 4

Chapter 1 : Found

Wind whipped across my cheeks, thunder roared in the air, as I was carried over the land I called home. I had already thrown up from the vertigo, passed out from shock and fear and awakened to find we were still flying. Now I just hung numb and freezing in the clutches of a massive white dragon.

At moments I could almost hear Logan's thoughts intruding, percolating into the edges of my mind before the faint whispers would vanish altogether. He had shown me *this* dragon. Had shown me his nefarious plans to decimate the city of Erasmus. Yet I had missed any signs of this, any signs he would attack the castle on the day of Shroding's coronation and instead of seeking to destroy Shroding he would send this vile beast after me.

The terror and heartbreak on Callum and Shroding's faces was imprinted in my mind, an ever-present companion on this endless flight through the sky. Shroding had told me he loved me, and then I was cruelly snatched from his grasp, ripped away into the night. Would I ever see him again? I had my sword, and though it was pinched between me and the monster's claw, I could wiggle it loose and cut myself free, but at what cost? I would surely not survive a fall from this height. Even if I did, I would land somewhere in the barren wilderness between Shamar and Golan, if our flight trajectory was any indication of where we were headed.

Thunder boomed across the night sky, and the dragon swooped low, making my stomach dip, before it thrust its massive feathered wings back, taking us up above the clouds. I closed my eyes against the pelting rain and slicing wind.

I could no longer tell what was below us as thick sheets of gray clouds permeated the air. The rain coated my skin in dark wet streaks. Was the rain actually dirt? I rubbed my fingers together; rough particles of sand textured the rain. No, not quite sand. Ash?

A new wave of panic seized my heart as the air grew dense, making it hard to breathe. The dragon's speed, already breakneck, increased, and I used the sleeve of my dress to filter the air as best I could as we zipped through the night.

It was unclear how long it had been from the time we passed into Golan territory till we were descending. The only clear sign the beast had dropped altitude was the popping in my ears. When the dragon dashed a sharp left my stomach dipped. There was, thankfully, nothing left for me to throw up, so I closed my eyes and gripped the slick scales of the dragon's feet. They were black, and though I could see where the scales turned to feathers further up, I could not reach them.

The view when we broke through the cloud cover was marred by the unending haze of ash Golan is known for. Never in my life did I expect to see this land, let alone walk upon it. But that was what I would soon be doing, as the dragon was making a straight shot for the worst and most volatile place in all of Golan. Mount Kidrisol. The blue volcano, rumored to be the reason for the ash covering the land.

Blue lava poured from the caldera, splintering out and down on three sides of the massive mountain. We were descending on the ocean side, the only part clear of the lethal blue molten rock.

I could smell the sulfur and feel the heat long before I could make out the details of the craggy gray-red rocks. With my bones frozen from the frigid flight I did not mind the heat as it slowly warmed me to the point where my teeth stopped chattering. I could not tell the time of day, as the sky was impossible to see through the haze. In fact I could only see the blue volcano because of the glowing lava; the haze everywhere else obscured my view, making it impossible to see what was actually ahead until it was too late.

When I could make out the cave opening I knew I had lost my chance to escape. The dragon hovered over the ground for a moment before it tossed me violently from its clutches into the dark opening.

I hit the ground hard but used my gift to protect against the worst of the fall, rolling along the ground. I came to a stop in the cavernous space, only to discover it was not as empty as I had anticipated.

The shriek of the beast rattled the air as it swooped up

into the sky, its once white wings and body coated in a sheen of gray. Was it leaving? I rose onto unsteady feet, my gown tattered around my legs and arms. I took in the not-so-empty cave, finding a bed, a wood-burning stove, along with a desk, table and chairs. Was this for me? Did someone actually live on the mountain? If so, who? And what did they want with me?

A massive thud shook the ground as the dragon's form blocked the opening. Lanterns burst to life in the space, blue flames illuminating the cave, casting it into a world of cerulean. The beast shuddered, its massive wings spreading out, and with an ear-piercing scream it morphed, feathers receding into scales, then scales to skin. In place of fangs and a snout were teeth and a nose. The screaming changed from the shill cry of an animal to the groans of a man in pain. Then it was over, the grotesque transformation completed, and before me in the shadowed blue of the cave stood a familiar naked man.

"*Logan,*" I rasped, throat raw from bile and icy wind.

His pale eyes, made black in the dimness, flashed to mine before shock had me passing out again.

———

"Sleep there." Logan gestured to the bed. He had clothed himself, sometime while I was unconscious, in a Krav suit, the thick leather adding bulk to his physique that would otherwise not be there. He was still as lanky and gaunt as he had been in my memory. When I awoke, I'd been in the same spot as when I collapsed. I exhaled, grateful he had not touched me. What I could not fathom was how he had been a dragon one moment and a man the next.

My eyes followed his gesture, cutting to the single bed in the space. I shook my head vigorously, crawling away from him on my hands and feet, my rear dragging along the rough clay ground.

"Fine," he sneered, pushing his white blond hair back from his face, smoothing it over his head in a practiced, controlled way, as if he could sense a single hair might be out of place and that was unacceptable. Nothing like the relaxed, smooth way Shroding performed the gesture. "Sleep on the ground, then, love."

While he busied himself with something on the desk, I reached for my weapon, my heart plummeting to the lava below and burning to ash when it was nowhere on my person. "You *touched* me," I accused.

"I touched your weapon—there is a difference," he scoffed, annoyed by my accusation, but not turning to face me. "Of course I would not let you keep a sword. Are you *actually* that ignorant?"

I glared. If I could shoot vibrations out of my eyes, he would have two small holes in his back by now.

"Tell me, love, is it Shroding or Callum who finds that helpless damsel thing more appealing?" he goaded me, glancing over his shoulder. I clenched my teeth so hard my jaw clicked. Slowly he turned, crossing his arms, and then leaned his hip on the table. The movement was so languid that chills slid along my back. He was a predator waiting for his moment to pounce. "Or... do you put on the show for both?" he drawled, unsmiling. His words could have been teasing if not for the unhurried, flat way he said them.

"Shut your traitorous mouth," I hissed.

He narrowed his eyes and came forward. I shuffled back till my head hit the wall behind me. He crouched and yanked my chin up. "Don't tempt me to do worse to you, love. These scrapes and bumps, from your tumble, were only lessened by your gift, which, if you haven't bothered to realize, you have no access to at the moment. So unless you want injuries that *break* instead of mar that pretty skin, I suggest you weigh your words more carefully."

I paled. "What did you do?" I demanded, trying and failing to stir up the power in me. It was as if the strings of my soul were gone, inked out by a thick black sludge I could not get past.

His tapered face was close enough that even in the strange blue light I could see his eyes were not natural. The pale yellow green was darkened in the center by a narrow vertical slit. As if he did not just act like a serpentine monster but actually was one. I supposed that made sense since he had been a dragon only a short time ago. Could he transform at will? Was it another twisted distortion of the Creator's power, like the Nephesh Maveth was to the Nephesh Berit?

I gasped as he snaked an arm around my waist and jerked me up from the ground. My legs swayed under me, and despite myself I clung to his shoulders to keep upright.

"*What did you do? What do you want? What are you going to do to me?*" he mocked in a displeased tone. "Base questions not worth answering," he hissed, dragging me the short distance to the bed. I pushed and kicked, but each attempt at resistance sent waves of exhaustion through me. He tossed me down hard, the bed creaking in revolt at the impact. I cried out as my injuries flared with their own protests. "Stay there, love. I have no further use for you... for now."

"They will find and kill you," I bit out. Thinking of how venomous Callum had been that day he spoke to Logan through our connection. *I will put an end to you,* Callum had threatened, and by the delighted gleam in Logan's eyes I knew he was thinking of it too.

"Ohhh," Logan purred, leaning down to run his fingers through my loose hair. "I'm counting on it."

"Haya, wake up." A hand gripped my shoulder, shaking me, as my body twisted against the restraints holding my wrists and ankles. "Strings, what did he do to you?" Shroding's voice broke through the haze in my mind, and I opened my eyes.

The blue room was alight with a warm golden glow as Shroding's strong jaw and dark eyes came into view. He was here? How? Asher was at my other side, cutting through the ropes around my legs.

"He used the serum on her; she isn't in any condition to fight," Asher explained to Shroding. Once my legs were free he checked my body for injuries, but other than being sluggish and unable to access my gift, I did not feel hurt. What had happened to the scrapes and bruises from the fall into the cave? "The marks on her wrists are superficial; he didn't keep her tied up like this normally."

"*This* isn't superficial." Shroding's eyes narrowed on my neck. I touched the spot with my freed hand, fingers finding a rough, jagged mark beside the one Logan had given me back in Coinania.

"He bit her again?" Asher hovered over Shroding's shoulder, looking at the spot.

My hand shook. Why? Why had he bitten me?

"He really is an *animal*," Shroding spat—full of malice. What would Logan gain from biting me again? Our connection still existed, even if blocked and the taint removed. Had he just planned to taint me again? Why? I rubbed my head, as it ached terribly. When had he done it? While I was sleeping? Surely I would have woken up when his teeth broke my skin.

"How did you get here so quickly?" I muttered. How could Shroding get from Romath to Mount Kidrisol in less than a day?

Shroding's flint eyes met mine as he lifted me into a seated position. "Haya, what are you saying? You have been gone for two months."

"No, the coronation was yesterday," I panicked, hiccupping with nervous energy. Shroding had to be mistaken.

"He took her memories," Asher reasoned, but I couldn't follow what he was saying. My memories? Logan could take them? How was that possible? Why would he do that? The fear of what could be lost in my mind terrified me. All I could recall was the night I arrived. What other horrible things had Logan done? I shuddered, and Shroding's arm tightened over my shoulder.

"Another use of the gift forbidden in Shamar for a long time." Shroding shook his head in disappointment, but I was not sure if it was disappointment over my lost memories, or over Logan's continued descent into darkness.

"Are you able—"

Shroding glanced at the ground uneasily, cutting me off with a vague answer. "Just because you can do something doesn't mean you *ever* should." Then he lifted me from the bed, and I peered down at the tattered green dress from the Celebration of Strings. Had I been in the same dress the last two months? "You're so thin..." Shroding murmured, a mix of anger and worry texturing his tone. "Are you hungry?" he asked, and I whispered "no," as I was too run down from the serum to even sense if I was hungry.

"Where is Logan?" I glanced around the room, the space different from when I had arrived. There was another bed, a dresser and a vase of wilted flowers that had not been there before. My sword lay on the edge of the other bed as if Logan had put it there, just out of my reach, to torment me. Asher grabbed it.

"Our team is fighting him near the caldera," Shroding answered as I wrapped my arms around his neck. The green dress, which had hugged my curves at the party, was loose, hanging awkwardly over my arms. Had Logan starved me?

"Team?"

"The order of Claw and Wing," Asher explained, and I glanced at Shroding for clarity, but Asher continued grimly as we walked towards the cave opening. "A lot has happened in the last two months."

"Haya, I have to go help them, but Asher will take you to base camp, and I will meet you there after we have dealt with Logan."

I frowned. If it really had been two months since I was on that balcony with Shroding, then I didn't want to be parted from him, especially not when he was about to go up against Logan. I didn't know who was on his team, but no one was as strong as Shroding, and if he was expected to lead the fight, I would not be able to wait somewhere safe while he fought for his life.

I pressed my face into his neck. "I can still fight," I whispered, breaking free from his hold, my feet touching the ground gingerly. I reached for my blade in Asher's hand. "If we have been apart as long as you say, then there is no way I'm separating from you now. I am a part of the king's guard, after all." I held the sword to my chest, waiting for his acceptance. We all knew I was in no condition to fight, but at least he could let me come with him.

His dark gaze dragged over me, and as he took in my less than pristine state, I was sure he would refuse me, but instead he nodded. "You are not playing fair." He stepped forward, and my heart hammered instantly, his proximity stirring my desire from the terrace on what only seemed like the night before for me. He cupped my cheek and kissed my forehead.

A boom shook the cave, and a roar, like a wild beast was loose on the mountain, stung our ears. Shroding pulled me to him, hugging me tight as he yelled over the thunderous rumbling to Asher. "Keep her away from the fighting. Let's go!"

Then we were sprinting through a tunnel around the outer part of the mountain. Heat and ash saturated the air, and I coughed against the foul sulfur burning my nose.

"Here!" Shroding shouted as we dropped into a tight rocky passage, which opened into a massive pit. At its bottom was a group of unfamiliar men and women fighting an all too familiar dragon. "Keep her up here," Shroding ordered, jumping and sliding down the clay and rock wall of the pit.

Wind whipped up, blowing the heat of the dragon's fire into our faces. The cave ceiling had three large holes where steam and smoke billowed out. Blue lava sloshed off to the far side of the pit, a good distance away from the fighting.

I wanted to ask Asher what was happening, but the battle below held both our attention. A dark-haired girl ran behind the dragon and threw four sharp blades into the backside of the beast. Its responding bellow had me covering my ears and closing my eyes, as if not seeing the monster would diminish the cantankerous howl.

When the cry subsided, two dark-haired men, one with long hair and the other with short, teamed up against the dragon. Yet it was the presence of Micah and Sir Liam that drew my full attention.

Sir Liam was on the ground, body crumpled to the side in a heap of metal and salt-and-pepper dreads. I could not tell from the ledge we were perched atop if he was breathing. Nor could I tell if he was injured, but from the rubble around him, he probably was.

The team from Claw and Wing were bloody and hunched, the fight having been going on for some time before Shroding found me.

A gust of hot air shot up past us, blowing my loose hair wildly around my face. Asher grabbed my arm and pulled me away from the edge.

"The steam can be toxic, if you breathe in too much," he shouted over the endless rumble of the mountain and the battle below.

Micah threw a spear at the dragon, distracting it long enough for the dark-haired men to slide under its haunches and slice through the white feathers of its legs. Red stained the white, spreading quickly. Sullying what might have been beautiful plumage if not attached to such a vial creature.

Staggering, Logan's dragon form rocked to the side. Its tail slashed through the air to steady its massive body. Black claws swiped, sending the spear flying and clattering to the ground. Logan swung its head, angling its mouth before a blast of flames poured out, charring the ground with a spray of vitriol. The dark-haired men rolled to shelter behind a boulder. The girl sprinted up the tail of the dragon, taking two more knives and slamming them into the base of one of his feathered wings.

Logan's dragon body fell back, wings coiling in as if it could protect itself from the damage already inflicted. The girl was thrown off and skidded across the ground in a cloud of dust. But I could not wait to see if she was okay, as Logan's hulking form smashed into the rock ledge where Asher and I stood. Sharp rocks pelted my face and head as the ceiling above us rattled from the impact.

Asher quickly drew us back into the tunnel, hoisting me into the safety of the passage even as the debris continued to fall. Dust and ash clouded my vision until there was no longer any light from the caldera visible. What had happened? When my eyes adjusted to the sudden darkness, Asher's leg and arm were pinned under the rubble.

www.ingramcontent.com/pod-product-compliance
Lightning Source LLC
Chambersburg PA
CBHW022305310726
48973CB00001B/214